SEEK AND YE SHALL FIND

At the sight of the man's gentle features, the lustrous, long brown hair, and the beatific smile, cool air rushed into Joseph's lungs. The prisoner's sole white garment seemed to glow radiantly as did the man's face, and Joseph saw that he was still captive, held by some force that would not let him go.

Then he heard the prisoner's voice, speaking the same words Joseph had heard him speak before:

Find me. Help me. Save me. And then I may save you.

Joseph reached out his hands toward him, but felt himself being swept up and away through a small hole, his body stretched and elongated, his bones splintering . . .

THE
SEARCHERS
—— BOOK TWO ——
EMPIRE OF DUST

CHET WILLIAMSON

AVON BOOKS ◆ NEW YORK

This is a work of fiction. Names, characters, places, and incidents either are the product of the author's imagination or are used fictitiously. Any resemblance to actual events, locales, organizations, or persons, living or dead, is entirely coincidental and beyond the intent of either the author or the publisher.

AVON BOOKS, INC.
1350 Avenue of the Americas
New York, New York 10019

Copyright © 1998 by Chet Williamson
Inside cover author photo by Ron Bowman
Published by arrangement with the author
Visit our website at http://www.AvonBooks.com
Library of Congress Catalog Card Number: 98-93172
ISBN: 0-380-79188-9

First Avon Books Printing: December 1998

AVON TRADEMARK REG. U.S. PAT. OFF. AND IN OTHER COUNTRIES, MARCA REGISTRADA, HECHO EN U.S.A.

Printed in the U.S.A.

WCD 10 9 8 7 6 5 4 3 2 1

To my old pard,
Joe R. Lansdale,
his own mighty self

What is pomp, rule, reign, but earth and dust? And, live we how we can, yet die we must.

—SHAKESPEARE, *HENRY VI*
PART III, V, ii, 27

Who then to frail mortality shall trust
But limns on water, or but writes in dust?

—BACON, *THE WORLD*

Chapter 1

Damon had never seen anything as huge as the desert sky. Driving on the level roads in the sunlight had been bad enough, but standing under the flat black of the night was worse. He felt as though all anyone in the world had to do was to turn, and they would see him.

The thought gave him a shiver, and the chilly night only made it worse. He had no idea that the desert could be so cold in July. But he walked on, toward the campfire, the liquid gleam in the eyes of the dozen people around it, and the three small tents pitched near it. Lucretia was muttering behind him, and he looked back and told her to shut up, then looked ahead at the ragtag crew waiting for him.

They didn't look like the type of people the Divine would want. They were a bunch of dirtbags, dressed in dusty jeans, sweatshirts, and jackets with holes in the elbows. Most of the men had beards and long hair, and the women were just as unkempt, with stringy and unwashed hair.

In contrast, Damon was dressed in his Lizard King look, spotless black from his leather vest to his boots. Lucretia was pretty impressive, too, in her tight red slacks and little black top under the satin jacket with the cabalistic designs stitched onto it.

The only response their wardrobe got from the motley throng was hostility. All of them were standing now, and

1

the largest of the men turned toward the patched tent in the center. "Ezekiel? Company," he said, then looked at Damon with suspicion.

Damon wondered about the bad vibes. After all, they knew he was coming. He had connected with them through their website, had seen through the usual bullshit they had thrown up as a front, and figured out what they were *really* about.

The Divine. The one the Catholics were holding prisoner because they knew that once he got free, the joy and liberty and blood that he would spill would wash their religion off the earth. This was the Main Man, the most powerful human being—if that's what he was—on the face of the planet, and maybe in the whole damn galaxy.

Rumor had it that a bunch of cultists in New York had almost found the Divine, but got messed over by a small army of mercs hired by the Catholics, but rumors like that were cheap and plentiful. A rumor that Damon *did* believe, however, was that the leader of this bunch of desert rats had the *talent*, the wild Fortean brand, that let him link minds with the Divine.

But he was with a gang of real nobodies. Hell, they didn't even have a name, and their website was just text, as low profile as you could get without dropping off the cyber-radar. But the key words were there for those who knew, who wanted to search. Unfortunately, he and Lucretia were the only ones who thought the trek to Arizona worth the effort, and Damon wasn't all that sure about Lucretia.

Ezekiel Swain was sure as hell taking a long time to get out of that tent, and the dozen pairs of eyes regarding Damon were becoming no more friendly. Damon gave them back glare for glare, until Ezekiel Swain finally appeared.

From his name, Damon had pictured the leader of this group as someone tall, thin, and cadaverous, almost biblical, like a younger version of John Brown. But what staggered out of the tent was a fat, bloated man in his mid-thirties, sweat popping from every pore, even in the chilly night. His red-blond hair was plastered over his forehead, and the khaki shirt he wore showed dark, wet circles under the arms and in the center of his wide, almost womanly chest. Beard stubble grew wildly across the terraces of his chins, and crooked teeth darted behind a pair of bulbous lips.

At first he seemed as unimpressive a picture as could be imagined, and Damon nearly cursed aloud the fate that had brought him to this desolate place and this tub of a man. But then Ezekiel Swain looked directly at him, and his eyes, though hung over by moist folds of flesh, were as piercing and intent and *knowing* as any that Damon had ever seen, and he realized why people followed Ezekiel Swain.

Then the fat man spoke, and Damon was repulsed all over again. "Don't tell me—you're Demon Damon. And this lovely lady must be Lucretia Borgia, right?" The words bubbled thickly, like a boiling pot of greasy stew in which the cook had tossed slimy meat and soft vegetables that should have been thrown away.

"I'm Damon, yeah. And this is Lucretia." He took the girl's hand and pulled her up next to him.

She held back at first, as if dreading to come any closer to the repellent Ezekiel. "My name's not Borgia," she said softly but firmly.

"Apologies, milady," Ezekiel said. Right.

Then from out of the tent stepped a woman the physical opposite of Swain. She was tall and slender, and though her hair was prematurely gray, Damon guessed that she was only a year or so older than Ezekiel.

"Jezebel," Ezekiel said, with a touch of affection, putting his hand on her shoulder in a proprietary way. "This is Damon and Lucretia not-Borgia. Damon? Lucretia not-Borgia? This is my sweet Jezebel." He rubbed her shoulder, and his sausage fingers stroked her swan neck as he grinned. "My only sister. Our parents had a biblical thing when it came to names. But the connections meant nothing to them—it was just the names they liked. 'Jezebel' felt so good in my father's mouth that it didn't matter to him that she was an evil queen devoured by the dogs of the street. Not that that will ever happen to my sweet sister.''

Jezebel Swain smiled at her brother and kissed him full on the lips. The sight brought a whisper of bile to Damon's throat.

"Tell me," Ezekiel said, turning back to Damon, "why have you come to join us? What do you expect to find?''

"You know what," Damon said, slightly annoyed, but not wanting to seem so. "The Divine.''

"Of course. Come to find God, haven't we? Or the Devil? Or something in between?''

"You said in your e-mail that he communicates with you," Damon said.

"Oh yes. *'He walks with me and he talks with me, and he tells me I am his own.'* Well, come into our humble abode.'' Ezekiel swept a massive arm toward the small tent.

Inside the tent there were two sleeping bags zipped together to create one large one, exactly what Damon was hoping not to see. The eight-by-eight-foot square tent was brightly lit by a Coleman lantern. The ceiling was five feet high in the center, and the four of them sat on camp stools in a circle.

"There we are," said Ezekiel, whose buttocks draped over and hid his stool. "Boy-girl-boy-girl, how civilized.'' In the bright light Ezekiel looked all the more repugnant. As if the weight wasn't bad enough, he seemed to have once been cursed with a virulent case of acne, which had left its tracks all too plainly.

Ezekiel opened a cooler, revealing a few cans of Hamm's beer and an assortment of cheap supermarket-brand soda. He opened a can of cream soda with a hiss. "Help yourself," he told them. "Have beer if you want— I can't drink it, dulls the contact.''

"With the Divine," Damon said.

"No," Ezekiel replied, after draining half of the can's contents. "With all the spaceships hidden behind Uranus."

"You got any Diet Pepsi?" Lucretia said in a whiny voice.

Ezekiel glared down into the cooler and shoved aside a few cans of the generic soda as though he were looking for diamonds among a nest of rattlers. "Gee whiz, missy," he said, "we seem to be fresh out. Can I offer you a Valu-Shop brand cola instead, in the ever so simple black-and-white can?"

"Is it diet?" Lucretia asked.

"No, it's not diet. I hate diet. Diet's got that shit that kills rats. This stuff's packed with real cane sugar, twelve teaspoons a serving—good, and good for ya, too."

Lucretia took the can from Ezekiel's outstretched mitt as though she were picking a slug off a rose, then sat holding the unopened can. "You gotta pull the tab," Ezekiel said. "Diet Pepsi's the only one that opens by mind control."

Damon took a birch beer. If Ezekiel wasn't drinking beer, he was damned if he was. All this time, Jezebel had not spoken a word, but now she looked at Damon. "I thought there would be more of you," she said, and he heard accusation in her tone. "You said in your phone call that there would be six."

"I . . . overestimated."

Ezekiel pointed a finger at Damon. "One . . ." Then he pointed at Lucretia. ". . . Two. So you overestimated by, um, two hundred percent, is that right? So what was the problem?"

"People had . . . other engagements," Damon said, hating how ineffective he sounded. "A lot of them are in the film industry, and there are a couple of big event movies shooting right now."

"Actors and actresses? Or grips and gaffers and caterers?"

"Yeah, them," said Lucretia. "The grips and all that."

"Well, we couldn't possibly have Tom Cruise under-gaffed," Ezekiel said. "He does need his best boy, too. Even though they had an opportunity to confront the only being on this earth that could pass for God. But I mean, when Tom Cruise calls . . ."

"Why couldn't you convince them?" Jezebel said. "I thought you were their leader."

"I . . . kept them together, but we didn't believe in for-mal leadership. It wasn't that kind of group."

"Well, that was your major screw-up," Ezekiel said. "The mob always needs a leader. See, around here, *I'm* the leader. Not because I'm smarter or braver or hand-somer than anybody else, but because I'm the one, see?"

"The one?" Damon said. "The one he speaks to?"

"That's right. Me and Jezebel, though he doesn't hit her nearly as strong as me. She's gotta work at it, but I just open up, and if he's trying to communicate, slam bam, I know it. I'm blessed with a wonderful family . . ." He squeezed Jezebel's leg, and she smiled. ". . . And a wonderful talent. Hell, I never met *anybody* could pick him up except me and Jezebel. Must be something in the blood, y'know? Power in the blood, man."

"So how does he contact you?" Damon asked. "I mean, do you actually *hear* something?"

"I hear him inside my head. There's a *presence* there, it *echoes* without going through my eardrums, if you can dig that."

"What does he say?" Damon was getting excited in spite of his reluctance to appear emotional. He knew that emotions were something that Ezekiel Swain would only use against you.

"He tells me things . . . *promises* me things." His hard, piggy eyes grew suddenly dreamy. "Wonderful things. Not always good things for other people . . ." He smiled, and it wasn't pretty to see. "But good things for me."

"He tells you where to go?"

"Yeah, he tells me. But that took a while. He wouldn't tell me where he was until he knew I had enough manpower to make it worthwhile. That's what I was hoping you were gonna bring to the party, Demon Damon, but all you bring along is Miss Lucretia here, who doesn't appear to be Michelle Yeoh.''

''I can take care of myself,'' Lucretia muttered, still picking feebly at the soda can tab, trying not to break a nail.

Ezekiel grabbed the can away, stuck a thick fingertip under the tab, and jerked up. A spray of soda geysered into Lucretia's face and hair, and she gave a gasp and wiped at it frantically. ''Oh yeah,'' said Ezekiel, ''we can see you're *American Gladiator* material all the way. And I've been meaning to ask, what the hell is that shit sewed on your jacket?''

Lucretia couldn't answer for a moment. Her mouth opened and closed like a fish, and then she said, ''*Symbols*, they're *symbols*, man, don't you know *anything*? *Shit!*''

''Watch your mouth,'' Jezebel said coldly, ''Don't you forget for a minute who's in charge here.''

Damon thought about saying something in Lucretia's defense, but forgot about it when Jezebel turned her basilisk stare on him. Sometime he could show these two that they couldn't pull this kind of shit on him, but not yet. Besides, Lucretia was acting like such a chump that she deserved to get reamed. What really offended Damon was the way her behavior reflected on him, like having a dog who pissed on your host's carpet.

''So what's the plan?'' Damon said, ignoring Lucretia.

''To write a whole new book of the Bible, my friend— the Revelation of Ezekiel. A book of total freedom and the release of the human spirit to realize its full potential, both for light and for darkness. But in order for that book to be written, the Divine has to be freed. Turning to the practical, the plan *was* to get more people for an out-and-out assault on the assholes holding him. But now we'll just have to find him and play it by ear, see what we're up against.''

"So where is he?" asked Damon.

"Northeast of here somewhere. We head that way, and then he'll speak to me again, get us closer, like a hound dog sniffing out a trail . . . you get a little closer, it gets a little stronger."

"So you don't know where he is exactly, then?"

Ezekiel looked at Damon as though he were the dumbest thing he had ever seen. "What, you want an *address?* I said he's *northeast.* We'll find him, Sunny Jim. Now, you guys bring a tent, like I said?" Damon nodded. "Then I suggest you set it up, or just bunk down in your van. We're taking off in the morning."

Chapter 2

Damon and Lucretia went outside and walked to their van, past the circle of people who continued to glare at them. Several had gone to their own tents, but half of them were still sitting around the campfire.

"I want to set up the tent," Lucretia said.

"What? I thought you hated that tent."

"I want to sleep in it tonight," she said, in a voice so firm that it made Damon sure that even if he found the Divine and understood the workings of the mysteries of life and death, he would still never understand women.

But he understood at least one woman when he woke up at 6 A.M. to find Lucretia nowhere in sight. Oh yeah, *now* he understood, all right. If they had slept in the van, she wouldn't have been able to drive away in it alone.

The foam pads they had brought along were so uncomfortable that he had been awake for an hour after they had gotten settled in. He had not heard Lucretia stir once during all that time, and wondered how she managed to get to sleep so easily.

Now he knew she had only pretended to sleep, waiting for him to nod off so she could take the keys and split. At least she'd been straight with him. She hadn't taken any of his money, and had left his duffel bag behind. He couldn't be pissed at her for taking the van, since they had rented it on her credit card.

But what he *could* be pissed at her for was dissing him. He looked around desperately, dreading the time when the others would rise and he would have to tell Ezekiel Swain that the only person he had been able to talk into coming with him had gone.

The reality was worse than the anticipation. When Ezekiel Swain heard the news, he laughed out loud. "Demon *Damon*! You dumb, handsome *schmuck*! The princess not only splits on you, she *takes* your *van?*" Then he laughed, like lava bubbling. Jezebel smirked, and the others laughed, too.

Damon could feel a blush burning his cheeks. He wanted to tell them all to go to hell, wanted to lash out at that fat, gross pig who called himself a leader and bury his fist in the man's doughy gut. But instead he smiled, because he was where he had to be, and he had to stay there. There was a way to use this.

"I told her to go," he said gently, but loudly enough for them all to hear. "She wasn't right for this . . . for *us*."

"Wait a minute," said Ezekiel. "You saying you *told* her to take off with the van?"

"Sure. It was her van. And you saw the way she behaved last night. She doesn't have the determination, the *spirit*, to see this through to the end. Everybody here is dedicated. I doubt there's a person among you who isn't ready to die if we have to, to find and free the Divine. But she didn't have what you all have, so I told her to leave. I'm sorry that I couldn't bring more people to help, but those like us are very few."

He could feel them listening now, actually responding to this shit. "To leave everything behind," he went on, "and come into the desert looking for someone we've never seen, not knowing what we may have to face when we find him . . . well, it takes strong people to do that. I'm sorry she couldn't handle it, but I'm glad I'm a part of it."

For a moment there was silence, and then Ezekiel started to clap, an amused, lopsided grin on his fat face.

"Very nice. Very nice indeed, Damon. How did you know that we respond so well to flattery? But you're right on one count—that chick was a real pain in the ass." He stretched and yawned, showing yellow teeth. "Let's get some breakfast and then get our butts in gear."

Breakfast was simply instant coffee and donuts, of which Ezekiel ate half a dozen of the cream filled. Damon took down his tent and put it and his duffel into one of the vans. "Come on, Demon," Ezekiel told him. "Since your old lady took your van, you're riding with me."

"Great," said Damon with a smile. "Where are we headed?"

"Due east, pilgrim." Somewhere, John Wayne rolled over. "Toward New Mexico." Ezekiel maneuvered his bulk into the front passenger seat next to Jezebel, who sat behind the wheel. Damon got into the back, next to a colorless woman who Jezebel introduced as Charlotte. Rodney, a big man who looked like an ex-biker, was on the mousy girl's other side. Two dour men in their mid-twenties were wedged in the rear seats. "That's Chang and Eng," Ezekiel said. "Now, you're probably thinking that they don't *look* like Siamese twins, but they're bound at the hip just the same."

Damon nodded to them, looking but not discovering if Ezekiel was speaking figuratively or not. The two men stared back. They did not speak.

Jezebel drove the van out a dirt road until she reached Route 40, then headed east. The northwestern Arizona scenery was sparse and beautiful, but Ezekiel didn't seem to notice it. A six-pack cooler was at his feet, and he opened a can of the generic soda and started guzzling it. When he wasn't drinking, he was either belching or talking nonstop.

The subjects included the country around them, the Anasazi Indians who had lived there centuries before, the Navajo who lived there now. He also talked about the Divine, and how when they found him and freed him, there was going to be "a whole new world on this old shitball we call Earth,'' and how the ones who freed the Divine were going to be kings and queens over all the countries of the world, or what was left of them after the wrath of the Divine was satisfied.

"He's been held down for a long time, man,'' Ezekiel said, ''like a genie in a bottle. And when he gets out, he's gonna be righteously *pissed*. Even though he gets a taste now and then.''

"A taste?''

"Of *blood*, Demon. He knows how to mess with people's heads. Man, he messed with mine—that was how I knew he existed.''

"What did he do?''

Ezekiel turned his ball of a head around to look at Damon. "Oh no, you're not gonna get me to incriminate myself. Besides, I wasn't the one who did the actual killing, was I, Rodney?'' He reached back with a fat hand and patted Rodney on the knee.

"Sonofabitch deserved killin','' Rodney replied heatedly.

"Enough said.'' Ezekiel tossed his empty soda can out the window. "Jezebel heard him that time, too, didn't you, baby?''

Ezekiel's sister nodded. "Loud and clear.''

"I keep telling her that if he came in that strong once, it can happen again—she just gotta work at it a little harder.''

Jezebel sighed as though she had heard this many times before, but didn't otherwise respond. It was as if she knew that if she didn't rise to the bait, Ezekiel would find new prey.

She was right. It didn't take him long to turn the dreary light of his antagonism onto Damon once again. Ezekiel berated him for coming alone, and for not having the strength of will to persuade others to come with him.

Damon didn't take the bait, either. He agreed he was not a proselytizer. "There were a few,'' Damon said, "who liked what they heard, but they just didn't believe enough. But *your* people, now, they've got a strong faith and commitment. It would be an honor to lead people like this. They'd probably lead themselves, given a direction." He smiled at Rodney and Charlotte, but only Rodney smiled back, a crooked, lopsided grin.

"And what about that little girlfriend of yours?" Ezekiel said. "I still think she was the one who made the decision to split, wasn't she? All she needed was the chance." Ezekiel's laugh cut into Damon's gut like a rusty knife.

He bit back what he wanted to say. "I'm just glad that *I* can be here. I'm just glad that I can serve you—and *him*."

Ezekiel laughed again. "Okay, okay . . . you're a good boy, Demon. Maybe we can get *some* use out of you. . . ."

So the day went on, punctuated by Ezekiel's mockery that made Damon appear reasonable and slow to anger, and roused Rodney's sympathy toward him. A few gibes made the big biker actually shake his head and look out the window, as if embarrassed by Ezekiel's sadism towards so sincere a follower.

Jezebel, Charlotte, and Chang and Eng seemed to take Ezekiel's attacks in stride. They had probably heard and received worse from Ezekiel themselves.

The vehicles frequently stopped when other routes crossed Route 40. Ezekiel told everyone to shut up for a minute and sat stiffly for anywhere from five to thirty seconds. Then he nodded and pointed straight ahead, and Jezebel drove on.

Just after 1 o'clock, they stopped on the outskirts of Flagstaff for food and supplies, and Damon made certain that most of the party saw how generous he was, chipping in fifty dollars of the eighty-dollar total, and how he carried more than anyone else when they loaded the vans. It didn't keep Ezekiel from ragging on him once they were driving again.

But it was all right. The fat man would stop singing soon enough.

Chapter 3

*T*hey stopped for the evening north of Joseph City, driving a few miles up a rutted dirt road, then turning onto what looked like a cattle path. It wasn't a road so much as bare scrub.

"There it is," Rodney said, and up ahead Damon saw a low adobe building forty feet long. If it ever had any windows, they were gone now, leaving square openings in its front wall. There was an open doorway at each end.

"Old cowboy bunkhouse," Rodney explained for Damon's benefit. "When I was ridin', we used to come out here and party."

"Enough history, Rodney," Ezekiel said. "I just hope the place has running water and ice machines."

Rodney, confused, thought for a moment. "Hell, no."

"I know, Rodney. I was joking. It will be sheer delight to live as the cowboys and the Hell's Angels did."

"I wasn't an Angel, Ezekiel," Rodney said. "I was a Pagan."

Ezekiel snorted as he opened his door. "I don't distinguish between turds by their shapes or shades of brown, Rodney."

Rodney got out of the van frowning. It was certainly not the first time Ezekiel had insulted his former colors, but if Rodney was like the few bikers Damon had known, the slur would not sit well, no matter how long ago Rodney had left his club.

The bunkhouse was a mess. The legs of half a dozen rusted metal cot frames were nearly covered with the years of sand and dust that had blown in through the open doors and windows. "Well," Ezekiel said, "this is really nice, Rodney. I'm glad you remembered this place. Gonna be another tent night, friends. Unless you care to sleep in the old bunkhouse here, Rodney."

Rodney scowled and nodded. "Yeah, okay."

"Stubborn, stubborn," Ezekiel muttered, then suddenly looked up. The stupid meanness vanished from his face, and was replaced by a look of transfiguration.

The air had been still, but now the wind stirred, making small whirlwinds of sand near Ezekiel Swain, and in that moment, Damon saw why the others followed this fat, repulsive man. He had become a prophet, a seer, one who hears the voice that others cannot, who is touched by the Divine.

Then the wind stopped and there was nothing in the air but heat. Ezekiel's face sagged into its usual rolls of flesh, and he smiled. In that smile Damon read not a joy of sharing, but a satisfied possession, the dog in the manger that has his own while the other mutts starve.

"Now, that was primo," Damon said, then shook himself in a way that was probably meant to imply an orgasmic shudder. "Okay, let's get camp set up. God, I'm starving."

After dinner, Ezekiel said that he wanted everyone in their tents soon after dark. When Damon looked at Rodney quizzically, the man said, "He's goin' out—into the desert to talk to the Divine. He needs it quiet. You know, he's out there, he hears somebody back here yellin' or somethin', it throws him off. It's hard work, I guess, communicating, I mean."

This was it, then. It would be tonight. The chance to kill Ezekiel Swain had come more quickly than Damon had expected. He had thought it over long and hard all day. He had loathed Swain from the start. What he practiced was bullying, not leadership, and he had made it all too clear that Damon, the new guy, was going to be his favorite target.

But what had really nailed the lid onto Ezekiel Swain's coffin was what had made Salieri hate Mozart, Rufus Griswold hate Poe, Judas hate Jesus. It was the thought of *Why him? Why is this fat, mean asshole visited by gods, while I, who am so much more deserving, have never even been an afterthought?*

But I will be heard. For this time, fate has given me the means. Jezebel.

It didn't matter if Damon didn't have the power to hear the Divine. Jezebel did, and Damon could control her. She was already insecure enough to let her pig of a brother push her around, and probably have sex with her, too.

The thought made Damon shiver, then smile. If she was that desperate, he could run her easily. And when he controlled her, he could handle the others, too. Hell, he could tell that Rodney was so sick of Ezekiel that he'd probably be willing to become anyone else's boy so long as he could get him to the Divine. They all followed Ezekiel like dumb dogs, and when dumb dogs lost one master, they got used to another one quick enough.

Sure, Jezebel had the link, so she could be queen if she wanted to be, but Damon was going to be the power behind the throne. And when they finally found the Divine, that power would be nothing compared to what the Divine would give him. Maybe finding him would take a little longer, since Jezebel's connection wasn't as strong as Fat Boy's, but Damon would rather find him in two weeks with himself as boss than in two days with Ezekiel Swain running the show. So Ezekiel would disappear into the desert night.

From his tent, Damon watched the others retire as Ezekiel walked away from the road in the direction of a mesa. It was hard for Damon to estimate distances here, but he guessed that Ezekiel would never reach it. With his weight, he'd be panting from exhaustion after a hundred yards.

Finally the last flashlight was turned off, and the only sound was that of the wind, which was picking up force every minute. Damon stuck his head out of his tent and looked in the direction Ezekiel had walked.

A gibbous moon lit the tents and the vans, but Damon could no longer see Ezekiel Swain. When he looked across the desert, he saw only the motion of the sands being lifted and tossed by the winds. No one moved around the tents, and he heard no voices, so he crawled out and crept on hands and knees to where he could not be seen. Then he stood up.

The earth was soft, so he could walk with hardly a sound. He patted the folding Buck knife and the small, thin Maglite in his pockets, then moved carefully and quietly toward where Ezekiel Swain had disappeared into the night.

Damon had been wrong about Ezekiel's stamina. It took a long time for the younger man to catch up with him at what Damon had thought was a large mesa, but proved to be only a small flattop just two miles from the camp. The soil was more sandy here, and the wind quickly erased his footprints.

Damon moved more slowly now, watching the fat man outlined against the sky on top of the little mesa. Ezekiel's back was to Damon, and he was looking up toward the moon, so Damon knew the only way he could be seen was if Ezekiel turned and looked down at him. Even then, his eyes would be blinded by the moon.

Damon figured the best way to do it was just to do it. The ground would soak up any blood like a blotter, and it would be easy to bury the man in the soft sand. He could use his hands to dig. So he crept up the side of the flattop, careful not to dislodge any of the loose rocks that peppered his way.

He was ten yards below Ezekiel when he heard, over the roar of the wind, the man's words. "Yes," he said. "Yes, I will . . . no, nothing, Lord. I will let nothing keep me from You, I swear to You. Just keep Your voice

strong. I will come. Now ... show me, please, Lord.
Please show me what I want to see. ...."

Damon felt a chill run through him. Ezekiel Swain
seemed like a sorcerer, calling up gods and devils, casting
spells on that mini-mountaintop. But there was nothing
Damon could see other than blowing sands, nor anything
he heard besides whistling wind. He crept closer.

Ezekiel seemed to be in a trance, standing with legs
slightly spread, arms out and partially raised, as though
presenting himself to whatever was speaking to him. Damon, now ten feet from Ezekiel, felt in his pocket for the
knife.

It was a nasty piece of work, with a tapered four-inch
blade and a solid wood-and-brass handle. Damon took it
out and opened the lock-back blade, which made a soft
but heavy click, clearly audible over the wind's howl. He
could see Ezekiel's shoulders tense, his head come down
slightly, as though ducking a bullet, and then the man
looked over his shoulder at Damon.

The moonlight made the pig eyes glitter before they
vanished into shadow, and Damon knew that in that second Ezekiel saw the spray of moonlight on the brushed
steel blade. The fat man drew in a breath as if to speak
or shout, but words wouldn't save him.

Damon closed the gap between them so quickly that
Ezekiel was barely able to throw up a hand to stop him.
It didn't do any good. Damon came down over his out-
thrust arm with a right hook, burying the blade to the hilt
in the folds of the fat neck, then pushing the knife back
and out, ripping the jugular and several layers of thick fat
like butter.

Damon jumped back quickly before the blood started
to jet, and watched as Ezekiel stood, his face filled with
shock, eyes as wide as the fleshy pouches around them
would allow. He clapped a hand to his neck, but his heart
continued to pump the blood through his pudgy fingers.
It was black in the moonlight.

The dying man seemed to stand there forever, looking

at Damon. So he stepped in again, punching the knife hard into the flabby softness under Ezekiel's breastbone, and tore downward. It was like ripping open a sack of hot manure. Thick, greasy wetness flowed over his hand. Damon staggered back, knelt, and savagely thrust his hand into the soft sand, as if ridding his skin of a painful acid.

Still Ezekiel would not fall. He stood, life leaking out above and below, emptying as Damon watched and thought, as if in a nightmare, that the juices coming out of Ezekiel Swain, his blood and bile and yellow fat, were mingling together in a stream that would creep around him and drown him.

"Go *down*, damn you!" Damon said through the nausea that choked him, and he pushed Ezekiel Swain with all his strength, so that Swain finally toppled. But now Damon could see his face in the moonlight, and it was even more terrible than his leaking body.

Ezekiel's eyes were glaring at Damon with the ferocity of the justly damned, and the nostrils of his bulbous nose were a second pair of flat black eyes beneath the true and burning ones. The wide mouth, made even larger by the blood that outlined the lips, was twisted in a snarl. It tried to form words, but only air wheezed from it. Blood still pumped from the slashed neck.

"Die, Fat Boy," Damon said, hating how his voice shook.

Then Ezekiel Swain's mouth stopped working, the blood slowed to a trickle, and the head lolled to the side. But as it moved, Ezekiel's gaze remained fixed on Damon, like a portrait in which the eyes follow you about, accusing even in death.

The blood and bile continued to dribble from the holes Damon had made. It was as if Ezekiel had been filled with juice that would ooze out of him indefinitely. If he waited for it to stop, Damon thought he might be there for days. So he looked around for a place to bury the man.

The mesa top was too rocky, but Ezekiel's body was

only a few feet from the edge of the incline that led to the desert floor. Damon steeled himself, then rolled the hideous carcass, like a huge beach ball stuffed with sand, toward the edge.

Ezekiel bounced down the slope, and his body came to rest near what looked like soft sand, white in the moonlight. Damon bounded down the incline. The sand was soft and deep, almost chalky in consistency, and he began to dig in it.

Digging a grave with his hands was more of a job than he had thought, but he continued to scoop up the sand, throwing it out of the hole he was slowly making. Finally there was a trench three feet deep—two feet to cover the body, and another foot of sand to keep the coyotes away.

Damon pushed and tugged at Ezekiel's corpse until it rolled face up into the grave. The bastard was still leaking, leaving a trail of blood and yellow slime. What *was* it, anyway, fat?

Damon didn't know and didn't care, but he did realize he'd have to erase any trace of it. At least the wind was helping, blowing over the wet spots and drying them the way sand blotters dried ink.

It was a hell of a lot easier to fill in the grave than to dig it. Damon just pushed with both hands, like a kid playing bulldozer on the beach, and soon only Ezekiel's face and round stomach were protruding. He paused, shaking his aching hands to bring the blood back to his fingers.

Then he stopped. There was a trace of movement in the grave. At first he thought it was the wind stirring the sand again, but as he looked more closely, Ezekiel's stomach seemed to be shrinking beneath the bloody shirt he wore. In a few seconds it vanished, and sand poured down into the cavity it had left.

At the same time, Ezekiel's face seemed to shrink, the fullness going out of it, as though the sand itself was draining it of its fat and moisture. The cheeks went flat, then hollow. The eyes pulled into themselves, and sand flowed into the sockets and filled the empty cheeks. The face was gone. A coyote howled over the roar of the wind. It sounded close.

Suddenly Damon felt very alone and very guilty and very scared. But before he could return to the relative safety of the camp, there were things to do.

He finished filling in the grave and retraced his steps up the flattop to examine the site of the killing. The blood and whatever else had leaked out of Ezekiel's body were already gone. The sand had soaked it up and blown it away. What a great place to kill a fat asshole. Let him leak all over, and the sand would take care of it all.

Damon headed back to camp, trying to keep from whistling in happiness. It couldn't have gone better. Soon this little band would have a new leader, and that leader would have a woman who could lead them to the Divine.

As Damon crept stealthily into the shelter of his tent, he would not have been so happy had he realized with what intensity he was being watched.

Chapter 4

*T*he panic started before dawn. Damon had slept lightly, anticipating the searches and suspicions the next day would hold. He was not disappointed.

Jezebel had not awakened until four in the morning, and was alarmed to find Ezekiel still gone. She took a flashlight and searched for him, but became scared when she heard the coyotes howling, and returned to camp.

She woke up Rodney, and the two of them went back out with a lantern, walking all the way to the flattop. They found no trace of Ezekiel, nor any sign that he had been there. When they got back they roused the rest of the party.

"Everybody up, c'mon," Rodney shouted. "Ezekiel's missing, man, we gotta find him. Let's go!"

The fourteen people split into seven pairs, and Rodney fanned them out in a shotgun pattern heading north. Damon was paired with Charlotte on the extreme right flank. Rodney and Jezebel, pale with worry, took the center route, which would bring them to the small mesa once again.

Damon was worried. What if he hadn't noticed something, like a pool of blood that the sand hadn't soaked up and blown away? What if his footprints had remained in spite of the wind? Rodney wasn't a total dummy. He was smart enough to know when Ezekiel was putting him down, and he might also be savvy enough to notice, under the bright sun, some disturbance in the sand where Damon had planted Ezekiel.

Some of the others were already looking at Damon with distrust. A stringy young man and his woman kept watching Damon from under glowering brows while Rodney gave them their orders. Though they said nothing, Damon could feel their hatred.

He and Charlotte walked their route, and Damon tried to be the picture of determination and fortitude. "I didn't come all this way," he told her, "to find Ezekiel and then lose him. He's got to be out here somewhere. People don't just disappear. . . ."

Charlotte, who apparently had needed only the proper conversational gambit in order to speak, went on at length about a cousin who had indeed just disappeared during a camping trip to Yosemite, never to be seen again. "That's when I knew," she concluded, "that there was more to life than I thought."

That launched into a story about how she had first found the Swains and learned about the Divine. By the time she finished, they had swept back toward the center as ordered, where they met the rest of the party at the mesa.

A chill went through Damon when he saw the others standing not fifty yards from where Ezekiel's body was buried. No one, however, seemed to have noticed anything, "Well," Rodney said, "at least there's no sign anything bad happened to him."

True enough, the absence of any coyote-chewed bones or shredded clothing was a relief to most of them, but not to Jezebel. She seemed a hair away from flipping out, and kept muttering, "We've *got* to find him, we've *got* to . . . let's look again . . . farther away . . . he must have gone farther away. . . ."

Damon, anxious to draw the group away from the mesa, agreed. "Jezebel's probably right," he said, as the others turned in surprise to hear the newbie express an opinion. "Ezekiel's a holy man, one who receives visions from the

Divine. And a holy man possessed . . . who knows where he might have gone? Maybe just kept walking until he couldn't walk any more.''

''What the hell are you saying?'' asked the man who had looked at him with such suspicion. ''That the Divine would lure Ezekiel out into the desert to his death?'' A sob escaped Jezebel, and she buried her face in her hands.

''No,'' Damon answered. ''If the Divine took Ezekiel into the desert, it was for a reason. To show him something, give him new wisdom, teach a lesson, not only to him, but maybe to us, too.''

''What kinda lesson?''

''About patience, about dedication, I don't know. But I do know that if Ezekiel's out there lost or wandering, we're not going to do him any good by standing around here.''

''Well, who the hell are *you* telling us what we oughta do? Funny, you ask me, you cruise in here and the next night Ezekiel disappears, man! What's *that* shit?''

''Okay, Ted, cool it,'' Rodney said. Then he looked at Damon with flat eyes. ''What you got to say about that?''

Damon spoke calmly, but with enough fire to show that he was unjustly accused. ''I came here to find the Divine. Why would I try and hurt the only man who can find him for us?''

Rodney nodded slowly, as did Charlotte and a few of the others. ''Then we'll just keep lookin'. Right, Jezebel?''

She looked up, her cheeks wet. ''Yes. We have to find him, we just *have* to.''

They spent several days widening the search, establishing a base camp at the old bunkhouse. Jezebel contributed nothing to the effort; she was too sick with worry over her missing brother. The others cleaned out the bunkhouse for her so that she would have an airy and open place to rest.

Once Damon was shaken when Aileen, Ted's girlfriend, suggested bringing in the police. He could just picture trained dogs going directly to the grave and digging like crazy in the soft sand. Fortunately, Rodney scotched the idea. There were too many of them who couldn't afford to be questioned by the law.

During the next few days, Damon insinuated himself among the others. It wasn't hard. He appeared to search for Ezekiel many long hours, and returned to the camp seemingly exhausted. What the others didn't know was that he spent most of the time resting in the shadows of buttes, or in small canyons.

At the end of four days, they were ready to give up the search. Some thought Ezekiel had been taken by the Divine onto the next plane of existence, while others figured he must have stumbled off a cliff. Whatever the answer, they had to go on.

Jezebel Swain was not sympathetic to this view. She pleaded for them to remain and continue the search, but Damon knew that they had wasted enough time here.

"We have to go on," he told Jezebel in front of the others. "Ezekiel is gone, and you're our hope now, Jezebel. You're the only one who can get us to the Divine so that we can free him."

"I don't know...." She shook her head. Damon thought she had lost ten pounds in the last few days. "Without Ezekiel...."

"You *have* to," Damon said, and the words made her jerk up her head and look at him, trembling. "We followed Ezekiel, but we're not here for him—we're here for the Divine. And you're the only one who can find him." He took a deep breath and shook his head. "You don't have to do anything but take us to him. We can handle the rest."

"But I'm not a leader, not strong the way Ezekiel ... is."

"You don't have to be the leader. We don't even *need* a leader—we're all here for the same purpose, right?"

"But Ezekiel said one person should make the decisions. What do we do if . . . *when* we find the Divine?'' Jezebel asked.

The opening was there, and Damon didn't have to leap in himself. ''I think *Damon* would make a good leader,'' Charlotte said. He could have kissed her. He had worked on her the way he had worked on the others, but she had been the most malleable. Except for Rodney and Ted, the others were born followers. They would fall in behind whoever turned out to be the Alpha dog in the pack, sniffing his ass.

But now Ted staked his claim. ''Why the hell Damon? Why not me? Or why not Rodney—shit, he's the strongest.''

''Yeah,'' said Rodney. ''But I ain't . . . I'm not the smartest. If we're gonna have a leader, and not just Jezebel, then I say Damon, too.'' That floored Damon, but he tried not to let his surprise show. ''He worked harder'n anybody lookin' for Ezekiel,'' Rodney went on, ''and he knows what's goin' on, and I think . . . well, he oughta be it.''

Ted made a noise of disgust, but said nothing more. Damon nodded. ''If that's how the majority feels, all right. But I won't lead you unless I know you want me to.''

''Okay,'' said Ted. ''Let's vote on it then. I say no, Damon's too new.'' He put up his hand. ''Who else?'' Aileen hesitated, then raised her hand. No one else did.

''Who's for Damon, then?'' asked Rodney. Everyone except Ted, Aileen, and Jezebel raised their hands. ''That's it. But what about you, Jezebel? You're the one with the power.''

''I don't care,'' she said, in a voice heavy with weariness.

''You're going to *have* to care, Jezebel,'' said Damon. ''You've got to do what Ezekiel would have—find the Divine—and we need to start now. We've waited long enough.'' He turned to the others. ''Let's strike camp. It's time to get moving.''

He was relieved to see the way they responded. All they needed was someone to tell them what to do.

As he was taking down his tent, Rodney came up and spoke quietly. "You know why I did that? 'Cause I saw you that night, saw you go out and come back." Damon felt ice all along his throat, down into his stomach. "And when we was out there—at that mesa—you buried him in the sand there, didn't you?"

Damon couldn't say a word. Rodney shook his head. "Man, I wanted to kill that bastard for weeks, but I didn't have the balls. You did, so you oughta be king shit. Lemme tell you, though. I want to find the Divine, only reason I put up with Fat Boy's bullshit. He can't find him no more. If Jezebel can, fine. If she can't, then you're toast, friend." Rodney smiled. "And don't think you can jump me the way you did Tubby. I'm big, but I'm fast. We make progress, we'll get along okay. Well?"

Damon smiled back. "Thanks for your continued support." Then he turned his back on Rodney and continued rolling up his tent.

That night, long after the cultists piled into their vans and headed east, a coyote trotted around the base of the small mesa. He was old, and had just been outrun by a jackrabbit, so now he was looking for carrion.

He stopped and sniffed. There was something dead nearby. The coyote snuffled the ground, and detected traces of blood in the sand. He dug tentatively, and the scent grew stronger. Meat was buried here.

He dug faster, and the scent continued to strengthen. The meat was deep, but the sand was soft. It flew from his paws, and he began to pant with the exertion.

The scent was powerful now, almost maddening to the starving animal. He dug as if in a frenzy. But when his claws finally scraped the surface of the meat, he yelped and leapt back.

Something was wrong. The meat was bad. Not rotten,

but bad in a way that the coyote could not understand. Though his stomach burned with hunger, he could not bring himself to approach this meat again.

He turned and ran silently away into the night.

Chapter 5

*O*ne week after the old coyote had uncovered Ezekiel Swain's corpse, Richard Skye sat in his office in the CIA headquarters in Langley, Virginia. On his computer, he was writing his monthly report to the deputy director concerning the field agents working under his supervision.

Three of his agents, he reported, were working separately, using simple covers to investigate the interconnected activities of the Russian Mafia in Ankara, Bucharest, and Azerbaijan. Their involvement with illegal drug transactions in order to penetrate the layers of the Mafia's bureaucracy had made it impossible for Skye to entrust the local governments with data concerning the operations. So the operatives were working under NOC, nonofficial cover, with fully developed legends, complex but artificial life histories and backgrounds.

As far as the governments of Turkey, Hungary, and Azerbaijan were concerned, the agents were dangerous drug dealers. If it was revealed that they were working for the Company, the resulting fallout would be unacceptable to national security, and if the agents were revealed to the Russian Mafia as anything other than what they were thought to be, there would be no opportunity for a rescue.

Agents Laika Harris, Joseph Stein, and Anthony Luciano were now on their own. Reports from them would be sporadic, as each contact increased the risk of their discovery. The operations could take a year or longer. It was altogether possible, Skye reported, that he might not hear from any of them at all during that time.

God, what a sack of crap, thought Skye, as he keyboarded in his code name for the deputy director. But it was an impregnable sack, lined with steel mesh. He hit the combination of keys to transmit the report, then sat back, interlaced his fingers behind his head, and permitted himself a rare grin, showing white, even teeth beneath his carefully trimmed moustache.

That would do it. The agents were now his to do with as he liked. And his goal, crystal clear to him, but hidden from everyone else except his true, secret employer for whom he had done a number of services in the past, was to find that goddamned prisoner.

He remembered when Mr. Stanley had first told him about the prisoner:

Consider, Mr. Skye, a man of near infinite power, whose abilities are so beyond ours that we might even consider him a god. But he is still a man who can be made a prisoner, and if he can be held, his power can also be harnessed. The man—or government—who is able to control this creature could have unlimited powers, Mr. Skye. And unlimited wealth.

It was a pleasing prospect for any man, most of all Richard Skye. Mr. Stanley had heard through his many sources that the Roman Catholic Church was holding such a man, if a man he was. He had been held for many years in many places all over the world, and what better way to ferret out his hiding place than to use the most sophisticated intelligence gathering agency in the world? Skye was a high-ranking member.

But not high enough. Three years before, he had been passed over for a deputy director appointment. Even though Skye had made the Company his life, apparently he had not kissed enough asses in his twenty-plus years of service to warrant the promotion. So he remained in field operations, hating those above him, coming to hate even his country, but not to the point of selling it out like Aldrich Ames, for a small bit of money.

No, the way to become Judas was to align yourself not with some enemy of your country, whose bureaucracies would prove to be just as stifling and unrewarding as your own, but to one of the true powers of this world, to an individual with so much money and influence that his only unrealized ambition was the amassing of still more. Such was Mr. Stanley, and if Skye were able to utilize his position in the Central Intelligence Agency to track down this supernatural paragon and deliver him into Mr. Stanley's hands, and if Mr. Stanley were able to harness this creature's power, well then, Skye would come as close as one could to sitting at the right hand of God.

But so far the quest had proved fruitless. Skye had been able to ascertain, from certain lower level informants in the Vatican, that the church was indeed holding a mysterious prisoner, but that was the extent of the information. No government in the world was more difficult to gather intelligence on than the geographically minute but influentially global bureaucracy of the Roman Catholic Church. By the time a functionary reached a certain level in Saint Peter's government, he was unturnable. No priest would betray his holy city for money when he sincerely believed that after thirty more years of wealth in this world, he would spend an eternity bubbling in the hellfire of the next.

The only thing known for certain about the elusive prisoner was that his presence had in the past been considered responsible for what people referred to as paranormal activity. It was a long shot, indeed, but since no cardinals were rushing forward to reveal the prisoner's whereabouts, the only other option was sending operatives into the field to investigate such events.

The trick was that such operations had to occur without anyone in the Company but Skye knowing their true objective. And what made such intelligence gathering even more difficult was having to do it within the borders of the United States, an action specifically prohibited by the CIA charter.

Still, Skye had found a way around the difficulties. He had recruited a team led by Laika Harris, a thirty-five-year-old African-American agent, highly experienced in field operations. The woman was a born leader, and Skye suspected she had to be in order to handle two such disparate personalities as the others on the team, Joseph Stein and Anthony Luciano.

Stein hadn't been in the field in years and was an out-of-shape desk jockey, but with a mind like a fifty-gig hard drive and a skepticism that quickly separated the bullshit from the truly paranormal occurrences. Unfortunately, they had seen more of the former than the latter.

Anthony Luciano was Stein's opposite in many ways, gullible and a believer in his Catholic faith, but of great use for such a group, since he was a master of B&E and surveillance. He was also a masterful killer, should he be forced to resort to using those skills.

The supposed rationale behind the operations was that the president was concerned with the way that leftist New Age beliefs in everything from crystals to cults, and fundamentalist fervor over demons and angels, were making the USA the world center of irrationality. The operatives' job was to visit "paranormal" sites, as representatives of the National Science Foundation, and prove their normality. Case closed.

What Skye was counting on was that there would someday be a case that *couldn't* be closed by the ops' investigative prowess, and when that happened he would set them looking in earnest for the elusive prisoner—them and a few of his attack hounds in the Company, relatively brain dead but loyal as dogs to Skye. This current report would ensure that when Harris, Stein, and Luciano had accomplished their actual mission, they could, if it became necessary, be quietly terminated to keep their superior's involvement permanently secret.

Unfortunately, the first operation had been unsuccessful, although Skye thought it had initially shown much promise. Peder Holberg, a sculptor who worked in iron, had disappeared in an explosion in a workroom in his New York City studio. Dozens of people had supposedly seen him enter the room, and there was no other way out, yet no traces of human remains had been found after the explosion.

The operatives had discovered a secret studio in a warehouse that held the ruins of the sculptor's last work, which had been destroyed at roughly the same time as the explosion in the main studio. After months of investigation, however, the agents had found that Holberg had indeed left the room before the explosion had occurred, unseen by the drunken and cocaine-snorting patrons of the arts. According to their report, he had booked passage on a cargo ship back to his native Norway but never arrived. His suicidal tendencies had undoubtedly driven him over the side. As for the sculpture, it was merely a work of modern art, and a ruined one at that.

Mr. Stanley had been greatly disappointed, though not surprised. It would have been a stroke of good fortune had their very first attempt proved positive, but both Skye and Stanley were realists enough to know that the search could take years, and the current operatives would have to be replaced before it was completed.

Harris, Stein, and Luciano were the best team Skye could gather, but already he was considering who might replace them when the time came. They could not remain indefinitely under NOC. But he had just bought at least a year of their usefulness, certainly long enough to look into a number of occurrences, the next of which would be the strange death in Arizona and a possibly paranormal phenomenon only a few miles away from where the body had been found. Perhaps one of these by itself would not bear investigation, but it was the combination of the two that bore looking into.

Skye's operatives had had enough R&R time. He began to write the directive that would take them west.

Chapter 6

"**W**hy the hell do we have to drive all the way to Arizona?" Joseph Stein said, turning in the front passenger seat and trying unsuccessfully to stretch his six-foot frame.

"Because the airports may be covered," Laika Harris replied from the backseat. "You know *somebody's* been trying to follow us."

"It was merely a rhetorical question," Joseph said. "As in bewailing my state."

"Well, keep your bewailing to yourself," Laika said, "or I'll make you trade seats before the next stop." She turned toward Tony Luciano, who was smiling at the exchange. "Make any more tails since we lost that one in Jersey?"

He shook his head. "Nope."

"I still don't think he was a fed," Joseph said.

Tony nodded his head. "He was, trust me. He drove like a fed."

"You lost him easy enough," Joseph reminded him.

"A *dumb* fed," Tony added.

"What would the FBI be trailing us for?" Joseph said, unable to drop the argument.

"I don't *know*, Joseph, but it was the kind of car the feds drive, and the method of the tail was right in line with their training—I mean, it was textbook. That's why he was so damn easy to lose." Tony suspected that the agent was young, and hadn't yet learned how to break the rules. He was glad he'd been able to help educate him. "Where do we make the switch?" he asked Laika.

She referred to a dossier on the seat beside her. "About fifty miles, after we get on 78. It's a rest stop set back from the road."

Tony nodded. "We get to hear the directive, then?"

"No," Laika answered. "More of Skye's cloak-and-dagger stuff. Not until we're over the Missouri border."

"Oh well, that makes sense," said Joseph dryly. "Missouri—espionage capital of the world. Come on, Laika, we'll never tell. Open the damn thing now and let's find out what goofy assignment we've drawn this time. Christ, he's probably got us going after a cactus in the shape of the Virgin Mary."

"Yeah," Tony said, "Or a haunted hacienda or something." Tony could feel Joseph tense, and he wished he had bitten his tongue. The mention of a haunted house couldn't help but remind Joseph of the woman he had killed in New York. A supposedly poltergeist-infested row of townhouses had turned out to be haunted by an all-too-alive pair of insane squatters whose baby had died of malnutrition. When Joseph and Laika had found their hiding place, the woman had attacked, and Joseph had had no choice but to shoot her.

Tony kept his voice light, going on as if he'd said nothing unusual. "Come on, Laika. Skye hasn't bugged the car. I checked. What's the difference if we know now or twelve hours from now?"

"Forget it," Laika said. "The orders say Missouri; we wait until Missouri."

And that, Tony knew, was the way it was going to be. Laika was the team leader, and she went by the book. At least, she had until she had given Skye that completely spurious report about their activities in the Peder Holberg investigation. They were all in on it now, not only working against the charter by performing internal operations, but going a giant step beyond that by conspiring to keep vital intelligence from their superior.

None of them trusted him. His reputation for cutting field agents loose had preceded him, and they also suspected that he had been responsible for planting the bug they had found in the warehouse that had contained Peder Holberg's final work.

But the main reason for their distrust was the mass poisoning of eleven Scotsmen in upstate New York. There had been one survivor, a man who had called himself Kyle McAndrews, and who had tried to kill them in return. *You, your organization, what difference does it make? You work for him, there's blood on your hands.* That was what he had said before he had tried to kill them, and they had killed him instead. He had, in so many words, accused Skye of the mass assassination.

What made the situation even more confusing, and, to Tony as a Catholic, compelling, was the mark identifying McAndrews as one of the Knights Templar, and a first-century wooden cup among his few possessions, a cup that now lay in a safe deposit box back in New York City. Further evidence from other sources suggested McAndrews' involvement in some way with a prisoner being held by the church. The more the operatives learned, the more it seemed that this prisoner was either descended from the bloodline of a Jesus Christ who had survived the cross, or—and this was what had truly stunned Tony—an immortal Christ himself.

As Tony thought about the possibilities, he broke the silence that had settled on them after Laika's last pronouncement. "You know what we *oughta* be doing? Looking for the prisoner."

"Damn right," Joseph said softly. "But no way we can tell Skye about it. Not yet anyway, not until we know where he stands."

"Sonofabitch stands over a pile of bodies," Tony said.

"We don't know that," said Laika coldly from the back. Tony glanced in the mirror, and saw that she was looking out the window at the trees whipping by. "Suspicion isn't certainty."

"But it's kept you alive more than blind trust would have," said Joseph, and Tony saw a thin smile crease Laika's dark and lovely face. Tony wished that he wasn't attracted to her, but damn it, a woman was a woman, and he'd never be able to look on Laika as merely his team leader. His hormones wouldn't allow it.

But he also wouldn't ever attempt to start any kind of relationship with her other than professional or platonic. Anything more was out of the question, even if she were willing, which he was sure she wouldn't be. *Get back on track,* boy, he told himself. "Maybe we'll stumble across him again . . . the prisoner."

"Could be," said Joseph. "After all, he had a connection to Holberg. Maybe some other so-called paranormal bullshit will draw us to him. Of course, it all depends on Skye's directives. The odds are long, I'm afraid."

Tony knew they were. Yet who would have suspected that Holberg's last work, once they had reconstructed it, would point the way to the prisoner? The damn sculpture had been a map showing precisely where Mister X was being held. But when the ops had gone there, he had been whisked away right under their noses, and they had been nearly killed by a stronger-armed force that seemed to be there for the same reason as they, to free the mysterious prisoner.

Two people had died that night, and on the body of one of them, the agents had found a list of cities and dates headed "*Locus hominus aeterni,*" or "Place of the one who never dies," which only added fuel to the theory that the prisoner was, to say the least, long-lived.

There was also a sheet of paper whose front and back were filled with numbers. They had identified it immediately as a book code, but without the proper book to check page, line, and word, it was impossible to decode. They could have sent it to Langley, but didn't want to tip their hand to Skye. As far as Tony was concerned, Skye knew next to nothing about the prisoner, and the ops wanted to keep it that way.

Tony glanced over at Joseph as he pulled another book from the backpack at his feet. "What are you reading?" he asked him.

"I'm trying to find out about what McAndrews said just before he died," Joseph said. "That word . . . or words."

"You still think it had something to do with that Andrea guy?" Johann Valentin Andrea was said to have been the head of the Priory of Zion, a group that wanted to put the bloodline of the Merovingian dynasty, supposedly descended from Christ, back on the thrones of Europe.

"Well, Andrea's Rosicrucian connections link nicely to the Templars, but I don't know."

"Still," said Tony, "it'd be kind of a roundabout way of delivering the message." He thought for a moment. "What if he was trying to say his own name?"

"What?"

"Sure. He said something like 'anda' or 'andra.' What if he was trying to say 'McAndrews?' Andra . . . Mc-Andrews?"

"First off," Joseph said, "his name probably wasn't McAndrews to begin with, and second, if you were dying, do you really think you'd try and say, 'Luciano?' I know *I* wouldn't."

"You might if I was around."

The second car was right where Skye had informed Laika it would be. They transferred their bags from one car trunk to the other, locked the keys to the first car in its trunk, and headed west on Route 78 again. "I think the leg room in this one is worse than the Chevy," Joseph said.

"Stop complaining," Laika replied. "We may have a bigger problem."

"I spotted it," Tony said. "It was with us when we got on 78. When we stopped, it pulled over. Further on, it picked us up again after we switched cars."

"What do you want to do, Laika?" Joseph asked.

"We can't lose them here. Let's get off at the next exit and get back on right away, as if we got off by accident. If they follow us, we'll know for sure."

"Then confront them?" Tony asked.

"First, let's see if we're just being paranoid."

The next exit was four miles ahead, and when they got off, the van followed them. But when they looped right back on, the van turned onto a state road and disappeared.

"Feel better?" Joseph asked.

"Much," said Laika.

A half mile behind the three agents' car, the driver of a 1995 Ford Taurus spoke into a cell phone. "I've got them again," he said. "We better stay further back from now on. They made us too quickly that time."

Tony, Laika, and Joseph did not notice the car following them, nor did they notice the six changes of vehicles behind them that occurred over the next day and a half. When they left their motel on the outskirts of Indianapolis the following morning, the driver who had watched their room all night from his car made another call for the next pickup. The surveillance they were under was handled professionally and systematically.

Chapter 7

They crossed the state line into Missouri in the late morning. "We're here, Laika," said Joseph, who was now driving. Laika ignored him, continuing to look out the window. "La-*ee*-ka?" Joseph went on in a singsong voice. "Did you *hear* me? We're in Mis-*sour*-i, and you know what Mis-*sour*-i is?"

"What?" Tony could see a smile creeping onto her face.

"The Show Me State," said Joseph. "So show me. . . ."

"Show *us*," Tony corrected.

Laika gave a small laugh and picked up her dossier from the floor. "You two, I swear, you're like a couple of kids. Okay, okay. Let me read it first."

Although Tony glanced back over the seat several times, he could not make out any of the small type on the four-page directive. Finally Laika looked up at him as if to caution him to wait, and he gave a sheepish grin and faced the road again. After a few more minutes, she spoke.

"We're going out to Arizona to investigate a mummy that's been found there."

"A mummy?" Joseph said, with more than a touch of sarcasm. "And no doubt the archaeologist who found it is suggesting that its discovery proves a link between North America and Egypt via ancient astronauts."

"An archaeologist didn't find this one—a hiker did."

"So what's the big deal?" Tony asked.

"The big deal is that the hiker who found the mummy had eaten lunch with him just two days before."

"Whoa," Joseph said. "Are you saying that the mummy wasn't old?"

"Brand spanking new. The mummy's name was Philip Lynch, and he was backpacking alone through the high desert."

"The Four Corners area," Joseph said.

"So where'd he find him?" asked Tony.

"Just a few miles south of the Navajo reservation, off a dirt road. Nearest town of any size is Joseph City."

"Never heard of it," Joseph said.

"No reason you should have," said Laika, flipping through the dossier. "It's hardly a metropolis. Anyway, the hiker met Philip Lynch in Winslow at a café; they ate together and chatted enough to exchange names. Turned out they were both going to the same area—up near the border of the reservation, near Louis Well. Indian roads, mostly, dirt or gravel, and both intended to take trails off of them."

"What's the difference between a trail and a dirt road?" Tony asked.

"You'll have to ask the hikers that. But two days after they meet, the hiker comes across Philip Lynch. At least, he *thinks* it's Lynch—the mummy is wearing Lynch's shirt, shorts, and hiking boots, and carrying Lynch's backpack. Though how a mummy got into all this is beyond the hiker. He gets back to civilization, gets the police, and they pick up the body and get it ID'd."

"How?" asked Tony.

"There's enough left of the fingerprints, and Lynch had conveniently left a set with a Flagstaff backpacking club. Apparently it's par for the course when they go into the back country alone."

"You have the medical examiner's report?" Joseph asked.

"Yes. The gist of it is that the tissues are completely dried out. Leached. Not a drop of moisture in the body."

Tony rested an arm on the seat back. "Could he have been burned somehow?"

"No. Not a trace of ash. And his clothes weren't burned, remember."

"Well, what about spontaneous combustion?"

Joseph snorted. "Spontaneous *human* combustion. SHC. It's a crock, Tony. Bodies don't burn by themselves. There always has to be an external heat source, since the human body's mostly water. For the body to burn, that water has to be vaporized away first, and it can't happen from the inside."

"Carl Sagan was wrong," Tony said.

"About what?"

"Life after death. Reincarnation in particular. He came back in you, Joseph."

"I can think of no higher compliment, Tony. But I have to decline the honor. Sagan would never have been swept away by the Holberg case and this whole prisoner thing the way I've been. But hell, we're off the subject. Was there any heat source near the body, Laika? Anything that might have . . . dried him out?"

"Just the sun," said Laika. "But whatever dried the hiker worked a lot faster than that."

"Did the M.E. have any conclusion?" Tony asked.

"No. Apparently he doesn't want to believe this is really Lynch's body. He has 'hoax possible' in his notes. Still, the fingerprints. . . ."

"That's how it strikes me." Joseph suddenly seemed to think of something. "What about blood? Any trace of it, or did the *chupacabras* get that, too?"

Laika's face clouded for a moment, then brightened as she chuckled. "Oh, the Mexican goat-suckers. Well, if it was them, they're pretty picky. All the blood *solids* were present, but no liquid at all."

"Stranger and stranger," Tony said. "That's one selective phenomenon. Can we rule out Joseph's vaporization?''

"We can't rule anything out," Laika said, "until we investigate ourselves. And even then, who knows? There's something else, too. Skye has it almost as a footnote, doesn't want us to investigate it specifically, but only if we suspect some connection. . . .'' She seemed hesitant to continue.

Tony prodded her. "And that is?"

"Between Winslow and Joseph City," she went on, "around the same time as the discovery of the corpse three days ago—and only several miles away from where it was found—someone made a huge design in a sandy area near the main highway, Route 40. It's a fairly well-traveled road, but no one noticed any lights or anything else the night before it appeared, or saw anyone or anything in the area the day before."

"Uh-oh," Joseph said, "sounds like the cereologist-baiters have found a new game."

"The what?" Laika asked.

"The folks who made the crop circles in England. Some here in the States, too. The people who went for it called themselves cereologists—"

"After Ceres, goddess of grain and the harvest." Tony grinned. "I just want to make sure you know you're not the only college graduate in the car."

"*Touché,*" Joseph said. "And do you also know that they were, and are, all fakes?"

"So I've been told. Seems natural to me."

"These designs in the sand are probably the same kind of thing," Joseph said. "Fakes."

"Maybe," said Laika. "But they sure weren't made the same way. As I recall, the crop circle people used wooden contraptions that they pushed in front of them, and grain, if it isn't pressed down hard, will spring back up again, so that you can walk through it and leave no trace. But these sand circles were fairly deep—up to eight inches where the sand was softest—and there were no prints of feet or vehicles approaching the area.''

''Ah, aliens coming down from the sky, no doubt,'' Joseph said. ''And what were the designs anyway?''

''There were two. A stepped pyramid and a triangle.''

For a moment, they all were silent. ''A triangle, huh?'' Joseph said thoughtfully. ''Those things get around.''

Tony knew they were all remembering the triangle of sculpted iron that had led them to the hiding place of the prisoner in New York City, and, most of all, the isosceles triangle drawn in Peder Holberg's dried blood that had pointed west-southwest, the precise location of Arizona from New York City.

''These symbols were used by the ancient Anasazi,'' Laika said quietly.

''An Indian tribe?'' Tony asked.

''Yes. Vanished centuries ago. But they left a lot of ruins behind. Mesa Verde's the biggest, but there are also sites at Chaco, Navajo National Monument, Canyon de Chelly—all over the southwest.''

''How come you're up on all this?'' Joseph asked.

''I had two courses in native American cultures in college. I enjoyed it, so it stuck.''

''You know what the symbols mean?'' Tony asked.

''Well, the triangle is associated with the sun and with corn, and can be a fertility symbol. If it points up, it stands for fire and the male sex. Down is for water and the female sex.''

''And which way is this one pointing?'' Tony asked. ''That is, if it's isosceles and has a short point.''

''It is and it does,'' Laika said, referring to the dossier. ''And if north is up and south is down, the short end is pointing up.''

''Fire,'' said Joseph. ''And the male sex.'' Tony knew what he was thinking: the prisoner was male.

''What about this pyramid?'' Tony asked. ''So what's the difference between a pyramid and a triangle on a flat plane?''

''A *stepped* pyramid,'' Laika explained. ''It's a common Indian symbol. It can mean rain clouds, or . . . a stairway to heaven, the steps to the next world."

"So we've got a stairway to the next world," said Tony, "and another triangle. That's triangle number three, in fact, if you count the one in Peder Holberg's sculpture and the one back at the warehouse pointing . . . here. Three triangles, three sides . . . a male symbol, and the prisoner was male. . . ."

"Don't let your imagination run wild," said Laika. "To paraphrase Freud, sometimes a triangle is just a triangle."

"Laika's right," Joseph said. "There are more coincidences in life than there are synergies. After all, triangles abound."

" 'Triangles abound,' " Tony repeated. "Sounds like a new-age gift shop." He looked back at Laika. "So what do we do first, boss?"

"We get through Missouri, Oklahoma, Texas, and New Mexico. Then we'll see the medical examiner, talk to the police, and view the body, after which we'll no doubt come up with a brilliant solution. Or not."

Tony's smile faded as they continued to drive. He thought about a desiccated, mummified body, then about Peder Holberg, the sculptor, and his apparent apport, when he was swept from his midtown studio in an instant to the warehouse in the Bronx, smashing into and becoming one with his sculpture, fragments of bone and blood and muscle blending into the iron, then finally dropping from it weeks later, as shards of yellow bone and powdery dry blood, forming the pattern of the triangle.

"There wasn't much moisture left in Peder Holberg, either, was there?" he said, almost to himself, but the others heard.

"There's no connection," Joseph said flatly, his hands on the wheel, eyes on the road.

"No? What happened to Holberg—and his body—was inexplicable. Same with this Lynch."

"It's only inexplicable because we haven't explained it

yet," Joseph said wearily. "There is no connection with the prisoner here."

"You don't know that," Tony said. "Maybe you hope there's not, but you can't know that."

Father Alexander sat and watched the desert night come slowly. The air was cool on the portico of the Mission of San Pedro, and a breeze was rising, blowing strongly enough that he was at last relieved of the musty smell of the mission's rotting interior.

He shivered, partly from the chill of the air and partly from the knowledge of what was going to come to this place in a few days. He wasn't sure when. He had been called from the Tegakwitha Mission at Houck, one of the few missions flourishing in these days of pagan returns. Even the whites were learning the Indian lore now, looking into the ceremonials as though these foolish practices would give them a glimpse into the beyond that they were incapable of finding in the true faith.

They needed him there, and he had been happy and full of purpose, feeling as though he were the last holdout against the Indians, like the Kit Carson of the stories his father had told him in Ganado when he lived there as a boy. His grandfather had been in the U. S. Cavalry and had filled his father's head with his exploits, and his father, a mostly unemployed house painter, had passed them on to young Alex.

He had quickly become infatuated with the idea of battling Indians, but he knew those days were over. Besides, he was a spindly boy who fared poorly at sports. But he learned there was another way to carry out his grandfather's work, and that was to change the Indians' souls, turn them from their dark gods, their peyote ceremonies, their kivas and their sweat lodges, to the living Christ, through whom even they could be saved.

He brought light to the heathens, but he brought more than that. The church brought education and cleanliness and warm clothing and blankets, taught the Navajo and the Hopi, who were his wards, how to care for themselves and let Jesus care for them. His grandfather, he thought, would be proud of him. While the old man had killed the Indians, his grandson had killed the Indian gods, the things that made them strong. Now they were little more than white men with brown skins, all brothers in Christ.

At the thought of Christ, he remembered what was coming, and he closed his eyes and prayed, asking for the strength to deal with it. The creature had touched him before, nearly seduced him to do its evil bidding, although he had struggled and won through, and no one ever knew how close he had come to sinning. No one ever knew that he had nearly been a murderer.

And now he waited again, here among the steep canyons of southern Utah, for his nemesis to return. He prayed that his years would not tell against him. The first time, he had been young and strong, but now he was old and bent with age. Still, his faith was that much stronger, and that was what was needed to keep the enemy at bay.

That, and prayer.

"West," Quentin McIntyre said thoughtfully. "Well, that certainly offers a lot of possibilities, doesn't it?"

Alan Phillips, assistant to the FBI deputy director, did not respond, knowing the question was rhetorical. Phillips had just performed the unpleasant task of telling his boss that the three CIA operatives had evaded their surveillance, thanks to a dumbass rookie screwing up royally what should have been as easy a piece of tail as a two-dollar whore, though Phillips hadn't used those particular words. This was, after all, the FBI.

"Skye's running them, damn it," McIntyre went on. "This isn't a rogue operation, at least to the extent that these operatives are on their own. Skye's behind it, steering all the way, but what the hell that bastard's up to I can't begin to guess." McIntyre took a sip from his coffee mug, then made a face.

"Cold, sir?" Phillips said, and, at McIntyre's nod, took

the mug, went down the hall, and refilled it with hot coffee. If he was going to be McIntyre's lackey, he'd be a good one. It was one way to rise in the ranks.

"I'd be willing to bet, though," said McIntyre, when Phillips returned, "that it's got some of that psychic crap mixed up in it. Skye's had a hard-on for that ever since that thing with the Russian psychics the sonofabitch disappeared."

"How deep do you want to go looking for them now?" Phillips asked. "They could be anywhere in the States, or out of it."

"Did our people get any photos before they lost them?"

"No. No sooner found than lost."

"And we can't get them from the CIA, that would tip off Skye. So all we've got is that shot of Luciano from the tabloid, that *Inner Eye* rag. Well, it'll have to do. Have it reproduced and sent to every field agent, along with descriptions of Laika Harris and Joseph Stein. Let's see if we can't get better pictures of the three somewhere— put an agent on that exclusively, but very low profile. I don't want anybody knowing we're looking for these people. And when you send out the data, tell the field to keep on the lookout. Maybe we'll get lucky, maybe not. And tell them to pay particular attention if they're in the vicinity of vaguely so-called paranormal occurrences."

McIntyre grabbed another newspaper off the pile sitting on his desk and began to go through it, looking for any small item that would trigger his deep database of a memory. His glimpse of the photograph of Anthony Luciano had led to the current investigation, and Phillips had seen McIntyre perform even more wondrous leaps from the most seemingly innocent mentions.

Phillips turned and left the office without another word. His boss was at work. There was something deep between McIntyre and Richard Skye of the CIA, but Phillips had no idea what it could be. There had always been a rivalry between the two agencies, and although the CIA had run plenty of operations inside the country, the feds had never liked it, even on the rare occasion when they were informed.

But this thing between McIntyre and Skye seemed to be more than mere professional jealousy. Phillips had the feeling that the deputy director hated Richard Skye. Whenever the FBI became aware of a domestic operation by the Company, they were always interested, since it was possible that it could be a rogue op, run for a traitor's own good. So it was possible that Skye had sent out a team of ops on his own, though Phillips doubted it.

There were too many ways that such an operation could be discovered. He had never heard of anyone successfully covering all the many clandestine bases. There was always something they had missed. From the intelligence that the bureau had gathered on Skye and his operation, it seemed to be sanctioned by everyone it needed to be sanctioned by. At least the cover did.

As for the *deep* cover, the actual operation within the United States, breaking that Company ice was nearly impossible for the bureau. Phillips could only hope that the king spooks knew what was wiggling in their own drawers.

In the meantime, he would do what he could to satisfy Quentin McIntyre. The odds of a field agent stumbling across these three ops were about as long as winning the Virginia state lottery, but hell, Phillips still bought an occasional ticket. So he'd do what McIntyre told him and more. If his number hit and the agents turned up, it would be one hell of a payday for him. McIntyre might not have been the kind of guy who thanked you for schlepping him coffee, but he knew how to recognize performance above and beyond, and that was precisely where Phillips intended to go.

Chapter 8

*T*hey were close now. They had been scheduled to stop outside of Albuquerque for the night, but had made good enough time through the day that Laika had decided to push on. She was driving now, and Joseph was dozing in the backseat. Laika had loaded the CD changer with all three discs of Birgit Nilsson's 1966 Bayreuth recording of *Tristan und Isolde*, and while listening to it kept her alert, it had been an effective soporific for Joseph.

Tony sat in the passenger seat, reading with the aid of a minilight that plugged into the cigarette lighter, and occasionally glancing into the right rearview mirror. "Don't you ever sleep?" Laika asked. It was long after midnight, and Tony had driven for most of the day.

"When I hit the sack," he said, "and not before. When I know I'm safe and sound—or when I know I'm as close to it as I can get and I don't have any choice, I sleep."

"Lightly, I'll wager."

"Yeah," Tony said quietly, thinking about the two times that sleeping lightly had saved his life, once in Beirut, another time in Montevideo. When much of your career was wet work, you had to learn to sleep little and lightly, or else you would sleep hard and long, and not wake up.

"Oh hell, look at that," said Laika, braking the car slowly. Tony saw a sign up ahead: ROAD CLOSED—DETOUR. An arrow pointed north. Laika swung onto the dirt road as directed and drove down it a few hundred yards until it came out onto a two-lane blacktop. Another detour sign with an arrow pointing up for straight ahead was prominently posted.

"Wonder how many miles this'll take us out of our way?" she said. "God, I remember one time my folks and I took a vacation out here when I was little. Triple A had routed us fairly far north of here, and there was a detour. We went over what had to be Arizona's highest mountain on a dirt road with no guard rails, didn't see another car for thirty miles. My dad had to replace the shocks in the next town. Needless to say, he was not pleased with Triple A."

"This doesn't look as bad as that," Tony said. "I'll drive, if you want me to. You've been going for four hours straight."

Laika agreed and pulled the car off the road. Tony got out and Laika slid over, but Tony murmured, "Excuse me a minute," and stepped away from the car and into the darkness to urinate. He listened for a moment, but heard only the car's engine humming softly. When he returned to the car, he got in, turned off the headlights, and switched off the engine. "You gotta get out a minute," he told Laika.

"I don't *have* to go," she said, and he heard the humor in her tone.

"Not for that," he told her. "For the silence . . . and the stars. Come on, look at this." He got out and Laika did the same.

They let their eyes adjust to the darkness, and he heard Laika whisper, "Wow."

"You betcha," Tony agreed. He had never seen the stars so bright. There was no moon, and the sky seemed a pall of black velvet with pinpricks in it and a bright light shining through from behind. A glowing haze swept across the roof of blackness. "The Milky Way," he said. "Ever see it so bright? Not a town anywhere near, and there hasn't been a car in miles. And listen. . . ."

There was only the desert breeze. No sounds of cars or planes or trains or distant cities. Just wind in the sand, blowing over the rocks. Tony felt as much at peace in that instant as he ever had.

And then a fist of light struck his eyes, and Joseph called from the open back door of the car. "Is this a private party, or can anyone stand in the sand and let gila monsters and scorpions crawl up their legs?"

"Thank you, Joseph," said Laika dryly. "You know how to make a moment perfect."

"Oh, *I* see—communing with nature. Sorry to wreck the mood, but I thought our goal was Winslow, not the middle of the desert . . . unless this *is* Winslow. After all, I have no idea how desolate these little Arizona towns are."

"All right, we're coming," Laika said, walking back to the car.

"Well, take your time," Joseph said, getting out and stretching. "I need to irrigate the sands a bit. . . ."

When they were all back in the car, Tony pulled onto the road again. Three miles away, there was another detour sign, this one pointing left. "Must be the road west again," he said, "and we'll turn south before too long."

But he found to his dismay that the road was dirt, and began to wind its way through high canyons whose tops they could not see from the car. "Why the hell," Laika muttered, "didn't Skye's itinerary mention this little hell-drive?"

"It's all right," Tony said. "I've driven on worse."

"I'd feel a lot better," Laika went on, "if we saw another car out here." She peered ahead. "Or even some fresh tracks."

"Those tracks are fresh, *kemo sabe*," Tony said. "I can see at least one set that hasn't blown away."

"Great," Laika said. "That makes me feel a whole lot better."

They rattled along for another few miles, dropping in and out of canyons and slipping on loose stones as Tony accelerated up the hills. They had just come around a bend in the road when Tony pumped the brakes. There was something ahead that didn't fit into the landscape, something whose whiteness gleamed in the beams of the headlights.

The drive had been so eerie and disquieting that the first thought Tony had was that it was a ghost, some desert phantom standing by the side of the trail long after midnight, and he shivered in spite of the fact that he knew it had to be real and solid. The white form defined itself as he approached, and he saw that it was a woman standing there, wearing a white T-shirt and khakis, waving to them.

"My God, who's that?" Laika asked, and he was glad she saw the woman too. "The ghostly hitchhiker?"

Tony continued to slow. "Pull over for her?"

In response, Laika opened the specially designed glove box and Tony saw the Glock 17 inside. "Just slow down for now. Joseph, you awake?"

"Yes, indeed," came the voice from the back. Tony also heard the click of the console in the center of the backseat and knew that Joseph was ready with a weapon as well, in case the girl was the bait in some sort of trap. Perhaps, Tony thought, the detour had been a fake. He pressed his elbow against his side and felt his own pistol nestled snugly under his jacket.

He slowed the car further, until they were only ten yards away from the girl. Her long though striking face was relieved but wary at the same time, and Tony saw a patch of red on the white T-shirt, just over the girl's left breast. A large black backpack with a sleeping bag strapped to it was sitting in the dirt at her feet.

"Pull over, Tony," said Laika, "but everybody be ready." She rolled down her window, and Tony stopped the car several feet away from the girl and watched the mirrors. "You stuck out here?" Laika asked her.

"Sure am," the girl answered, in a soft contralto. "Think you could give me a ride?" Tony glanced at her and saw a cut above her forehead, probably the source of the blood on the shirt.

"Where are you headed?"

"Anywhere. I'm just doing the area, but I could use a place that's got a motel and a restaurant."

Laika gestured to the girl's forehead. "What happened?"

Her face soured. "Oh, I hitched a ride with a truck driver . . . didn't work out too well. He got a little . . . aggressive, and I grabbed my backpack and jumped out, while he was still moving. That's when I got this." She touched her forehead, and Tony could see the blood had dried. "He stopped and came looking for me, but it was dark, and I ducked into some brush."

Laika nodded, and Tony sensed some sympathy from the team leader. Laika had had her own problems with an abusive man, James, her ex-boyfriend, who had gone down in a shower of bullets when he had tracked them to the prisoner's hiding place in New York. "Climb in the back," she said. "We're heading for Winslow."

"Oh, that's great," the girl said, snatching up her backpack and running to the door Joseph had opened for her. "There's a bunch of motels there."

By the glow of the dome light, Tony could see that she was young, probably in her early twenties, and she was prettier than he had first thought. Her hair was chestnut brown, and her face and arms were deeply tanned. Even in the dim light, Tony could see that her eyes were a sky blue. Her face was a long oval, with a small nose and a wide mouth that didn't seem as if they should go together, but did nonetheless, and very nicely, too, he thought.

He smiled over the back of the seat at her, and she smiled back, then pulled the door shut, dropping them into darkness again. Tony started driving.

"I was really lucky you guys were coming by. I haven't seen a car since I jumped out. I'm Miriam . . . Miriam Dominick."

"Glad to meet you, Miriam," said Joseph. "I'm Kevin,

this is Florence, and our loyal driver is Vincent." The names were their National Science Foundation covers. "Wow, that's some heavy backpack," he said as he hoisted it onto the back ledge. "Collecting arrowheads?"

She laughed. "No, that's my camera equipment. I'm photographing the country, as much of it as I can possibly see—the towns, the desert, the canyons, just whatever catches my eye, defines the place for me."

"You a professional?" Tony said.

"I've sold a few things, but I can't support myself yet. I'd like to, though. This trip is kind of a crack at it, get a few hundred rolls shot and see what happens."

"There's always *Arizona Highways*," Joseph said.

"One of the toughest to get into," Miriam said. "I've looked at it all my life."

Suddenly they were all jarred by the uneven boards of a bridge that crossed a gully. "My God," Joseph said, his voice vibrating, "what the hell is that?" Then they were over the bridge, and he laughed. "I can't believe some of the—"

But Miriam interrupted him. "Stop the car," she said in a low, tense voice. "Please stop . . . right now. . . ."

Tony took a quick look at Laika and saw her dark face in the dashboard lights look at him for a moment, then nod sharply. He hit the brakes, and the car slid to a stop in the dirt. Laika turned to the girl. "All right, why?"

The girl sat there, her head down, eyes closed, a grimace on her face as though she were in pain. Then a strange sound came from ahead, a low rumble, followed by a clatter, the sound of falling rocks. It lasted for several seconds, then died away.

Tony looked at the road ahead and saw, just beyond the headlights' reach, brown dust floating toward them. Then he looked back at Miriam.

She looked up suddenly, her eyes opened, her mouth took in a breath like an emerging swimmer gasping for air, and then she let the breath out slowly and looked at

Laika almost apologetically. "I knew something was coming, but I didn't know what."

"Pull ahead," Laika told Tony, and he obeyed, driving slowly toward the dust, stopping when it became too thick to see. It took several minutes to settle, and during that time they got out of the car, Miriam with them, and started walking into the dust with flashlights.

There were rocks all across the road, most of them smaller than a foot in diameter, but a few were larger, and a half dozen were boulders six feet across or more. The rocks had fallen from a steep cliff to their right, and some of the larger stones were on the extreme left of the road, at the edge of an embankment. Tony's light showed a steep dropoff, and from the looks of the crushed vegetation, some of the larger rocks had gone over the side and down into a canyon below. It was all too obvious that if they hadn't stopped when Miriam had told them to, they might have been caught in the avalanche, and either been crushed or pushed over the side.

Chapter 9

"**G**ood call," Joseph said flatly, shining his light down over the embankment.

Laika looked at Miriam as though she were hiding something. "How did you know?" she asked. "Why did you stop us?"

The girl gave a self-effacing smile and shook her head. "I don't know how I knew," she said. "I just did. It happens now and then. I just . . . *know* things, *see* things. I mean. . . ." She struggled to explain it. "I didn't know about the rocks, but I just knew there was something dangerous up here, that we had to stop, that if we stopped we'd be all right." She laughed nervously. "And we are."

"Yeah," said Laika, giving Joseph a sidelong look. It was, Tony thought, probably due to their recent experiences together that Joseph didn't look more scornfully at Miriam than he did. It was quite remarkable how seeing inexplicable things could change even the most devout skeptic, a category into which Joseph had comfortably fit until recently. "Think we can start clearing the road enough to get through?" Laika asked Joseph, shining her light upward.

"Probably," Joseph said. "Slides like this don't happen very often. All the loose stuff's probably down by now."

So they set to work, picking up and tossing the rocks

over the side, pushing the larger ones until there was enough room for Tony to maneuver the car around them. In a few miles they joined a blacktop road again where a detour sign pointed left. "More like it," Tony said, and felt the tension flow from him as the tires traveled smoothly over the road.

There had been an uncomfortable silence in the car ever since they had left the rock slide, and Tony tried to break it by talking about what had to be on all their minds. "So, Miriam, this has happened before? Your, what would you call it, premonition?"

"Yes," she said. "I get feelings about things . . . it's as if something tells me not to go somewhere or do something. Sometimes I learn that I might have been harmed if I had—like the rock slide? And other times, well, there doesn't seem to be anything bad that happens."

"But it might have," Tony suggested, "if you'd acted against what you thought."

"Or maybe not," said Joseph. "Premonitions are funny things. We have a pretty selective memory when it comes to coincidences, but our memories get faulty concerning the noncoincidences, which, let's face it, are a lot more plentiful."

"What do you mean?" Tony asked.

"Well, lots of times people have bad feelings about things—getting on planes, going on trips—but when they do, and they arrive safely, they forget about the bad vibes they felt. But that one time out of a thousand when something really does go wrong, when there's an accident or a flat tire or something, they remember the premonition."

Miriam nodded. "I see what you mean, um. . . ."

"Kevin," Joseph said.

"Kevin, sorry. But my . . . experiences aren't like that. I love to travel, and I never have premonitions, just these . . . *things*. And they are so sure, so certain, that the people around me know, and they can vouch for it. I just figure it's a present from God."

"You're religious, then?" asked Joseph, and Tony

hoped that he wasn't going to start one of his agnostic harangues.

"I was brought up Roman Catholic," Miriam answered. "I'm kind of lapsed, but it's been more the result of circumstances than any willful denial. I still believe in what I learned. It's just that it's hard to attend mass when you spend a lot of your Sundays in the desert, or on the rez."

"The rez?" Tony said.

"The Indian reservation. I try to photograph there as much as possible, though it's hard. The Navajo aren't very cooperative, and unfortunately I've never been able to break through their reserve and make any real friends among them, except for a few I've met in some of the towns."

"I'd think they'd be impressed," Joseph said, "with somebody who can predict rock slides."

"You're making fun of me," Miriam said, though not angrily.

"No, just skeptical, that's all."

"Kevin," Tony said, using the cover name, "you really saw it, so how do you explain it?"

"It's possible Miriam might have actually heard the beginning of the slide, or sensed the trembling of the earth ahead. To me that's more likely than a visitation from the spirits."

"Just one spirit," Miriam said. "God."

Joseph chuckled. "Ah, the main man himself."

"My mother always told me it was a gift, and not to be scared of it. It would come in dreams, too. I would see things, and the next day I would see them for real. A person, or a pattern, or an animal . . . and there it would be, and I would remember it."

"And did you ever tell anyone about these dreams?" asked Laika. "Or could it have just been dèjá vu?"

"Oh no, I told people—my mother, my sister, my friends. And they would see what I had dreamed about, and they would know I was telling the truth."

"It's a wonder," said Joseph, "that you never tried to use this in any way, you know, become another Jeane Dixon, only a *real* one, of course."

"Oh no, it's nothing that *I* do. I mean, I can't sit down and make predictions, or see what horse will win a race, or what stocks will do well. When it comes, it comes; and when it doesn't . . . well, I'm just like everybody else."

"I can't believe that," said Tony, intending it to sound as flirtatious as it seemed.

He heard her give a little laugh, though he couldn't see her face in the mirror. *Score one, ace,* he thought, and smiled in the dark.

Once they got back on 40, it took only another hour to get to Winslow. Still, it was 2:30 in the morning when they entered the town. "So," Laika said to Miriam, "can we drop you off anywhere before we try and find a place for the night?"

"Or what's left of it?" Joseph said.

Miriam seemed slightly uncertain. "Well . . . maybe I could just go where you're staying. I mean, one motel's pretty much the same as another, and I did want to spend a few days shooting around here. . . ."

From the corner of his eye, Tony could see that Laika wasn't pleased at the prospect, and he knew why. It was never a good idea to get friendly with civilians, even possibly psychic ones. But dumping her somewhere else would seem suspicious, and Laika must have realized that, since she nodded and said, "Sure, that's fine."

They pulled into the parking lot of the first chain motel they saw, and registered in four singles, which seemed to surprise the clerk, who thought he was seeing two couples. They were all in the same hallway, though not in adjoining rooms.

Tony received a call in his room five minutes after he closed his door behind him. "Come down," Laika said into the receiver, and hung up.

Joseph was already in Laika's room when he got there. "We'll just go for a few hours sleep," Laika said. "Let's be ready to head out at nine—the hospital first, then we'll go to the site where the body was found." She paused, as though she wasn't sure what to say next.

Joseph filled the gap. "What about the girl?"

"What do you mean, what about her?" Tony said.

"She's going to be around here for a few days, and so are we."

"So what? She doesn't know who we are. And if she knows our covers, it doesn't matter. A lot of people are going to know Doctors Kelly, Tompkins, and Antonelli before we're finished here. From the National Science Foundation, big deal."

"What are you saying, you want to date her?" said Joseph.

"Date her? Hell no, but if we run into her again—and we probably will, if we're staying in the same place—so what?"

"We want to stay as low profile as possible," Laika finally said. "And this girl's a photographer."

"So? She's interested in rocks and Indians, not us. What are you saying, you want to terminate her because we picked her up?"

"Of course not," Laika said. "I just don't want any of us to fraternize with her further."

"Fine," Tony said, "But I'd have thought we'd jump at the chance to deal with a genuine psychic."

"She's not genuine," Joseph said wearily.

"Hey, if it weren't for her, we might be at the bottom of a goddamn canyon right now. And you heard what she said about the other times."

"Yeah, what she *said*," Joseph replied. "Okay, maybe her little premonition saved our asses, but how many times that we don't know about has she hitched a ride, pulled the same 'Stop the car' stuff, and nothing happened? And then she says, 'Oh gee, I'm sorry, I was so *sure* something bad was going to happen.' Tony, all we've got here is one coincidence and a little anecdotal evidence, and that's nothing."

"I have to agree with Joseph," Laika said. "But the main point is that even if she made aliens come down and dance the boogaloo on our car roof, we're investigating a mummified corpse, not some nineties Bernadette with visions, no offense, Tony."

"None taken," he lied. "And no fraternizing, I get it, okay?"

"Okay," said Laika. "See you in the morning, right?"

Tony and Joseph went in different directions when they hit the hall. Typical, Tony thought. That sonofabitch could be such a know-it-all. Tony had seen what had happened in the car, he had known there was something other than a coincidence going on there. The fact that she was Catholic helped convince him.

Tony always felt that people of his own faith, so rich in ritual and mystery, were more susceptible to the other mysteries of this world as well. One of his mother's aunts was born with a caul, and family history told of her predicting not only the death of her own mother and father, but the crash of the *Hindenburg* as well. What was so difficult about believing that a Catholic girl could have a premonition of danger, especially when the results were so impressive?

But Tony felt more than just a fascination over Miriam's psychic abilities. He had been drawn to her in a way he had always tried to avoid. In Tony's profession, women were something to be kept at arm's length, and sex was recreation rather than an expression of love, something fleeting and enjoyable to both parties. The woman had to know going in that it wasn't going to be anything lasting, and there were always a lot of women who were willing to play by those rules.

Love and wet work didn't mix. They gummed each other up so badly that neither could thrive. You loved somebody, you started wanting to come home to them, so maybe you got a little too cautious, and that could be as dangerous as being too reckless. But the worst thing that

Tony could imagine was having somebody who loved him left alone after he was killed.

It was what had happened to his mother, and he had watched her shrivel up and lose the will to live after his father had died in an accident at work. She had lasted for seven more years, and seemed to grow more and more transparent each time he was able to visit her, which was generally two or three times a year. She had quit smoking, but started again after she lost her husband, and was up to two packs a day when the lung cancer hit her at age sixty-three. When it happened, she welcomed it, refusing chemotherapy. "I just want to be with Frank," was all she said about it. Tony wasn't with her when she died, and he never stopped wishing that he had been.

So he had always tried to stay away from Miriam's type, the type he suspected he could feel more for than just companionship and desire. But in spite of his better judgment, in spite of what Laika had just said, he wanted to see her again. There was something about her that he couldn't shake.

Besides, the Company didn't have any right to run his private life, as long as it didn't interfere with his current op, and neither Laika nor Joseph had the right to tell him what to do, either.

Chapter 10

*T*hree hours later, the cultists rose with the dawn. Things had changed among those who had followed the late Ezekiel Swain. The days that had passed since they had hit the road again had been full of frustration and tension.

Jezebel, after much concentration, had felt that they would reach the Divine by going east, so they traveled in that direction on Route 40, stopping every twenty miles or so to let her get the psychic scent again. Rodney drove and Jezebel rode shotgun, with Damon right behind her, frequently querying her as to whether or not she had it. "Yeah," she would say, "yeah, it's okay."

But it wasn't, as it turned out, not by a long shot. God damn it, the bitch couldn't sniff out a bad container of yogurt in a heat wave. They had driven and driven and driven, and were nearly to the New Mexico line, when she had shaken her head and said, "Wait . . . wait, wait, wait, please, just stop. . . ."

She had gotten out of the car, and Damon had been ready for her to point dramatically to one of the half dozen rusty trailers around which a bunch of Indian kids ran. But instead of making some magnificent gesture of discovery, Jezebel stood for a moment as if listening, then put her head in her hands and started to cry.

"What?" Damon said, feeling the presence of all the others behind him, sensing their expectation and anticipation. "What's wrong?" But she only kept crying. "What the hell is *wrong*, Jezebel?"

She looked up, her cheeks streaky with tears. "I don't have it anymore. . . ." she whimpered.

"Have *what?*" Damon asked, near panic. Jesus, had she lost the power to sense the Divine altogether?

"The *trail*," she said. "We went too fast . . . there were too many roads . . . I missed Him. . . ."

"Too many roads?" Damon said. "Jesus, we were only on one road, Route 40 all the way!"

"No, I mean . . . too many off 40 . . . listen . . . it was on one of those that I lost it, it *must* have been. I just have to stop, you know? I'm not as good as Ezekiel was, I want to be, but I'm *not*," and she started to cry again.

"Okay, okay, jeez, knock it off. So you're saying that you want to go back the way we came and stop at all the crossroads so you can pick up the trail again?"

She shook her head. Well, that was good, anyway, Damon thought. Maybe she could just stick her stupid head out the window like a dog, and get a whiff as they passed each crossroad. "No," she said. "We need to go back to where I started . . . *then* start again. I have to stop everywhere . . . wherever there's a possibility He might be . . . I mean, it's no use in getting it—*if* I can get it—where there's no road. But He could be anywhere . . . in any direction."

Oh, Jesus. He thought about all the exits they had passed, and all the different directions off all of them. First to backtrack and start over, and then to stop and get out and let her get the vibes or the message or the radio waves or whatever the hell it was that she was picking up . . . it was going to take days, maybe even *weeks*. Damon started to think that maybe he had made one large economy-sized mistake when he had offed Ezekiel. His sister was apparently not in the same Daniel Boone league.

"Shit," he muttered, and then swung a fist at the side of the van. "*Shit!*" No one said anything about his outburst, though Ted shifted angrily, as though he wished he had the balls to. But Damon had quickly won most of them over to his side. Rodney seemed to be standing by him, and that muscle helped. "You can't go backward?" Damon asked Jezebel.

"No, I *can't!*" she shouted at him. "And who the hell are you to get pissed off at *me? I'm* the one who can talk to the Divine, not you!"

It was, Damon realized later, one of those defining moments that dictate where the power lies. But at the time he acted purely out of instinct, walking up to her and putting his face so close to hers they nearly touched.

"And what the hell does that make you, Jezebel? A tool, that's all! A vessel! Your brother not only had greater power than you, he was a *leader*. But you not only have a mere fraction of his ability, you snivel when you fail. You cry and cower and want to give up. Well, I won't let you do that to *them*!" He waved a hand, indicating everyone who was watching. "And I won't let you do it to me, and I won't let you do it to yourself!" He stepped back from her, pleased at the way her face had gone pale and her head had dropped slightly in submission.

"Now, you pull yourself together," he went on in a softer voice. "We'll take a rest, and then we'll turn around and go back the way we came, and stop whenever you want. We'll do whatever we have to do to help you find the trail of the Divine. But we expect you to be strong. Only strength will do it. If you already think you're beaten, we'll never find the one we seek. Be strong, girl. Be as strong as Ezekiel would have wanted you to be."

Her face started to tremble, and he held up a hand. "No! Let his name and his memory put steel in you, not bring you to tears. You do this for *him*, if not for us."

Jesus, he thought, it sounded like bad melodrama. But it had the desired effect. Jezebel's lower lip stiffened, and she straightened her head. "All right?" he asked her, and she nodded sharply. "Let's go, then." Damon turned and looked again at the others. A few, Ted among them, seemed restless, as though they wanted to protest Damon's control of the situation.

But how could they? He had taken matters in hand and dealt with them, and now they were ready to proceed again. They were once more on the trail of the Divine. How could they protest anything that gave them that result?

They couldn't, and Damon walked to the van and opened the door for Jezebel. It was not so much a gesture of courtesy on his part as it was tucking away a very valuable item that he owned.

Tony, Laika, and Joseph met promptly at 9 o'clock, had breakfast in the coffee shop, and drove to Winslow Memorial Hospital, on the northeast side of town. There they asked to see the hospital administrator, a Dr. Ward, to whom they showed their false credentials, which identified them as being from the Division of Special Investigations of the National Science Foundation. "We've been sent," Laika said, "to investigate the condition of the body of Philip Lynch, the hiker who was found."

"Ooo. . . ." Ward said, as if she had mentioned something indelicate. "That's going to be difficult. You see, we released the body to the custody of the family, and, uh . . . well, considering the circumstances, they chose to have it cremated."

Laika closed her eyes for a moment, then opened them and looked at Ward. "You didn't receive any request from the foundation to hold the body until we arrived?"

"Well, yes, but not until two days ago. The body had already been cremated here in Winslow, and the ashes sent to the family in Tucson. I'm sorry."

"We'd like to talk to the medical examiner, then. I assume an autopsy was done. Were photos taken?"

"Uh, I'm not really sure, you'd have to ask Dr. Petrie."

Dr. Martin Petrie looked like what Tony imagined as a desert rat prospector. He was in his sixties, and his white beard was in sharp contrast to his deeply tanned skin. "Damn goofiest thing I ever saw," he told them in his office. "The man looked mummified. If I'd have come across him in some ruins, I'd have sworn he was a seven-hundred-year-old Indian corpse. But don't take my word for it. . . ." He opened a desk drawer, took out a large envelope, and handed it to Laika. "See for yourself."

The three of them looked at the photos. Some were close-ups and others were shots of the entire body lying on a steel autopsy table. There was also a series of photos of the body, clothed in a T-shirt, shorts, and boots, lying in the sand.

"Those are the police photos," Petrie said.

Laika looked up at the man. "May I see the autopsy report?" Petrie handed a couple of stapled papers across the desk to her, and she quickly looked through them. " 'Cause of death unknown,' " she read. "There were no signs of any wounds or blunt trauma?"

"Not that I could find," Petrie replied. "Would've been hard as hell to spot any bruises on that skin, though—you can see it's like dried leather. But none of the bones beneath were broken, and the skull was intact . . . there was just no *juice* left in the man."

"His weight was 22 pounds?" Joseph asked in disbelief.

"Like I said, just like a mummy."

"Look, Doctor," Tony said, "if all the fluid was missing from his body, it had to get out somehow. Otherwise, it means he'd have suffered total dehydration over a period of less than two days, since that's when he was last seen. And that's impossible."

Petrie shook his head. "There were no wounds . . . not even a little hole where a vampire could have stuck a straw."

"You *did* check for bite holes in the neck, of course," Joseph said wryly.

"Of course," Petrie returned with the same smirk. "Nary a toothmark. But believe you me, it was something more than the desert sun that dried out this poor fellow.''

"Could he have been exposed to some other source of heat?" Laika asked.

"Like a giant fruit dryer?" Petrie said. "I doubt it. Any heat intense enough to evaporate all the fluids from the body in such a short period of time would leave some sign of burning, and this guy's hair wasn't even charred, not to mention his clothes. The man just dried up, that's all.''

"What about radiation?" said Joseph, thinking aloud.

"Don't see how," said Petrie. "Never heard of any kind of radiation that would do that, and even if there was, how did this Lynch fellow stumble across it out in the back country? Some scientist with a secret lab under the desert? Hell, sounds like one of those Mickey Mouse funnies I read when I was a kid. So, you starting to see why I put, 'Cause of death unknown'?''

The three agents visited the Winslow police station and met an Officer Bryant, who showed them the police file on the case and more copies of the photographs taken at the scene, along with the deposition of the witness who had found Lynch's body. There were no surprises.

The hiking trail on which Donald Vance had found the body ran through an abandoned ranch just south of the vast Navajo reservation. Vance had returned to town and gotten the police, who thought at first that Vance was trying to hoax them by putting clothes on an Indian mummy. But when Dr. Petrie had found that the teeth had modern amalgam fillings, and after the fingerprints had matched Philip Lynch's, they were convinced that it was no hoax.

"There's no mention of any footprints," said Laika.

"Between the time Mr. Vance found the body," Officer Bryant said, "and the time we drove back there, there was one helluva storm rolled in. If there were any footprints, they'd been washed away."

"And you found nothing at all suspicious?" she asked.

"Nothing except a dried-up body. That was sure suspicious, but I can't tell you how it got that way. You want to check the place out yourselves, I'll take you out there in the four-wheel—it's about twenty miles of dirt road."

"Fine, thanks. Dr. Antonelli and I will come with you. But I'd like Dr. Tompkins to look into another matter—those large sand designs located near here?"

"Oh yeah, those . . . you head toward Joseph City on 40, you can't miss them—about a mile east of Hibbard on the left. Though with everybody traipsing around out there, I don't know how much is left to see."

As it turned out, there wasn't much, just as there wasn't much to see on the hiking trail, up which Officer Bryant easily maneuvered the four-wheel, dodging around rocks and bumping through ruts that would have gobbled up a less sturdy vehicle. When they arrived at the site, there were absolutely no clues to be seen, and after only minutes they drove back to Winslow.

When Joseph had returned, they thanked Bryant and drove to a restaurant. There they had dinner while Joseph told them that his trip had been futile. "The designs themselves were almost all trampled away by gawkers. The only thing I learned was that they must have used something damned heavy. That wasn't just soft sand they made the patterns in—it was a mixture of soil and sand, not like sand castle sand."

"Could you tell how deep the designs were?" Laika asked.

"Like I said, they were pretty well kicked in, but there were a few places that looked to be damn near the eight inches in the report. Think we ought to report it to Skye?"

Laika shook her head. "It wasn't requested, and I don't think we should give our friend Mr. Skye any more than he specifically asks for."

"So we struck out," said Tony. "No body, and no magical UFO sand circles."

"No body," Laika agreed, "but those photographs

were convincing enough. And I sure as hell can't come up with an explanation for Mr. Mummy, can you two?''

Tony smiled. "I liked the giant fruit dryer theory. That body looked like a plum after it became a prune."

"Drier than that," Joseph said. "Once I toured the Mutter Museum in Philadelphia—medical anomalies, and other similar goodies—and they had two dried bodies, cut down the middle and split apart, with all the dried organs in place. Dry as a bone. That's what those photos reminded me of. And no, I have no idea how it might have been done."

" 'Been done?' " Laika said. "You're implying, then, that it was an outside act."

"Well, I doubt suicide," Joseph said, "and it hardly ranks under natural causes."

"Got it," said Tony. "The same aliens who made the designs shone the sun's rays through a giant magnifying glass. *Poof.*"

Laika finally chuckled. "We're looking for *rational* explanations, Tony. I don't think Skye would want that one leaked to the press."

"Speaking of which," said Joseph, "there were plenty of tabloid toads out at the landing site, but why aren't any reporters sniffing out this Lynch death?"

"Bryant told us on the way back," said Tony. "They reported it to the press as heat stroke, and fortunately nobody had the curiosity to check the death certificate. Just another hiker who stayed out in the sun too long, happens all the time." He looked at Laika. "So what's next, boss?"

She sighed. "Unless something happens overnight, I think we ought to visit Lynch's family in Tucson, see if he had any enemies, what his work was, if he had any medical condition that would make him susceptible to. . . ."

She seemed to be searching for the right word, and Tony helped her out. "Prunization."

Laika gave an exasperated laugh. "All right, for want of a better term."

"What medical condition could even begin to cause something like this?" Joseph asked, not amused. "But it seems to be the only path to follow. Okay, Tucson it is."

Chapter 11

At midnight, an hour after Laika, Tony, and Joseph went to bed, a sixty-three-year-old Navajo named Ralph Begay came stumbling down a road that had once been loose stone, but had now been reclaimed by dirt, like so many of the Indian roads on the reservation. Begay had had too much to drink, as he often did, and was unsure as to whether or not he was even on the right road home.

Jesus, he thought, turning the white man's god into an epithet, the only use to which he ever put it. All these damn roads looked alike, especially in the moonlight. He'd be lucky if he made it back to his place on the rez. It wouldn't be the first time. He'd spent a lot of chilly nights wrapped up in the serape he wore, sleeping out in the open before he sobered up the next morning and made his way home. That was why his arthritis was so damn bad.

But it didn't ache now. That's how he knew he had enough to drink, when his joints stopped feeling so damned painful and his elbow didn't hurt when he bent it to lift the glass to his mouth. Unfortunately, by the time he got to that point, he was stinking drunk, and they threw him out of the Longhorn or Boots & Saddles or the Dewdrop Inn, or any of the other dozen bars in and around Gallup that he frequented.

And he drank whisky. He was proud of that—of not

being one of those damn wino Indians who bought a three- or four-dollar bottle and sat in an alley or on a curb, swigging away until it was empty. Hell no, Ralph Begay could afford to sit in a bar like a white man and toss back shots at a buck and a half or two bucks each until he was properly stewed and feeling no pain. *Then* they could boot him out and he'd be none the sorrier. He'd have forgotten, for a time, about the betrayal.

But you looked at it another way, and if it hadn't been for the betrayal, he wouldn't be able to afford the whisky. He'd be respected, but he still wouldn't be able to afford to get rid of the pain. Nah, thought Ralph Begay. Whatever it took to get the whisky was worth doing, and the others could just go to hell if they didn't like it. His wife would still take care of him.

Ralph nearly tripped in a rut, and stopped for a second to regain his balance. For a moment he thought he heard something shuffling along behind him, and thought— quite logically, it seemed to him—that it must be his shadow following along, catching up to him.

Then he realized how stupid that was, and thought about Coyote. Coyote, that trickster of the animal world, often delighted in tormenting men, and if there was one thing Ralph Begay didn't need, it was more torment. So he started walking again, faster than before, and his own footsteps shuffling along in the dirt covered the sound of any others nearby. When Ralph no longer heard them, they slipped from his mind.

He felt pretty sure now that he didn't know what road he was on, and he'd probably have to spend the night outside. He had just decided to start looking for a ditch or culvert in which to curl up, when he heard a strange noise ahead to the right, and saw lights in the sky.

He rubbed his eyes to try and make them more clearly define the blurring lights, but they would not, so he stepped from the road and walked closer, across the scrub and rocks and sand. In his youth, Ralph Begay's eyesight had been phenomenal, but now the cataract in the right eye and the glaucoma in the left had taken away his ability to even find the Pleiades, let alone count every one of the seven star-maidens. Maybe if he got closer he could tell what the lights were. Now he didn't even have a sense of their distance from him. They might have been a hundred yards or a hundred miles.

Whatever and wherever they were, they also gave off a sound, a heavy throbbing. Maybe they were demons, and the lights were their flashing eyes, and the sounds were their huge hearts beating. Maybe they had come for him, and he was walking right into their trap. He didn't know, and in his drunken state, he scarcely cared. If they were demons he would talk to them, ask them what they wanted. Maybe he would ask if they had any whisky.

But then it seemed as if the demons were moving away as he drew nearer. Yes, that was what was happening, all right. They must have been scared of him, Ralph thought. You never could tell with demons. Sometimes they were brave, and at other times they were cowards. He had been lucky enough to confront a pack of cowardly ones.

Or at least he thought he was lucky, until he came over the rise and saw in the moonlight below what they had left behind in the sand.

It was the outline, cut into the rocky sand, of a giant bird, its wings spread over a distance of several hundred yards, from one end of the shallow basin to the other. Ralph Begay had seen the symbol before, in petroglyphs and on pottery. It meant many different things, but to Ralph, whose guilt caused him nearly as much pain as his arthritis, what he read into it was that his soul was soon to be carried away by a great bird, and that before that occurred, he must die.

So be it. He might as well keep trying to get home, though, so that he could wait there in relative comfort for the bird to overtake him.

As he stood looking at the shape in the sand, he became aware of other lights close to the ground, farther away. It was the highway, he realized, and then he remembered this basin where the demons had done their artwork, and by combining the two landmarks he had his bearings again. He knew where he was and how to get home.

He headed back in the direction of the dirt road he had been on. Once there, he would walk northwest and turn right at the first crossroads he came to. Another three miles and he would be back at his house, and Mary, his wife, would help him undress and get him into bed and maybe hold him until he fell asleep. He had dismissed the thought of sleeping out in the desert tonight. When death came for him, he wanted to be in his own bed.

He had walked a mile, considerably sobered by the sight of the symbol in the earth, when he thought he heard the footsteps shuffling behind him again. Old Coyote, or something else? He paused, but this time the shuffling did not stop, and he turned slowly, afraid to see what might be behind him.

When he finally saw his pursuer closing upon him, the sight drove the last doubt from his mind. It was one of the ancient ones, come back to punish the man whose mouth ran with the truth to outsiders, who told the secrets to those who had no business knowing them. Ralph Begay stood rooted to the spot, a condemned man before a bullet-pocked wall. Guilt breeds resignation.

Ralph fell backward onto the ground, his attacker with him. Then a feeling he had never had overcame him. It was as though the essence was being drained out of him, as though his consciousness was sliding from his body in a thousand different places. This sensation lasted until his blood dried up, leaving only its solids in his brain, which, unable to absorb the stuff that allowed its synapses to send their messages, died instantly.

It was good for him that he could not know what happened next to his body.

Tony Luciano looked up at the motel room ceiling, and the jagged line the yellow light made as it reached in over the top of his room's curtains. No light had been added to or taken from it for hours, and he expected no change until the dawn, which was coming, he feared, far too soon.

He had slept lightly when he'd slept at all, and now was fully awake. Often he would go for weeks at a time with just two or three hours of sleep a night. If he was on a solo assignment, he used the time as effectively as possible against his enemies; if not, he devoured piles of books while most of the citizens he was charged with protecting slept. It was a combination of that "protection" and his metabolism that kept him awake.

For many years, his primary charge had been killing. Assassination, termination, prejudicial intervention—there were many different names for his specialty, but they all dealt with the taking of human lives. For a long time, he didn't mind. He was good at it, and at first he thought, with a simplicity born of faith in God and his country, that this was what he had been intended to do, that it was part of a divine plan, that those he killed deserved killing.

But as the years passed and the body count increased, his innate intelligence crushed such fables like cyanide pellets in a panicked mouth. The ambiguities multiplied, the questions increased, the doubts bred. The ghosts of his kills, not exorcised by the ritual of confession, spoke to him, neither accusing nor cursing, but only querying through their mere presence. They were shadows in his memory, predecessors sent ahead to scout the territory beyond life, bound to him more closely than family or lovers could ever be.

They teemed now, still many hours before dawn, and he saw their eyes again, saw that they retained the knowledge of why they died, but that they were unsure into what black lake they were sinking. Though most had been ready, none was prepared, and it had been the same with him in their killing.

He finally threw off the covers and swung his feet over the side of the bed, not bothering to tell them to go away, for they would not. Instead, they could walk the night with him, have a cup of coffee, sit where there was food and light, until, sated with these comforts of a world they had left, their silent voices withdrew, leaving him as alone as he could ever be.

He dressed and opened the door of his room. From the second-floor balcony, what might have been the first light of dawn hung low over the desert in the east, far surpassed by the incandescence of the bright neon of the Tumbleweed Coffee Shop across the street. Dusty pickup trucks were parked in front of it, and a figure in white moved behind its broad windows, going from counter to booths and back again. The promise of early morning bacon and a dark eye of coffee looking up from a white china cup set him moving.

Inside the aluminum frame, the Tumbleweed was structured like a classic diner, with the counter in front of him, spanning the entire width of the building, and booths to either side against the front wall. Automatically, Tony surveilled them all, and was pleasantly surprised to see Miriam Dominick occupying the far left booth. Though facing him, she was not looking at him. Her head was resting on her left hand, while a white mug was hovering, perched on two fingers of her right hand, over the formica tabletop. The string of its teabag dangled in the air.

His first response was to go to her immediately, but Laika's caution over further contact with her made him hesitate. Then Miriam raised her head from her hand and looked out the window into the night. When Tony saw her eyes, Laika and her warning were forgotten.

" 'Morning," he said, raising a hand as he closed the gap between them. He felt like a schoolboy finding his beautiful teacher, for the first time, outside of school.

She turned and looked at him, and for a second there was blankness. Then came recognition that lit her face like firelight. "Vincent, right? *Is* it morning?" she asked, with a smile that drove all his ghosts back to the dark wells deep in his brain.

"It must be, it's after midnight." He nodded to the

empty vinyl bench across from her. "Taken?"

"Please, sit down," she said, and reached out her hand to shake his. He took it, sat, and grinned, wishing to hell he had brushed his teeth.

"Couldn't sleep?" he offered, signaling the waitress, who returned a weary smile and drew out her order pad, walking with a movie gunslinger's crawl to their booth.

"No, I. . . ." Miriam shook her head. "Bad dream," she said, and then the waitress was there, turning over Tony's coffee cup and filling it at his nod. Maybe the coffee breath would mask the lousy taste in his mouth.

With a glance at Miriam's buttered muffin, he ordered a bagel and cream cheese. But when the waitress asked if a frozen bagel was okay, he amended his order to what he had really wanted, two eggs over easy, bacon, and wheat toast. "That we can handle," the waitress said, and moseyed back to the opening behind the counter.

"Bad dream, huh?" he said, picking up the conversational thread as Miriam drew up the string of the tea bag and lowered it delicately to her saucer.

"I don't know if it was *bad*," she said, "but it was . . . haunting. All too real."

"One of your visions?" he said, with a smile that he hoped told her he doubted, but was willing to be convinced.

Her face grew serious, and she nodded, then looked out the window again toward the motel, as though seeing her dream's birthplace would help her recapture it for Tony. "I was in the desert," she said softly. "It was night. I heard something overhead, like . . . like a fluttering of wings, only much louder. I looked up, and I saw . . . it wasn't a bird, but it was the *shape* of a bird, an outline, like a petroglyph?"

She looked back at him, and he sensed pleading in her eyes, a painful desire to be understood and believed. "Those Indian drawings," he said, nodding, held by her gaze.

"Yes . . . and the shape came down—*over* me—until I

was inside it. And when I looked all around, it was as though the shape had *dug* itself into the sand . . . the shape of a giant bird, its wings spread. And then I rose up, until I was high overhead, looking down at it . . . a giant bird, there in the sand. . . .''

Her eyes were far away, looking into that middle distance, the place of dream and vision and possibility, and then, in another second, she came back, shaking her head and smiling apologetically. ''It must sound silly,'' she said.

He shrugged. ''Most dreams sound silly, but that doesn't mean there isn't a deeper meaning to them. Dreams are . . . profound, somehow. Glimpses into ourselves, I think. I don't know that I really believe in prophetic dreams, but I think that dreams can tell us a great deal . . . about the dreamer.''

''Really?'' He saw a mild challenge in her smile. ''And what would that dream of mine tell you about me?''

He chuckled. ''I think I'm being put on the spot. Well, dreams are made up of our waking experiences, there's no other possibility there. As my colleague Kevin, a true rationalist, might say,'' Tony said, using Joseph's cover name, ''output depends on input. You can only get out what you put in, with variations owing to the dreamer's creativity and imagination. I'd suggest that your dream was the result of several pieces of data that were fed into your brain, to continue the analogy.

''We were talking in the car about prophecies and visions, so it's not unnatural that you would have a dream that seemed like one. As for its content, you must have heard about the design in the sand found near here the other day, and your subconscious mind developed the bird image coming down from the sky. You said you've seen the design in petroglyphs, and it's been used a lot in those *Crow* movies. Also, you had a fairly traumatic experience earlier, what with that trucker, so all in all, it's no surprise you had a dream—or *vision*, if you will—like that.''

She stuck out her lower lip for a moment, as though it

were an organ capable of judging the validity of argument, then pulled it back in as she smiled. "Several objections, counselor. First of all, *what* design in the sand?"

"You haven't heard about the Indian designs?" he said.

"I haven't heard about anything. I was in the back country before I ran into you, and I spent all day today south of 40 shooting Saguaros. I can show you six rolls of film to prove it. As for those *Crow* movies, I've never seen them—I don't like violence."

"But didn't you see anything on TV about the designs? The triangle and the stepped pyramid?" He was fishing now, unsure whether there had been any local television coverage.

"I was exhausted when I got back today," she said. "Took a hot bath and crashed. My dream woke me up, and here I am." She held out her hands, fingers spread.

Tony had no doubt that she was telling the truth. Still, a dream was a dream. "Okay," he said, "but it could be just coincidence. Like Kevin said, do you know how many times—"

He was interrupted by the waitress, who set down his plate of eggs and bacon with a studied flourish, asked, "Anything else?" and left before Tony had a chance to answer.

"Give the lectures a rest, and eat," Miriam said. "And let me tell you about my day amid the Saguaros."

He did as ordered. It was the most pleasant breakfast he had had in a long time.

Chapter 12

*A*n hour and a half after Tony Luciano started eating his eggs, Laika Harris was awakened by the telephone in her room. The clock read 6:15.

"Dr. Kelly?" said the voice at the other end, which, she immediately knew, was coming from Langley. *Skye.*

"Yes, sir?" She tried to sound more alert than she felt.

"I received your report. As it turns out, you may have an opportunity to observe a body similar to Mr. Lynch's firsthand, after all. Whatever phenomenon was responsible for the first death was thoughtful enough to repeat itself, as we were informed early this morning."

"There's been another. . . ." She wasn't sure whether or not to call it a killing. ". . . death?"

"Yes. And in your vicinity, too. One might almost see a pattern forming, if one had a suspicious nature."

He gave Laika the name of the dead man, Ralph Begay, and the location where the body had been found, then told her that it had been taken to Gallup General. "One of those interstate things," Skye said. "The body was found in Arizona, but the nearest major hospital was in Gallup. I did, however, make certain that the body would not be returned to the family until representatives of the National Science Foundation's Division of Special Investigations had an opportunity to observe it. So may I suggest that your next stop be Gallup? You are expected. And I wouldn't worry about rushing—I doubt there will be any further deterioration of Mr. Begay by the time you arrive.''

There was a click, and Laika found herself listening to a dead line. It was like Skye to hang up with no acknowledgment from his underling. He gave his commands and expected them to be obeyed. It was an attitude that made him so hated and so efficient.

But he had said that there was no rush, and Laika was prepared to take him at his word. She fell back into bed, knowing that she would not sleep again, but relishing the rest nonetheless.

"I don't know why we can't at least give her a ride," Tony said over his second breakfast, a bran muffin and a cup of coffee. "I mean, she said she was heading there next—wanted to take some photos of the Indians around the pawn shops and bars and all."

"You just couldn't wait to see her again, could you?" said Joseph.

"Hey, I told you I ran *into* her, that's all. I mean, Christ, she was right over there in that booth, so what am I supposed to do, ignore her?"

"That was a possibility," said Laika.

"You want to look suspicious? *That* would be suspicious. People out here are friendly, Laika." Tony knew the only reason she didn't reprimand him for using her real name was that no one could hear them in the booth where they sat. "Giving her a lift to Gallup can't do any harm, can it?"

"Why should we?" Joseph asked.

"Why shouldn't we? Besides, I *like* her, okay? Wanta hear me say it? I really happen to *like* her. And she knows a helluva lot about this area, about the Indians . . . she could be useful."

Joseph smirked. "You're thinking with something other than your brain, Dr. Antonelli."

"Yeah, well, at least I got something besides a brain!"

"Boys, boys," said Laika calmly, but with an undertone of force. "Don't make me play den mother, all right?" She frowned and looked down at her empty oat-meal bowl, then back up at Tony. "Okay, Dr. Antonelli, how much did you tell this woman?"

Tony shrugged. "Our covers." Before Joseph could open his mouth, Tony went on. "It's not like anybody else is going to know around here. I mean, that's what covers are *for*, for Chrissake."

"Was she impressed?" Joseph asked.

"Well . . . yeah, I guess, I mean, *I* don't know. . . ."

"All right," said Laika matter-of-factly, as though she had made up her mind some time ago. "We'll give her a ride."

"Oh, Jesus Christ!" Joseph exploded. "Why, Laika?"

"Like Tony said, why not? Do you have a problem with it?"

"She's a New Age airhead, that's my problem."

"She's not a New Age airhead, she's a *Catholic*," Tony said.

"Sorry, make that an *Old* Age airhead."

Tony reached across the table, grabbed Joseph's wrist, and squeezed. "You can insult me all you like, Joseph, but goddamn it, don't you insult my faith!"

"And don't you get grabby. Let *go* of me, Tony."

"Do it," Laika said. "Right now." Tony released Joseph, who started to say something, but Laika cut him off. "And both of you, shut up. Not another word. The woman can come with us to Gallup. The ground rules are that we don't say any more about our mission than comes up in normal conversation. We take her to where she wants to go, we say goodbye, and that's that. Under-stood?"

Joseph drove. He wanted to have something on his mind, he told Laika, besides listening to Little Miss Psy-chic. Laika rode shotgun and watched Tony and Miriam Dominick in the rearview mirror.

She didn't mind the woman's company. In this business

she ran into few other women, and what she liked about Miriam was that she didn't seem to pry. She didn't ask them about their jobs or why they were in the high southwest, or how long they had worked for the National Science Foundation, or what exactly was the Division of Special Investigations, anyway.

Instead, she talked about the land as one who loved it and was familiar with the buttes and mesas and deserts and the people who lived in them. She talked of how the rocks had been sculpted over the years by wind and water, and of the ancient Anasazi and the Sinagua and the present-day Navajo and Hopi and Zuni. Her words showed respect for the Indians, and a sorrow for what had befallen many of them in the past few decades. Sheepherding had been reduced dramatically, and alcoholism, drugs, and even gangs had all taken their toll on and off the reservations.

"Still," Miriam said, "many people walk in the old ways. They try to preserve what they had—and what they still have. I try to record as much of it as possible, but it's hard. Most of them distrust Anglos, and it takes a lot of patience even to make a little inroad."

"Anglos?" Laika said.

"White people. It was a term my grandfather used. He claimed to be a quarter Navajo, but I believe it was wishful thinking. Still, my family's been out here forever. It used to be Dominique, but somewhere along the way it got anglicized."

"And Catholicized?" Joseph asked.

Laika watched Tony's face harden, but Miriam seemed nonplussed, and Joseph's question held no malice that Laika could hear. It almost seemed as if he were being won over in spite of himself, and wanted to enter the conversation, no matter how awkwardly. "Oh no," Miriam said, "we've always been Catholic, back to France, I guess."

"So," Joseph went on, "you, um, have any more of those visions lately?"

"You're baiting me," Miriam said with a little chuckle.

"Maybe a bit," Joseph said, "but it isn't every day a . . . visionary saves my life."

Laika couldn't get what Joseph was driving at. He didn't sound sarcastic. Tony looked as though he were about to start in on Joseph, but Laika gave him a look in the rearview mirror that he read clearly, and he settled back.

"Well," Miriam said reluctantly, "I had a dream last night." She told them then, about the shape of a giant bird in the desert. From Tony's expression, Laika felt certain that he had heard the story already, probably in the coffee shop the night before. It made little impression on her. After all, people were always having dreams.

She saw an exit off Route 40 for a town called Lupton, and Joseph glanced at her. "Isn't that where . . . ?" he said softly, leaving it unfinished.

She nodded. It was the closest town to where Ralph Begay's mummified body had been found. They were within the boundaries of the reservation now. In another mile they would cross into New Mexico.

Then she saw a dozen or more cars parked near the northern edge of the road, and some on the southern side. People were standing and pointing down at something Laika could not see, and the talk of visions and premonitions inspired her to tell Joseph to get off at the exit there. At the bottom of the ramp, they crossed under Route 40 and discovered even more cars parked on a small road identified as 118. As they pulled onto the shoulder, Laika could see what had so fascinated everyone.

Etched in the gritty sand of the desert floor was a bird, curved wings spread wide, its head featureless, so that no bill was visible. At the base of its thick body was a flaring tail, curved and pointed at the ends, like the wings. Wing tip to wing tip, Laika estimated, the crude drawing spanned a quarter mile.

"Holy shit . . ." Tony said softly, as they climbed out of the car.

"I see the cereologists of the southwest are at it again," Joseph tried to say lightly, but Laika heard tension in his voice. She glanced at Miriam, but the girl was only standing there, looking at the figure and the people moving around its border, her eyes fixed but dreamy.

"This is the same thing you saw in your dream, isn't it?" Tony asked her, and she nodded.

"Come on," Laika said, "I want to look at this."

They walked down a steep slope toward the drawing. The thick, deep lines in the sand that comprised it were several hundred yards away. Other people were coming and going to the drawing as well, many taking photos and videos. Laika didn't see any TV crews yet, but knew that they would appear eventually.

Laika stopped a man with a camera who was walking toward the road, and asked him if he knew when the drawing had been discovered. "Early this morning," he replied. "Just after dawn, people were coming by and noticed it. The cars started stopping, and . . ." He swept his hand around at the dozens of people walking to, from, and around the drawing. ". . . you see it."

When they finally reached the giant pattern, Joseph knelt and examined the trench carefully. "No tread marks," he said. "Of course, whoever did this could have used tires without a tread."

"Look around," Tony said. "You see any entrance or exit tracks? How'd they get out here in the first place?"

"Maybe they flew, Dr. Antonelli," Joseph said dryly. "They do have things called helicopters now, you know."

"I don't see any backwash," Laika said, looking around. "As powdery as this sand is, you'd think some would show if a chopper came in. Besides, that'd be an awful lot of money to spend on a practical joke."

Joseph said, "Maybe they just drove in and swept their tracks clean behind them when they left. After all, you didn't see the paths the crop circle makers used to get in to the fields, did you?"

"No," said Laika, "but that was because the wheat

sprang back up on its own. These trenches wouldn't fill
in by themselves.''

"Okay, you got me, it was pixies,'' Joseph said. "Or
angels, or spacemen, or Steven Spielberg. And Miriam
predicted it all in her dream.''

"Are you saying she didn't?'' Tony asked. "I mean,
at least *that* much seems obvious. You heard it yourself,
and I heard it late last night, when she couldn't have
known anything about it . . . even before it was made,
probably.''

"I really didn't know anything about it,'' Miriam offered. "I was just as surprised as all of you were.''

"I'm sure you were,'' said Joseph. "I'm not suggesting
collusion here, I'm just saying that as great a coincidence
as it seems, that's what it is—coincidence. People dream
all the time, and sometimes what they dream about comes
true. That doesn't mean they're prophetic.''

"What about her premonition?'' Tony asked. "That's
two coincidences in a row.''

"Sure, and sometimes *that* happens. Sometimes somebody hits *three* in a row, or four, or more, and if they can
prove it, they win a column in a tabloid as Madame Souv-
laki, who sees all and knows all.''

"You're probably right, Kevin,'' Miriam said, address-
ing Joseph. "It's just coincidence. But sometimes coincidences can be pretty strange.''

Laika got the feeling that the girl was just saying the
words, trying to keep the peace. As for herself, Laika
wasn't a believer in coincidences. She liked explanations
for things, and when she didn't get them, she went looking, assuming something was wrong. When, in a foreign
city, she came across the same person twice in two days,
that was more than a coincidence, and finding out why
might save her life.

At the very least, Laika believed that whatever else
Miriam might be, she was not, as Joseph put it, a New
Age airhead.

As they started to walk back to the car, Miriam stopped.

"This is why you're here, isn't it? You're investigating these sand drawings for the Science Foundation?"

Several mouths opened, but Laika was the first to figure out what to say. "It's another matter. One that's taking us to Gallup. Not to say that this might not fall into our purview eventually, but now we're just curiosity seekers, like the rest of these people."

Miriam nodded, then asked, "Does it have something to do with that hiker they found?"

Laika tried to keep a poker face. "Hiker?"

"The one who got all dried up." She looked at their solemn faces, then grinned. "Oh jeez, it's not like it's a big secret. News travels fast among the nomads out here. I heard about it from a girl who heard from a friend of the guy who found him."

"Well, I'm glad security's so tight," Joseph muttered.

Laika nodded and started walking again. "That's the one."

"They found another one in Gallup?" Miriam asked.

"Near here, actually. We're going to Gallup to see the body." What the hell, Laika thought. The girl knew they were investigators, and they had to be investigating *something*. She might as well know the truth. It wouldn't matter. So she'd hit on a lucky guess. So what?

Laika felt a sudden twinge as she thought, shit, maybe the goddamned girl's psychic, after all.

"By the way, Dr. Kelly," Joseph said, as they neared their car, "does the bird stand for anything in particular in Indian lore?"

She looked at him with a wry smile. "The eternal," she said, and was pleased to see his face grow serious. "The great bird would carry away the dead to the eternal dwelling place."

Laika knew what he and Tony were thinking: *Locus hominus aeterni*, Place of the one who never dies. It seemed as though the prisoner would not leave them alone.

*   *   *

As Laika, Tony, Joseph, and Miriam got back into their car, someone watched them through mirrored sunglasses from behind the wheel of his own dusty car. He was a big man with heavy features, and his skin was a deep reddish-brown, the color of the desert sands in certain forbidding light.

From beneath the dashboard, he brought a pair of binoculars, and noted the operatives' license number as they pulled away. He saw them pass under the highway to get back to Route 40. Only after they disappeared around the abutment did he pull his car onto the road to follow.

Once on Route 40, keeping a quarter mile distance between them and himself, the man punched a number into his cellular phone and spoke into it. "I think," he said, "I've found some people you've been looking for."

Chapter 13

They dropped Miriam Dominick off at a small hotel on what used to be Route 66, and still was the main drag through Gallup. Tony wasn't impressed with the town. It seemed like a stretch of restaurants, transient hotels, bars, pawn shops, and tourist traps. There were a lot of Indians on the streets, a few sitting on curbs and stoops, some with cans of soda, some with bottles in brown paper bags. None of them looked happy.

"You've, uh, stayed here before?" Tony asked Miriam, as he walked her to the door while Laika and Joseph stayed in the car.

"Sure. Not a thing to worry about. It looks a lot cruddier than it really is."

He wondered whether or not he should tell her where he and the others would be staying in Gallup, but only for a moment. If Laika and Joseph got pissed, so be it. "Look, if you want to get hold of us . . . for any reason, we'll be at the Gallup Inn, for one night, anyway, maybe a couple, depending on what we find." There. The die was cast.

"Okay, Vincent. Well . . . I hope I see you again."

"Yeah, me too." He smiled and headed back to his partners.

They stopped for a quick lunch and then drove to Gallup General Hospital, where they showed their IDs and asked to be taken to the body of Ralph Begay. A middle-aged man in a dark suit came out and introduced himself as Mr. Austin, a hospital administrator. "I'm sorry, Doctors," he said, "but the body has been turned over to the family."

"This is getting to be a habit," Joseph muttered.

"Mr. Austin," Laika said, so tightly and officiously that Tony was glad she wasn't talking to him, "were you not instructed by the National Science Foundation to retain this body until we arrived to examine it?"

"Yes, Dr. Kelly, we were. But when it comes to dealing with the Navajo, we're limited to how much we can do as a hospital. If the foundation had spoken directly to the police, it might have been a different story, but when the family requests the body, we as a facility can't refuse it."

"Where's the body now?" Joseph asked. "Cremated?"

"Oh no," Austin replied. "It would have been taken to Red Water, the village on the reservation where Mr. Begay lived. There's a tribal cemetery there. The Navajo like to bury their dead as quickly as possible."

"Do you think he's been buried already?" Tony asked.

"Possibly. I sure wouldn't waste any time in getting out there. But I ought to caution you that it's not very likely they'll let you see the body."

"Was a cause of death determined while the body was here?" asked Laika.

"Yes." He handed her several sheets of paper. "Here's a copy of the report. The cause of death was extreme dehydration, but the reason for it is unknown."

"And no foul play was suspected?"

"There was no sign of violence."

"Just how dehydrated was Mr. Begay?"

Austin seemed to be getting to the point where he no longer liked Laika's tone. "I think you'll find that all in the report," he said coldly. "I'm sorry we weren't able to help you further."

"Thank you for the information," Laika said, just as coldly, then turned her back on the man and stalked out. Tony and Joseph followed.

Back in the car, Tony found the village of Red Water on the detailed topographical maps in their dossier, while Laika and Joseph pored over the medical report. "Identical to the hiker," Joseph said. "No photos, though."

"Well, why should they take photos?" Laika asked. "They're not of a suspicious mind around here. Maybe they're used to finding dead Indians."

"An Indian mummy, in this case," Joseph added. "So do we have any legal rights on the reservation—as members of the National Science Foundation, that is?"

"I suspect," Laika said, "we'll be greeted with the same respect they'd afford a drug dealer. Or Custer."

Red Water was worse than Tony had imagined. The town, such as it was, consisted of one long street with houses on either side, and two side streets with scattered dwellings. The whole village was no larger than a few acres. Everything was exposed to screaming sunlight, for the only vegetation was low brush and a few short, decorative trees struggling for their lives, planted in front of some of the houses.

The buildings were all of one story, and mostly made out of weathered, unpainted planks. Roofs were flat or slightly slanted, and Tony noticed that rubber tires were sitting on a few of them, either for storage, or, as he suspected, to hold the roofs on in the event of a windstorm. Most of the windows were open and without screens, and Tony saw no air conditioners, though a few box fans sat in some of the windows, whose sills, when they were painted, were nearly all blue.

Some of the houses were in clusters with other structures. On one lot there might be a house, then a small round or hexagonal hogan with a sloped roof, and next to it a small trailer or another outbuilding.

On the side streets were a few rusty mobile homes, and

even a school bus with painted-over windows. He wondered if anyone actually lived in it.

A few of the houses had rudimentary porches, and some people were sitting on them, as if trying to catch a whisper of the breeze that stirred the dust. To the porch sitters, Pepsi seemed to be the drink of choice. A number of children played in the streets and in the areas between the dwellings.

A car was parked at every third house or so, with the exception of one house where plaster or adobe, painted light green, covered the wooden planks. There, four cars were parked, all of them older than ten years. A black station wagon sat nearest the house. A long and narrow wooden box hung over its dropped down tailgate.

"Looks like a party," Tony said.

"Or a funeral," said Joseph.

They parked, which consisted of pulling off the dust of the main street onto the dust in front of one of the houses, and walked to the house with the cars. The few windows were all open, and three men were standing in the shade of a wood-planked porch. Two were drinking Pepsi, and one drank something from a chipped coffee mug.

"Is this the Begay house?" Laika asked. The men, somewhere in age between thirty-five and sixty, only looked at her. "I'm looking for Mrs. Begay," she went on. "Mrs. Ralph Begay?" Still the men said nothing. Tony thought he saw one of them nod slightly. "Would you please tell her that three doctors from the National Science Foundation's Division of Special Investigations are here to speak to her?"

The men looked at Laika, then at each other, and one of them went inside through the open door, where Tony saw less than a dozen other people standing, talking quietly. In a minute the man came back out with an elderly woman wearing a long-sleeved black blouse and a long dark blue skirt. Her face was deeply lined, and the hair on the top of her head was sparse. Around her wattled neck hung a large necklace made of small discs of turquoise and other stones, and from her ears dangled large, finely engraved silver earrings.

"Mrs. Begay?" Laika said, and the woman nodded. Laika went on to introduce their party and apologize for their coming at such a sad time, but that in the interests of science and to prevent other deaths similar to Mr. Begay's, it was imperative that they be allowed to examine the body before it was buried.

Mrs. Begay shook her head and looked pointedly at the wooden box in the station wagon. "The coffin is nailed down. It cannot be opened again."

"Mrs. Begay," Laika said, "I can't stress too strongly the importance of this. Now, we represent the government, and—"

"No," Mrs. Begay said flatly, shaking her head. "You mean nothing here. This is Navajo land. The People's affairs are not your affairs. What happened to my husband is between him and the gods, that is all."

"She's right," one of the men said. He was the biggest and probably the youngest, and wore a tan sisal cowboy hat and a red-and-white striped shirt. "You have no authority here. Why don't you stop bothering my aunt on the funeral day of her husband? The coffin is nailed down, and it stays that way, that's all. Leave us in peace, now."

Mrs. Begay turned and walked back into the house, and the men turned away from the three operatives and sipped their drinks. Laika, followed by Joseph and Tony, started walking back toward the car, but she turned and moved a few steps closer to the station wagon and the wooden coffin inside it. They stopped near enough for Tony to see the big nails in the coffin. The men on the porch were watching them warily.

"Want me to steal the wagon?" Tony said softly to Laika.

"Sure," Joseph said, "and start another Indian war."

"Let's go," Laika said, walking to the car and getting behind the wheel.

"Why don't they have the coffin inside?" Tony asked.

"Looks like a wake, but without the main attraction."

"As I recall, the Navajo have a traditional fear of the dead," said Laika. "They don't like a dead person inside the house. In fact, they try to get them outside if they're definitely going to die."

"Tenderhearted," said Joseph.

Laika shook her head. "It's just their belief. They like to have someone else bury the dead, too. Odds are whoever's driving that station wagon isn't part of the family." She sighed. "We'll head out of town and stop up on that butte overlooking it. From there we can see where the coffin goes."

"What, you mean to find the cemetery?" Tony asked.

"Right."

"And what good'll that do?" Then it hit him. "No way. You're kidding, right?"

"We have to see one of these bodies, and if the family won't cooperate. . . ." She shrugged. "It's necessary."

"One little problem," Joseph said. "Getting caught doing something like that on Indian land? Our covers would be busted for sure. No government agency is supposed to operate around here without permission from the Bureau of Indian Affairs."

"Hell, Joseph," Laika replied, "we're not even supposed to be operating in this *country*, so it's a little late to worry about such niceties now. Besides, we'll cover him up again. No one will even know we were there."

Tony didn't like the thought of rifling a fresh grave. It almost seemed like sacrilege to him. Still, he wouldn't buck Laika on this. She was right. They had to see what the hell they were up against.

They drove onto the butte, from which they could see the house. In less than an hour, the people came out and piled into the cars. One of the older men on the porch walked to the station wagon, closed the tailgate, and started the procession, which seemed to head straight out into the desert. The ops followed.

Three miles north, the cars turned onto another dirt road

even less traveled. Tony could see the cemetery about a half mile away. "Good enough," Laika said. "Tony, where does this road come out?"

Tony consulted the maps. "Joins a paved road in three more miles."

"All right," Laika said, driving on. "That's how we'll come back after dark."

Chapter 14

*I*n Gallup, Laika, Tony, and Joseph bought two shovels, a small digging iron, and a crowbar, then had dinner. They returned to their motel, where Tony got an infrared camera and three pairs of goggles.

When it grew dark, they drove back out to the reservation and came down to the cemetery road from the north, the long way around, so that they would not have to go through Red Water. The road to the cemetery blended so well into the desert that Tony, who was driving, would have missed it had Laika not told him to turn.

It was the saddest graveyard Tony had ever seen. The natural vegetation was sparse, mostly sagebrush and yucca, with an occasional clump of rabbitbrush, its yellow flowers closed tightly against the chilly night. A withered juniper stood at the entrance, next to a wrought-iron gate that seemed never to have been attached to a fence. Tony thought there once might have been a sign above it, but now there were only rusty bolts.

There were hundreds of graves, the more recent ones covered with foot-high mounds of earth. Small decorative picket fences, only a few inches high, surrounded many of the graves, and plastic flowers adorned most of these. The sun and dry air would have leached real flowers dry in a day. Although there were a few actual gravestones, most of the markers were metal plaques stuck in the dirt with names and dates spelled out with snap-in letters.

There were even a few faded plastic toys on what Tony assumed were children's graves.

There was no sign of a caretaker's house nearby, and although they could see an infrequent car pass on the dirt road a half mile away, they felt confident that there would be no more visitors until morning. In fact, the few passing cars seemed to speed up as they drew nearer to the cemetery. Maybe Laika had been right about that fear of the dead, Tony thought.

They found Ralph Begay's grave easily enough. It was near the back of the cemetery, and the earthen mound was darker than those of older graves. There was only a wooden stake with Begay's name written on an attached piece of brown cardboard. With little ceremony, they began to dig.

Uncovering a grave, even a fresh one, was a tough job. Tony and Joseph were sweating by the time they had finished bringing the mound to ground level. "What I wouldn't give for a backhoe," Joseph muttered, as his spade dug into the clods of dirt.

Laika took her turn, too, and after an hour the blade of her spade scraped against the wood of the coffin. "This is a helluva time to say it," Joseph said from where he sat on the edge of the grave, "but I think the batteries in my goggles are failing. It's a lot darker than it used to be."

"Same with me," said Laika. "I think we can use flashlights in the grave, though. There shouldn't be a glow, and if there is, maybe people driving by will think it's just another ghost."

Tony, next to her in the grave, grunted his agreement. He didn't like this any better than he had liked their nocturnal visit to the graveyard in New York City, when they had uncovered a crypt that held not corpses, but a living though extremely elderly priest, entombed there as punishment for his attempt to free the prisoner they had sought. Under the trees or out in the desert, a graveyard was the one place that gave Tony the creeps. He wasn't afraid of anything or anybody living, but the dead were another matter.

They all took off their goggles, and Laika, standing on top of the coffin, turned on a flashlight and got a foothold in the earth at the end of the open grave. "Open it, Tony," she said.

He fit the curved end of the crowbar under the lip of the coffin lid and strained upward. The nails shrieked as they were jerked out of the wood, and all three of them jumped at the sound. They looked at each other and smiled uncomfortably. Then Tony reached down and opened the lid, pulling it up and propping it against the dirt sides of the grave, while Laika shone the flashlight inside.

"My God," Joseph said softly, as close to a prayer as he ever came. The man inside the coffin had been dressed in a white shirt and clean denim pants. Someone had wrapped a bandanna around his neck. He wore no shoes or socks.

But it wasn't his clothing that elicited Joseph's comment. Rather, it was the condition of his corpse. The flesh was uniformly brown, not the natural tan of a desert dweller, but the dark, muddy brown of an exposed tree root. The texture was similar to a root's as well, fissured and dried. But unlike a root, the skin showed no signs of ever having held an ounce of moisture.

Tony had seen many bodies, and the unpleasantness of such contact had always come from the smell of the fluids and gases issuing from the tissues. In the case of Ralph Begay, however, there were neither fluids nor gases. The corpse did indeed look like that of a mummy.

The eyelids had tightened and pulled open, revealing the sunken eyes. They looked, Tony thought, like white raisins, with little bugs where the pupils had been. The lips had drawn back from the teeth, and even though they had been poorly taken care of, they appeared obscenely white as they protruded from the brown gums.

"Like jerky," Joseph said. "What the hell happened to this guy?"

Laika snorted, unamused. "Total dehydration." She knelt by the body and undid the shirt buttons, then drew back the cloth. "Look, not a sign of burning. There's no charring, no ash, no sign of spontaneous or nonspontaneous combustion." She closely examined the man's neck and chest. "I don't see a sign of an entry wound anywhere here. Come on, Tony, help me get off his pants—I want to check the whole body, just in case. Joseph, hold the light."

Ralph Begay's naked body weighed so little that Laika turned it easily in her hands. Every now and then Tony heard crackling sounds, though whether it was the dry flesh cracking or the bones breaking, he wasn't sure.

"I think we can rule out vampires and *chupacabras*," said Laika. "No signs of puncture wounds, not even small ones. Even if there were, that wouldn't explain why even his bones are dry. What could suck out the marrow, along with every other drop of moisture?"

"A *super chupacabras*?" Joseph suggested.

"Let's get a few tissue samples. And then some photographs."

"It's bad luck to take pictures of the dead," a voice said.

They had all looked up at the first word, and now saw a tall Indian, shading his eyes against Joseph's flashlight with one hand and holding his own light with the other, which he now turned on and shone at the three of them. He was wearing a dark-colored cowboy hat, a denim jacket over a blue work shirt, and jeans. A badge shone over his breast pocket.

"Not specifically photos," he went on, a smile playing over his heavy lips. "But anything connected with the dead is out of bounds. Especially the kind of thing you're doing here."

The three operatives looked at each other and then back at the man. Tony had a gun, but he didn't feel threatened enough to go for it, especially since the man was wearing a badge. The decision might be made to protect their covers by killing this stranger, but it was Laika's to make, not his, and he knew she would try every other option first.

"Let me introduce myself," the man said in his deep voice. I'm *Officer* Joshua Yazzie, tribal policeman." He tapped his badge and smiled. "And who might you be, and why are you digging up graves?"

Laika straightened up and reached for her wallet, Tony was relieved to see, rather than her concealed pistol. She took out her NSF ID and handed it up to the big man. "I'm Dr. Kelly, and this is Dr. Tompkins and Dr. Antonelli."

Yazzie looked over the ID and handed it back. "If you're here on archaeological business, you're a little premature." Then he frowned and eyed the corpse of Ralph Begay. "Though from what I see of that poor guy, maybe not. At any rate, maybe you'd like to climb out of there so we can discuss this on even ground."

As they got out of the hole, Yazzie went on. "And let me warn you, it had better be a good story. Grave robbing on Indian land, whether it's fresh graves or old ones, falls under federal jurisdiction, and if you had permission to do this, I think we'd have been informed of it, and I don't think you'd be doing it in the dead of night."

"Did you see our light?" Laika asked.

Yazzie nodded. "I don't believe in ghosts, unlike many of the People."

"I thought *you* were one, at first," said Tony, trying to make conversation. "You crept up on us pretty quietly."

Yazzie shrugged. "Hey, I'm an Indian, right?" Then he chuckled, a throaty sound like a lion's warning rumble. "Now, who's got the best reason why I shouldn't turn you over?"

Standing by the side of the grave, Laika explained how Begay's strange death was the second in a week, how they had been unable to examine either of the bodies, and how this was a desperate attempt to observe one of the victims.

"Victims of what?" Yazzie asked.

"We don't know. But we want to find out, so that it doesn't happen again."

Yazzie shone his light down into the grave and shook his head. "Scarcely dead for a day, and he looks like a damn mummy. You're right, somebody *should* investigate this." He looked back at Laika. "And they have, you know. The Anglo police have started to look into it."

"You don't sound as though you expect much from that," Laika said.

"When the Anglos investigate on Indian land," said Yazzie, "it's like first-graders building a computer—they don't know where to start, they don't know how to get their information, and nobody takes them seriously, not on the reservation, anyway. Present company possibly included. Now, you've committed a pretty dreadful crime here—robbing an Indian grave, stripping the corpse. . . ." He shook his head. "But you had valid reasons. So I'll tell you what—you get Mr. Begay dressed and put him back where he belongs, exactly as he was, and I'll see if I can get the Bureau of Indian Affairs to approve of your investigating on Indian land."

"Why would you help us?" Laika asked. "After this?"

"I don't like my people getting turned into mummies. And there's something about you that makes me think you'd be more effective than the Anglo police."

"Can't you tribal police investigate things yourself?" Joseph asked.

"We don't have the manpower or the resources. Or access to National Science Foundation investigators."

"So why should we go through you?" Laika said. "We could get clearance ourselves, couldn't we?"

"Sure," said Yazzie. "And by the time you cut through all the red tape, there may be a dozen more deaths like this one. Besides, I want to keep an eye on you three. What you've done here . . . well, this is not a good thing. So, where are you staying?"

"The Gallup Inn," Laika said.

"Tell you what. You give me your IDs, and I'll take them up to the Navajo Area Office in Window Rock first thing in the morning, vouch for you, and get you clearance to investigate . . . *legally*. Then I'll meet you at your motel."

Laika hesitated, and Tony knew that she was wondering if their IDs would pass muster with a governmental agency. But she must have come to the same conclusion that he did, that the Bureau of Indian Affairs wasn't real heavy on the investigatory end. If their IDs could pass muster with anything short of a Senate committee, the local BIA shouldn't prove too big a hurdle. Laika took her ID back out and handed it to Yazzie, then gestured for Tony and Joseph to do the same.

"All right, then," Yazzie said, "get Mr. Begay covered up again."

"I don't suppose that we could take some photographs and tissue samples first?" said Laika.

"That would *not* be a good idea. Consider this a purely visual surveillance, and one that you will not discuss with anyone else."

The ops put the dead man's clothes back on him and fit him back into the coffin. It took less time to fill in the hole, but when they were finished, it was only a few hours before dawn. They drove Yazzie to his car, which he had parked on the main road before jogging back to the cemetery.

"White," Joseph observed. "Shows the dust pretty well."

"It needs to be washed," Yazzie admitted. "But in a white car, it's harder to see you coming in the desert. Crimestoppers' tip number 358."

"Dick Tracy," said Tony.

"Ah, a well-read man." Yazzie got out of their car and opened the door of his own. "I'll see you tomorrow around noon. Till then, stay out of trouble."

Chapter 15

"**I** think we got lucky," Joseph said when Officer Yazzie was safely behind them.

"I don't know *what* we got," Laika said. "I was surprised, that's for sure. Surprised that somebody was able to sneak up on us like that. It was my fault. One of us should have watched."

"It wouldn't have done any good, Laika," said Joseph. "He's an Indian."

"I think that qualifies as an ethnic . . . something-or-other," she said.

"Not a slur. It's a compliment."

"It's a stereotype," said Tony.

"Tell me about it while you cook me some spaghetti sauce, pal," Joseph said.

"Fine—I know you can tell me where to get the cheapest ingredients."

"See there?" Joseph said with a laugh. "There's nothing wrong with knowing how to cook spaghetti sauce, or knowing how to save money, or being stealthy—they're all stereotypical, but they're not *negative*."

"Mmm-hmm." Laika nodded. "And I got *tons* of rhythm. I'm not worried about his stealth, I'm worried about his cooperativeness. He caught us grave robbing, and how it ended up was that he volunteered to *help* us. That doesn't make sense to me."

"It did when he suggested it," Joseph said. "He

doesn't want to see any more dead Indians, and he knew we were connected with the government. As far as he's concerned, we're more than legit, in spite of what we were up to tonight.''

"I think you're right," Tony said. "He seemed on the level to me. But what about that body?"

"A completely unnatural death," Laika said, "and I can't find a rational answer for it. It looked identical to the photos of the first victim."

"There's that *victim* word again," said Joseph. "Like the cop's line from *Plan Nine From Outer Space*—'This man's been murdered, and *somebody's responsible*.' So you think there's a killer involved?"

"Yes. Someone who did something to these two men. Two deaths like these have to be more than just a coincidence.''

"Then he's on the move," said Tony. "Looks like he's traveling east."

"You're the map man, Tony," Joseph said. "Where could Mr. Prunization go from Gallup?"

"Well, he could keep going east into New Mexico, northwest toward Canyon de Chelly on Indian roads, or north from Gallup on Route 666."

"Ooo, the Route of the Beast," said Joseph. "That's the one *I* predict. . . ."

They got to the Gallup Inn an hour before dawn. They had decided to remain in the area, finding out as much as they could about Ralph Begay and those who knew him. What they could learn, they realized, depended on how much Joshua Yazzie was willing to help them. Three Anglos on their own weren't going to get a lot of information from the dour and taciturn Navajos.

Joseph Stein flopped down on his bed as soon as the door of his room closed behind him. It had been a long day and night, and the energy expended in digging and filling in the grave reminded him all too well of his forty-plus years. What the hell was he doing in fieldwork? He had been, if not happy, at least content with his desk job.

Still, for better or worse, there was no going back now. He was in this until the end, whatever the end might be. Joseph hoped that it would have something to do with the prisoner. The symbols of eternity in the sand pointed that way, at any rate. But hell, maybe *every* Indian symbol could be read as a sign of eternity.

He made himself undress, and left a wakeup call for ten o'clock, which would give him five hours of rest, then turned off the lights and closed his eyes. He was asleep in moments.

And in his sleep he dreamed. There was no period of blackness. The dream came instantly, the moment he dropped off. He went from lying in a Gallup motel bed to floating under the dome of a dark sky, black with touches of blue where dim lights from below shone off of it. It was the blue-black, he thought, of Elvis Presley's hair, and he chuckled in the dream at the simile.

He was not frightened, although he seemed to be suspended with only a vast abyss beneath him. He knew he had been here before, but then he had been on a narrow bridge of rusting iron, under the same dark sky. And because he knew this was a dream, he had a dreamer's fearlessness. He could fly, he could fall, and nothing could harm him.

Joseph looked around, ready for whatever would come next, and then he heard a voice, as soft as the breath of whatever God might be, form the words, "Find me. . . ."

He knew it was the prisoner. It was the same sweet, angelic voice that had spoken to him in that other dream. Hearing it, all he could think about was finding the man, freeing him, helping him, however he could. He looked up, then down, and it was down, far below, that he saw the keyhole.

That was the first image that sprang to his mind. Whatever it was he was looking at, it was round, with a smaller shape attached to it, straight lines that spread out slightly from the circle, then were joined by another line. Yes, an

old-fashioned keyhole. That was where the voice had
come from, asking Joseph to find the speaker. All right,
then. Maybe Joseph himself was the key.

He willed himself downward, toward the shape, and
that will dropped him as if on an elevator, slowly and
safely toward the keyhole. As he drew nearer, the darkness below took on a sandy brown color, and resolved
into a gritty texture, and he knew that he was drifting
toward the floor of the desert.

Though the keyhole was covered with sand, its outlines
stood out clearly. There was one small hole that appeared
slightly above the center of the circle, like a misplaced
nipple on a breast, and it was toward that hole, only an
inch across, that Joseph descended. For the first time,
panic hit him as he realized that he could not pass through
that hole, and that he might be crushed in the attempt.

He need not have worried. The dream-stuff he had become slipped through the tiny hole as smoothly as sand
slipping through an hourglass, and he found himself in a
large room whose walls were of a black so flat that no
light could reflect from them. Instantly his throat locked,
and though he tried to breathe, there was nothing to enter
his lungs.

Look for him! his mind screamed. *Find him, and you
will breathe!*

Joseph whirled about and saw the prisoner.

Immediately, at the sight of the man's gentle features,
the lustrous, long brown hair, and the beatific smile
wreathed by the soft beard and moustache, cool air rushed
into Joseph's lungs. He felt saved, cleansed, released from
all the rigors and terrors of life. The prisoner's sole white
garment seemed to glow as radiantly as did the man's
face, and he saw that the man, although free of the chains
that had bound him in Joseph's previous dream about him,
still was a captive, held by some force that would not let
him go to Joseph, although he knew the prisoner wanted
to. Nor could Joseph draw any nearer to him.

Then he heard the prisoner's voice, speaking the same words Joseph had heard him speak before:

Find me. Help me. Save me. And then I may save you.

And the desire rose in him, stronger and deeper than any he had ever known, to save this man and be saved by him. Joseph reached out his arms toward him, but felt himself being swept up and away, through the small hole, and this time it hurt. His body stretched and elongated as it was forced through the narrow passage, and he could feel his muscles contract, his bones splinter, his skull collapse, and with what was left of his brain that was being crushed and forced through the hole, the thought came to him, *Strait is the gate, and narrow is the way, which leadeth unto life. . . .*

Then he was through, and the maddening pain had ceased, bright only in memory. As he was swept away from the chamber and up into the darkness, he got a glimpse of another structure but was unsure of whether he was seeing it in his dream or in his imagination. It seemed not fully realized, even in the loose structure of dream, but was there, somehow, somewhere.

It was the front of a building that faded from view as quickly as it had appeared, a wide structure with a doorway and a humped top, with another opening in the hump from which something hung suspended. There were other details which his mind scarcely had time to register before it was gone, swallowed up in the darkness into which he flew.

His eyes opened, and he was awake.

His body was covered with sweat, and he still remembered the terrible pain of being forced through the narrow hole, though no pain actually touched his body now. Though he wanted to recall the prisoner's voice and appearance, and the way he had felt in his presence, Joseph struggled most to remember that last image he had seen in his dream, the building, the humped top, and what hung there.

Slowly it came, like the memory of something seen in

the split-second illumination of a flashbulb. A bell had hung within the rounded top, and there were smaller humps, two of them, on the roof line on either side of the main one. A door had been in the center of the structure, and between it and the roof were lines . . . boards . . . timbers. A railing. It had been a balustrade. And there to the left, more lines, leaning against the wall. A cross.

A mission, then. That must have been it. He had seen a Spanish mission. But the only mission that he could remember was the Alamo, and he had only seen it in photographs. Still, that was what it had looked like. He would have to look at a picture of it again, refresh his memory. But he felt fairly confident that what he had seen was not the Alamo. It had been more open, the door recessed beneath the balustrade. At least, he thought that was how he remembered it.

But if there was one thing of which he did feel certain, it was that the prisoner was near. He had been in New York when Joseph had had his first dream, only a few miles away. So it seemed likely that he was close by now. Joseph didn't think it possible that so strong a dream impression could be sent over vast distances.

"Jesus," he muttered, "listen to yourself." He gave an exasperated sigh as he considered the idiotic places to which his imagination was taking him. A year ago he never would have even considered the strength of dream images as something to be transmitted, and now here he was, sounding less like his late hero, Carl Sagan, and more like Marianne Williamson or Deepak Chopra.

Still, the force of the prisoner's personality was such to make Joseph doubt if he could have come up with something so . . . godlike. But maybe that was why, he thought. Maybe his disbelief in God and the gods had been masking a need for the divine, the infinite. Maybe he was at that point in his life now where he realized that he was all too mortal. As a result, he hungered after immortality, even though he would not admit it to his waking self.

Or maybe the sonofabitch was really sending him dreams, telling him where he was.

And maybe he'd better try and get some sleep before he tried to explain this all to his colleagues in the daylight.

Chapter 16

"*I* think it's a coincidence," he told Laika and Tony, over a late breakfast in the Gallup Inn's coffee shop, "but I thought it's something that you should know about, if for no other reason than to keep an eye on me if I start cracking up."

"I don't think you're going nuts," Tony said. "Your previous dream was, what's the word, visionary? It fit in with the windows we found in the church where the prisoner had once been held. And the fact that he was imprisoned within lead walls . . . we saw that at the church, *and* at the deserted office building where he was imprisoned."

Laika put down her cup and eyed Tony. "So you think the dream wasn't just a coincidence, a construct of different elements?"

"Look," Tony said, "even though this area has missions, I don't recall us driving past any since we got here, do you? As for this keyhole-shaped room with the little hole, where'd *that* come from? Does that have *any* significance for you, Joseph?"

"Not a bit. But it doesn't mean my dreaming it was the result of some outside force. Maybe when my subconscious was thinking about the prisoner, it was only natural to think of him as being under lock and key—so I saw a big keyhole."

"What about the smaller hole?" Tony asked.

Joseph wiggled his eyebrows up and down. "Sexual, no doubt."

"Or a *sipapu*," Laika said softly.

"A who?" asked Joseph.

She frowned, then shook her head and looked out the window. "Oh, nothing. Just more Indian mumbo jumbo." Her eyes narrowed. "And speaking of Indians. . . ."

Tony followed her gaze and saw Officer Yazzie pulling into the parking lot in his big white dusty car. He got out and set his dark cowboy hat on top of his stylishly cut hair, then walked toward the lobby. "Go get him," Tony said to the others. "I'll sign the tab."

When Tony stepped into the lobby two minutes later, Yazzie was talking with Laika and Joseph. "Dr. Antonelli," Laika said to him, "Officer Yazzie's given us some good news and some bad news. The good news is that the BIA is allowing us to investigate these deaths all we want on Indian land. But the bad news is that it's conditional."

"On what?" Tony asked, knowing when to give the set-up.

"On our being accompanied at all times by a tribal policeman." She looked up at a grinning Yazzie. "And guess who that tall, dark, and handsome gentleman is?" It occurred to Tony that of the three of them, only Laika could get away with the "dark" line.

Tony stuck out his hand and shook Yazzie's. "Howdy, colleague."

"I'm glad you're taking it so well," Yazzie said, tongue firmly in cheek.

"We got a choice?" asked Tony.

"No, but frankly, you're better off with me than without me. You try to talk to the People on your own, you won't get very far. But maybe I can sort of ease the way. They'll be more likely to tell me things they wouldn't tell you alone."

"What's this 'People' stuff?" Joseph asked. "That's

not the first time I've heard it, and it sounds more than just generic.''

"It is. The Navajo refer to themselves as *Dineh*, which means 'the People,' with a capital P."

"No ego problems there," said Joseph. "Is that what these Anasazi called themselves, too?"

Yazzie shook his head. "Navajo aren't descended from Anasazi—that's the Pueblo Indians, Zuni and Hopi. Navajo come from Athapascan tribes, from the north."

"So 'the People' are a mite cliqueish, huh?" asked Joseph.

"I think you learned that when you visited Ralph Begay's family." Yazzie smiled at their startled looks. "No, I wasn't checking up on you—I just figured you'd go there first, ask for permission. And last night proved you didn't get it. Believe me, you won't be any more persuasive in other areas. You're going to be glad I'm around." He shrugged. "What do you want to do first?"

The four drove in Yazzie's car to Red Water, the village where Ralph Begay had lived. The cars that had been so numerous the day before were gone, except for a 1980 Dodge Dart whose rocker panels were nearly eaten away by rust. A Navajo woman in her forties was sitting in a white resin chair on the porch. She was wearing a short-sleeved red-checked blouse and a long green skirt. "Can I help you?" she asked in English.

"We'd like to see Mrs. Begay," Yazzie said. "I'm Officer Yazzie. I'd like to talk to her about her husband."

The woman stood up. "She's my mother-in-law," she said. "I'm Ella." Then she looked suspiciously at the three ops.

"These folks are from the government," Yazzie said. "They're all right."

Ella seemed to take his word for it, for she nodded and led the way inside. Mrs. Begay was wearing a long black skirt and a long-sleeved black blouse. Her face was a map of wrinkles, like a slab of rock crisscrossed with fault lines. "Mrs. Begay?" Laika said, but the woman only looked at her.

"Mrs. Begay?" Yazzie repeated.

"I'm Dorothy Begay," the woman finally said, looking now at Yazzie's brown face and the badge on his chest. It seemed, Tony thought, as if she wasn't going to talk to the white-eyes, and apparently even Laika fit that category.

Yazzie introduced himself and the ops, and then asked if it would be all right if they would ask her some questions. She nodded, but kept her eyes on Yazzie, not even looking away when Laika spoke to her.

"Mrs. Begay," she said, "your husband's death was quite out of the ordinary, and the foundation is investigating the possible causes. The first thing we have to rule out is foul play, so can you tell us if your husband knew anyone who would have wished him ill?"

Dorothy Begay frowned even more deeply, then closed her eyes for a moment. "No." Tony knew in an instant that she wasn't telling the truth, and the sour look on the daughter-in-law's face only added to his certainty.

"Are you sure?" Yazzie asked, and the old woman looked stubbornly into his eyes.

"He had no enemies," she said.

Laika asked a few other questions about Begay's medical history, and about his drinking habits, but according to his wife, he never drank to excess, nor did he have any adverse medical conditions. Tony was sure they weren't going to get a thing out of the old woman, and Laika must have felt the same way, because she thanked Dorothy Begay and led the way outside.

On the porch, Yazzie turned to Ella. "Your mother-in-law didn't feel like talking. Anything you could add?"

Ella chewed her upper lip for a moment, then nodded and beckoned them toward the car, away from the house. "I don't know what happened to him," she said, when they were out of earshot of the house, "or *how* it happened, but he was my father-in-law, and if anybody did anything bad to him, then they ought to pay. He was a sad and unhappy man, and he didn't deserve to die like he did." She nodded firmly. "He did have enemies, though. He made a lot of them when he talked with John Reece."

"The mystery writer?" asked Tony. He had read a half dozen of Reece's novels, but had stopped after they became repetitious.

"Yes," Ella said. "Reece met my father-in-law in a bar in Gallup—the Wet Moccasin, real politically correct name. Ralph was active in the village ceremonials with the other elders. The young people aren't very interested anymore—oh, for the annual festivals the tourists go to, sure, they can make some money dancing and all, but not the real thing. Tourists don't see that, they don't know. But Ralph knew about the real thing, and that was what Reece wanted."

Ella shook her head. "My father-in-law liked to drink, and Reece bought him plenty. The more he drank, the looser his tongue got. He told Reece a lot. They met again, many times, and every time Ralph told more. Reece paid him for the information, and then he used it in his books. But the other elders found out about it."

"How?" Yazzie asked.

Ella shrugged. "You can't keep these things secret. Somebody saw Reece giving Ralph money, or overheard him talking to Reece, I don't know. But when they found out, Ralph was banned from the ceremonials. And he was pretty well shunned by everybody but his own family, and even some of them. His brother, in particular."

"Why was that?"

"Uncle Kee's a medicine man. He didn't like the idea of Ralph giving away his secrets. He wouldn't even come to his funeral."

"You think this Kee would be angry enough to do something about it?" Joseph asked.

"He *did*," the woman answered. "He was the one who got my father-in-law banned."

Yazzie nodded. "Yes, but anything more than that?"

"Kee told Ralph, when he found out about it, that the gods would punish him for what he'd done. I think," Ella said slowly, "that he might have put a curse on him. But the shunning was enough of a curse. Ralph had no friends outside the family, so he started drinking more and more, and with what John Reece had paid him over the months for information, he had enough to do it. He left behind a fair amount." She smiled thinly at Yazzie. "For a Navajo."

"Does your Uncle Kee live here in Red Water?" asked Yazzie.

Ella pointed down the bare dirt road. "The street to the left. He's in the blue house at the end."

"Could you introduce us?" Yazzie asked.

"You don't want me to. Uncle Kee refuses to have anything to do with any family members who still associated with Ralph."

"Does that mean that you're . . . shunned, too?" Tony asked.

"Just by Uncle Kee," she said. "No big loss."

Kee Begay's house was painted blue, all right, though much of it had chipped off, revealing the bare boards underneath. On the dirt in front of the porch was a two-foot-wide plateau of sand an inch high, with large, dark feathers encircling it. Several stones and the claw of some bird were arranged in a pattern on the sand.

Yazzie knocked on the torn screen door, while the ops stood a few yards behind him. Behind the mesh screen, Tony could see a shadowy figure, and heard a deep, resonating voice speaking, he assumed, the Navajo language.

After a minute, Yazzie turned and beckoned them onto the worn boards of the porch, as the screen door opened and Kee Begay came out. He put a round-crowned, broad-brimmed hat on as he stepped into the sunlight, and glowered at the ops out of a craggy, fissured face. He wore glasses whose heavy black plastic frames and thick lenses made him look like a Svengali of owls.

"I don't like talking to white folks," were his first words after Yazzie introduced them. "Or to those with them," he added, nodding to Laika. "But I've learned that if you don't talk to them, they come back and keep bothering you, and I like being bothered less than I like talking. What is it you want to know about?"

"Your brother, Mr. Begay," Laika said.

"I don't have any brother. You may mean a man with the same last name as mine, a man called Ralph, but he's not my brother, alive or dead." Kee Begay fished a pack of Winstons from his pocket and lit one with a butane lighter.

"Well, at any rate," Laika said, "we're looking into his death."

"Why?" Begay asked quickly.

"Well . . . it was suspicious, and we want to learn what killed him."

"I know what killed him. A betrayed spirit. An angry spirit. I heard how he died. People don't just die that way. He was sucked dry, the same way that he helped that white story teller to suck the *Dineh* dry. They took away everything from us, and now they won't even leave us our secrets, the things most sacred to us. This Ralph Begay got what he deserved."

"But the same thing also happened to someone else," Laika said. "A white hiker died the same way. Would the spirit have done such a thing to a white man?"

"It would have," Kee Begay said, "if the white man offended it, or if he discovered things about the *Dineh* he shouldn't have known. The gods cannot stay silent forever. They speak from time to time. They spoke to Ralph Begay. And they speak in the sands."

"You mean the drawings," Tony said, thinking of the giant images made in the earth nearby.

The old man nodded. "These are signs. Signs that the gods are alive and awake." He looked out into the harsh desert, at the loose soil, the sandstone rocks, the sparse vegetation that managed to cling to life in such a cruel environment.

"There is something here. Something that has no love for betrayers. . . ."

There was something, and love was the farthest thing from its mind. Its intent was as dark as the blackness in which it lay.

It reached out, pressing its thoughts against the heavy shell that encased it, using all its prodigious energy to push through, probing with mental tentacles, trying to sense who was out there, who were the ones that it could reach, could speak to, could seduce. Who was there who would free it from its leaden prison?

It felt the strong one, the one who spoke to it. It had heard the man's prayers and curses, his yearnings and tantrums, and it had responded, telling the man, as best it could, where it was, drawing him closer.

But the man had changed somehow. He was different, weaker, but it could sense the fire in him, the desire that was still there, the need to find what beckoned him, entering first his dreams and then his thoughts. He would come.

It struck out with its thoughts again, and found the woman. A stupid woman, not strong at all, but at least it was able to touch her, rattle her mind from time to time, shake her, and say, *Here! Here I am! Find me!* Her mind seemed closed to him now, however, as thick and obtuse and unyielding as the lead that was its prison. If she would only listen, it thought, open herself, maybe it could speak to her more clearly.

It pushed out anew, a sailor on a sea of thought, and found the one it had touched several times before, the man who doubted. And there was someone else now, near to the man, another woman, one who had felt his presence, but remained unaware. It felt a shudder of pure joy ripple through its earthly body as it considered what strength she might have, if she only knew.

But she would have nothing like the strength of the man. The man could be its mightiest disciple of all, if he could lay down his doubts and his fears.

That was something to think about, and the prisoner had nothing if not time to think.

Chapter 17

*R*ichard Skye set the steel balls swinging on their strings, staggering his release of the first and second so that the five balls made a jerkily rhythmic sound as they tapped against each other.

The executive toy had sat on Skye's desk for the past fifteen years. It was the only item in his office that was not work related. There were no family pictures, for Skye's parents were dead, and he had never married. There were no sports items; Skye played no sports and rooted for nobody. A daily workout in the Company gym gave him all the exercise he needed. There were no novels on the shelves. Although Skye was an avid reader in his spare time, the books were all nonfiction, and concerned government and politics.

But there was something about the wooden framework and the five steel balls each descending from two strings that Skye found oddly comforting. He seldom thought about it, but when he did, he assumed that it appealed to his sense of order, that no matter how chaotic the rhythms of the swinging balls seemed, there was always a pattern, and the balls always came to rest as they had been before.

Now, as he spoke to Agent Harris on the phone, they were making a *tack*-eta *tack*-eta rhythm, the force of the falling balls at the left passing through the central ball and driving the balls at the right end upward, and the descent of those balls causing the ascent of the left balls, and so on. It was soothing, relaxing, predictable, quite unlike his life.

If Harris wondered what the clicking was, she didn't ask. It was just as well. Skye liked to keep his people guessing.

"Your investigations," Skye told her, "will from now on include the sand circles that have been done and any future ones."

"They aren't really circles, sir," Harris said. "They're patterns in the shape of—"

"Yes, Agent Harris, I *know* what they are." Skye hated to be corrected, and he was certain Harris knew that. "But sand circles are what the popular press is calling them, no doubt to tie them in with crop circles. Therefore, I will describe them as *circles*, if that's all right with you."

"Sorry, sir. We have already seen the . . . circles."

"Yes, but I want you to take photographs, soil samples, talk to the people who seem most interested in the phenomenon. Theorize how it might have been done, and then check all the resulting avenues—do I have to explain this further, Agent Harris?"

"No sir, of course not."

"I'm so glad. Now, anything to report on the other phenomenon?"

He listened as she told him about the visit to the Begay family, and of Officer Joshua Yazzie's intrusion into their investigation. "Did you run a background on him?" Skye asked.

"Yes, and he checks out. He's been a reservation cop for seven years."

Skye didn't tell her not to get too familiar with the man. He knew she wouldn't. "Continue to investigate Begay," he said. "And the . . . circles, until further notice."

He hung up and sat back. The balls had stopped moving. He stroked his thin moustache as he thought about the sand designs. It was probably foolish to have the agents investigate them, but the two deaths were bizarre enough to be paranormal events. And if they were, it was also possible that there was some connection between them and the patterns.

Besides, if the patterns had been made by hoaxers, Skye felt certain that Joseph Stein would sniff them out. The man was a mountain of skepticism, with enough knowledge to expose any fraud he might suspect. Yes, it was best to turn them loose on it and get it out of the way. Afterward, they could concentrate all their attention on these dried-up corpses. Then maybe, just maybe, they could lead him to the prisoner he and Mr. Stanley sought so earnestly.

Skye allowed a small smile of anticipation to bend his lips. Then he picked up the end steel ball and let it fall, to start the most simple pattern of which his toy was capable.

"So we're splitting up tomorrow," Laika told Joseph and Tony, after she had explained to them what Skye had ordered. "Joseph, you and I will go to the sites of the sand drawings and see what we can find that we haven't already."

"Jesus, Laika," Joseph said, "that's just bullshit stuff and you know it—the kind of crap kids do."

"Skye wants it done, we'll do it. Maybe he thinks there's some sort of connection between the two. And maybe there *is*, for all we know. But if it's a hoax, we'll debunk it as fast as we can. That's our job."

"Sorry," Joseph said. "I forgot—'Ours is not to reason why. . . .' "

"What about me?" Tony asked.

"I want you to go into Gallup and hit the bars where Ralph Begay hung out. Start with this Wet Moccasin place Ella Begay mentioned. Find out where else he might have had a drink. See if the bartender or anybody he knew has any information. And while you're in there, one other thing—check the air service centers and see if any of them rent or charter helicopters, and if any were out around the times of the sand drawings."

"Gotcha."

"What about the chief?" Joseph asked.

"You mean Officer Yazzie?" Laika said, and Tony heard a chill in her tone. "The second site's on the reservation, so we'll have to ask him if he wants to go with us."

"Dandy."

"He was helpful today," she replied. "We never would've gotten to talk to anyone without him."

"I, uh. . . ." Tony began. "Listen, Laika, I was wondering if I could get a helper of my own for tomorrow."

Laika's face betrayed nothing, but Tony saw that Joseph immediately knew who he meant. "The girl," Joseph said disgustedly. "You want to take Miriam along with you, don't you?"

"*Yeah*, I *do*," Tony said. "She knows Gallup, I don't."

"Well, use some of those newfangled street maps and phone books," said Joseph. "I hear secret agents find them quite useful."

"Why don't you just shut up, and—"

"She's not *going*," Joseph said.

"You heading this team now?" Tony said.

"No," Laika said, finally speaking. "*I* am. Try to remember that." She cocked her head at Joseph. "Okay?"

Joseph threw his hands in the air. "But, jeez, that *girl*. . . ."

"She knows this town," Tony said, "she knows a lot of the Indians, bartenders, pawn shop owners . . . and she knows what we're doing here. We've got covers—hell, that's what they're for, so we can work with people, right? I mean, we're not wearing disguises and staying in the shadows, are we?"

"All right, Tony," said Laika. "I don't see how it could hurt, and it might help." Joseph's jaw dropped, but before he could protest further, Laika went on. "What Tony's doing is in line with our covers. If the girl is a good resource, we'd be foolish not to use her." She looked narrowly at Tony. "As long as *she* didn't suggest it. Did she?"

Tony shook his head. "It was my idea."

"It was a good one. Call her."

"Yeah," Joseph said, "call her. I'll be in my room if anybody needs *my* opinion on anything." He strode to the door of Laika's room, yanked it open, and slammed it shut behind him.

"He's edgy," said Laika.

"Yeah. Think it's the dream?"

She nodded. "Could be he's starting to believe in things he doesn't want to believe in."

"Including Miriam?" Tony asked, thinking of the woman's uncanny predictions.

"Maybe," Laika said after a moment. "Maybe."

Miriam Dominick agreed to go with Tony, who would pick her up at her hotel the next morning. Laika liked the girl, although she was slightly concerned by the hold she seemed to have over Tony. When he talked about her at breakfast, he was beaming.

Tony's psych profile, which she had read in detail, indicated that he was extremely independent when it came to women. His sexual liaisons were frequent, with little emotional involvement. But his feelings toward Miriam, if Laika was any judge, were quite the opposite. He reminded her of a teenager with his first crush. She should have realized that when guys like Tony fell, they could fall very hard.

Joseph, on the other hand, was acting like a spoiled child who wasn't allowed ice cream for breakfast. He said little, concentrated on the menu, the window, and the titles on the table's jukebox selector, and only picked at his bagel and oatmeal. When the meal was over and they left Tony, Joseph fell into the driver's seat of the car with a long sigh.

"Don't tell me," Laika said. "You're not happy."

"Laika," he said wearily, "we've got a self-proclaimed

psychic on our team, and I'm going out to investigate some assholes who do crop circles in the sand, because our boss apparently takes such bullshit seriously. Yes, I admit I'm a little piqued this morning.''

"All you have to do is prove they're manmade, and we're finished with the drawings.''

"Not that easy. You know what happened with the crop circles? By the time the hoaxers came forward and actually showed how they did it, a whole cottage industry had sprung up. People were writing books and magazines about this crap. And instead of saying, 'Oh yeah, boy, we got fooled, are we suckers,' they said that just because *some* of the circles were hoaxes doesn't mean they *all* were. If people want to believe, they're going to believe, even if you turn on the lights when the medium's got the luminescent ghost puppet over his hand. 'Oh, look what the spirits did to your hand, oh Great Bamboozle!' ''

Laika laughed in spite of herself. "The only one we have to convince is Skye. From there on, it's up to him to educate the masses.''

Yazzie was where he'd said he would be when Laika had talked to him the night before. His big white Plymouth was parked along Route 118, just off the exit from Route 40. He was leaning on the car, and he waved when he saw them.

There were dozens of cars parked along the road, and several vans that Laika thought might contain video crews. As they joined Yazzie and walked toward the drawing itself, she saw many people taking photographs, and two men with video cameras. The videographers were accompanied by necktie-wearing men with microphones and designer hair, who were interviewing some of the onlookers.

"We'd prefer to stay out of camera range," Laika told Yazzie.

He nodded. "The badge won't let any of them near you. This is reservation land, after all.''

"And you're a reservation cop," Joseph said. Yazzie grinned.

As they drew closer to the giant drawing, they saw that it had been defaced in many places by footprints, and that people had been digging in the trench. There were some holes that were over three feet deep. A man in a baseball cap with a cartoon drawing of an oval-faced, slit-eyed alien was sitting on the edge of one of the holes, sweating profusely and holding a shovel across his lap. "What are you digging for?" Laika asked him.

"You a reporter?" the man asked in return, in a flat Texas accent.

"No. I'm. . . ." She was about to utilize her cover and say that she was with the government, but then she remembered the government conspiracies most saucer nuts believed in. "We're just curious about all this. You think it's, uh. . . ." She pointed upward.

The man snorted a laugh. "What else would it be? As for what I'm digging for, it's glass."

"Glass?" Joseph said, and then nodded. "Ah, fused sand, right?"

"You betcha. I know for certain that this thing couldn'ta been done without *enormous* heat and pressure, and if I find some glass, that'll prove it."

"Well, good luck," Joseph said, and they walked on. When they were at least a hundred yards from the sight-seers, Joseph took some samples of the sandy soil in glass tubes. "I know what I'm going to find," he said. "Sand."

"I take it you don't think this was made by aliens," Yazzie said.

"Nope. Do you?"

"Nope. I have to go with that medicine man—Indian gods." Then he chuckled to show he was joking. "Nah, probably just some coyotes."

"Pretty damn big coyotes," Joseph said, straightening up and putting the cap on the tube.

"Not real coyotes—tricksters. In the Indian legends?"

Laika nodded. "The eternal prankster, like Till Eulen-spiegel or Punch or Brer Rabbit."

"Indian kids can get pretty bored if they're out of work," Yazzie said, looking at the broad expanse of desert and the thick trench cut through it in the shape of a bird. "Still, this is a massive piece of work. Don't know how they'd do it in one night."

"Maybe we should ask Tagore over there," Joseph said, pointing to a man who was seated in the lotus position on the sand, near the center of the giant bird's chest. He was wearing no shirt, and his sunburnt chest was an angry red in contrast to his brown arms and neck. A tattered knapsack sat next to him.

" 'Morning," Laika said. "You look like you've been here awhile."

"Since it happened," the man said in a voice as dry as the sand. "I saw it happen."

"You *saw* it?" Joseph said. "When it was made?"

The man nodded and tried to lick his lips. From the knapsack he took a plastic bottle of tepid water and drank just enough to moisten his mouth so that he could speak more easily. "I'm gonna be on television," he said. "The guys with the cameras? They're from local NBC and ABC stations. They think it might be on the national news. I won't get to see it, though. I'm not leaving here until they come." He looked up at the cloudless sky. "And then I'm going with them."

Laika knelt next to him. "When did you see it? That night?"

The man nodded. "It was late—early in the morning, I don't know when. I was on my way, gonna go down to Mexico, goin' without my lights, you can do that here, you know. It's so cool, no cars, just drivin' through the dark . . . and then I saw it. I saw the mother ship. It was just so quiet, man . . . and so goddam big. . . ."

The man was tripping, Laika thought. He might have been on drugs at the time, but now he was zonked out on exposure and heat exhaustion. He was flying high, and he was going to crash hard. But before she helped him, she had to find out what he had seen. "This mother ship," she said, "what did it look like?"

"Oh, Christ, it was big, and lights all around, like in *Close Encounters*, you know? And then it sent down the baby ship, man, and I watched it, and it made the bird, it just skated over the surface, and wherever it went it drew the picture, man."

"Can you describe it?" asked Laika.

The man thought for a full minute before he answered. "No . . . it was just lotsa lights and *big*, and like, quiet, but I heard this, like, low *roar*, like something under the earth. . . ."

"Maybe the creatures came up from under the desert," Joseph said, earning a dirty look from Laika, and a look of interest from the man.

"Maybe they *did*," he said, then frowned. "But I saw 'em fly away. But maybe they *came* from under the ground, like the center of the earth, where it's hollow inside. . . ."

"I think we ought to get Ignatius Donnelly here to a hospital," said Joseph.

The man waved an arm weakly. "Nah, I'm okay. They're gonna come back, and I wanta *be* here. I think they'll take me then."

"Yeah, I have a hunch they will," said Joseph. "But they're going to take your corpse if you don't get out of the sun and get some liquids into you."

"He's right," Laika said. "You're sick. You need some medical treatment or you're going to get sicker."

"I don't know who you are," the man said, more testily, "but I'm not goin' *no*where!"

"Afraid you are," said Yazzie. "You're on Indian land, and I'm Officer Joshua Yazzie. Now, by my authority, I'm telling you that you either submit to us, get in our car, and let us take you to a doctor, or I'll have to call an ambulance, and you'll be financially responsible for that."

"Oh yeah? Well, you're gonna have to *carry* me out of here . . . chief!" the man snarled, swaying slightly.

Yazzie looked down at him with seeming amusement. " 'Chief.' Nice. Never heard that before." Then he looked around to make sure no person or camera was watching them, leaned down slowly, as though he were going to whisper in the man's ear, and cold-cocked him on his right temple with the heel of his fist.

The man's eyes rolled up and he fell into Yazzie's waiting arms. Yazzie swept him up as easily as if he were carrying a baby, and smiled at Laika and Joseph. "I didn't want him to make a scene and attract attention, and it was only a matter of time before he lost consciousness anyway. Can we all agree that he fainted?"

Laika looked at the man's forehead. There was no trace of a mark. "Dead away," she said.

"Keeled right over," Joseph added, with an appraising look at Yazzie that told Laika he wouldn't use the *chief* appellation again, even behind Yazzie's back.

"I'll take him into Gallup—it's the closest hospital," Yazzie said. "You two find enough to amuse yourselves here for a while?"

Laika nodded. "When we get finished, we'll go to the first site. West on 40, a few miles this side of Winslow." When Yazzie and the man he carried were out of earshot, Laika looked hard at Joseph. "What do you think?"

"About what Looney Tunes said? I don't take it seriously at all. The guy was driving in the dark, probably going down to Mexico for peyote buttons. I don't think he saw shit."

"He thinks he did."

"Yeah, and he also thinks that the earth is hollow and that ET is coming back for him. And his description sounded like he really has seen *Close Encounters* too many times—he even mentioned the movie. The dude is not stable."

Laika and Joseph walked the entire perimeter of the drawing, but could find no spot where entrance or egress had been made to the whole. Much of the area had been trod upon, but the marks were deep enough that mere feet could not have erased them. Still, they both wished that they had investigated before hundreds of people had tramped around. If there were any clues, they were long since gone.

They talked to several people on their circuit of the giant bird, but in Joseph's words, most of them made the sunburned man look like Martin Gardner. Three men wearing white shirts and ties called themselves *silicalogists*, a play on the British cereologists, and had several battery-powered devices with switches and gauges, supposedly able to measure energy bursts remaining from extraterrestrial intrusions. They too were proud to boast that the television people had interviewed them.

When Joseph asked them if they had received any positive indications, they were quick to show him the needles jumping to the right of their gauges. But when he asked to examine their instruments, they declined, saying that they were too delicate for inexperienced people to handle. Joseph nodded smugly and walked away with Laika. "Their fingers were always on the bottom of the box," he said. "That's where the button is to make the needles jump. God, what a bunch of lamers. They're even too obvious for the Fox Network."

Chapter 18

*T*ony met Miriam Dominick in what passed for the lobby of her hotel. Two Indians, both wearing cowboy hats, were sitting on a sofa, and Miriam had been occupying a chair six feet away. When Tony entered, she was leaning forward as though she had been listening to the Indians, though Tony had heard neither one talking.

When she saw Tony, she smiled, stood up, and said, "See you later, fellas," to the Indians, who merely looked at her, following her with their eyes as she left the room.

"Friends of yours?" he asked.

She nodded. "I met them both a couple of years ago. They live here, share a room."

"Not on the reservation?"

"Not every Indian lives on the rez. It's up to them, where they're most comfortable. Danny and Silas like it in Gallup." She sighed. "There's not as much liquor on the rez."

"They alcoholics?"

"Yes. It's not a universal addiction among the Navajo, but there are a lot more than there should be." She shrugged. "I used to think maybe I could do something about it. I know better now." Then she brightened. "So what are we doing today? Looking for places where this man hung out?"

Tony had told her on the phone the night before about

Ralph Begay and his drinking habits. "Yeah. Let's start with the Wet Moccasin."

It looked a little more upscale than most of the town's many bars. A hand-painted sign hung out front with the bar's name and a picture of a tan moccasin dripping water, whose painted drops ran along the bottom of the sign and down the brick wall. The front window was tinted a dark brown, with a neon Budweiser sign glowing behind it. There were no Indians sitting on the steps, as was the case with so many of the other bars.

Even at ten in the morning, the bar had a few customers. Three white men in T-shirts and cowboy hats sat in a booth nursing beers and sandwiches, and Tony guessed that they had gotten off nightshift work. Two elderly Indian men were sitting at a small round table, a pitcher of beer between them, and several people, white and Indian, were at the bar.

Behind it was a big white man with a dark tan. He glanced up from the morning paper when Tony and Miriam entered, and his eyes remained for a moment on Miriam before he looked at Tony and asked, "Help you?"

"Maybe . . . I hope so," Tony said. "Did you know Ralph Begay?"

The bartender's face clouded. "He came in here, but I didn't know him. He just died. But maybe you know that. Who are you?"

Tony showed his National Science Foundation ID. "We're working with the police investigating the death."

"Oh yeah? Why? Something funny about it?"

"Should there be?"

The bartender shrugged. "Hey, drunks are dying all the time. Liver, heart, you name it." Apparently the man hadn't heard about the mummification, Tony thought. It hadn't been in the newspapers.

"And you help them right along, don't you?" Miriam said to the man. Her voice was pinched and angry.

The bartender looked at her in disgust. "Hey, excuse me, but alcohol sales are legal, okay? You don't like it, go tell your congressman, don't bust my balls."

"When's the last time you let an Indian walk out of here drunk, jiggling his pickup truck keys?" she responded.

"I don't *do* that! They have enough, I don't serve 'em!"

"Oh yeah, you're a real philanthropist, aren't you?" Miriam growled. Tony was amazed at the change that had come over her.

"Look, lady," the bartender snarled back, "why don't you just shove your bleeding heart up your—"

Tony's arm shot out and grabbed the bartender by the front of his shirt. He heard cloth rip as he pulled the man across the bar so that their faces were only inches apart. "Let's try and be civil, okay?" Tony said in a low voice.

The man's face flushed under his deep tan, and his right hand fumbled under the bar. Tony grabbed it, pushed it back, and was rewarded with the sound of a cut-off baseball bat clattering to the floor behind the bar.

Then he released the man and held up both hands. "No need for that," Tony said, moving his hand slowly to his hip pocket and taking out his wallet, from which he withdrew two fifty-dollar bills. "That's for the shirt," he said, dropping the first one on the bar. "And that's for civility," he said as he put the second on top of the first. "I apologize. My colleague and I can get a little hot tempered. Now, can you tell me anything about Ralph Begay?"

The money seemed to mollify the bartender. He stuck it in his pocket, straightened his torn shirt, and gestured to the men in cowboy hats, who had stood up menacingly, to sit back down. Then he cocked his head at Tony. "He came in here for years, never talked to me except to order drinks. He always had beer. Then, after he hooked up with that writer guy, he bought whisky."

"You mean John Reece?" Tony asked. The bartender nodded. "Does he come in here often?"

"No. Every few months. I think he kind of cruises the

bars. Gathering, whaddyacallit, information?''

"Local color," Miriam said, her voice hard.

"Whatever."

"You ever hear what they were talking about?" Tony asked.

"I don't eavesdrop."

"Anybody besides Reece particularly friendly with Begay?"

"No. The Indians didn't talk to him after he got pally with Reece. They don't like Reece."

"What a surprise," said Miriam.

"What *is* it with you?" the bartender said, glancing at Tony, who didn't move. "I mean, the guy writes books, the books bring tourists here, and the Indians sell their blankets and jewelry and shit, so what's wrong with that?"

"He exploits them," Miriam said. "He tells secrets they don't want known."

"Well, hey, there's a price for everything, isn't there? Welcome to the real world. I get to see it pretty good from here."

"Did Begay ever drink too much?" Tony asked, getting back on track.

"Almost always. He didn't drive, so I let him drink a little more than the ones I know do. But when he got too plowed, I'd stop serving him. He'd just go on down the street then—there are some bars that keep selling until the Indians fall off their stools. I don't do that." He frowned at Miriam. "Believe it or not, honey. I don't care." Then he looked back at Tony. "You wanta know what Begay was like when he got really blotto, ask there."

Tony looked at the Indians at the table. "They know him?"

"If they did, they wouldn't tell you shit about him. Not even if you were Secretary of the Interior."

Tony tried anyway, but the Indians disavowed any knowledge of Ralph Begay. In whatever front they put up for the two Anglos, Begay had never existed.

Outside, Miriam looked sheepishly at Tony. "I'm sorry I blew up in there. That guy probably wasn't as bad as some. Still, liquor's a big problem with the Indians, and the blame has to go right down the line. He was right about one thing." She gestured to an Indian sleeping on the sidewalk twenty yards away. He could have been anywhere from thirty to fifty. "Drunks *are* dying all the time. And nobody's doing anything about it."

Miriam removed a camera with a telephoto lens and took several pictures of the man. "Looks like *you* are," Tony said.

She shook her head sadly. "*Arizona Highways* doesn't run photos like that."

They checked all of the bars for two blocks on either side of the Wet Moccasin, but the story was always the same. The bartenders knew who Ralph Begay was, but nothing more about him than the fact that he was usually drunk by the time he left their establishment. None of the Indians admitted knowing him, and the white patrons, although they recognized the name, had never spoken to him.

They had a late lunch in a back booth of one of the bars that served sandwiches. After they ordered, Tony noticed tears in Miriam's eyes. His hand sought hers before he'd even realized it. "What is it?" he asked, surprised at finding himself so concerned. "What's wrong?"

She gripped his hand gently. "I'm sorry," she said, her voice choking. "It's just that . . . they're such *good* people, the Navajo. And to see them the way they are here, it just gets to me. And we haven't even seen what's happened to a lot of the younger ones, drugs and gangs. . . ." She shook her head. "I love this country so much, but I hate what's happened to the people whose country it was—and still *is*."

"I'm sorry," Tony said, thinking of the drunks and the town of Red Water. There were places in New York City that rivaled it for poverty, but the racial inequality seemed almost genocidal.

They talked for a long time about the problems of the Indians, and let go of each other's hand only when the food came. But even as he ate, he couldn't help looking at her as she took small bites of her sandwich. "You eat like a bird," he said. "My mother used to say that, but I never understood it till now."

"I think I must have a small stomach. It doesn't take much to fill me up. Where do your parents live?"

"They both passed away," he said.

"I'm sorry."

"They had a lot of good years together. But they . . . couldn't live apart. Mom didn't last too long after Dad died."

"It must be wonderful to have a relationship like that— even if there's pain at the end. Are you married?"

"No. Never. How about yourself?"

"Never found the right man. They all wanted more than I could give." She thought for a moment. "Or less, if that makes sense."

He nodded, thinking of some of the women with whom he had been involved, and of how they wanted to give him more love than he wanted to take. He had never wanted to make anyone a widow.

Why then did he find himself thinking that he had never wanted anything more than the love of the woman sitting with him now, this gentle, compassionate, yet fiery and dedicated woman?

"Haven't you ever used your . . . special abilities to find the right someone?" Tony asked her.

"No. I've tried, but it doesn't seem to work for something like that. I just have to take my chances like everybody else."

Take chances. Everybody had to, and even if his chances gambled with life and death, why should that stop him from loving? It wasn't fair, not to him, not to the women he might have loved.

Wait a minute, he thought. Don't be so damn ready to

hold out your heart. He had done that only once before, and it had scarred him and killed another.

It had been in Brussels, nine years earlier. She had been his contact. He had always made it a strict rule not to get involved with fellow agents, but during their first meeting, he knew that she was the person for whom he had been searching all his life, and he could tell she felt the same way. By their second meeting, his first true love affair began, so strong that he never thought about how it would end.

It had ended in blood, two weeks later. They were leaving her flat when two men on a motor scooter drove by, one of them firing a machine pistol. Tony recovered, but the woman died, and he vowed that he would never know such pain again. He had never loved a woman since.

"Sometimes it costs a lot to love," he said, as much to himself as to Miriam. "There are a lot of sad endings."

"They don't all have to be sad."

"Don't they? Nobody lives happily ever after. There's always a widow or a widower, a dearly departed and a mourner."

"But living how many years alone, compared to all the happy years spent together? Fear shouldn't stop love. That's surrendering to death years before it comes."

She was right, but he couldn't tell her that death could claim him anytime, turning her happy years into months or even weeks. Still, for him to deny love was like denying life itself. And who was he to do that?

He took her hand again, and the look in her eyes told him how she felt.

He spent the rest of the day in a waking dream, holding her hand as they walked through Gallup's streets. Still, he fully performed his assignments, checking the air services in town to discover that two of them rented helicopters, but that they had all been in hangars on the nights in question.

At Miriam's hotel, Tony thanked her for coming with him, then added, "Maybe I could call you tonight—depending on what Dr. Kelly has planned for our team.''

"I'd like that," she nodded.

Tony glanced at the desk clerk, whose face was buried behind a newspaper, then at the two Indians still sitting on the lobby sofa, and decided not to try a kiss. "Goodbye," he said, and walked out. He looked back several times, just to see her standing there smiling at him, her face alive and glowing, while the Indians only stared at him, their expressions unreadable.

Chapter 19

*A*t dinner that night, Tony reported on his failure to turn up anything at either the bars or the air service centers, and Laika and Joseph told him about their visits to the two sites.

"I sent the soil samples to the lab," Joseph said. "They'll have the results in the morning."

"What do you expect to find?" Tony asked.

Joseph shrugged. "If there was enough traction, maybe traces of vulcanized rubber from tires. If there isn't any, it won't prove that tires *didn't* make the tracks, though."

"So what's on the schedule for tomorrow?" Tony asked, hoping that there were no plans to leave the Gallup area.

"We still don't know what killed Begay or the hiker," Laika said. "So we keep investigating. Tomorrow I want you two to take Yazzie and hit the towns near where Begay was found dead, see if there's anyone who might have seen him on those back roads, and if they did, find out who or what else they saw. While you do that, I'm going to visit a professor of anthropology at the University of New Mexico over in Albuquerque and learn what I can about mummification."

Laika paid cash when the bill arrived, and they drove back to the motel and went to their separate rooms. It was 9:30, and Tony called Miriam at her hotel and asked her if she wanted to meet him somewhere.

She was quiet for a moment, and then said, "Why don't I just come over there?"

He felt his heart start to beat faster. "Sure, that'd be fine," he said, and offered to drive over and get her, but she said she would take a cab.

After he hung up, Tony brushed his teeth and took a quick shower, then dressed in clean clothes. He wished his heart would stop beating so fast. After all, she was just one more woman. After tonight he would probably never see her again.

There was a knock at the door. Tony checked his hair one last time, and opened it. Miriam stood there, dressed with a simplicity that only enhanced her natural beauty. She was wearing a white linen blouse with a scoop neckline, and a dark red skirt of Indian design that stopped just below her knees. Her legs were bare, and her small feet wore brown leather sandals. Her only jewelry was a gold chain around her neck, from which hung a gold cross, an inch wide at the crosspiece. Her ever present backpack was slung over her left shoulder.

Tony moved aside, and she entered the room, letting the backpack slip to the carpeted floor. When the door clicked shut, she turned and faced him, her mouth open slightly, expectantly. Her ice-blue eyes looked into his, and before he knew what was happening, his arms were around her, circling her possessively and lovingly, and her mouth was on his.

The kiss ended, and she drew back from him, but allowed his arms to remain around her. "I didn't . . . intend for that to happen." Then she smiled. "At least, not that fast. Maybe being so tired has impaired my judgment."

"I think your judgment was very good." He drew her to him again, but this time she moved away.

"Let's not go so fast, Vincent. Can we just . . . talk?" She sat in one of the two easy chairs on either side of the table near the bed, and Tony took the other.

They talked for a long time about their lives, and when the silence finally came, it was rich between them. He drank in the sight of her, convinced more than ever that she was what he had always wanted in a woman, and dared to think that she felt the same about him.

He got up and stood next to her chair, looking down at her and resting his hand on her shoulder. "Stay with me tonight, Miriam. Please."

She put her hand on top of his, and her look made him feel his heart would break from wanting her. "If I do," she said softly, "will you hold me? Nothing else. Just hold me all night long."

To his surprise, he found the suggestion completely acceptable. Lust was a part of what he felt for Miriam, but the greater need was to do what she desired. And if that was for her to be held chastely through the night, then that would be his desire, and he would hold her as tenderly as he could.

"I would love to," he told her, crouching at her side. He took her hand and pressed his lips against the back of it, then stood up.

He turned off the light so that the only illumination came from the night light he always plugged into the wall, as he never slept in total darkness. Then he stripped to his boxers and got into bed.

Only then did Miriam begin to undress. Tony felt a tightness in his throat as she revealed her small and lovely breasts. Her waist was slender and her hips slight. She dropped her clothing and slipped under the covers next to him, wearing only a pair of panties and her gold cross. Then she moved into the crook of his arm as though she belonged there.

Though he was aroused by her warmth against him, he only kissed her scented hair and moved his other arm across her body as she nestled closer to him. He wanted to say something, but could not decide what, so he remained silent, cradling this woman he thought he loved, thinking how wonderful it was to just hear her breathing softly, beside him in the night.

*   *   *

At the same time Tony Luciano was falling asleep with Miriam Dominick in his arms, Father Alexander, on his cot inside the Mission of San Pedro, awoke. He had been plagued with terrifying dreams for the past few nights, but it was not a nightmare that had awakened him. Rather it was the sound of a vehicle rattling up the dirt road toward the mission.

Painfully, Father Alexander sat up on the cot. His back had been bothering him, and the condition had been exacerbated by the narrow canvas strip he slept on. He pulled on his robe and slippers, and padded outside onto the portico.

A large panel truck was coming up the slight rise on which the mission stood. Had it not been for its headlights, the old priest could not have made it out amid the darkness of the canyons that surrounded the old building where he stood. It was moving slowly, laboring as though it carried a heavy burden. That much was certainly true, he thought. It bore perhaps the greatest burden in all history, and now that burden would be his.

The van stopped directly in front of the portico, and Father Alexander walked down the three wooden steps to greet those inside. Three men climbed out, dressed in cowboy hats, plaid shirts, and jeans, but Father Alexander knew who they really were. Clothing could not disguise from him the fact that these were men of God. He knew his own.

He nodded a welcome, and the driver took off his hat and bowed slightly. "Father Alexander?" The old priest nodded again. "I'm Father William, and this is Father Donald and Father James. We're a little late. Took a wrong turn back there, nearly ended up over at the dam."

"These desert roads are confusing," Father Alexander said with an understanding smile. "The debris in the slot canyons can get washed out by flash floods so that you would swear they were roads, if the occasional boulder doesn't get in your way. I thank God you've arrived safely. And, um. . . .'' He looked toward the body of the van.

"Yes, he's there," said Father William. "And he's done no harm on the way, as far as we can tell."

"But you couldn't tell very well now, could you?" the old man chided.

"No. That's why we were chosen, after all. He cannot touch us."

"Nor me," said Father Alexander. "We are blessed in that at least." He said a silent prayer, asking God to forgive him for lying to these young men. He *had* been touched, though he would not be again. His faith would keep him strong.

"I'm not sure that it's that much of a blessing, Father," said Father William, "if our immunity to the creature's wiles makes us the perfect ones to be his keeper." He smiled at the others. "I can imagine more pleasant ways to serve God."

"But few so important as this," said Father Alexander. These boys must not think this was all a lark. Their task was dangerous and deadly, not only for them, but possibly for the entire world.

"No. I suppose you're right. Shall we take him to the kiva tonight?"

The old priest shook his head. "In the morning. I'm sure you're all tired, and it will be safe. You were not followed?"

"No, Father," said the fresh-faced young Father Donald. "We've been driving for days, mainly to throw off anyone who might have been on our trail, but believe me, nobody's behind us."

"Good. Come inside and have something to eat. There are cots to sleep on. Now that you're here, maybe we can move something better in," Father Alexander said, thinking of his back.

The cots didn't seem to keep the young men from sleeping soundly, although Father Alexander found it impossible to return to his own slumbers. What he had been waiting for and fearing had returned, and its presence kept him awake as though his canvas cot had been replaced by a bed of thorns.

Long after midnight, he arose quietly and walked outside. The van sat in the starlight, looking like a wide, heavy tombstone. Father Alexander approached it slowly and gingerly, as though he expected its doors to burst open and a horde of giant maggots to emerge from its interior.

But nothing of the sort occurred. The desert night was silent. Yet as he turned to go back to his cot, he thought he heard a whisper, a voice both inside and outside his head that said one word:

Alex . . .

He froze for a long moment, but the voice said no more. He walked into the mission without turning around and looking back.

Father Alexander was very much afraid to look back.

Chapter *20*

Nearly two hundred miles southeast of the Mission of San Pedro lies Canyon de Chelly, a national monument near the New Mexico border in northeastern Arizona. The sandstone canyon stretches for twenty-six miles, and is a protected national monument. Since the canyon is within the Navajo reservation, and Navajo families live and farm on the canyon floor, visitors must be accompanied at all times by a Navajo guide or a park ranger.

The people who had followed Ezekiel Swain, and who now followed his sister Jezebel and their new leader, Damon, did not know about the regulation, and would not have cared if they had. They got into the canyon in the first place by ignoring a sign that read, INDIAN ROAD: RESIDENTS AND PARK SERVICE OFFICIALS ONLY.

There were only six of them now, and Damon was having trouble holding even them together. Frustration had driven the deserters away, and most of it had come from the slow and tentative pace Jezebel's psychic searching required. Also, as Damon had to admit, he did not have the power over them that Ezekiel Swain had possessed. But then, Damon did not have the *psychic* power that Swain had shown and of which Jezebel had only a fraction.

Some of the cultists had come to Damon and Jezebel and told them they were leaving. Though he had tried to persuade them to stay, first by flattery and then by telling them that they were traitors to the Divine, they still left, angry and bitter. Chang and Eng had slipped out one night in their van, leaving only a single van for the six who remained and all their gear.

Though Damon had expected Ted and Aileen to be the first to leave, they had hung in there. They still looked on Damon as an interloper and an adversary, but remained, Damon was convinced, in hopes that Ted could take over the leadership of the tiny band.

With Rodney by his side, however, that was damned unlikely, and Charlotte had stayed as well. Damon could tell the woman wanted him but was too damn shy to say anything. She just hung around him whenever she could, which was often. The six of them drove, ate, slept, and practically shit together, and Damon was getting as sick of it as the rest of them.

Jezebel, who had seemed such a witty smartass when he had first met her, was a damp rag without her brother around. Her indecisiveness when they came to a crossroad was driving Damon insane. She would get out, look around, close her eyes, and then open them again. Sometimes she would see a little dust devil blowing toward one of the roads, and then she would nod in that direction. Once she had noticed that the leaves on a piñon oak were rustling when there was no wind to be felt, and then she had motioned in that direction, and they had driven on.

Shit, Damon had thought, *he* could look for things like that. You didn't have to be psychic to see a goddamn dust devil. Soon she'd be cutting open jackrabbits and examining their guts for signs. If they didn't soon get some indication that the Divine was near, he was going to kick her ass.

And now here they were on some stupid Indian reservation, after zigging and zagging for days, but always moving north. Rodney had said that back in the late seventies, when Damon was in *kindergarten*, for Chrissake, his motorcycle gang had stayed in this canyon several times without getting hassled by the Indians.

"They were scared of us, man," Rodney said, as they drove along through the dark, the canyon walls growing higher on either side. "Peaceful little Navajos, and here comes a bunch of bikers. Hell, I guess they thought we'da scalped them if they bitched." Rodney thought for a moment. "Some of the guys probably woulda, too."

They stopped the van about a half mile into the canyon and set up camp a hundred yards off the dirt road. They had three tents, the one Jezebel had shared with Ezekiel and now slept in alone, a two-man tent Ted and Aileen slept in, and the pup tent Damon had brought. Charlotte slept in the van, and Rodney just tossed an air mattress and a sleeping bag on the ground.

The day had been annoying all the way around, and everyone's patience was short. As they set up their tents, Ted and Aileen eyed Damon with undisguised hatred, while Jezebel sat on the ground, as though too weary to do anything else.

"Why don't you get up off your ass and help?" Damon said to the woman. "Or do you expect Charlotte and Rodney to set up your damn tent *every* night?"

"I don't mind," Charlotte said quickly, picking up a hammer to drive in the pegs.

"Well, damn it, you *should* mind," Damon said, wrenching the hammer from her hands and throwing it at Jezebel's feet so that it nearly hit her. "If you can't bring anything else to this party, at least pull your own damn weight!"

"She *is* bringing something else to the party," Ted said. "You forgot who's got the power to bring us to the Divine."

"Well, then, why doesn't she use it?" Damon answered. "We're wandering through the desert like the Israelites behind Moses—maybe forty years from now she'll finally hone in, huh?"

"It's not her fault!" blurted Aileen. "If Ezekiel hadn't been killed—"

"What?" Damon shouted. "You don't know he was killed, you dumb bitch!"

"Doesn't she?" Ted said coldly. Damon glanced at Rodney, but the look the big man gave him in return told him that Rodney hadn't betrayed him.

"What the hell do you mean by that?" Damon said. "Come on, man, spit it out—you think *I* had something to do with Ezekiel disappearing?"

"Well, you tell me. Everything was fine till you came. Ezekiel would go out in the desert all night sometimes, but he always came back. Then you come along, he gives you some shit—the same kind of shit that we all learned how to take because he was our *leader*, damn it—and that night he disappears and doesn't show up again. And he didn't get lost, man! You ever heard of a psychic getting lost?"

"So you think I killed him and buried him out in the desert?" said Damon. "That what you think?"

"I think it's real possible," said Ted.

"Why the hell do you think I came out here, Teddy? To lead half a dozen raggedy-ass assholes like you and Aileen around the desert? Well, think again! I came out here to find the Divine, and you think I'd be goddamn stupid enough to kill the only person who can find Him for us?"

"You knew Jezebel could," said Aileen accusingly.

"Yeah, and I also knew that she wasn't nearly as good at it as Ezekiel was—and you sure proved *that*, lady," he added in a loud aside to Jezebel, who had gotten to her feet and was looking at him like a little girl whose favorite doll he had broken. "What, you believe this bullshit?"

"Ezekiel was alive," she said, "and when you came, he died."

"You don't know that he's—"

"He's *dead!*" she screamed. "I *felt* it . . . I *feel* it . . . I *know.*"

"And then you became leader," Ted said bitterly. "Just took over."

"It was right," said Rodney in his gravelly voice. "He should have."

"Why?" asked Ted, nearly in a rage.

"Because that's the way it should be," Rodney said. Damon knew what he meant. Damon had killed the king, and it was only right that he should become the king himself. But did that mean he was going to tell the truth about what he'd seen? Damon stiffened, ready to fight.

"Damon's the smartest one of us, and he didn't do a thing to Ezekiel," Rodney went on. "I hardly slept at all that night, and I had my eye on Damon's tent almost all the time. He hardly moved. If he'da gone after Ezekiel, I woulda seen him."

A wave of relief swept through Damon, and he grinned at the others. "All right, happy? Now, let's finish making camp, if the psychic princess wouldn't mind."

"Come on, Jezebel," Charlotte said, picking up the hammer at Jezebel's feet, "I'll help you."

Ted and Aileen turned away from the others and got their tent, and Rodney helped Damon set his up. "What was that for?" Damon asked him.

"Saving your ass? Hey, all I want now is for those of us who are here to stick together. We already lost too many, but we'da lost everybody, me included, if old Ted was leader of the pack. Nobody can stand that prick's guts. He's even worse than you."

"Thanks. You think we got enough muscle left to liberate the Divine . . . assuming we ever find Him?"

"Dunno. Shit, they could have a small army holding him, for all we know. But if we believe, we got no choice in the matter. Can I make a little suggestion, though? About *her?*" He jerked his head toward Jezebel, who was awkwardly helping Charlotte raise the tent. "Get her under your thumb more. I mean, she didn't take a leak that Ezekiel didn't have something to say about it."

"Why? She doesn't mouth off, or anything. That just now, that was way out of character for her—Teddy Boy was pushing her."

"Yeah, but when Ezekiel controlled her, it somehow, like, focused her more. She needs that, she needs somebody to replace what Ezekiel was to her."

"And what was that?"

"Shit, just about everything—brother, father, lover . . . yeah, they did it, all right, musta been a real trick with his blubber gut. About time somebody filled that gap in her life, know what I mean?"

Damon watched Jezebel for a moment as she bent over to try and hammer in a tent peg. "The prospect isn't unpleasant," he admitted.

"Hell, no. She's a good-looking woman. You took Ezekiel's place, so take it the whole way. See, it's like she never grew up. Ezekiel did her thinking for her and gave her everything she needed, including sex, the sick bastard."

"What about the others? Jezebel starts yelling, you think Ted's not going to try to stop me?"

"First of all, she's not gonna yell. And if she does, you think I'm gonna *let* Ted try and stop you? Besides, Aileen already thinks he's got the hots for Jezebel himself, so if he gets too involved in her sex life, Aileen won't be happy about it. As for Charlotte. . . ." Rodney shrugged. "Charlotte wouldn't squash a scorpion if it stung her on the ass."

Damon watched as Jezebel zipped open the flap of her tent and stepped inside, zipping it shut behind her. "I don't know, Rodney."

"Hey, man, don't make me sorry I backed your ass now, okay? I'm concerned with just one thing here, and that's getting that woman in the right frame of mind to get us all to the Divine. That's what it's all about, and nothin' else matters."

Damon straightened up and looked at Jezebel's tent that was to be his tent, too, from then on. He squared his shoulders and walked past Ted and Aileen, who were eating from cartons of yogurt they had bought earlier that day, and past Charlotte, who was pounding the final stake to secure the tent. "Good enough," he told her, then gestured toward the van. "Go bunk down yourself."

Then he zipped open the door of the tent and stepped through. Jezebel was lying on her back on top of her sleeping bag. She was wearing only a T-shirt and panties, and looked up at him as if she had been expecting him, but didn't feel either happy or sad about his presence, or know what he was going to do.

Damon put on his Mr. Cool face, zipped the door shut, and got on his knees next to her. Her lips were cold when he kissed them, and she didn't respond at all, but he liked a challenge. He ran a finger down her cheek and whispered, "Daddy's home. . . ."

All in all, he enjoyed it and thought she had, too, though it would have been better if Ted and Rodney hadn't been yelling at each other outside.

When Gary Chee heard the shouts, he switched off his flashlight and rode his horse in darkness. There weren't any houses right around there, so he wondered who the hell it was making all that noise.

Shouts were something that you didn't hear much of down in Canyon de Chelly. Most of the Navajo who still lived there were summertime farmers, like Gary Chee's parents. Their houses weren't palaces, but the families who lived in them during the farming months were sober and hardworking, unlike some of the Indians who lived in the small towns on the rez on the government dole. Farming gave you some pride, and for a season let you live the way your fathers did. The only problem was, Gary hated farming. That was why he had become a guide.

It wasn't a bad life. He hung around the visitors' center with the other guides, sitting in the shade, drinking Pepsis, and shooting the shit, until his name worked its way up to the top of the list. Then he met the people he was going to guide, found out how long they wanted to stay in the canyon, hopped in their car while they drove to an access trail, and away they went.

He would guide them down into the canyon, along the floor, and past some farms and herds of sheep, and usually end up at one of the ruins. Then they would head back. A hike lasted a minimum of three hours, and Gary charged twelve bucks an hour, and usually got a ten-dollar dip. Most days he made two and sometimes three trips, so he could salt away a good bit during the tourist season, more if he stayed with his folks on the canyon floor.

Most of the Anglos he guided were nice enough, though they were pretty stupid when it came to knowing much about the Navajo. But he had his gracious answers ready for even the dumbest questions and remarks. That was how he got his tips.

The last family he had taken down that day had been more than pleasant, but totally clueless. The father had thought the Navajo and the Anasazi were the same, so Gary had gently corrected him by telling him that the Navajo considered the Anasazi "the ancient enemies," and keep their farms as far as possible from the ruins. The teenaged son thought that the "desert varnish," the marks made by oxide-rich water flowing down the canyon walls, was put on by the park service to preserve the stone. Fortunately, the mother filled him in, and Gary pretended not to hear. If you made your people feel *too* stupid, it could hurt your tip.

The mother had been far and away the sharpest of the trio, and a pretty good-looking lady, to boot, but a little careless, as it turned out. At the end of the day, Gary was walking out the door of the visitors' center, getting ready to hike the two miles back down into the canyon to his folks' farm, when a ranger hurried out after him and told him that he had a phone call.

It was the husband of the family he had taken down on the last trip of the day. They had gotten back to their motel and discovered the wife's wallet was missing, and figured that it must have slipped out of her pocket on the hike through the canyon. She thought it had probably happened where they had sat to rest on a log about halfway in. If Gary was willing to go back and try to find it, the man would pay him fifty dollars, and if he was successful, another fifty. Gary agreed and told the man to meet him at the visitors' center when it opened at eight the next morning.

By the time he had hiked down to the floor, it was already dark. So he had dinner, and then, at 10 o'clock, saddled his father's horse and rode to the trail they had hiked that day, riding slowly along and shining the bright flashlight back and forth. He wondered about what he might do if he found the wallet and discovered that it was stuffed with money. Then he decided he would give it back. He'd been honest all his life. No need to change now.

When he heard the shouting, he turned off his light, tied the horse to a tree, and walked softly toward the sound. It was some kind of camping party, and by the flashlights they were whipping around, he could see they were white people, and they looked pretty ratty.

The hell with them, he thought. He wasn't about to tell them that they were trespassing on Navajo land and to get out. He doubted they'd take the advice kindly. He trotted back to the horse and rode away, not turning on his light to look for the wallet until he knew he was out of sight of the camp.

He rode deeper into the canyon, and the walls began to rise steeply around him. The place he was heading for was about three miles in, at the bottom of an overlook which offered no access trail to the floor.

Only a hundred yards before he reached it, Gary thought he heard something up ahead, and he drew his horse up and listened. The dead silence had been broken by the sounds of rocks rolling from the top of the cliff. Slides occurred occasionally and were generally of no concern, since most of the houses were built far from the canyon walls. Maybe the Anasazi had built their cliff dwellings where rock slides could sweep them off their ledges, but the Navajo had been a lot smarter than that.

But there was something about the sound that had puzzled him, a softness among the peppery rattle of the stones. It was the sound a deer or other large animal might make falling from the top of the cliff. There were few deer in or around the canyon. Although the park service had made attempts to reintroduce them, they generally wandered away to the Lukachukai Mountains, or the higher parts of the Defiance Plateau.

Gary thought about a stray sheep but doubted one could climb as high as the place he thought he had heard the slide start. They were just domestic sheep, not mountain goats, and whatever it was hadn't made a sound in its descent. Most sheep would bleat their asses off if you looked at them sideways.

Finally he thought, God, what if it's a person? It would be just like some dumb tourist to want a shot of Canyon de Chelly by moonlight and lean too far out over the edge of the overlook. But hell, people were even noisier than sheep, and he hadn't heard anyone yell.

Everything was quiet again, and he guided his horse toward where the sounds had come from. But then he saw the log on which the family had rested that day and remembered his main reason for coming out tonight. He whipped the light ahead, looking at the cliff face, and saw some loose stones at the bottom, about thirty yards away, but saw not a trace of man or deer or sheep. It had just been a little rock slide, then, nothing more.

Then he played the light about the log and saw something gleaming warmly at him from the ground behind it. Polished brown leather? He climbed off the horse and walked toward it, flashlight in one hand, reins in the other.

Then he grinned. Hello, a hundred bucks, he thought, crouching and picking up the brown leather wallet. He stood up and looked at the cards first, and saw on the Indiana driver's license the photo of the woman he had met today. Out of curiosity he looked in the currency sleeve and found seventy-two dollars and some travelers' checks. Good. He wasn't going to be tempted.

He put the wallet into the pocket of his denim jacket and snapped the snap so that it wouldn't fall out. Then he put his left foot into the stirrup and vaulted back onto the horse. Tomorrow morning he'd see the grateful Anderson family again and collect his hundred dollars. He wouldn't be surprised if there was a little bonus besides.

Just as he turned the horse, it began to get skittish. It snorted, jerked its head, and then reared up so that Gary almost toppled from the saddle. "Hey!" he shouted. "Easy! Easy, boy!"

They were his last words. Suddenly he felt something leap onto the horse behind him, and the old animal gave a shriek of terror, twisting like a rodeo mount, then rearing up again.

What felt like claws dug into Gary's shoulders from behind, and he found himself falling backward, losing the reins, his feet slipping from the stirrups. He waved his arms once, in panic, and the horse galloped madly away into the darkness, as Gary's back struck the ground.

Or *was* it the ground? It felt as though he were lying on something brittle, a construction of sticks, but when he tried to push himself up, he found that whatever he was on was clinging to his back like a suction cup to a wall.

Then the thing's arms came around him from beneath, and he felt one clawlike hand over his heart and saw the outline of the other coming down upon his face, blotting out the stars, and then everything.

Chapter 21

*T*ony Luciano awoke instantly, as he always did. There was none of that slowly coming out of sleep for him. If he was awake, there was a reason, a sound, a bit of unexpected light, an unwelcome visitor. And if it were none of these, if he had slept just enough that he was rested and then woke up, what the hell, he might as well be awake.

Immediately he realized that what had awakened him was Miriam. She was moaning in her sleep, and her breath was coming in quick, panting gasps. He touched her forehead with his fingertips, hoping it would gently wake her, but she remained immersed in her nightmare. His fingers came away damp from her perspiration.

Then he said her name softly in the dark. The second time she seemed to hear him, and she hitched in a deeper breath. He felt her stiffen, and in the dim glow of the night light he saw her eyes open. She looked at him for a moment as though she did not understand where she was. Then, as she recognized him, she let her breath out slowly and melted into him with a shudder.

"Bad dream?" he asked.

She didn't answer for a moment, and when she did, her voice was a rough whisper. "I saw it again. The drawings in the sand. And this time I saw . . . what made them." She drew away from him again, just far enough to look into his face. Her breath was as fresh as if she hadn't been

157

asleep at all. One more point in her favor, Tony thought.

"What did you see?" he asked her. "Tell me."

"It was the most realistic dream of the three," she said, turning on her back and looking up at the dark ceiling as though it were a screen on which she was playing back the images. "I was standing high on a ledge, and off in the distance there were two stone towers."

"You mean, towers that were built of stone? Or natural towers?"

"Natural. They were weathered, like sandstone. Chunks had broken off them, and I remember, one was taller than the other. And then . . . it wasn't like it was happening at the towers, but *near* them, like I was seeing two different places at once? Anyway, it was night, and I looked up in the sky and saw something moving, like a huge white cloud lit by the moon. And it was getting bigger and bigger, as though it was dropping toward me.

"Then it broke apart, and I saw that the cloud wasn't a cloud at all, but a flock of white birds, like doves. And they dived to the earth below me, so that they were just hovering over it, and they began to fly over the sand in patterns, weaving and twisting all around. I kept thinking that they were all going to collide with one another, but they never did.

"Finally, they rose, back into the sky, going up so fast that I could barely follow them, until they looked just like a cloud again. It drifted up and up, higher and higher, until it was gone. Then I looked down and saw what they had done.

"It was . . . an animal in profile. Crude, almost like a cave drawing, you know? I couldn't tell what it was supposed to be. Maybe a bear, or something. But the weird part was that there was a line from its mouth to its chest or stomach; again, I couldn't really tell. But at the place where the line touched its body, it looked like an arrowhead."

"An arrowhead?" Tony said. "So was this line like a . . . a curved arrow?"

"I don't think so . . . I don't really know."

"What frightened you so badly then? Just the dream itself?"

"At the end, the animal . . . it started to move. The whole desert began to shift, like this gigantic beast was starting to rise right out of the sand." She pressed against him again. "That was what frightened me awake."

Tony put his arm around her and held her closely. "Well, you're not the only one with bad dreams," he whispered.

"You?"

"No. Dr. Tompkins. He's gotten what seem to be prophetic dreams now and then."

"What are his about? Monsters in the sand?"

"No. A prisoner. A man in . . . in a cell who wants to speak to him." Tony stopped himself from saying more. "It's okay. They're just dreams, whatever they're about. You're here with me now, and there's nothing that can hurt you. No animals, nothing." He kissed her forehead gently. "Just go back to sleep."

For a moment she looked up at him, and her eyes gleamed in the dim light. "I'm so glad I'm here with you," she said, then closed her eyes and nestled her head back against him.

It had been 1:30 in the morning when Miriam had awakened Tony. An hour later, Tony was still awake, looking at the glowing red numerals on the clock radio bolted to the bed table. Next to him Miriam was sleeping soundly, a soft snore coming from her slightly open mouth. Far from being disturbing, it was a rhythmic, soothing little sound that would have lulled him to sleep had his mind not been so busy.

He had not comforted her with the old saw that it was only a dream, because he did not believe that it was. With the other evidence of the girl's power of prophecy or out of body experiences, he thought it very possible that her dream had been another vision of reality. If another sand drawing was found that matched her dream, even Joseph would have to admit there was certainly something going on here that was inexplicable to science.

However, there was something else besides Miriam's psychic abilities that was keeping Tony awake, and that was the realization that he had fallen in love with her. Miriam Dominick seemed to be everything he had ever wanted in a woman. She was self-reliant and independent, yet also devout and compassionate. She was one of the easiest people to talk to that he had ever met, and to add to the mix, she was very lovely.

She is a lovely person, he thought, as he lay in the dark with her. He wanted the night to go on forever, thought that he would be content to hold this woman in his arms every night, as the years passed and they grew old together.

Then he remembered what he had never really forgotten, that he was an operative with a job to do, and another to do tomorrow, and another next year, and so on down the years, and that there was a good chance that one of those jobs could kill him and leave Miriam alone. How could he ask a woman to lead a life like that?

But then he realized it was her decision to make, if she felt or would someday feel about him the way he did about her.

Another thought occurred to him then, a less generous one. The fact that he was an operative with a team affected and possibly endangered by his actions and his contacts made it imperative that he know as much about those contacts as possible. And Miriam Dominick was one of them. There was always the chance she was not what she seemed. With Skye at the controls, *nothing* might be what it seemed.

She seemed to be sleeping soundly, and he slowly slid his arm from beneath her neck and got out of bed, thankful it was one of those commercial motel beds that wouldn't have made a squeak if elephants had been mating on it. He stood for a moment, listening to her breathing as it continued undisturbed.

Her backpack lay just inside the door, and he picked it up and took it into the bathroom. He closed the door behind him and turned on the heat lamp. By its reddish glow, he examined the contents of the backpack.

Two cameras were on top, a Pentax K1000, which Tony knew to be a good but older model, and a newer Nikon. There was also an assortment of five lenses, a lead film packet with four rolls of exposed film, and a dozen unexposed loose rolls.

Tony examined the wallet next. There was a VISA card, a social security card, and an Arizona driver's license with Miriam's photo and the address of an apartment in Kingman. The date of birth told Tony that Miriam was twenty-seven. He also found a library card, a prayer card to St. Jude, and several photos of a younger Miriam and a cheerful-looking older couple Tony figured were her parents.

Further down in the backpack was a clean, rolled-up T-shirt and a pair of panties, which made him happily think that she had come intending to spend the night with him. There were also several letters from her mother. They had been addressed to general delivery at different northern Arizona and New Mexico towns, and the envelopes had a Tucson return address and postmark. They were mostly news about family and the neighborhood, with frequent admonitions to be careful when she was "out in the middle of nowhere," and assurances that Father Andrew and all her mother's friends would offer up prayers for her safety.

At the very bottom were three books, a worn Bible, a thick Maeve Binchy paperback novel, and a paperback edition of *My Partnership with Christ*, by Michael La-Pierre. Tony examined them all. The small black leather-bound Bible had an inscription from Miriam's grandparents, and the other two books had been stamped by a used bookstore in Flagstaff. Tony looked more closely at the LaPierre autobiography.

Although Tony had not read the book, he had heard a

lot about LaPierre. The man was a right-wing populist hero who had contributed millions over the years to a wide assortment of religious-right causes. On the rare occasions when Tony channel surfed, he had come across the man as a guest on various programs on ChristNet, the Reverend Richard O'Brien's cable network. LaPierre had heavily funded O'Brien's unsuccessful presidential bid back in 1992, and the LaPierre Foundation now financed a series of anti-abortion ads that made the DeMoss commercials look positively liberal in comparison.

Though Tony disapproved of abortion personally, he felt that it ought to be left up to the individual. He had seen enough of the effects of tyranny in some of the countries in which he had operated. Though he knew he should obey the church in every way, he still had difficulties resolving some of the tenets of Catholicism with his own fairly liberal social views. Despite his faith, he disliked pronouncements and any language that smacked of self-righteousness, and Michael LaPierre had created a public image founded on those.

Still, there was no denying the man's charisma. He had aged handsomely and was an articulate and persuasive speaker, and his book had sold in the millions over the five years it had been in print. It was the usual rags-to-riches story. LaPierre's father had been a poor fisherman on the Gulf, but his son, through smarts and hard work and, most important, LaPierre claimed, a close association with Christ, was able to get a scholarship to Tulane. When he was graduated with an MBA, he borrowed money to start a small fleet of shrimpers, which over the next ten years somehow grew into a worldwide trading corporation.

LaPierre had expanded into a dozen other areas, and now LaPierre International had its hands in everything from computers to banking to media, and Michael LaPierre was the third richest man in the United States, constantly traveling around the globe for both business and spiritual reasons, opening a new factory in Thailand or a new foster care facility in India.

Tony flipped through the book. It was a long one, nearly 500 pages. He saw that Miriam's bookmark was halfway through, on page 250. For some reason, the number gave him pause. Then he remembered. Page 250—"250-17-4." It was the first series of numbers of the book code message that they had taken off the dead body of a member of the group that had nearly killed them in New York City, a group whose primary purpose had seemed to be to locate and free the mysterious prisoner.

The ops had thought that the key book, without which the code was unbreakable, might be a religious book of some kind, since everything about the prisoner seemed steeped in religion, and the dead man was also packing a Bible. According to the numbers, the book had to be at least 452 pages long and have at least 34 lines per page. *My Partnership with Christ* qualified.

The chances were long, but Tony turned off the light, crept back into the room, slipped his wallet from his pants pocket, and went back into the bathroom. There he turned the heat lamp on again and took a reduced copy of the book code from a hidden sleeve in his wallet. Then he began to check.

250-17-4. On page 250, the fourth word in the seventeenth line was *The*. A propitious beginning, he thought, much better than *Reagan* or *perversions* or *anti-Christians*, other words to be found on the same page.

He went on. *19-2* indicated the second word on the nineteenth line of the same page. It was *Lord. The Lord*—so far, so good.

293-4-3 was *did*. *26-6* gave him *not*. *29-10* was *die*. With three more words, he had the sentence:

The Lord did not die on the cross.

This was the book. It had to be. He felt his heart pounding so hard that he was afraid Miriam would hear it in the nethe next room. Although he knew he should stop, return the backpack to its previous spot, and rejoin Miriam in bed before she woke up, he had to do just one more sentence, to prove to himself that the words weren't just a coincidence, a simulacrum of the infinity of monkeys and typewriters writing Shakespeare.

He flipped through the pages, reading the numbers, counting the lines and words, until he had another full and cogent sentence:

He was placed living in the tomb.

Tony's mouth felt as dry as sandpaper, or as sand, the same sand that had been used as a canvas by whatever had made the drawings of which Miriam had dreamed. But those drawings were far from Tony's mind now. All he could think about was Christ, his savior, who had supposedly risen from the dead, now never having died at all, and about what it meant to both Tony's personal salvation and to the world.

He wanted to go on decoding, but he thought he heard a sound in the other room, and he whipped the heat lamp switch to the off position and listened in the silence.

"Vincent?" It was Miriam's voice, and from the muffled nature of it, he was sure she was still in bed, her face against the pillows.

He opened the bathroom door a crack. "I'll be there in a minute," he whispered, then shut the door and placed Miriam's things in her backpack. Finally he put the code back into his wallet and opened the door.

He carried the backpack low, on the opposite side from the bed, and crossed to the door. She did not look up. He let the backpack slip to the floor and jiggled the security chain. "Just wanted to make sure the door was locked," he said, sliding his wallet underneath his pants.

Then he climbed in beside her. "You okay?" he asked, and felt her nod. He cupped her chin and raised her face so that he could kiss her. He had intended it to be brief and gentle, for what he had read in the bathroom had taken his mind far from lovemaking.

So it was with surprise and a bit of a shock that he felt Miriam extend the kiss, her lips parting. She molded her body to his own, and he moved against her, instantly filled with desire for this wonderful woman who trusted him enough to lie with him, and now enough to love him.

They made love, and it was long and soft and sweet, and he placed the book and the code, the dead men and the sand drawings, his partners and their mission, far back in his mind, until he forgot about them. He even forgot about the prisoner, forgot everything but the two of them.

He made love to the woman he loved, Christ forgotten. The gold cross between them pressed itself into their flesh, and the cold metal grew warm from being couched between their bodies.

Chapter 22

A t 6:30 the next morning, Tony opened his motel room door and looked both ways, preparatory to letting Miriam slip through with her backpack. It had been she who'd insisted on leaving that early, so as not to be seen by "Vincent's" colleagues, Drs. Kelly and Tompkins.

Just before she went through the door, she kissed him deeply and held on to him tightly.

"I want to see you again," he told her.

"When?"

"All the time," he said, meaning it. "In the morning when I get up and when I go to bed at night, and all the time in between."

A blush reddened her cheeks, and she shook her head as though confused by his words. "Vincent, I don't . . . I don't *do* this kind of thing. I mean, I didn't intend for . . . *any* of this to happen, but I think that I want to see you again, too. I don't mean just, like, *see* you, but more like, well, what you said." She shook her head again. "I feel like such an idiot."

He kissed her on the tip of her nose. "You're not an idiot. Look, I don't know exactly what's going on today, but if I can take you along, I want to. You were a big help yesterday. Were you going to go out and shoot some pictures?"

"Tell you what," she said, "I'll hang out at my hotel until around noon. Give me a call when your plans firm

166

up." She smiled, and he felt like he was in high school again. "Truth is, I could use a little more sleep."

"You're sure you can get back okay?"

"I'll be fine," she said, and kissed him again. "Good-bye, Vincent." Then she was through the door and walking down the hall. She didn't look back, but he didn't take his eyes off her until she turned the corner.

Then he quickly got dressed and went outside. He saw her diminishing figure two blocks away, heading for her hotel closer to the center of town. He kept watch until she was gone from sight, and then he watched the spot where he had last seen her.

He took a deep breath and finally looked away. Jesus, he was in love. Goddamn, he *loved* this woman, it was no use denying it. He felt like some stupid puppy mooning outside the window of a girls' dorm, waiting for a glimpse of his sweetie at the window. But he couldn't help it. He wanted to run after her, never let her out of his sight again.

Then he shook his head in self-disgust. He was too damn old to feel like this, and too damn smart.

No, he wasn't.

Best to get his mind off her, he decided, and onto work, what he was out on the street for. He didn't know where the hell he was going to find a copy of Michael LaPierre's *My Partnership with Christ* in Gallup at 6:40 in the morning, but he figured he had better start looking. He could've asked Miriam for her copy, but their farewell at the door hadn't been the right time for a line like, *Gee, I'm out of reading material. Got anything good?* So he started walking toward the center of town.

Within blocks he came upon an all-night grocery with a small wall of magazines and two wire paperback racks, one of which was filled with tracts and religious books. There were two copies of LaPierre's book, and he bought them both, to the apparent approval of the proprietor, who tried to proselytize Tony to join the Christian Coalition on the spot. Tony paid for the books, declining membership.

*   *   *

Laika was lying in bed, watching the local morning news, when the phone rang. It was Tony, or "Dr. Antonelli," who told her that he had something very important to share with her and Dr. Tompkins, and wondered if they could meet for breakfast as soon as possible.

Laika agreed. It was 7:30, and they had been scheduled to meet in an hour anyway. Tony said he would be in the coffee shop across the street.

At 7:45 she met Joseph coming out of his room and they went to the coffee shop, where Tony sat in a back booth. He looked grim. "All right," Joseph said, "what's the big deal? Miriam call you with another dream?"

Tony's face changed subtly then, and Laika thought that he might be trying to hide something. Then his expression grew fixed. "Yeah, she had another dream. But that's not what I want to talk about now. It's the book code—I cracked it."

This *was* something, Laika thought. Even Joseph seemed startled. "You cracked it?" Laika said. "What was the book?"

Tony reached onto the bench seat beside him and brought up two copies of *My Partnership with Christ*. Joseph snorted in disgust. "Jesus, *that* guy."

"Right, that guy," Tony said. "I got two copies because I thought two of us could decode it at once, but I couldn't wait. I started in my room . . . and finished." He held up several sheets of writing on motel stationery.

"What does it say?" Joseph asked excitedly.

Tony looked around. The nearest people were two truckers at the counter who were discussing baseball scores. A vacationing family was three booths away, chattering over a Triple-A guidebook, arguing about where to go that day. "I think it's a bunch of shit," Tony said in a low voice. "It sounds nuts."

"Let us offer a second opinion," said Joseph, holding out a hand. "Give."

Tony handed him the papers, and Joseph set them on

the table where both he and Laika could see them. As she read, Laika began to feel more and more disconnected, as though this entire thing were happening to someone else. It was just too weird, even after what they had seen. Tony was right: it couldn't be true.

The message stated that Jesus had not died on the cross, that he'd been alive when he was taken down, that the Roman soldiers had been unable to kill him, either by crucifixion or by stabbing him in the side. However, they'd assumed that although he was not dead, he would die from loss of blood, and had allowed his family and friends to take him away, with the stipulation that he be placed in a tomb and allowed to die there.

They had placed the living Jesus in the tomb and set two Roman soldiers to guard it, but Jesus himself had rolled away the stone, overcome the soldiers, and rejoined his disciples. He'd told them to travel the world, spreading his gospel, and said that he was going to do the same, by going to lands far to the east. Then he'd walked away, and not been seen again by that generation.

He'd traveled to India, to southeast Asia, and even, some said, to the Americas. By the time the immortal Christ had returned to the Holy Land, hundreds of years later, Christianity had taken over the Roman Empire, and the papacy had been firmly established. Jesus came before the Pope in the year 502, declared himself to be the still-living Christ, and told the Pope to have one of his courtiers strike him with a sword to prove it. When the sword did not harm him, the Pope knew the claim to be true.

But the Pope reasoned that if he admitted that this man was Christ, his own power and the power of the Roman Catholic Church would be severely diminished. So he declared Jesus to be an impostor, a demon sent by the antipope, and ordered him imprisoned in St. Peter's deepest crypt.

One lie had led to another, and one cover-up had led to centuries of cover-ups. As later popes had learned what their predecessor had done, they had to become accessories in the imprisonment, for were Jesus ever freed, it would be learned that it was a pope who had imprisoned him and other popes who had acquiesced to his continuing imprisonment. The papacy would be revealed as a corrupt institution that had buried away its own god in order to preserve its temporal power. Papal infallibility would be a joke and the power and wealth of the church destroyed.

For nearly 1500 years, the message went on, the church maintained its hold on Jesus, with the tacit approval of every pope. At intervals, the holy prisoner was moved from country to country, always in a lead box, for reasons unknown. Likewise, he was always imprisoned in lead as well.

Then followed the information that the accompanying list was of the cities and other locations where Jesus had been held captive over the centuries. The message ended with a charge to the reader to obey the will of God and do everything possible to find and free the captive Jesus Christ, in order for his kingdom to come to pass upon the earth.

When Laika finally looked up from her reading, Joseph had finished and was gazing out the window. Tony was looking at Laika expectantly. "What do you think?" he said quietly.

"You're sure it's correct?" she said, then waved the question away, realizing how stupid it must sound. Of course it was correct. Random words wouldn't tell a story like this. "This would explain the list, then," she said.

"It explains a lot more than that," Tony said, sadness in his voice. "It's amazing . . . yet somehow terrible." He passed a hand over his forehead, shielding his eyes from her. "I don't want this to be true, yet in another way, I do."

Joseph turned from the window and looked at Tony. "What you're saying is that you want your faith in Jesus Christ fulfilled, and that would happen if he turned out to be an actual living entity, and not a dead first-century prophet. But what you *don't* want is for the faith in which you were brought up and the church in whose tenets you believe to be revealed as nothing but a pack of self-serving priests who have lied to their flock for a millennium and a half." He nodded brusquely. "I can see the pull of emotions there."

"You cut right through, don't you, Joseph?" Laika said in a biting tone.

"He's right," Tony said, his eyes still hidden. "Damned if I do, damned if I don't. Still, all in all, I'd rather have Jesus."

"Isn't that the title of one of those Baptist hymns?" Joseph said.

"What the hell is it with you?" Laika asked him. "I thought you were the one who bought all this prisoner stuff."

"I buy the possibility that there is a prisoner and that he may be the descendant of the historical Jesus. That's unlikely but possible, and I've admitted that. What I won't admit is that some divine personage, the so-called Son of God, has been walking the earth for two thousand years— wait, make that walking the earth for five hundred and pacing his cell for another *fifteen* hundred." He tapped the decoded message with two fingers. "Frankly, I think this is a wide load of shit."

"It tells us one thing for sure," Laika said, "and that's that those people in New York were after the prisoner to free him. And if it *is* true, it would explain why the Catholic Church is holding him."

"Christ," said Joseph, "he's an apostate or something, a goddamn heretic they're scared of. Or maybe the descendant of Jesus, I don't know—but he's not Jesus!"

"What about the wooden cup McAndrews had?" asked Tony. "Or dare I say the *grail*?"

"It's a first-century wooden cup," Joseph said. "That's all. I admit, I jumped to some conclusions myself about that cup." He smiled. "I'm better now. Listen, that coded message tells us so much, don't you think it's possible it might have been planted for us to find? As a red herring, to throw us off the scent?''

"If they wanted us to find it," said Tony, "why write it in a book code for a book that we didn't have?''

"More than that," Laika added, "would they have sacrificed one of their own people like that to get it into our hands? Weren't there other ways?''

"No ways that wouldn't raise questions. What were they going to do, leave it in an envelope marked 'CIA' when they left after our shootout?''

"The coded message may not have been intended for us in the first place," said Laika. "Maybe it was meant for a . . . new recruit.''

"Don't you mean a new *acolyte*?" Joseph said. "If these people believe this stuff, they probably have a whole hierarchy of arcane titles, like the Fifth Level Knight of the Blue Cross.''

Tony leaned on the table and glowered at Joseph. "Excuse me, but aren't you the guy who's been having the dreams about the prisoner? Wouldn't you like to finally find out just what the hell . . . or heaven . . . he is?''

"Yes, I would. But I'm not so desperate as to believe irrational—and *impossible*—messages.''

" 'For God, all things are possible.' ''

"Don't quote scripture to me, Tony. I wasn't born yesterday.''

"That's enough, Dr. Tompkins," Laika said. "I don't pretend to know if this story is true, but let's find out if it's at least valid. It's time for some Net research, unless you know, Dr. Antonelli, anything about this reference to an 'antipope' in the year 502?''

Tony shook his head. "They didn't cover that in my parochial school.''

"Parochial is right," said Joseph. "So are we taking this seriously?''

"Enough to find out whether we *should* take it seriously, okay?" She turned back toward Tony. What he'd said earlier about Miriam Dominick had stuck in her mind, and now that Tony's main news had been delivered, she wanted to learn more. "You said that Miriam Dominick had another dream? Last night?"

Tony hesitated, then nodded.

"How do you know? Did you talk to her this morning?"

"Yes."

"On the phone, or . . . at closer range?" said Joseph. Laika shot him a look, but Tony responded immediately.

"I spent the night with her. I was there when she had it."

"Aren't there church rules against that?"

Laika pointed a slim finger at Joseph and bared her teeth. "Not a word. Not another goddamn word." Her hot gaze held him until he looked away. Then she glanced back at Tony. "Was that wise?"

"Maybe not. It happened, and I'm not sorry. Besides. . . ." He tapped his head. "I checked her wallet. Got her social security and driver's license numbers. We can run a make on her."

"I thought you already—" Laika's glare cut Joseph dead.

"We will," she said. "What are the numbers?" Tony gave her the numbers from memory. They could all memorize short strings of digits easily. "And what was the dream?" she asked. "If it has some bearing on this, that is."

Tony told her about white doves coming down to a place near two stone towers, and making an outline of an animal with a line running from its mouth to its chest, ending in an arrowhead. "Does that mean anything?" he asked her. "Is it a symbol?"

She nodded. "It's called a heart line. It's sort of wishful thinking, a drawn prayer for a successful hunt."

Joseph spoke again, but now his voice was softer, more contemplative. "A hunt for an animal . . . or maybe a man."

Chapter 23

While the three were sitting in the coffee shop, two hundred miles north of Gallup, the young priests and Father Alexander were climbing into the panel truck that held the leaden casket. The old priest looked back at the forbidding container with apprehension, but when he felt and heard nothing, he relaxed a little.

"Don't worry, Father," Father James reassured him, sensing the older man's concern. "He's snug as a bug in a rug in there. Not going to pop out."

Father Alexander forced a smile and nodded.

"Okay, Father," said Father William, who had slipped behind the wheel. "Which way?"

Father Alexander guided them on a circuitous route among the narrow canyons. In some places there was scarcely room for the vehicle to get through, and once they had to get out and move some fallen rocks out of the way. The sides of the canyon rose like straight walls, so steep and high that the canyon floor was in constant shadow except for those rare occasions when the sun was directly overhead.

Father William looked up at the strip of blue above them as he threw the last rock out of their way. "Do these canyons ever get flooded?" he asked.

"Every now and then," said Father Alexander. "Believe me, if they do, you want to see it from up there." He pointed to the rim high above. "Not as often, though, since they put the dam in. Now, if *that* would go—well, I imagine the water would be pretty high in here.''

They got back into the truck and continued to drive through the narrow slot canyon until it widened out into a flat-bottomed bowl a hundred feet across. Above them the walls of the canyon broadened and then partially came together again over them, as though the priests were at the bottom of a huge bowl.

In the center of this bowl was a circle of fitted stones thirty feet in diameter, and several inches higher than the floor, and near the middle of that circle was a rectangular opening eight feet long and five wide. The top of a wooden ladder stuck out of the dark hole.

A heavy stone slab lay next to the entrance, and a black sheeting that apparently covered the bottom of the slab extended up for several inches on each side of it. A heavy metal ring was attached to the top of the slab. A thick cable ran upward from it to a small metal crane powered by a gasoline engine. Just outside the stone circle, a large wooden cross had been erected. The upright was twenty feet high and the crosspiece ten feet long.

''The kiva,'' Father William said, as the priests got out of the truck.

''Yes,'' said Father Alexander. ''An Anasazi ceremonial chamber. Probably built sometime between 1000 and 1100. The priest who tended the mission back in the 1880s found it. He had been told about our prisoner by another priest who had been involved in one of the holdings. The kiva struck him as being an ideal place. A few Indians were with him when he found it, but they were afraid of the structures of their ancient enemies, particularly kivas, steeped as they were in ceremonialism. The priest had the cross put up to mollify them. It was used, for a short time only, for several weeks in the late 1950s.''

''That was when you were involved with it,'' said Father William.

''Yes.''

"Why did they move it so quickly?" Father Donald asked.

"There was . . . an incident. A novice died under mysterious circumstances, and it was thought best to move the creature in case it had infected one of its keepers."

"Do you think it had?" asked Father William.

"No. I think it was merely a coincidence. But all those who were suspect are either dead or long gone now, and the four of us have been entrusted. With God's help, we will not fail."

"Amen," muttered one of the priests, and they all crossed themselves.

Then Father Alexander took a flashlight and led the way to the opening. He climbed down the ladder and the others followed. The floor of the kiva was twelve feet deep, and when Father Alexander shone the light around the subterranean chamber, the others could see that it measured thirty feet across, the same as the stone circle above. Every square inch of the room, from the floor to the walls to the ceiling, was a flat black that seemed to suck in the feeble glow of Father Alexander's flashlight.

"Lead, of course," said Father Alexander. "Everything is coated with it, from those pillars, which are set into stone sockets to support the roof, to that stone bench, which, as you can see, encircles the room. The vaults and firepits have been filled in so that the floor is level, and the antechamber there . . ." He pointed to the southern end of the kiva. ". . . sealed off. That was how the Anasazi entered. Even the little *sipapu*'s been filled in. No possibility of escape, even of thoughts."

" '*Sipapu*?' " repeated Father James.

"Ridiculous notion," Father Alexander snorted. "It's just a little hole in the floor. But the Pueblo people thought they had come up through it into this world from the underworld. An insane religion." Father Alexander looked around and smiled grimly. "Oh, yes, he'll be cozy and safe enough down here, I suppose. Well, let's get to it."

Father William brought the truck as close as possible to the entrance, and then Father Donald and Father James spread out a large mesh net next to the stone slab. The priests lugged the leaden casket out of the rear of the truck and set it on top of the net, then drew the sides of the net around it. Father Donald unhooked the cable from the ring in the slab and attached it to the reinforced steel rings on the corners of the mesh netting.

Father Alexander started the engine and the crane slowly raised the netting-wrapped casket aloft. He maneuvered it so that it was directly over the hole, and the other priests swung it around so that it would fit through. The old priest carefully lowered it to the floor of the kiva. Then the younger priests descended into the chamber, detached the cable from the netting, and climbed back out as Father Alexander raised the heavy cable.

"There's no way we can let him out?" Father James said. "Just to walk around down there?"

"They do it in some of his prisons," Father Alexander said. "But it requires more complex mechanisms than we have available. Besides, I've never been convinced it'd do him any good. He's not like you and me. He feels no need to stretch his legs. Best to keep him doubly secured, in both kiva and casket. Two strong layers of lead are better than one. He's quite used to the dark, as you might imagine."

Father Alexander looked into the darkness of the kiva and addressed what lay within, uncertain whether it could hear him or not. "Aren't you? Oh yes, a creature of darkness! Why do you not repent? Even you can be redeemed, yes, even you! If you would send your thoughts free of your prison, let it be *that* message that is spoken. That you are heartily sorry for what you have done, and that you will obey the laws of God and the truths of this, our holy church!"

Then he heard it, a series of low laughs, like a string of faraway mortar fire, one after another, deep and thrusting.

He glanced in sudden panic at the other priests, but they were only looking at him, and their faces showed that they'd heard nothing. "Can he hear you, do you think?" Father Donald said, but the old priest heard his words only dimly over the rushing of blood in his ears and the ever growing laughter of the beast in the kiva.

"No," he was able to say, and hoped that they did not notice his voice trembling. "Cover it!"

He turned and walked back toward the controls of the crane as Father William attached the cable to the metal ring in the slab. Then Father Alexander rammed the control lever so that the slab was jerked upward. When the other priests had positioned it over the hole, he lowered it, faster than he should have, so that it slammed down into position, the lead sheeting sealing any gaps between slab and entrance and cutting off the sound of laughter.

"That should do it," Father William said, grinning.

"It should." But as Father Alexander turned off the engine, he thought he heard, in the sudden silence of the canyon, an echo of an unholy laugh.

Laika gave the coded knock, and Tony opened the door. She didn't speak until she was inside the room and the door was closed.

"Miriam Dominick checks out clean," she told him. "She seems to be exactly who she says she is. Graduated from college four years ago, lived with her mother and father in Tucson, while she worked at a bank for two years. Never married. Good credit risk, but she never owned anything big, like a car, to test it.

"For the past two years, she seems to have been bitten by wanderlust, traveling alone around the southwest, taking pictures. During that time, the lion's share of her credit card purchases have been for photography equipment. Her last two tax returns show 1099s from six different magazines—none of which I imagine you've ever heard of, because I hadn't—paying her for photos. Mostly a hundred dollars each or less. Lowball markets, no *Ari-*

zona Highways. She's had no arrests, either.''

"You didn't find out anything about her—" Tony paused. He wasn't sure of how to bring it up.

"What, relationships?"

"No," he said impatiently. "I don't care about that. I meant her . . . psychic tendencies, for want of a better term."

"Government agencies and banks don't generally record that, Tony." The knock sounded at the door, and Tony opened it for Joseph to enter.

Laika filled him in on Miriam. "I've found some things, too," he said. "It seems that the book code message is at least internally sound. It mentions the year 502 and an antipope. In that year, the pope was Pope Symmachus, the one and only—I guess the name just never caught on the way 'John' did. Anyway, during this time there was another priest named Laurentius who also claimed to be pope, so the followers of Symmachus called Laurentius the antipope. And the St. Peter's reference fits too, since Symmachus was the first pope to make St. Peter's Church his base of operations, and did some expansion to it."

"That proves it, then," said Tony.

Joseph shook his head. "All it proves is that whoever might have concocted this story did their homework with information that I could pull off the Internet in less than an hour."

"And speaking of time," Laika said, "we'd better get going. Yazzie's supposed to meet you two at ten, and it's almost that now. And I've got to get to Albuquerque."

Tony was trying to figure out if there was any reason he could give for wanting to bring Miriam along, when there was a knock on the door. "Yeah?" he said, thinking it was the maid, but ready for anything.

"It's me," came a rough voice. "Yazzie." When Tony opened the door, they saw that the policeman's usually pleasant demeanor was now grim. "I know we were supposed to meet in the lobby," he said, "but I thought you'd want to know as soon as possible. Another corpse was found this morning. Dehydrated to the point of mummification, apparently just like the other two.''

"Good God," said Laika. "Where?"

"Up at Canyon de Chelly. Northwest of here, in Arizona. It was a Navajo guide. The first tour group of the morning found him. I was in the office when the report came in, and made arrangements right away that the body wasn't to be moved until we could examine the scene.''

"Thanks," said Laika.

"No problem. I just wanted to keep you from robbing any more Indian graves." He didn't smile, and Tony wasn't sure if he was joking. "But there's something else you're going to be interested in, too. Seems there was another one of those drawings made during the night, just a few miles away from where the body was found. Big sonofabitch, not in sand this time, but down in a wash, a quarter mile long was the report."

Tony felt Laika and Joseph's gaze resting on him. "Do you know what it was of?" Laika asked, looking back at Yazzie.

"Another Indian design. An animal with a line from its mouth to its breast. I think they call it a heart line."

"Do you know," asked Tony, as offhandedly as he could, "when the drawing was first reported?"

"Not till after sunup," Yazzie said. They were all quiet for a moment. "Is something wrong? I mean, other than another drawing and another corpse?"

"No, Officer Yazzie," Laika said. "Not at all."

"Well, good. I asked the tribal police to try and keep tourists away from the drawing until you three had a chance to look at it."

"Thanks again," Laika said. "I think this means we'll be changing our plans today. I have to call the university and reschedule a meeting. Dr. Antonelli," she said, turning to Tony, "why don't you call your friend, Ms. Dominick, and see if she'd be able to come along with us today?" Joseph's face clouded, but he didn't speak, and Laika turned back to Yazzie. "She's sort of become our unofficial photographer. We should just be a few minutes, Officer.''

Yazzie understood the dismissal, and retreated to the lobby. As soon as he closed the door, Joseph whirled on Laika. ''Now *you? You're* buying into this psychic seer stuff?''

Laika ignored him, and looked at Tony. ''What time did Miriam tell you about her dream?''

''At 1:30 in the morning. I looked at the clock.''

''She's got a flawless track record so far, Joseph,'' Laika said. ''And her background check was as clean as a nun's. We're supposed to investigate unexplained phenomena, and this woman's predictions or OBEs or whatever you want to call them are certainly inexplicable at this point. Now, I'm not willing to admit that they're paranormal, but I couldn't swear they aren't, at least until we get some more information, and the only way we can do that is by observing her.''

''She's not a goddamn guinea pig,'' Tony said.

''I don't mean that. If there really *is* something to her predictions, she might be of help to us. And if not, she can certainly take as good photos of these scenes as any of us can.''

''Okay, fine,'' said Joseph sulkingly. ''You're the boss.''

''Thank you for concurring, but I wasn't asking for your permission. Tony, call Miriam, and both of you meet me in the lobby in ten minutes.''

A three-year-old dark blue Buick sat near the rear of a deserted service station. The two men inside watched as Joshua Yazzie and Joseph climbed into Yazzie's white Fury, and Laika and Tony got into a cream-colored Camry. When both vehicles had pulled into the late morning traffic, the Buick followed.

Several blocks away, the Fury and the Camry stopped at a transient hotel, and Miriam Dominick came out and got into the Camry's backseat. The cars headed north on Route 666, and again the Buick followed, staying back just far enough so as not to lose the operatives.

One of the men in the Buick dialed a cell phone. "They're on their way north, to the drawing, and to investigate another body that's just been found . . . yes, dehydrated . . . yes, it *is* a coincidence. Still, things seem to be working out the way we'd planned it. Oh, and the girl is with them . . . yes, I thought you would find that interesting. . . ."

Canyon de Chelly was a big, sprawling spiderweb of a canyon, and Yazzie and Tony parked their vehicles at the western mouth. Two tribal policemen, wearing cowboy hats and badges, were waiting for them next to a large truck with big wheels. When Yazzie introduced himself and the others, the officers informed them that the medical examiner had already been and gone, and that another officer had remained with the body.

The officers got in the cab while the others piled into the truck's open bed and sat on the metal benches along the sides. The truck pulled away, bouncing up and down on its big tires every time it hit a bump, which, in the absence of roads, was twice a second. "They call them shake-and-bakes," Yazzie told the ops. "The truck shakes you while the sun bakes you."

Even though the sun was shining brightly, Tony thought, it wasn't really that hot. The altitude made a big difference, and once you were a few hours north of Phoenix, the weather was pretty pleasant. He couldn't understand why everybody retired to hot, dry Tucson or Phoenix instead of the far more comfortable Flagstaff.

They traveled through the beds of dry washes, as well as through some that were still damp. "Where's the water come from?" Tony asked Yazzie.

"The sky. It does rain here, you know. These washes turn into streams, then dry up again after the rain stops. It rained up here a couple days ago."

They drove out of the wash onto sand as dry as any Tony had seen. The contrasts were amazing, he thought, and with the red sandstone walls rising on either side of them, he could easily see how Miriam had fallen in love with this country. She was looking around as though the canyon floor were a wonderland, and he smiled at her joy.

"I haven't been down here on the floor in years," she told him, hugging her backpack. "It would be so wonderful to actually live down here."

"For a vacation, anyway," said Yazzie. "But I had relatives who farmed down here during the summer, and it was rough going. Helluva way to make a living."

They passed a larger shake-and-bake coming out of the canyon, loaded with tourists. They looked a little worse for wear, and Tony wondered if it was the jerkiness of the ride, or if they had glimpsed the desiccated corpse.

In another ten minutes they saw a tribal policeman sitting on a log, and something dark brown and shriveled lying near him. The truck stopped and they got out. "Holy hell," Yazzie said, as they stepped over to the body.

"Yeah," said one of the officers. "His name was Gary Chee. His wallet was in his pocket, what was left of it."

"What do you mean, 'what was left of it?' " Laika asked.

"Take a look." The officer on the log reached into a leather pouch and took out an object in a plastic bag. It looked like a wallet, but was somewhat shrunken, the leather wrinkled. Laika opened the bag and involuntarily jerked back her head from the smell. Tony, a few feet away, could smell it easily. It smelled like something long dead.

"There's another one," the officer said, taking out another bag. "This one belonged to Mrs. Rachel Anderson. It was in his shirt pocket. We found the Andersons when they showed up at the visitors' center asking for Chee. He guided them yesterday, she lost her wallet, and that's what he was out here looking for last night. He found it."

"And something else," said Joseph, looking at the body.

Laika slipped on a pair of latex gloves and gingerly examined Gary Chee's wallet. The leather was dry but gleamed with traces of a fatty residue. The paper cards were all yellowed and curled, as though they had been dipped in lard and then allowed to dry in the sun. She dropped the object back into the bag and sealed it shut, then knelt by the body.

There was a smell to it as well, sour and pungent. It took her a moment to realize the truth. "It isn't the body that smells," she said. "It's his clothing."

The denim jacket the corpse wore, along with the flannel shirt and jeans, were stiff and yellowed with dried moisture. "My God, what happened to him?"

"It's almost like," Tony said thoughtfully, "the moisture was sucked out of him right through his clothes.

That's what's on the clothes, all right—dried body fluids.''

"We don't know that yet," Joseph said shortly. "Not until we run some tests."

"Want to put some money on it, Dr. Tompkins?" said Tony. "I'd be willing to bet that those tests show the presence of blood, bile, fat, and any other juices that you can find inside a body. It's like the guy went through a goddamn wine press.''

"How can you. . . ." Laika looked over at Miriam Dominick, who was standing back from the others. Her tanned face had gone pale, and her mouth was slightly open. "He was a human being. Have any of you prayed for him? Or said a word of sympathy?" Miriam's voice was tight and choked.

"Poor fella," said Joseph. "You wanta get some shots of Mr. Chee here?"

Laika saw Tony ready to rip into Joseph, so she took the initiative, speaking quickly: "I'm sorry, Miriam. But we're here in a professional capacity. We don't intend to be callous, but we don't have much time for spiritual matters. Now, I'd appreciate it if you could take photographs of Mr. Chee's remains from various angles after we finish examining it. Do you feel well enough to do that?"

It had been the right thing to say. For all her compassion for the dead man, she could not bear to have the others think of her as less strong-willed or strong-stomached than they. Without another word, she rummaged in her backpack and took out a camera. Laika noticed with some amusement that Tony started toward her, but then changed his mind and knelt beside the body.

Gary Chee was very much in the same condition as Ralph Begay had been. His skin was dried and browned until it resembled old leather. The lips had drawn back from the teeth, and the eyelids were wrinkled pouches, puckering to show the dried eyeballs.

But unlike Begay's body, which had been prepared for burial by the family, Gary Chee's corpse seemed more shrunken, drawn in on itself. "The connective tissues have dried and receded," Laika said. "It's drawn the joints together. Look at the fingers—they're like claws."

"There's not a drop of fluid in the whole body, is there?" Joseph said, crouching on the other side of the corpse.

"No," she said. "I'm wondering about the internal organs."

Joseph slipped on a pair of latex gloves and pressed against the corpse's shirt over its midsection. "Very hollow. I can touch the spine." He sniffed quickly several times. "That smell of vomit is probably bile. And the urine smell is mousy and pungent, more like the pores of a uremia patient than the smell of sterile urine. And I'm betting the fecal odor isn't coming from the anus, but directly from the bowel. Hell, you could probably stick his liver, his kidneys, and the rest of his guts in a shoebox with room to spare."

As Joseph continued to stare at Gary Chee's wizened face, Laika thought about how much more she liked him when he was involved in a practical puzzle like this rather than trying to refute anything that smacked of the supernatural. That was their job, after all, but Joseph seemed to take it too damned seriously, as though any suggestion of a higher power undermined his own worth as a human being.

Joseph went on, as if talking to himself. "But what in the name of . . . what could suck the moisture out of a man's body like this, right through his clothes?"

"Aliens."

They turned around to see one of the tribal policemen, his eyes hidden behind sunglasses, looking down at them. "Sure, the same ones been making those big sand paintings. They do it to cattle, don't they?"

"No, they don't," said Joseph with a tinge of impatience. "So-called cattle mutilation has been shown time and again to be just the combination of natural decomposition and scavenger activity."

"Oh yeah? Well if it's scavengers, why aren't they eating the good meat instead of the eyeballs and tongues and . . . well, the private parts and stuff?"

"Because there aren't many scavengers that can bite through cowhide," Joseph said, as though explaining it to a child. "So they take what they can get, which is soft tissue, like eyeballs and tongues and testicles and anuses and other orifices."

"Yeah, well, maybe," said the officer. Then he brightened. "But scavengers didn't do *this*."

Joseph seemed to realize that there would be no victory today, so he threw up his hands. "You got me there, Officer. Doggone, I guess it just *has* to be aliens, then."

The policeman turned and walked toward his colleagues, seemingly proud of his debating skills. When the cop was out of earshot, Yazzie said, "I don't think he gets off the reservation enough."

"You don't buy the aliens theory?" Laika said with a smile.

"Nope. Or the Navajo spirits. I think it was just a really big kid with a really big magnifying glass."

"So you don't have a pet theory?" she asked.

"If I had a tenable theory for this," Yazzie said, "I'd be a professor of pathology somewhere, not a tribal cop. This is the most puzzling thing I've ever seen."

Laika returned to her examination of the body. She lifted the right hand and looked at the fingernails through a strong magnifying glass. "There's something under his nails."

Joseph held the dead hand, while Laika gently dug underneath the brittle fingernails, one after another, with a small blade, scraping the debris into a small plastic bag. She sealed it and looked at the contents through the clear plastic. "They look like flakes of skin," she said, "but dark, and very dry. Almost like his own."

Joseph shook his head. "There's no sign of any wound, though. We'd see if he had scratched himself."

"That's so bizarre," Laika said, holding the bag up to

the sky so that the light shone behind the small dark shreds. "It's like he . . . scratched a mummy or something." She turned to Tony. "Dr. Antonelli, would you please take some more samples? Hair, tissue, clothing, some of the soil? Perhaps Ms. Dominick could help you."

Tony rewarded her with a smile and walked over to Miriam, who was looking less upset than before. Laika and Joseph began to walk around the site, looking for anything that could give them a hint as to the cause of Gary Chee's fate. Yazzie joined them, his eyes on the ground.

Laika noticed the marks of horseshoes in the dirt. "Chee's horse?" she asked Yazzie.

"Almost certainly. It went back to his family's farm."

"So whatever got Chee might have scared the horse."

"A good possibility."

Laika followed the horse tracks for a short distance until she saw a pile of loose rocks at the base of the canyon wall. She walked up to it and kicked over one of the flatter stones. The narrow leaves of the yucca plant that had been crushed beneath it were still green.

"Do you think this was a rock slide?" she asked Joseph and Yazzie.

"Looks like it. Recent, too." Yazzie pointed at the plant Laika had uncovered. "Might have happened last night. The flowers are closed, see? But I don't know what a rock slide would have had to do with Chee's death."

Laika looked at the pile of rocks, at the body thirty yards away, and at the hoof prints. Then she looked high above, to the top of the canyon wall.

"Hey!" she yelled over to the tribal policemen leaning on the truck. "Do any of you know a good tracker?" She started walking toward them. "Anybody who could follow a trail?"

"What?" said the officer who believed in aliens. "You mean, like in the movies?"

"Yeah. Someone who can spot broken twigs and misplaced pebbles and tell me the height and weight of the guy who did it.''

One of the other officers spoke. ''Old Sam Bitsosie is a helluva tracker. Lived here in the canyon for, oh, forty years, I bet.''

''He still alive?'' asked the cattle mutilation believer.

''Oh yeah, lives in Chinle.''

''Okay,'' said Laika. ''That's who I want.''

''To track what in particular?'' Yazzie said. ''If you don't mind my asking.''

''Not at all. Something was in this canyon last night with Gary Chee. It got in here, as Mr. Chee would attest, if he could, and it left. I want to know where it came from and where it went, and maybe a tracker can tell us that.''

''I'm starting to wonder about you, Dr. Kelly,'' Yazzie said. ''Are you a scientific investigator, or a cop? You seem more interested in the perpetrator than in the phenomenon.''

''That's because I think the perpetrator *is* the phenomenon.'' Laika turned back to the other policemen. ''Would this Mr. Bitsosie do a job for us if we paid him?''

''Probably. I got a cell phone. Want me to give him a call?''

''Yeah, see if he can get out here right away. Two hundred dollars for the rest of the day. Cash.'' Laika turned to Tony. ''Dr. Antonelli, would you come over here a moment?'' She led him to the base of the cliff where the rocks had fallen. ''This may sound goofy,'' she said in a low voice, ''but I think there's a link here. Something fell from the top, and whatever it is might be the thing that did this to Chee.''

''Something fell from up there?'' Tony said, looking two hundred feet up at the edge of the cliff. ''And then walked away? Does that seem likely?''

''For Chrissake, does *any* of this seem likely? I suspect whatever might have done that to Chee might also be able to take that fall unharmed. Go with Yazzie and the other cop to get the tracker, and start him here. See where he ends up.''

''What are you going to be doing?''

''Going to the site of the new drawing with Joseph and Miriam. I want to see what else she might have been close to in her dreams.'' Laika smiled. ''Besides you.'' Tony blushed and she slapped him once on the shoulder. ''Let's go.''

''He says four!'' the tribal cop called from the truck.

''What?'' said Laika, walking toward him.

''Four hundred he wants to come out here.''

''Three,'' Laika said, and watched as the Navajo spoke into the phone.

''He says to tell you four,'' he said after a moment. ''He says he's seventy-eight years old, and if he's gotta come out here and start ... screwin' around in the dirt, it's gotta be worth it. And he said if it isn't, to go and track yourself.'' He held his ear back to the phone. ''And he says if you're from the government, you can *afford* four.''

Laika smiled ruefully. ''Tell him four, if he can get out here within the hour. A minute later, and it's three.''

''Mr. Bitsosie?'' the policeman began, then said, ''Hello?'' He clicked the phone shut. ''He must've heard you. Guess he's on his way.''

Chapter 25

*T*he old tracker arrived in forty-five minutes. By then the body of Gary Chee had been taken away, and Laika, Joseph, and Miriam had left with a policeman to look at the sand drawing at the eastern end of the canyon. Yazzie and Tony had agreed to meet them for dinner at Abner's, a roadhouse northeast of the canyon on Route 12.

It didn't take long for Tony to wish he'd gone with the others. Sam Bitsosie, a short, wizened, and ill-tempered old man whose face looked not dissimilar to the dehydrated Gary Chee's, demanded his four hundred dollars immediately. Tony gave him two hundred and said he'd pay the rest at the end of the day. Bitsosie bellowed, "Bullshit!", and said that he wanted it now and if he didn't get it that Dr. Antonelli could buy himself a goddam bloodhound. A tentative truce was reached when Officer Yazzie offered to hold the money.

"All right," Tony said. "Someone was killed right around here. Can you tell me where?"

"What do I look like, Houdini?" said Sam Bitsosie. "No, I can't just tell you—I have to look around a little." He walked around the log, then moved in the direction of the rock slide, and stopped after walking ten feet. "Here, right here."

"How do you know?" Tony asked.

"What, are you blind? I'm the one who's seventy-eight,

191

sonny. See here, where the marks of the hooves are deeper, and there are more of them? Something jumped on this horse, maybe to attack the rider, am I right?''

''We don't know. We're asking *you* to figure it out. Can you tell where the attacker came from?''

Bitsosie gave a broad and theatrical shrug. ''Gallup?''

''No,'' said Tony with a sigh, ''I meant where . . . right *here*.''

''I *know* what you meant, it was a little joke, okay? Lemme see.'' The old man walked around, looking at the ground, kneeling now and then with a loud moan. ''My knees,'' he kept saying. ''Shoulda asked *five* hundred.''

At last he led the way to the rocks. ''Over here. He came from here. It's hard to tell, because you big-footed cops have been walking all over the place.''

''I'm not a cop,'' said Tony. ''I'm a scientist.''

''You still got big feet, sonny. But this is it. I don't know where he was before this.'' Then Bitsosie looked up at the side of the cliff, and saw the empty places where the stones had been. ''Maybe he *rode* down.''

''What?''

''On the rocks. Coyote coulda done that, you know.''

''You serious? I mean, about riding down?''

''Well, everybody's gotta come from somewhere.'' He looked at Tony and grinned. ''Take me—I'm from Ganado.'' The grin vanished. ''Another joke.''

''Okay,'' said Tony, ''so the attacker started there, came over here, attacked the victim. Then what?''

Bitsosie eyed the ground. ''Too many flatfoots tromping around. Have to go out. . . .''

He started moving in ever-widening circles around the spot where he said the attack had taken place. The old man's path reminded Tony of one of those spiral Indian designs. At last, thirty feet from the center of the circle, Bitsosie stopped and bent down.

''Here it is. I can pick up his track here. He was going this way.'' He pointed deeper into the canyon, along the base of the cliff. ''Okay?''

"Okay," Tony said, "let's go."

"Wait a minute, you want me to keep going?"

"You're a tracker. You want the rest of the money, you track."

Bitsosie looked at Yazzie as if in appeal, but Yazzie nodded. "That would seem the minimum requirement," he said dryly.

Bitsosie replied with a string of profanity in a combination Tony had not heard before, then started walking up the canyon, his eyes on the ground. Tony and Yazzie followed.

"Can you tell us anything about him?" Tony asked, after they had gone a few hundred yards along the canyon base.

"Yeah. He was moving slow. Sort of shuffling. And he was pretty heavy. But it may not be the same guy."

"You mean, as the one who came down the cliff?" Yazzie asked.

"Yep. Those tracks weren't as deep as these. I mean, it *could* be the same guy, because the boot marks look like the same size, but if it is, he's carrying something pretty damn heavy."

Tony stored that one away in the *weird shit* section of his mind as one to lay on Joseph and Laika. He thought about how much water the human body had in it, and how all that moisture would be pretty heavy, were it all to be drawn out. But what would the attacker carry it in? A barrel? The even more confusing question was why? What would anyone do with . . . man juice?

"Well, looka here," said Bitsosie, pointing to a trail up the cliff. There was a natural cut through the sandstone, and flat stones had been placed to facilitate easy access to the canyon from above. "He went up here. Slow, too. Bet he was pantin' when he reached the top." He fixed Tony with a stern glare. "Just like a certain old Navajo would be if some white-eye sonofabitch made him climb up there."

"You want the rest of your money?" said Tony. "We

can go as slow as you like, but we've got to stay on this trail. I want to know where this . . . person went.''

Yazzie, the holder of the money, nodded in agreement. ''You turn against your own people like this?'' the old man said.

''Two of my people have died, maybe because of what the person you're tracking did. I want to find him.''

''Well, you might have another one of your people die on you, you make me climb up there.''

''Come on,'' said Yazzie. ''We'll go at your pace.''

Grumbling, the old tracker started climbing the steps nimbly, in spite of the complaints of ill health that he continued to make.

Twenty minutes later, they reached the top of the cliff. There was an overlook fifty yards away, where several tourists were peering into the canyon and taking pictures. A sign at the top of the trail informed all that access to the canyon was forbidden without a guide.

Bitsosie kept his eyes on the loose stones that led to the road, and stopped at the edge of the blacktop. ''That's it,'' he said. ''Stops here. Even I can't track on a paved road.''

''Can you tell which way he went?'' Tony asked.

''Yeah—either that way,'' Bitsosie pointed down the road, ''or that way. Now, where's my money?''

Yazzie took the bills out of his pocket and handed them to the old man. ''All right, damn it,'' Bitsosie said. ''I'm an old man, and I'm not going to walk down there again. Here, sonny.'' He handed Tony a ring of keys. ''The silver one's to my car. I'm going to sit on that bench over there and count my money while you two walk back down and bring that car back up to me. Unless you want another dead Indian on your conscience, white-eyes.''

Driving along on the floor of the canyon had been an experience that Joseph never wanted to go through again. The truck bounced enough through the dry sand, but when it hit the washes it was spine rattling. By the time they approached the eastern end of Canyon de Chelly where it met Monument Canyon, Joseph's buttocks felt as though he had been initiated into several dozen fraternities at once.

The drawing was flush with the canyon floor, so they saw the two towers of Spider Rock first. Joseph heard Miriam gasp, and when he followed her haunted gaze, he saw the two stone towers, one shorter than the other, rising to the sky, and remembered what Tony had told them about Miriam's dream.

"Are those the towers you saw in your dream?" Laika asked.

Miriam nodded dully, then seemed to grasp the implications, and blushed deeply. "Vincent told you?"

"Yes," she replied. "Don't be concerned. We're only interested in this from a . . . scientific viewpoint."

"Then you know about the—" They came over a rise then, and saw the drawing of the heart line in the damp sand of the wash. "Oh, my God. . . ." Miriam said.

"Vincent didn't tell you about this?" Joseph said, trying to keep the doubt out of his voice.

"No . . . no, he didn't, just that there was another drawing."

"But this is what you saw, isn't it?" asked Laika.

"Yes, it is . . . the beast . . . and the line to its heart . . . the arrowhead . . . *everything.*"

"Including the towers," Joseph said.

"Yes."

Laika glanced at Joseph. If he read her look correctly, she was impressed. So was he, but he wouldn't admit it. He still did not, could not, allow himself to believe in an out-of-body experience. It would give too easy an explanation to his own bizarre dreams about the prisoner.

If he tried hard, he could believe that the extraordinary coincidences between what he'd dreamed and what he'd later seen to be true were exactly that, nothing but coincidences, if in an amazing series. But if he allowed himself to believe that Miriam had some kind of psychic

power, then it would be easy to believe that he himself
had the same, and that was something he didn't want.

Strange mental powers existed only in the realms of
fiction and fantasy, areas in which Joseph had spent many
pleasurable hours. Though he knew that in reality such
things were rubbish, they could be sheer delight when
confined to the imagination. Joseph's collection of books
and videos, as well as his writings for fan magazines,
attested to his fascination with the genre.

Still, he wrote for skeptical publications as well, and
kept the two areas of interest totally separate, as a breeder
who fancies both Siamese cats and flightless birds. Now,
when it seemed that the two were merging into one disquieting reality, he struggled all the harder to keep them
apart.

Miriam's dreams and visions could be nothing more
than coincidences, as were his own. As the truck pulled
to a stop just yards away from the drawing, he jumped
down, anxious to investigate, to get to practical work.

This drawing was different. It was slightly larger than
the others, but what differentiated it most from its predecessors was that it was made in damp earth instead of
dry sand. "This should resolve the tread mark question,"
Laika said, as they walked toward the deep ruts in the
earth. He knew what she meant. Tread marks might not
show on dry sand, where gravity would pull the loose
sand down to cover them. But with wet earth, any tread
marks would be easily seen.

There were none. The ruts were nearly a foot wide and
seven inches deep, and as smooth as though a giant hand
had drawn in the earth with a massive pencil. "Still could
have been tires without treads," said Joseph, refusing to
give up his motorcycle theory.

Laika made no comment, but led the way around the
massive drawing. High on the canyon rim, dozens of people were standing against the railing, looking down at
them and the drawing. "I think the silicalogists are out in
force," Laika said.

"Yeah, well, let's hope we can prove to them this is just another hoax," said Joseph. "They don't want to hear it, but they'll be better off knowing the truth."

Miriam walked next to Joseph, just behind Laika. The tribal policeman tagged along behind. "Do you think there's any connection between the drawings and the deaths?" Miriam asked.

"I would think it's an incredible coincidence if there's not," replied Joseph. Then he snorted a laugh. "Of course, we've seen a lot of coincidences lately."

They continued to walk slowly around the huge drawing, stopping from time to time for Miriam to take pictures. When they reached the head, they stepped inside the drawing to examine the line from the beast's mouth to its chest. The arrowhead was as gigantic as the rest of the work. Two of the three straight lines that formed it were twenty feet long, while the base of the arrowhead was nearly twice that.

"These angles where the lines meet are nearly perfect," Laika observed. "Just a little overlap here."

"Where the motorcycle went a little too far," said Joseph.

"Dr. Tompkins," Laika said, "if you think it was a motorcycle that made these trenches, how did it get here? Unlike sand, tracks in wet earth can't be easily brushed away, you know."

"Dr. Kelly, there *were* no tracks in or out," Joseph said. Then he pointed skyward. "Death from above."

"Your helicopter theory?" Laika asked.

"Absolutely. When you eliminate the impossible . . . well, you know. A helicopter with some sort of mechanism attached to a chopper is damned improbable, but not impossible. Or maybe it just dragged something heavy in the sand."

"There wouldn't be any prop wash visible here," Laika admitted, "but there would have been at the other two sites. And wouldn't someone have noticed a helicopter in a place as heavily infested with tourists as this?"

In reply, Joseph called back to the policeman. "Hey, Officer, what happens to this end of the canyon at night? Anybody come to the overlook?"

The officer shook his head. "The access road's closed after dark."

"And does anybody live around here?"

"Used to, but no more. Some folks live back that way a bit," he said, gesturing to Canyon de Chelly, "but hardly anybody in Monument Canyon."

"So is it possible that if a helicopter flew over this area in the middle of the night, no one might have seen it?"

"Possible," the Navajo said.

Joseph looked at Laika. "You got a better explanation?"

"I haven't."

Joseph turned to Miriam. "Ms. Dominick?"

Miriam seemed to think a moment, even closing her eyes for a few seconds. "No," she said. "I really have no idea."

After they had completely circled the figure, and seen no way by which a vehicle could have gotten to the drawing over the wet earth, Laika turned to the Navajo policeman. "Could you take us back now? We'd like to see the drawing from the overlook."

Chapter 26

A thousand feet above where the two operatives, the policeman, and Miriam Dominick were getting back into the truck, a man named Taylor Griswold stood with a pair of powerful binoculars, looking down at them. A number of other onlookers were doing the same.

Many were taking pictures and videos of the drawing below, and the first video crew had arrived and were interviewing tourists, asking what they thought was the origin of the giant beast. When they asked Taylor Griswold if he thought the drawing was proof of alien intrusion, he told them not to bother him, in language that ensured his face would not be televised.

Only when the truck started moving westward did he start back on the path to the small loop road where his rental car was parked. He got in and dialed a number on his cell phone. He was calling the New York headquarters of the tabloid newspaper for which he worked, the *Inner Eye*.

When the automated operator answered, he punched in the extension of his assistant, with whom he was immediately connected. Then, from a notepad, he dictated to her his feature story, improvising the part about this most recent "incontrovertible evidence of artisans from beyond our solar system, and possibly our galaxy itself."

Griswold's story covered all three sand drawings, and also talked about "a series of recent deaths in which bodies have been drained of their blood. Authorities have been strangely silent on the matter, but the government has sent a secret team of psychic investigators to the area.

"Your reporter has spoken with these people, and learned that the deaths and the drawings are related, and may be some kind of alien blood sacrifice by which these otherworldly creatures derive the inspiration to create their monumental works of art.

"Does this mean that our popular conception of the peaceful alien offering us technology and wisdom may be replaced by a startling reality of bloodthirsty aesthetes, a race of 'Vampicassos' who are willing to slaughter our comparatively primitive race in order to feed their appetite for art? We pray that it is not so, but the evidence coming from the ancient southwest is anything but comforting."

Griswold was pleased with *Vampicassos*. It didn't flow as well as the *Vamparazzi* handle that he had used in his story SECRET BLOOD CULT CHASED PRINCESS DI TO HER DEATH, but it would do. Most of the dummies who read the rag ought to know who Picasso was, for Chrissake.

He closed the phone and thought for a moment. Laika Harris and Joseph Stein were at the bottom of the canyon, and if they were there, Anthony Luciano wouldn't be far away. He had first come across them in New York City, when they had spotted him, taken away the film he had shot of them, and given him a goofy warning to stay the hell away from them, as though they thought he actually believed the crap he wrote about.

No, he didn't believe in *that* shit, but there were *some* things he believed in. He believed that the bodies were something worth thinking about, although he thought the drawings were an elaborate hoax. And he believed in money, and now that he had fed the news machine, it was time to fill in the main man, the one who was searching for truth amid all this crap.

He dialed a number and waited as the call was shuttled along several lines to make tracing impossible. Finally a muddy voice with a strong burr grunted a few syllables, and Griswold identified himself. There was silence for nearly a minute, and then a different, crisp voice said, "Aye?"

"I've found them," said Griswold. "The three of them. In Arizona."

"Why are they there?" The Rs rolled slightly, just enough to cause an audible break between words.

"Two reasons. One is giant drawings in the sand . . . and mud now, it looks like. Like big crop circles. The other is dried corpses. That's the one that shows promise. No explanation so far."

"Could be his work. Stay on them. I swear before Christ that one of them has a connection to the one we're searching for. And they've still got something we want. But we can't take it until they lead us to him."

"Don't worry," Griswold said. "I'll stay as close as I can."

"You lost them before."

"Yeah, well, I found them now, okay?" There was a cold silence at the other end. The longer it lasted, the more uncomfortable Griswold grew. "Look, I'm sorry . . . I won't lose them, really." There were another few moments of silence, and then the sound of the phone being hung up.

Shit. He had pissed the guy off. But he had apologized. Everything was still okay. And he *wouldn't* lose those three this time. Odds were they would come up here to see the thing from above, and he could pick them up when they left. Trailing them was going to be tricky on these skinny, curvy roads, but he would do it. He couldn't lose them now, he just couldn't. There was too much at stake.

It was mid-afternoon when the shake and bake with Laika, Joseph, and Miriam arrived back at the western end of the canyon. Tony and Joshua Yazzie had already left in Yazzie's white Fury and Sam Bitsosie's 1972 Dodge Dart, which Tony was driving up to the rim of the canyon where the old man was waiting for him.

The policeman dropped off Laika, Joseph, and Miriam at their Camry, and they drove to the south rim road until they reached the left turn that would take them to the path that led to the Spider Rock overlook. Cars were parked everywhere along the small loop of road near the path, but Joseph squeezed into a space that had just been vacated, between a mobile news truck and an old VW van with Ohio plates.

Laika and Joseph opened their doors, but Miriam leaned forward over the backseat. "Would you mind terribly if I just stayed here in the car? I hate to say it, but I think the sun's kind of gotten to me. I feel a little sick."

"An old desert rat like you?" Joseph said.

"No, it's all right," Laika said. The girl did look pale, and there were droplets of sweat on her forehead, despite the coolness of the car's interior. "You want to keep the engine running so the air stays on?"

"No; if you just open the windows, I'll be fine."

"We'll leave the keys," Laika said. "That way you can start the air if you need to."

"Thanks," said Miriam, with a sickly smile. "This has happened before. I'll be okay in a little while. You want to take my camera?"

Laika shook her head. "We have some gear in the trunk." She popped the lever and Joseph took out the camera bag. "We shouldn't be long," she told Miriam, then smiled. "Especially if there are many reporters out there."

When they were out of earshot, Joseph said to Laika, "And what if there *are* a ton of newsfolk waiting for us, 'Dr. Kelly?' "

"I don't think any of them will recognize us from being down below. It was too far. And if they do, we leave."

In his car, parked only three spaces behind the operatives, Taylor Griswold slowly sat up, thanking what gods there were that Harris and Stein hadn't spotted him. He knew that they were tough people, and that although they had let him go once, next time he might not be so lucky.

He watched them disappear down the path to the over-look, but noticed that the girl was still in the car. Who the hell was she anyway? And what was she doing now?

She seemed to be looking all around her, as though searching for someone. Griswold ducked down in his seat again so that she would not spot him, and watched as she got out of her car and started walking back toward his.

There was nothing to do but fake it, so he leaned his head back against the seat, closed his eyes, and opened his mouth as though he were sleeping. After he heard her footsteps pass by him without slowing, he opened his eyes and watched her in the convex plane of the outer rearview mirror.

She walked back past several more cars and then stopped at one, a dark blue Buick. A door opened and she got in. Even though Griswold sat up and looked through the rear window, he couldn't see who she was with or what she was doing.

Miriam Dominick sat in the Buick's backseat and looked at the man beside her. He was in his mid-twenties and wearing a dark gray polo shirt and khakis. At last he smiled and kissed her, and she returned the kiss. When the greeting was over, another man, who was sitting in the front seat, turned around to look at them. "God's peace, Miriam," he said.

"God's peace, John," Miriam replied, then turned to the man in the backseat. "God's peace, David."

"God's peace," he said. "So, do they trust you?"

"Vincent Antonelli definitely does, and I think the woman, Dr. Kelly, does. I'm not so sure about Kevin Tompkins."

"Whatever his name is, it isn't Tompkins," David said. "He looks like a Jew, and they don't trust anybody. Watch him. They're like serpents. Have they broken the book code yet?"

"Yes." Miriam looked out the window, away from David. "I did what I was told to. Antonelli found it in my backpack."

"When you spent the night with him?" David's voice sounded cold, but tinged with repressed excitement.

"That was the plan. But we didn't. . . ." She turned and glared at him. "It was *your* idea, wasn't it?"

"Are you sure that he cracked the code?"

"He followed me the next morning, then turned off into a store. I backtracked on him. He bought two copies of the book."

"That's pretty definitive," said the man in the front seat.

"And I think the whole thing was unnecessary," Miriam said, looking out once more. "For Peter to lose his life back there, to . . . allow himself to be shot down just to get the list and the coded message to them . . . they know the trail is fresh again, they'd have kept searching anyway."

"Fresh?" said David. "We know the papists brought it west, but beyond that?"

"It's near, I'm sure of it. The one it speaks to has been having dreams again, visions about 'a prisoner.' Tompkins."

John in the front seat nodded. "The Jew. It makes sense that it would speak to a Jew, doesn't it?"

"And I think that these . . . mummification deaths might somehow be its doing, too," said Miriam. "So far, they have no explanation. But what's *really* scaring me is the fact that they keep occurring near the drawings."

David shrugged. "That's a fortunate coincidence, as far as we're concerned. A double 'event' to lead these three on. Besides, Miriam, you're the one calling the general locations. Remember, *God works in mysterious ways, His wonders to perform.* Maybe He's giving us these bodies as a bonus, to keep these three on the trail."

"The important thing now," John said, "is that they fully believe you are psychic. But you say this Jew has doubts?"

"I think he *wants* to believe, but he doesn't let himself. He's a very strange man. But I think their belief is strong enough that the . . . final suggestion will work, once we've pinpointed the location of . . . of it."

"It better," the man said. "We've gone to a lot of trouble with these drawings. Not to mention the rock slide."

"I've seen their faces," Miriam said. "I know that it worked. Dr. Kelly believes in my . . . powers, and Vincent . . . Dr. Antonelli . . . would follow me to the ends of the earth."

"I have no doubt," said David. "I'm sure he's fallen head over heels in love with you, good papist girl that you are."

"I'm not a papist anymore, David, you know that."

David smiled thinly and nodded. "You've seen the light. And pretty soon we'll show that light to the rest of this country."

"I should go," Miriam said. "I don't know how long they'll be." She looked at David, uncertain what to do, but he leaned toward her and kissed her again. It was a lingering kiss, but a cruel one. His mouth was rough against her lips, and she wondered if he could taste Vincent's presence there.

At last she pulled away. John had been watching from the front seat. "God be with you," he said.

"And also with you," she replied automatically as she opened the door and got out. As she walked back to the Camry, she could feel tears in her eyes, and wondered why, when everything was going as planned, she should be so filled with sorrow.

Laika had been right. None of the newspeople looking down on the huge drawing at the overlook had recognized her and Joseph as the investigators who had been far down in the canyon earlier that day. Joseph took several photographs, and they started back to the road.

Laika had not discussed Miriam's purported abilities

any further with Joseph. She had the feeling that even if Miriam had successfully predicted the license plate numbers of the next hundred cars to drive past, Joseph still would have called it coincidence, and that was a mistake.

It was one thing to be skeptical, but although Laika had started out that way when their shadow operation had begun, she had seen enough to make her believe that there were things in this world that science and skeptics could not fully explain, and maybe Miriam's strange predictions were among them.

But there was more to Joseph's denials than just stubborn skepticism. Laika somehow felt that he was a vessel for those very talents he dismissed in others. Maybe, she thought, that was why he was so adamant in his disbelief. It would be damned hard for a stone atheist to realize suddenly that he had the power to heal the sick and raise the dead.

When they arrived at the car, Miriam was still in the back seat. Though her eyes looked tired, some color had returned to her cheeks and her forehead was dry again. "Feeling better?" Laika asked.

"Much. I just needed some time out of the sun, I guess. When I'm in the back country I always find some shade and lie down for fifteen minutes every few hours or so. Guess it just sneaked up on me."

"Surprised you didn't see it coming," Joseph said offhandedly, though Laika read the message and was sure that Miriam did, too.

"Being hungry might have something to do with it," said Laika. "It's almost five. Why don't we head for the roadhouse—Abner's, was it? We can see if Vincent had any luck with the tracker."

Abner's was on Indian Road 12, east of the monument, but because it was reachable only by a labyrinth of dirt roads, Joseph decided to play it safe and drive west to Chinle, then northeast on IR 64 until he hit 12, and then head southeast. With the tourist traffic along the canyon rim drive, the entire trip took nearly an hour.

*   *   *

Tony and Joshua Yazzie, after returning Sam Bitsosie's car to him, had stopped at the visitors' center and various businesses and residences along the road to Chinle, asking if anyone had seen any suspicious person the night before, possibly carrying a large container of some sort. No one had. By the time they gave up the search and left for Abner's, they were a considerable distance behind the car with Joseph, Laika, and Miriam.

Chapter 27

At 5:45 in the afternoon, four unhappy people drove into the dusty parking lot of Abner's roadhouse. The arguments of the previous night, ending in Damon's sharing Jezebel's tent and sleeping bag, had proved too much for Ted and Aileen, who were found missing the next morning.

Damon had awakened in the early dawn next to a sleeping Jezebel and decided in retrospect that it hadn't been all that great. In fact, it had been pretty shitty. There was some excitement that had come with dominance, but the woman was really the worse for wear.

She had lost a lot of weight since Ezekiel had disappeared and resembled one of those skinny, skanky lowlifes in a CK commercial, only older. In the brightening light of dawn, she wasn't much of a turn-on. And her face was thinning, too. Her nose was looking positively beaky, and her eyes were starting to get that haunted, sunken look he had seen in pictures of starving kids in Africa. The whole thing was starting to suck.

Then he climbed out of the tent and saw that Ted and Aileen's tent was gone. He looked around a little, just in case they had moved it somewhere else—but no, they were gone, all right.

Damon walked over to the bulk of Rodney's sleeping bag and prodded the man with the pointy toe of his boot.

Rodney shot up to a sitting position, blinking away sleep. "What the. . . ."

"That was a hell of an idea you had last night to unify us," Damon said. "Teddy Boy and Aileen have hit the goddamn trail."

"What?"

"They're gone. And if I hadn't been sleeping with the keys in my pocket, they probably would've stolen the van. Great idea, Rodney. You get me laid and end up losing a third of our party. *Hell* of an idea."

"Shit. Aw, shit. . . ." Rodney flopped back onto his air mattress. "That dumb sonofabitch."

The day went downhill from there. The van felt a little less crowded when they got on the road, but the tensions among them were greater now than it had been when Ted and Aileen had made up part of the equation. Damon felt hate flowing from everyone who was left.

Rodney was pissed at himself and at Damon for throwing his bad advice up to him; Charlotte was pissed at Damon for rewarding her devotion to him by banging Jezebel; and Jezebel, instead of warming to Damon for his domineering ways, seemed rather to ooze hatred for him. It wasn't, he thought, a bunch of happy campers.

And instead of focusing Jezebel's spindly powers, Damon's actions of the night before had diffused them, if her indecisiveness at every crossroads was any indication. But now, instead of becoming weepily frustrated, Jezebel was growing angrier at her inability to sense the direction of the Divine.

They had driven all around Canyon de Chelly, finally escaping the tourists when they got on the Indian roads north of the canyon. But Jezebel couldn't seem to make up her mind which way she wanted to go, so they stuck to the largest roads, and eventually found themselves heading south again.

"There's *something* down here, damn it," Jezebel said. "I feel *something* on this road, I know it. . . ."

They had driven slowly down IR 12, stopping at every

dusty crossroads and letting Jezebel sniff for spoor or whatever it was she was doing. At last they saw a shabby little roadhouse with a Pepsi sign hanging from a post with ABNER'S beneath it. "Jesus," said Rodney, "could I ever use a beer!"

"You and me both," said Damon, happy to find something he and Rodney could agree upon. It seemed their dream of finding the Divine was blowing away as quickly as the dust that swirled around the van as Rodney pulled it into one of many vacant spaces in front of the roadhouse.

There was a rusty soft drink cooler outside. Next to it, pressed against its cold metal, lay a skinny yellow dog. Charlotte hurried ahead so that she could pat it, but as she leaned down, it raised its head and gave a soft, rumbling growl deep in its throat, and she stood up again and walked around it.

Inside there was a counter on the left and booths on the right. Both went three quarters of the way down the building until they were stopped by the kitchen, which had a door in the middle of the wall and two windows on either side, one for the counter man and one for the booth waitress.

As the four entered, the cook, a short Navajo woman in an apron and a white paper hat, passed two plates through to the counter man, who took them to two cowboys sitting on stools next to the door. These men were in their fifties, Damon guessed, though the desert sun might have weathered them beyond their years. They looked at Damon and the others, and the closer one eyed him up and down, as though he didn't quite get the black leather pants and vest. "Howdy, cowpoke," the man said, then chuckled and turned to his just-delivered plate, as though not expecting an answer.

Damon stopped dead. He had had quite enough shit from the world and the gods today, and now he was getting more from this skinny brown-as-a-nut hick asshole who was digging into a plate of what looked like jackrabbit and beans. " *'Cowpoke?'* " he said.

Then he felt Rodney's hand on his arm, tugging at him to come along to the booth near the back that Jezebel and Charlotte were staking out. "Come on, man," Rodney said softly. "No point."

Damon went with him, turning his head and holding the gaze of the cowboy, who had looked up from his plate and watched Damon with a challenge in his eyes. Damon sat in the booth with Jezebel, on the seat facing the door and the cowboys. He kept watching the man as intently as the man was watching him. Without looking at his plate, the cowboy picked up a forkful and chewed it, his mouth open, still watching Damon.

"Christ, what a moron," Rodney said.

"Him or me?" said Damon.

"Both of ya. Twenty years ago I woulda done the same dumb macho bullshit. But it ain't worth fightin' about. Ignore him."

Damon snorted and looked away from the cowboy, checking out the rest of the place. Besides them and the cowboys, only four other customers were there. They were Navajo men seated near the front, wearing work shirts and jeans and talking quietly. The Navajo counter man was pouring coffee from a big silver urn.

The kitchen door opened, and a tall boy in his late teens came out with a tray full of burgers and sandwiches, which he took to the Indians in the booth. On his way back, he stopped at Damon's table and handed them laminated menus. "You can bring two beers right away, pal," said Rodney. "What do you ladies want to drink?"

"No beer," the boy said flatly.

"Whaddya mean, no beer?" asked Rodney.

"You're on the reservation," the boy said. "No alcohol served."

"Jesus holy Christ," said Damon. "You telling me we can't get a beer anywhere in this godforsaken shithole?"

"Aw shit," muttered Rodney.

"I'll just have a Coke," Charlotte said, trying to still the waters.

"Pepsi okay?" the boy asked, a little nervously.

"Not for me," said Damon. "Goddamn it, I want a *beer.*" It had been one of those days, and things weren't going to get any better. He knew the law was the law and he should just forget about the stupid beer, but he had gone beyond the point of being rational.

He felt as if his whole life were slipping away from him, and something in him perversely made him want to shove the rest of it over the edge. He couldn't have a damn thing that he wanted in his life, not a group to follow him, not the Divine, not even a lousy beer. He had screwed up everything he had tried. If he hadn't killed Ezekiel Swain, they probably would have found the Divine ages ago. It just wasn't fair. He was righteously pissed, and somebody was going to pay for this world of shit in which he now found himself.

"I'm sorry," the Indian kid was saying, "we don't *have* any beer, and if we did, we couldn't *sell* it. You want something else to drink?"

The world went red before Damon's eyes. "I just want a beer . . . one goddamn teeny-weeny bottle of beer. That's what I want."

The grizzled cowboy who had been playing peekaboo with Damon had spun around on his stool. "They ain't got no beer, Mr. Rubber Pants. You deaf along with being queer, sweetheart?"

Damon started to get up, but Rodney was out of his seat before he could stand and pushed him back down. Damon was trembling with rage. "Hell with him," Rodney said coldly, "and hell with the beer. You order a Pepsi and somethin' to eat, and we'll get the hell outta here."

"Aw, looka that, Buddy," the cowboy said to his friend, who had also turned and was grinning at Damon and Rodney. "His honey hadda stop him from playin'.

Probably afraid them two dykes they're with might get hurt.''

Damon saw Charlotte's face blush a burning red. Rodney, keeping his hand clamped on Damon's shoulder, turned and looked at the cowboys. "I'm not his *honey*," he said in a low, even voice. "I'm his *friend*. And these ladies aren't *dykes*. And we're just gonna sit here and relax now and have a little something to eat." Then Rodney turned his back on them and sat back down.

The cowboy was silent for a moment, and Damon tried to look at his menu through the red haze that was still blinding him. But then the cowboy clucked his tongue and spoke again.

"Ain't nothing sadder than an old biker that's turned into a peter puffer."

He said something after that, but Damon never heard it. A roar from Rodney drowned it out as the man jerked himself out of the booth and ran like a tank at the offending cowboy on his stool.

The cowboy scarcely had time to spin partway around before Rodney was on him, smashing into him with a force that slammed them both onto the counter and then slid them off the end onto the floor. Rodney reappeared, getting to his feet. He was holding the cowboy by his shirt front and began to smash the back of the man's head onto the end of the counter.

The cowboy kicked his feet and smacked at Rodney with his fists, but the fists quickly became open hands as the man grew weaker. Then the cowboy's friend Buddy got into the action.

He grabbed a glass sugar container, ran to Rodney, and smashed it open on Rodney's head. Rodney, dazed, dropped the cowboy and staggered back, blood running from a cut over his eyes. By that time, Damon had jumped Buddy from behind, wrapping his arms around the man's neck and jaw. Buddy staggered backward, having enough presence of mind to bite the forearm that was pressing into his face.

Damon howled with pain and jerked his arms away just as the man swung around and landed a lucky roundhouse on Damon's temple. *"You little pussy!"* Buddy yelled, and hit Damon hard in the gut, then pushed him so that he tripped on the stools and fell partly onto the counter.

The cowboy was up again. He shook his aching head to clear it, and then went after Rodney, who was blinking like he didn't know what country he was in. The cowboy ripped a big key ring off his belt and laid a vicious backhand rake across Rodney's face with the ends of the keys. Rodney screamed in a voice that shivered the spines of the watchers. The fighters didn't have time to be impressed with Rodney's vocal range.

As the cowboy got set to slash Rodney again, Jezebel stepped in. In one quick move, she picked up a big glass shard from the broken sugar container and came up with it under the man's chin before he could strike again. The sharp point buried itself in the soft spot beneath his jaw, angled up the back of his throat, and slipped right into his brain. His fist spasmed open, and the keys fell to the floor. The cowboy followed them a moment later.

Damon wasn't doing much better than the cowboy. Buddy had shoved him behind the counter and into the coffee urn, knocking it over so that the top came off and scalding coffee cascaded out in a brown sheet. The heat of it made Damon hiss in his breath as he fell into trays of cutlery below it, sending the silverware clattering to the tile floor.

Buddy leaned over the counter, grabbed a handful of Damon's long hair in his wiry fingers, and yanked up hard. Damon's head snapped back on his neck and his fingers scrambled frantically for something with which to hit the attacker above him. They closed around the handle of a serrated steak knife.

Damon didn't even look. He just rammed the steak knife into the air, hoping that it would come in contact with some part of the man, and it did. The blade slid into

Buddy's left eye socket, slicing the eyeball open as easily as a razor blade through a hard-boiled egg.

The shock and the pain were so great that Buddy didn't even yell. His fingers remained clenched in Damon's hair as though he had suddenly turned to stone. When Damon saw the damage he had done, he released the knife handle, horrified by the sight of Buddy's dripping eye and the other untouched eye glaring in fury at him.

The knife stayed where it was, and the fluid ran down the handle. "I'm gonna kill you sure, you goddamn son-ofabitch," Buddy finally said between clenched teeth, and grasped the knife handle with his free hand. Slowly, with a grating animal growl escaping his throat, he slid the knife out of his blinded eye, gazed at it for a moment with the one that remained, and then, with a bellow of rage, reached further over the counter to try and cut Damon's throat.

"Uh-uh," Damon heard someone say, and a second later he saw Rodney grab Buddy around the neck with both hands. Rodney squeezed so hard that Buddy, lying halfway across the counter on his stomach, was unable to do anything. His right eye bulged, and his left eye pulsed jelly. Both fists opened, freeing Damon and the steak knife, which dropped onto Damon's forehead, the blade lightly scoring his flesh.

Damon grabbed it by the handle before it hit the floor and stuck the blade just under Rodney's choking fingers, directly into the soft half circle right above Buddy's collarbone. A shower of blood sprayed down upon Damon's face, and he closed his eyes and laughed wildly. *That* had taken care of the stupid shit, all right. If he wasn't deader than hell now, he would be in another few seconds.

But when Damon blinked his eyes so that he could see again, he saw that Rodney's face, a red blur behind and above Buddy's, was bleeding too, oozing blood from several slashes that made his cheeks and nose look as though a lion's claws had raked across them. As Damon watched, he saw Rodney's eyes roll up till only the whites were

showing. His fingers unclenched from around Buddy's
neck, and Buddy's head lolled like a heavy fruit over Damon.

Damon regained his footing and stood up behind the
counter. Rodney had fallen over onto the floor, his feet
kicking. Charlotte and the four Navajos were still sitting
in their booths watching the action, the Indians stolidly,
Charlotte in a daze, her mouth open. Jezebel was standing
over the dead body of the cowboy, kicking it savagely,
and holding in one hand the glass shard with which she
had killed him. The jagged glass had cut the heel of her
hand, and her blood was trickling unnoticed across her
palm and dripping off the ends of her fingertips.

But it was the actions of the counter man that held
Damon's attention. He was at the end of the counter next
to the kitchen, talking rapidly but softly into a telephone.

It was time to go. They had unloaded a storm of shit
and two people were dead. Damon ignored the counter
man. What was done was done, after all. He ran up to the
front end of the counter and around it and grabbed Jezebel's arm, wary of the glass dagger she was holding.
"Let's go," he said.

She glanced up at him, seemed to recognize him, and
gave the dead cowboy one last solid kick. Then she ran
for the door. Damon knelt and shook Rodney, but the poor
guy wasn't going anywhere. His eyes were glazed, and he
seemed loopy from loss of blood. He had saved Damon's
ass twice over, but there wasn't anything Damon could
do for him now. He dug the keys out of Rodney's jacket
pocket, then stood back up and looked at Charlotte.

"Let's haul it," he said, and headed for the door. But
when he looked back he saw that she was still sitting in
the booth, her mouth agape. "Come *on*, man!" he called,
but she just shook her head slowly. Fine then, the hell
with her, she was going to act like a goddamn moron.

Damon raced out of the roadhouse and over to the van.
Jezebel was already in the passenger seat and had flung
the driver's door open for him. He climbed in, fumbled

with the keys, and started the engine. He backed out, then started to pull onto the road, getting ready to head northwest.

But then he saw another car approaching from that direction, and was afraid it might be the police, so he pulled the wheel the other way and drove southeast.

Shit, shit, shit. Down to two now, and all he had wanted was a goddamn beer.

Chapter 28

"*L*ooks like somebody's in a hurry," said Joseph Stein, as he saw the big van tear out of Abner's parking lot. "I hope that doesn't bode ill for the quality of the food."

But as he steered the car into the dirt parking lot, a tall Navajo in an apron came running out of the roadhouse, and Joseph lowered the window. The man pointed down the road after the van and shouted, "They're gettin' away! They're murderers—they killed two people!"

That was all Joseph needed to hear. "Call the police," he shouted, as he hit the accelerator and drove back onto the road.

"I did!" Joseph heard the man say, as he tore after the van.

The road was straight, and he could see that the van was half a mile ahead of him. He was closing fast. The car had a big engine, and the van probably didn't, and was hauling a lot of steel and seats and impact beams besides.

Laika reached beneath the front seat for Joseph's Glock 17, then took out her own from the glove box and jacked rounds into the chambers. Then she looked back at Miriam Dominick and smiled. "I know what you're thinking," she said. "We're not the police, so why are we doing this. Well, Miriam, we're trained for this kind of thing. National Science Foundation work can get more exciting than you'd ever imagine—especially in our division.''

Joseph would have laughed if he hadn't been so intent on driving. He estimated the distance between them at six hundred yards. Another few minutes and he'd be right on their ass.

Back at Abner's, the four Navajos had finally sprung into action. Two were trying to stop Rodney's bleeding, while the others were examining the cowboy and his buddy to make sure there was nothing they could do for them.

The counter man, the waiter, and the cook were all standing over Charlotte where she still sat in the booth. The counter man was now holding a short baseball bat and looking at Charlotte as if he expected any minute for her to go as berserk as her friends had.

Charlotte looked around the roadhouse once more, as if trying to understand what had happened to her dream. Finally she came to the conclusion that it had assuredly ended, drowned in a bath of stupidity and blood and dead men.

She looked up at the suspicious face of the counter man and tried to smile, to show him that she meant no harm. She gave a little shrug, then said apologetically, "I don't know what happened . . . we were a *religious* group. . . ."

"Can't you go any *faster?*" Jezebel spat out, venom in her voice.

"It's a goddamn *van*, not a sportscar," Damon shot back. The car in the rearview mirror was getting closer, and he realized that there was no way he could outrun it. He looked ahead frantically for a side road, anyplace they could get off and maybe try and escape on foot, or lose their pursuer in a labyrinth of dirt roads. The van handled great on dirt.

Just as he topped a small rise, he saw a chance. Fifty yards ahead, a road led off to the right straight through the scrub. The crest of the hill kept the van from the sight of the car behind them, and there was enough cover from a small stand of piñon pine that they would be hidden for a while, perhaps long enough to lose the car.

Damon twisted the wheel and the van lurched off the road and bumped over a small ditch, and then he was on the dirt road, heading down it as fast as he could. But when he glanced in the rearview mirror, he let out a curse. The dust was rising heavily over the tops of the trees. The people in the car would see it for sure. He couldn't slow down now.

Then he saw the dirt road split up ahead and he got an idea. The road had been curving slowly to the left and the new road broke to the right. As he reached the fork, he turned left and reduced his speed to less than ten miles an hour.

"What the hell are you *doing?*" Jezebel shrieked. "You want them to catch us?"

"Relax, I just don't want to raise any dust here. Maybe they'll think we went the other way." He hoped the left-hand fork might bring them around again to the main road, though he ached with the pain of driving so slowly. When he was fifty yards from the fork, he slowly increased his speed, still trying not to raise the telltale dust. The road kept curving, and in another few minutes he saw the main road again. They had just made a big U-turn.

"Home free, baby," he said, and hit the gas. It was a mistake. The van's rear wheels skidded in a patch of loose sand and the vehicle fishtailed, then skidded to the left. Damon flung the wheel in that direction, but it was no use. The van slid off the road, its left rear wheel slipping into a ditch just big enough to trap it.

Damon pressed on the gas pedal, but the wheel only spun in the sand. "God *damn* it!" he said, opening the door. "Take the wheel," he ordered Jezebel, who slid across into the driver's seat. "I'll push the bastard!"

He ran to the back of the van and saw that it was wedged nearly a foot deep in the sand. He fell on his knees and started to scoop out the loose sand with his hands like a dog trying to dig its way under a fence. Jesus, he thought, as the sweat ran down his face, how the hell did this all happen? And he thought for the hundredth time that he never should have killed Ezekiel Swain. He'd be damned if this wasn't purgatory.

The wheels suddenly spun, kicking sand up into his eyes. Jezebel had hit the pedal. "Damn it, not yet!" he shouted. "I'll say *go!* Jesus. . . ." He started digging again, even more tense than before, expecting to get sprayed with sand again any second. It would be like her, he thought, to tear off and leave him alone to face the cops.

Then, for an instant, he sensed that something was behind him, and the thought crossed his mind that the cops were here, that they had caught up with him and were about to clamp their steely fingers onto his shoulder. But when the contact came, it didn't feel like flesh at all.

Instead, Damon suddenly felt as though someone had emptied a basket of sticks over his back and shoulders. But that sensation lasted for only a moment. The pain followed fast.

The sticks seemed to form themselves over the back of his body, pressing him down into the sand so that his eyes and nose and mouth were stuffed with it. Then the flesh of his back and buttocks and legs tingled as if covered with a quilt coated with electric needles.

He tried to rise, but he had barely enough strength to bring up his head out of the sand. When he did, something wrapped itself around his face, and a stench as of something long dead filled his nostrils. He still had enough sight left to see that it was a hand, but a hand whose fingers could have been made out of brown dried leather stretched over dry yellow bones.

Damon barely had time to croak out a scream before the thin fingers slipped into his mouth and scuttled down his throat.

*   *   *

"What's the matter?" Jezebel shouted through the open window of the van. "I didn't do anything." She waited a moment, but heard no reply. Then she looked in the rearview mirror and saw Damon's booted foot sticking out from behind the van. It was twitching, kicking up the sand around it. What the hell was wrong with him? Was he having a fit or something?

Joseph stopped at the fork in the dirt road and looked down both for a moment. Then he jumped out of the car, examined the road surfaces, and got back in.

"The road not taken," he said, nodding to the right hand fork and steering the car to the left. "You don't need a Navajo to track a heavy van on a sandy road."

In another hundred yards they could see the van ahead. It wasn't moving. "Nice work, Daniel Boone," said Laika. She hefted her pistol in her hands. "Looks like they're stuck."

The hell with him, Jezebel thought, and hit the gas again, but once more the wheels only spun in place. Then she detected movement in the mirror and saw the pursuing car bouncing along not far behind. It was all too clear that she wasn't going to be able to get the van moving before the car caught up to them. She'd have to try and escape on foot, then.

She got out of the car and headed toward the brush on the left, looking over to see what the hell was wrong with Damon. That was when she saw it.

She stopped running and froze in place, and the head of the thing on Damon's back rose up, and the eyes, dark stones deep in furrowed sockets, looked at her. The leathery lips split into a mockery of a smile, and at that moment Jezebel Swain knew what this creature was.

"Ezekiel. . . ."

Chapter 29

As Jezebel watched in horror and fascination and with a touch of wondrous love, the creature that was still somehow Ezekiel Swain began to stand up. The rapidly diminishing body of Damon came along with him, like a corporeal shadow. Damon's back seemed cemented to Ezekiel's chest, Damon's legs to Ezekiel's, and their arms to one another's.

Damon was still alive. His eyes continued to move, and Jezebel thought she could hear a high-pitched sound coming from his mouth like a balloon when air slowly escapes it through a pinched opening. But his body was shrinking. She recalled a high school science film in which time-lapse photography showed grapes becoming raisins in several seconds.

Damon's eyes shrank in their sockets, the whites vanishing. His cheeks sank in, his stomach became a hollow concavity under his leather vest, and his arms and legs withered.

And all that fluid, those juices and secretions, blood, bile, mucus, lymph, urine, marrow, the oils in Damon's skin, the water in his stomach, every drop of moisture that he had carried in tissue and bone was being drawn through his skin, being sucked out of him by the dry and ravening flesh of Ezekiel Swain.

The moisture was filling up Ezekiel like a sweating water bag. His skin, dry and brittle and brown only moments before, had become a pale gray and was starting to ooze with the wines of life he was drawing from his victim. Jezebel saw his features forming and expanding, the face becoming fleshier, the arms and thighs pushing through the rags that hung off his shoulders and from his waist.

The larger he grew, the fuller his flesh became and the more Damon withered. The skin of his face, neck, and hands was darkening as his body seemed to implode. His ligaments lost their elasticity and contracted, drawing up his legs and arms so that he remained attached by his back alone to the parasite that had already sucked its host's life away.

Damon became less and less, and Ezekiel more and more, until the need for the bond between them was no longer there and Damon fell from Ezekiel Swain like a dry husk, a seed pod from which all the contents have floated away on the wind. Damon's body scarcely made a sound when it hit the ground.

Jezebel could hardly breathe. There he stood, her brother, her lover, back from the dead, oozing, seeping life, glistening with stolen juices in the setting sun.

"Dear God," she heard someone whisper, and when she looked beyond Ezekiel, she saw two people, a black woman and a white man, both staring at Ezekiel and both holding very deadly looking guns.

Laika could scarcely believe what she had just seen. They had stopped the car twenty yards behind the van, planning to come up fast on foot on either side, but by the time they got out, cautioning Miriam to remain inside, the man in the leather vest was almost certainly dead.

Still, Joseph had glanced at Laika to see if she wanted to shoot, but she had given him the signal not to fire. She knew this was the killer they had been searching for, and that they were seeing it kill again. Part of her wanted to open up on it with her weapon, but another part, perhaps the scientist that she was portraying and had in a sense become, wanted merely to *watch*, to observe, to see what had been done, and how.

So they watched and marveled and trembled until the creature had finished feeding, and let its prey fall empty. It was then that Laika had spoken the words the woman had heard.

The woman, her blouse spattered with blood, looked at Laika and Joseph, then back at the bloated, slightly swaying figure of the predator as though she were both drawn to it and repelled by it, and Laika wondered if it would attack her next. But the thing seemed to be content, rocking happily like a man who'd had too much to drink and was pleased with the situation.

When the woman looked at Laika again, she asked in a quavering voice, "Who *are* you?"

Joseph said softly to Laika, "I don't think that the old 'your worst nightmare' line is going to have much impact after this."

"Put up your hands and lean against the van," said Laika, pointing her gun at the woman. Both she and Joseph walked slowly toward the woman and the man, his gray and greasy flesh swollen like a water balloon filled to bursting.

The woman did as Laika had ordered but kept her eyes on the obese swaying figure. "Ezekiel," she said to it. "Help me . . . you have to help me. . . ."

Laika heard what might have been a low laugh, a thick gurgling sound like oatmeal boiling, and the great head, as fat and round as a playground ball, seemed to shake back and forth. If the woman was looking for help from this Ezekiel, it didn't look like she was going to get it.

"What's your name?" Laika asked the woman, who shook her head as though she didn't understand. "Come *on!*" Laika barked. "Your name! Quick!"

"Swain . . . Jezebel Swain," she said.

Laika looked at the creature that stood before them, sated and smiling. "And you? Who are you?"

The words came haltingly, bubblingly, as though from

a deep well with lava at the bottom of it. "... A follower...." Dark fluids dripped from the man's lips and down over his jaw with every word.

"Who? Who are you following?"

"The ... Divine. He calls ... I answer. Must go ... free Him." The dark, wet laugh came again, and Laika bit back a shudder.

"You know him?" she asked Jezebel Swain.

The woman nodded. "He's my brother. He's Ezekiel." She looked at the dead and desiccated man on the ground, and her eyes widened as if in realization. "It was Damon ... *Damon* killed him."

Killed him? Jesus, what was going on here? "That's Damon?" Laika asked, and the woman nodded again. Then Laika looked back at Ezekiel Swain, who, if his sister was any judge, was dead and somehow made alive again. "Where is this Divine?" she asked him.

Ezekiel Swain turned slowly around, raised a right arm the thickness of a tree, and pointed north. "Divine," he said, "in holy place."

Joseph took a step toward Ezekiel. "*What* holy place?" he said. "What does it look like?"

The man's eyes, as wet as if they were brimming with tears, got an even more faraway look, as though he were trying to figure out how to convey the image. Then he seemed to think of something, and he sang softly, *"Davy ... Davy Crockett,"* then hummed a few notes.

Laika looked at Joseph, and wondered if he got it. His next words told her he had. "Davy Crockett ... at the Alamo. A mission? A Spanish mission?"

Ezekiel Swain's head bobbed up and down like a buoy in a calm sea. "*Holy* place," he said. "Called me. Had to answer. No matter what ... matter what...."

Still keeping his gun trained on the strange siblings, Joseph walked to Laika's side and spoke softly to her. "You know who he's after. You know who's ... responsible for him."

She nodded. "You saw the mission in your dream. He sees it too."

For a moment, Joseph looked sick. "My dream is . . . a coincidence. But everything else . . . what we just saw him do, the draining of that man's body, the fact that this thing's sister says he was dead and now he's alive again . . . it *has* to be connected to this prisoner. It's the only truly paranormal thing that we've actually seen, along with the apport of that sculptor back in New York. There's *got* to be a connection."

"You got religion real fast," Laika said, with just a trace of smugness.

"I believe in what I can see, and I can see this. I'm not saying it's supernatural or paranormal—it could be natural and normal in a way we simply don't know anything about. But we're never going to understand the processes behind it if we don't find this prisoner." He looked at Ezekiel Swain. "And this . . . *guy* may be the way to do it."

"I was having the same thoughts," said Laika. "We'd better do this fast."

But Ezekiel Swain was already moving. He was shuffling away toward the north, ignoring the pleas of his sister to stay and help her. Laika caught up to him easily. She didn't think the threat of the pistol would have much effect on him, so she used another tactic.

"We can take you to your master," she said, "to the Divine. It will take you forever on foot, you can see that. There are mountains and deserts between you and your master, places where there are no . . . where you wouldn't be able to feed. But we can go much faster in a car. We'll take you, if you want us to."

Please say yes, she thought. Otherwise they would have to try and force him to go with them, and she wasn't sure just how easy that would be. She wasn't even sure they could kill him, if it came to that.

The shuffling figure stopped, the huge head turned toward her, and the swimming eyes regarded her. Then Ezekiel Swain looked ahead at the desert and the hills beyond. "Long way," he said. Then the head moved up and down. "Yes. . . ."

"All right. Come back to the car. We'll have to hide you there. Other people will be coming who won't understand. Hurry."

He did, moving faster than she would have thought possible. "Open the trunk," she called to Joseph. Laika glanced at Miriam, who, wide-eyed, had been watching all the activity from the backseat. This was going to take some major explaining. Still, even if the girl talked to someone, the operatives would be long gone.

Laika put out a hand to help Ezekiel Swain, but thought better of it and drew her fingers back from that suppurating flesh. "What are you *doing?*" asked Jezebel Swain, as she saw her brother clamber heavily and awkwardly into the spacious trunk. He seemed indifferent to the accommodations, concerned only with reaching his goal. Jezebel took a few steps toward him, but Laika waved her off with the gun. Laika could hear a siren from the direction of the roadhouse.

"Dr. Tompkins," she said to Joseph. "Can you put that into the trunk, too?" She pointed to the dried body of the young man. Joseph knelt and lifted the corpse, careful to touch it by its clothing.

Its lightness made it seem to float upward, and he carried it easily to the trunk and set it in next to Ezekiel Swain, who was lying, sated, on his back, his body resting diagonally across the trunk, his head against the closed rear seat-back, his eyes looking peacefully at the bottom of the backseat ledge.

"Close it," said Laika. Then she turned to Jezebel Swain. "All right, listen to me. You just keep your mouth shut about what happened here. Damon ran away after you got stuck, understand? And we caught up with you, and that's all that happened. I don't know what went on back there at that roadhouse, but if you go along with what we say, we'll try to help you eventually, even though you have to go with the police now. You get what I'm saying? If you care at all about your brother, don't say a word. Because if they find out about him, they will take him and poke him and prod him and cut off pieces of him, and make whatever is left of his life a living hell. Got it?''

Jezebel Swain nodded. The sirens grew louder, and Laika saw a big white car coming down the road. They were only fifty yards away from it with no cover. The driver would spot them for sure. She hoped it was Yazzie and Tony.

Laika had Joseph watch Jezebel Swain, while she opened the car door and looked in at a pale Miriam. Laika tried to smile, to indicate some stability in the midst of all this insanity, of these things that could not be. ''Okay, I know you've see a lot of weird things going down, but strange as it may seem, everything *is* under control. Just sit tight and don't say anything when Officer Yazzie gets here, all right?''

Miriam nodded. ''All right.''

''And by the way,'' said Laika, slipping her weapon into the glove box again, ''don't worry if you hear anything in the trunk behind you.''

"There they are," Tony said, pointing to the rental car and the van on the dirt road up ahead to their right. They had pulled into Abner's only a few minutes earlier to find the place in chaos, with two dead men on the floor and another one badly wounded. The proprietor had been talking a mile a minute, but he and Yazzie had finally comprehended that the killers had driven south, and that a man and two women in a dark green car had gone after them.

Since they were late for their dinner with Laika, Joseph, and Miriam, and the Camry wasn't in the lot, it was natural for Tony and Yazzie to assume that the pursuers were their colleagues. So Yazzie had hit the siren and the lights, and they had headed south.

Now Yazzie swung the big white Fury onto the dirt road, kicking up a cloud of dust behind them, and brought the car to a sliding halt next to the other two vehicles. Joseph was holding a weapon on a woman who was spattered with blood. Laika was standing near the car, and Tony was relieved to see Miriam, seemingly unharmed, in the backseat.

"Well, Dr. Tompkins," said Yazzie, walking up to Joseph and eyeing his Glock. "The National Science Foundation sure gives its scientists enough firepower."

Joseph smiled. "Have to be ready for any contingency, as the present situation so aptly proves."

"You know firearms are illegal on Indian land?" asked Yazzie.

"Special government permit," Joseph said. "I think you'll find it passes muster."

"I'm sure I will."

"We don't know what went down back there," Laika said, "but this van took off as we were coming in, someone yelled that they had killed some people, so we chased them. Fortunately, they got stuck, and we caught up."

"They?" asked Yazzie.

"There was a male, but he escaped, ran into the brush. Dr. Tompkins tried to follow him, but he got away. Probably hiding in some canyon by now."

Yazzie took a pair of cuffs off his belt, cuffed the woman, and read her her rights. After he put her in the back of his Fury, he returned to the others. "Thanks for the help," he told Joseph and Laika. "Anything else you can tell us about this woman?"

Laika shook her head. "Just that she said her name was Jezebel Swain. We didn't look in the van at all."

Yazzie nodded. "So what did you find out over at Spider Rock?"

"Nothing much. Another drawing, that's all. In the mud of the wash this time. We called the foundation to report in, though, and they told us we're being taken off the case."

The news came as a huge surprise to Tony. What did it mean? Had Skye actually pulled them off, or was Laika faking it to get rid of Yazzie?

Apparently Yazzie was surprised, too, if his scowl was any indication. "Why?" he asked.

"We're being sent to Maine. There have been several cases of livestock being slaughtered, but the tooth and claw marks don't seem to be from common predators, so we're going to investigate. I don't know if the foundation will send a new team out here or not. We got the facts, but as for theories. . . ." She shrugged. "We did tell them that you've been a great help. They were noncommittal, but I suspect that if a new team is assigned, they'll contact you.''

"You're not at all upset about taking it this far and having to leave it?''

"If we got upset every time something like this happened,'' Laika said with a long-suffering smile, "we'd be gobbling Prozac like M&Ms. It's SOP, that's all. Standard operating procedure when you work for Uncle Sam.''

"We might have to get you to testify on this case, you know,'' Yazzie said.

"Here's how to reach us through the DC office.'' She handed him one of their fake business cards, and he took it. "Phone, e-mail, address are all there.'' Then she stuck out her hand. "It's been a real strange trip, Officer. Thanks for all your help.''

"My pleasure, Doctor. And speaking of strange trips, Dr. Antonelli can fill you in on what our tracker found. You ever need to get hold of me, the Bureau of Indian Affairs will know where I am.'' Then he shook their hands, tipped his cowboy hat to Miriam, got in his car, and headed back toward the roadhouse.

"Okay,'' Tony said, "will someone please explain to me just what the hell is happening?''

"I'll make it quick,'' said Laika, with a quick glance at Miriam, still sitting in the car. "We're after the prisoner. The person who killed and mummified those men knows where he is. And that person is in the trunk of the car, along with one of his victims.''

"What?''

"I'll fill in the details later. Miriam has seen everything that's gone on today. But she *doesn't* know about the prisoner. We're heading north—that's where the thing in the trunk says the prisoner is.''

"Holy shit,'' Tony said softly. "I missed a *lot*, didn't I?''

"All right,'' Laika said, when the three operatives were back in the car, "we've come to the parting of the ways,

Miriam. We ask you not to talk to anyone about what you saw today. But I think you deserve an explanation. The man in the trunk is the result of a private corporation's genetic experiment gone terribly wrong. It's something that we had suspected from the first, and that we now know to be true.''

Miriam was nodding, trying to understand, a solemn look on her face. The windows in the car had been up the entire time, and the engine had been running. Laika knew the odds were long that she had heard any of the conversation beyond the occasional shouts.

"He'll be taken care of," Laika went on, "and there will be no more killings. But you *must* remain silent about what you've seen. National security could be at stake.'' Laika hoped that the woman was as patriotic as she was religious.

"I will," she said. "I won't say anything, I promise.''

"That's good. I knew we could trust you. Now listen, you know what we have in the trunk. We've got to head north with it to a government facility there, and we don't have the time to take you back to Gallup. So we can either say goodbye here, or you can tag along with us until we stop tonight—probably just for a few hours at a motel— and then maybe get a bus back to Gallup.''

Miriam glanced at Tony, and in the look that passed between them, Laika was afraid she saw the answer. "I've got my backpack," she said. "It's got everything I need. So I'd like to go with you as far as I can.''

"Good enough," Laika said. "Let's go.''

By the time they passed Abner's, there were two police cars and an ambulance outside it. They looked for Yazzie's Fury but didn't see it. Maybe, Laika thought, he had taken Jezebel Swain to wherever the local jail was.

Laika knew that they had to have better directions than simply "north." Within a few miles she had regretted her invitation to bring Miriam along with them for any distance. What she should have done was just dumped her by the side of the road.

But she knew how Tony felt about her, and this way he and Miriam would have a chance to be with each other, if only for a few miles. Laika thought about what she had to do and how the presence of Miriam might prevent it.

The first thing was to talk to that creature in the trunk and try and get a better handle on where this mission, if mission it was, was located. The second was to get rid of the dried-up corpse who was shoulder-to-shoulder with its killer in the trunk. And the third was to use the online resources of the Company to pinpoint the location of this mission. The sooner the better, for all three objectives.

"Dr. Tompkins," she said to Joseph. "I want a deserted side road."

She caught Tony's quick look of panic in the rearview mirror and knew what he was thinking, that Laika had it in mind to terminate Miriam. She caught his eye, gave him a smile of reassurance, and shook her head slightly so that he knew the woman was safe. It was, she suspected, proof of Tony's loving concern for Miriam that he should have even thought of that. Laika had never, *would* never, terminate an innocent, even if it meant her own life.

A dirt road led them up among some rocks, out of sight of Route 12. Among the rocks the soil seemed loose and sandy, and Laika had Joseph pull off the road. The car handled fine on the loose earth, and they drove back another thirty yards until she told him to stop.

"Vincent, stay here with Miriam," she said. "We won't be too long."

Joseph left the motor running and the air conditioner fan on high. Then he and Laika took their pistols, got out of the car, and walked around to the back. "I want to bury this Damon character. We don't need his body, and I'd rather not be hauling around a corpse in the car."

"If we believe his sister, we've got *two*," Joseph said, nodding at the closed trunk.

"Then I want to talk to a dead man." She handed Joseph the extra set of keys. "Go ahead, open it. I'll cover you.'' And she stepped a few feet away from the trunk, her weapon poised.

Joseph gingerly unlocked the lid, threw it up, and stepped back. But Ezekiel Swain only lifted up his massive head and looked at them, an act, Laika thought, that must have taken great strength. His head seemed like a beach ball stuffed with wet sand.

He was peaceful enough, so Laika stepped up to the trunk. ''We want to bury this one,'' she said, gesturing at Damon. ''Do you want to get out and . . . stretch?''

The great head nodded, and the mouth smiled. As it did, a yellow, viscous fluid trickled from the lower lip. Slowly Ezekiel climbed out of the trunk, and when he stood at last, a good half pint of the same fluid ran out of a wound in his torso, splashing onto the sand.

Ezekiel pressed his hand against the opening until the liquid stopped running between his fingers. Then he looked at Laika. ''Hadda take . . . a leak,'' he said, then laughed that unpleasant rumbling laugh.

Laika could tell that Joseph was as uncomfortable as she was in the presence of this dead-alive creature. And the fact that it was doing one-liners made it even more bizarre. That even a vestige of humor could exist in such a thing seemed horrible. She would have preferred it to be voiceless and zombie-like. It would have been far less disconcerting.

Ezekiel Swain seemed to sense their discomfort and shuffled several steps away from the trunk, as if to give them room to take out the body without coming too close to his replenished, saturated flesh. Joseph lifted out the dried corpse effortlessly, and set it down where the ground was loose and sandy. Then he took a multipurpose tool from beneath the trunk floor, unfolded the spade, and began to dig.

Laika and Ezekiel Swain watched until Joseph had dug a hole four feet deep and three in diameter. Damon's shriveled corpse required no larger space. When Joseph stepped out of the makeshift grave, Laika was surprised to see Ezekiel Swain move to Damon's body and pick it up.

The round, moist face looked down into Damon's dried brown one. "You killed, buried me. In sand," the voice said. "Goes around . . . comes around."

Ezekiel stepped to the edge of the hole and dropped his arms so that the leathery body fell into it. "Go 'head," he said. "Cover up—he won't be back."

Joseph started to scrape the loose sand back into the hole, while Laika found the courage to approach Ezekiel Swain. The smell of urine and bile and other fluids was sharp and pungent, but she tried to ignore it. "But *you* came back," she said.

"Yeh." He nodded slowly. "But *I* . . . am *special*."

"In what way?"

"Divine. I hear Him. He talks me, tells me where is. Ordered me come, to Him." Ezekiel's shoulders rose and fell, and Laika interpreted it as a shrug. She thought she could hear the sound of moving waters with every motion. "When He ordered, had to go, go out, of grave."

"But were you dead—truly dead?"

Ezekiel pointed to a gaping tear in his throat. "Cut me here. . . ." His hand moved down to the wound from which the fluid had run. "And here. What *you* think? Grave took *juice,* out of me. Drained me dry."

Joseph, who had been listening, stopped digging and looked at Ezekiel. "What was your grave? Sand?"

Ezekiel nodded again. "Soft. White. Chalky. Juice ran out, sand took the rest. But he called. That night, He called. Had to answer."

"And you fed, didn't you?" asked Laika. "From the hiker. The old Indian. And the one on the horse, right?"

"Don't know. They there, when I needed. Divine provided. He calls. So loud and clear." The laugh broke through again. "I was going, faster than Jezebel. He calls her, too. But I hear better. She was in car, I still keep up, she go so slow."

Laika couldn't figure out if the crudeness of his con-

versation was due to impaired mental abilities or to the
fact that getting air to form words was physically difficult
for Ezekiel. She suspected the latter, if for no other reason
than that she refused to underestimate the abilities of this
creature.

"Were you after them," Laika said, "your sister and
Damon? Or were you after the Divine?"

"Both. They went, toward Divine." He pointed with a
finger like a sausage toward the grave that Joseph had
nearly filled in. "Wanted him. See him die. Now want
see Divine." Ezekiel raised his head and looked at the
sky to the north. "Divine. In a hole, too. Near church."

"The holy place you mentioned," Laika said. "What
can you tell us about it?"

"North. Way north. Days to walk, many days."

"Can you feel it enough to point to it? Exactly?"

Ezekiel closed his eyes, though tears still ran from
them. Then he raised his thick arm and pointed. Joseph
took a compass from his pocket and lined it up with the
direction indicated.

"Maybe three degrees west of north-northwest," Joseph said. "I can get an exact bearing from this location
online when we get to a phone."

Laika asked Ezekiel, "Is there anything else you can
tell us about the church? What kind of land is around it?"

Ezekiel kept his eyes closed. "Canyons. Many canyons.
High, narrow. Water close. Lotta water." He opened his
eyes, but he appeared still to be seeing what he was talking about. "And Divine. In the ground."

"Anything more?" asked Laika, but Ezekiel Swain
only shook his head. "I've got one more question. The
sand drawings . . . are you or the Divine responsible for
them in any way?"

Ezekiel looked at her, and she thought his ignorance
was unfeigned. "Sand drawings?"

"Giant designs in the sand—Indian designs."

He shook his head. "Don't know. Nothing."

"All right, then. It's time to get back into the car, in

the trunk. You cooperate with us, and we'll be with the Divine tomorrow, understand?''

Ezekiel looked at Laika and smiled, looking like the most repulsive Toby mug imaginable. ''I'll be . . . *good* boy. . . .''

Laika could only imagine.

Chapter 31

*T*hey came across a motel just a few miles north, near Round Rock. When they got out of the car, Laika went back to the trunk and leaned down to the crack. "We'll stay here until morning," she said. "Will you be all right?"

The voice came out as round and as wet as an echo in a well. "Much bigger . . . than a grave." Laika shuddered and headed for the office.

The motel had only six rooms, but they needed only three. Laika thought it wise to have Tony and Joseph room together. She didn't want Tony spending another night with Miriam and put her own room between the two men and the girl.

She told Miriam that they would be staying there that night and leaving the next morning at sunrise. Laika had asked the Indian desk clerk about public transportation when they'd checked in, and he'd said a bus passed through every morning around eleven, heading south to Gallup.

After Miriam was in her room, Tony and Joseph went into Laika's through their adjoining door. Joseph plugged his laptop into the phone jack and made the proper connections, while Laika tried to answer the questions that had been boiling within Tony for the last hour.

"The guy in the trunk—who the hell is he?"

"His name is Ezekiel Swain. And he seems to be the

239

wild west version of Peder Holberg. Just as Holberg was given certain knowledge by the prisoner, so the prisoner speaks to Swain.''

"Which is how we got the information about the mission that I'm trying to find," said Joseph, hitting the laptop's keys.

"Swain is, to all intents and purposes, dead," Laika said. "He's showing two wounds, either of which would have been fatal, but he still got up out of his grave and walked from somewhere on Route 40 up to Canyon de Chelly. He received an order from the prisoner, and by God, he obeyed it, dead or not. He even seems to have found a way to . . . revitalize himself by drawing fluids out of the living and using them to fuel himself.''

"Is he susceptible to injury now?" Tony asked.

"I'm not sure," said Laika. "Why?"

"Because according to the tracker, whatever sucked out Gary Chee's insides might have fallen down into the canyon on that rock slide and then walked—make that *shuffled*—up to the road again.''

"That wouldn't surprise me," said Joseph. "His body would have been lighter and less prone to damage when he fell in." Joseph shook his head and frowned. "I wonder what the hell leached it in the first place. It may have been the soil he was buried in. We'll never know what the content of that soil was, but it sure wasn't friendly.''

"So he got up and walked, because of a command from the prisoner," Tony said. "I wonder if it was the same kind of force that apported Peder Holberg several miles to become one with his sculpture.''

"It was certainly something we don't understand," Laika said.

"And," said Joseph, tapping the keys on his laptop, "we don't understand how it did what it did. It just drained every drop from that Damon character. And as for Swain, he just puffed up with Damon's fluids. Instant Jabba the Hut—just add water.''

"Is it processing yet?" Laika interrupted.

Joseph nodded. "I fed it the vector with a ten-mile margin of error to either side, the topography, and as good a description as we could get of the church. I asked for all Spanish missions within the parameters." The laptop beeped softly, and Joseph read the ghostly letters on the screen.

"We're in business," he said. "Only one match. The Mission of San Pedro. It's up in Utah, near Canyonlands National Park, out in the middle of nowhere . . . wait, I take it back, there was a ghost town called Hadley close by that nobody's lived in for over fifty years. Same with the mission—it went nonoperational back in 1939."

"That's pretty far north for a Spanish mission," Laika said.

"An outpost of progress, I assume," said Joseph. "It makes sense. Where more convenient for the Catholic Church to hide him than in one of their own deserted properties, whether it's in the middle of a city, like that abandoned office building, or the middle of the desert in an abandoned mission?"

"*Near* an abandoned mission," Laika said. "Swain said he was in a hole in the ground. How easy is this place to get to? Accessible by road?"

"It's not on any *major* route, but if you could get there sixty years ago, I'd guess you can still get there on dirt roads."

Tony shook his head. "Not necessarily. The desert takes back roads pretty quickly."

"But they had to get the prisoner in there," Laika said. "And they had to go in first and prepare the place for him. I'm betting there'll be roads, and if there are, Ezekiel Swain can get us there."

"What about the sand paintings?" Tony asked. "Is there any way they tie in?"

"Not that I can see," Laika said. "Swain seems to have no knowledge of them, or that's what he wants us to think. But it's been damned strange that wherever there's a killing there's a drawing not too far away."

"There wasn't one when Swain killed Damon," said Joseph.

"True. Or maybe there is one and we're just not aware of it yet." Laika sat down on the bed and put her hands on her knees. "There's another problem we've got, whether we find this prisoner or not. Ezekiel Swain."

"Mmm." Joseph nodded. "Jolly boy himself. Apparently he needs to keep drawing fluids from other people to keep functioning."

"And that makes him murderous," said Laika. "There's no way he can ever go free. But what do *we* do with him?"

"Could we turn him over to . . . some other agency?" suggested Tony. "Or the Company itself?" He shook his head and answered his own question. "I guess not, because Skye would find out about the prisoner. He'd know we didn't give him all the information we had."

" *'Oh, what a tangled web we weave,'* " quoted Joseph. "Not to be too brutal about it, but why don't we just cut off Swain's supply of sheep after he takes us to San Pedro? Put him in restraints and leave him that way until he dries up and blows away."

"If he does," Laika said. "He dried up in his grave, but he didn't blow away. It's probably our best bet, though— imprison him somewhere." She smiled. "Maybe where they're keeping the prisoner—if we free him."

"Let's not count our chickens," said Tony, but Laika could see that he was excited at the prospect. "I think there's another problem, though. What about Swain's sister, Jezebel? What if she talks?"

"Who's going to believe her?" Joseph said. " 'Oh officer, this guy killed my brother, but he came back from the dead and killed *him* and sucked all the blood and everything else wet from his body.' Okay, and where's the body? 'I don't know.' And where's your brother? 'I don't know, but he went to look for the Divine.' Yeah, right."

"Won't they listen to her story a little more carefully when Yazzie tries to bring us back to testify at her trial and can't find us?" Tony said.

"We'll be on confidential government business," said Laika. "Unavailable. Just like for real." She stood up and walked over to the laptop. "Before we get some sleep," she said, "download all the maps you can of the area. . . ."

Miriam Dominick removed the small pair of earphones and pulled away the tape that had held the contact microphone to the motel room wall. Though the conversation had been two rooms away, the door between Laika's room and Joseph and Tony's had been left open. The microphone was highly sensitive and had picked up the sound vibrations, converted them into an electronic signal that ran through a miniature amplifier which filtered out extraneous noise, and then entered Miriam's earphones. She had heard the entire conversation.

She placed the earphones, the mike, and the amplifier into the small false bottom of her backpack and slowly opened the door of her room. There was a phone booth across the parking lot, hidden from the rooms the agents were in by a cattle truck with high, slatted sides. Miriam ran to the phone, pushed in a quarter, and dialed.

She spoke quickly, telling everything that she had heard, including the general location of the Mission of San Pedro. The voice on the other end repeated the information, then said, "The final contingency goes into effect now. Everything will be ready. Understood?"

She hesitated for only a moment, then said, "Yes."

"God be with you."

"And also with you," she responded, but spoke into a dead phone. The other party had hung up.

She hurried back to her room and saw that the two doors down from hers were still closed, the curtains still drawn. She slipped into her room and closed the door behind her.

She lay on her bed for a long time, while the night came on and the sky grew dark. She did not sleep. She thought about Vincent Antonelli and Florence Kelly and Kevin Tompkins. She thought about what the Bible said and what she had been taught. She thought about her part in all this.

And then she thought about Vincent Antonelli some more.

Tony Luciano didn't sleep well, either. He wanted to see Miriam again, to be with her alone before they parted. He didn't even allow himself to think that it could be forever.

But with Joseph in the next bed, turning fitfully from time to time, Tony could not bring himself to get up and walk out of the room and knock on Miriam's door. The sense of disapproval he received from Joseph made him feel like the time he was a kid and his father had forbidden him to see a Jewish girl he liked. One Saturday night he had crawled out his bedroom window to see her, only to find his father waiting for him on the ground.

No, he couldn't see her tonight. He had jeopardized his career enough, not to mention jeopardizing Miriam by drawing her into things about which she should know nothing. Maybe they would get a chance in the morning to say goodbye, and he could tell her how he felt then.

Chapter 32

At 3 A.M., the approaching lights stirred Agent Daly from the semi-catatonic state of restfulness in which he was able to place himself. He called it sleeping with his eyes open, relaxing with all his senses alert.

"Hey," he said softly. "Lights." The man in the passenger seat and the other one in the back woke and cleared their throats. Daly patted the weapon in his lap and knew the Indian in the backseat would have his ready as well. The approaching vehicle was coming down the mountain, from the west. As it drew closer, Daly could hear the whining of springs, the thud of abused shocks. It sounded like some damned beat-to-shit pickup, not the operatives' car.

Finally it passed in front of them, and that's what it was, all right, a pickup with three or four Navajos sitting in the back, their arms resting on the sides, probably heading off to some early morning work on the other side of the mountain.

Daly eased back in his seat and let the weapon rest on his lap again. He knew they hadn't seen his Blazer, no matter how good their eyes were. Nobody would have seen it even in broad daylight, with the cover they had. And when somebody finally saw them, well, it would be just a little too late.

The Indians went back to sleep and Daly looked out into the dark. It was a clear night, and through the trees ahead he could see the lights of a few stars. Though he glanced at the rearview mirror, he couldn't see his face, only the darker shadow of his head against the blackness. It was just as well. He was sick and tired of looking at that long white scar running down the side of his face.

He had taken that wound for his country, the same way he had turned himself into a death machine, working in the gyms and in dojos and on the pistol ranges until his skill equaled his muscular bulk. He had been given the nickname "Popeye" for his thick arm muscles and had welcomed it. But other than his nickname and a salary that was far less than he thought it should be, the government hadn't given him much. And when he had been assigned to Richard Skye, he knew things were going to go downhill fast.

Skye was a bastard, best known for his expertise at getting his people into shit situations and his lack of skill at getting them out again. Or maybe it was that he just didn't give a damn, that agents were expendable as far as he was concerned.

Popeye Daly didn't intend to be expendable. Fortunately he had received what he considered "non-trust" assignments from Skye, shadowing agents Skye apparently didn't trust, and now Harris, Stein, and Luciano were on the list. He had crossed their path before, when they were sent—ironically enough, by Skye—to investigate the deaths of eleven men Daly had assassinated.

That mass assassination was his first job for his new employers, those to whom he owed his real allegiance, since they were the ones paying him real money. They had made their approach by opening a Swiss bank account in Daly's name in which they would be able to make deposits only, no withdrawals, and showed their good faith by depositing $100,000 just to get his attention. It was nearly two years' salary, and it worked.

Their goal was to find a certain prisoner being held captive by the Roman Catholic Church, and Daly was told that their efforts to find him would be highly illegal, but also highly profitable. When he asked them why they'd chosen him, they'd replied that they needed someone within the CIA, as they had received intelligence that a CIA functionary was also searching for this prisoner for his own ends.

When Daly asked why he should betray his government, the answer was simple: *for more money than you ever thought you would have—and for the freedom to spend it in perfect safety.* When they told him the name of the leader of their efforts, Daly knew they were telling the truth.

His activities with them had put an additional $250,000 into the Swiss bank account, and if the current mission went as planned, there would be another $2 million deposited within the week. Skye had unknowingly been a big help, assigning Daly to keep an eye on the three operatives, thus sending him right where the action was. His employers lost no time in putting him to work once he had informed them he was in the area.

Yeah, everything was going like a goddamned script he had written himself. And when his wacko employers finally caught up to whoever was being carted around in that lead coffin, Daly would make one final report back to Skye and disappear from the face of the earth, another agent lost in the line of duty. Daly could vanish and forget all about Skye and the CIA and the crazy assholes who were paying him all this money.

The truth was, he didn't like them any more than he liked Skye. He distrusted fanatics in general and religious fanatics in particular. He had no doubt that they would pay him, for they had been prompt when he had killed the eleven men in New York, but he didn't want their relationship to become anything more than business. To their credit, they hadn't tried to convert him. Maybe they thought him a lost cause, an already damned soldier that they might as well use.

Christ, he thought, they were so full of shit. There was no hell to be damned to, no heaven where their God would reward them when they died. There was only this world, here and now, and when you died, that was it. The only thing that made sense was to get as much money as you could and enjoy what life there was. That was how Daly was betting it. From everything he had ever seen in his life, that was how the odds lay.

He kept his eyes open, but got lost in his dreams again, dreams of disappearing forever.

The soft rap on the door woke Tony from his dream instantly. He scarcely had time to recall it before he was out of bed, and then it was lost forever to wakefulness.

It was Laika, and she called through the adjoining door that it was time to go. While Joseph was in the bathroom, Tony rapped quickly on the wall of Miriam's room. He wanted her to know that they were up and getting ready to leave. He wanted to be sure that he could say goodbye. When he was dressed, he went outside and was happy to see that her door was opening into the desert dawn.

She looked out, and her face showed a mixture of joy at seeing him and sorrow at the knowledge that it might be for the last time. He took a step toward her, and suddenly she was in his arms, and he was telling her that he would be back, that he loved her, and he would come back for her when everything was over. He scarcely knew what he was saying, and heard her voice, too, telling him that she loved him and she didn't want him to leave, but she understood, and she wanted him to come back, and they were both talking at once, and then they were kissing, and he wanted it to last forever.

But then he heard a door opening, and they broke the embrace, and as he turned he saw Laika coming out of her room with her overnight bag. She looked at the two of them and smiled and said good morning. "Is Kevin up?" she asked him.

"He'll be out any minute," Tony answered.

As if on cue, the door opened and Joseph stepped out,

taking in the scene with his usual air of cynical omniscience. "Everybody ready?" he said.

"Which way are you headed?" Miriam asked.

"North on 191," said Laika, "for as long as it—"

She broke off and stared at Miriam. Tony turned and looked, and saw that the girl's eyes were rolling up, and she had started trembling. Her entire body shook, and Tony grabbed her, afraid she would fall. "Miriam," he said. "*Miriam.*"

Her breath was coming in sharp, quick pants, as though she couldn't draw in any air, and her mouth was open wide with the effort. Her eyes showed only the whites, and her nostrils flared. Tony knew it wasn't epilepsy, but didn't know what else it *could* be.

All at once it stopped. Miriam slumped in his arms, her eyes closed, and he held her tightly. In another few seconds her eyelids fluttered, she took a few deep breaths, then opened her eyes and looked up at him. "Oh, my God," she whispered, as if still seeing the horror of whatever it was that had driven away her consciousness. Then she shook her head, slowly at first, then more rapidly. "No," she said, "no, please, you can't go . . . not that way. Oh God, no. . . ." Tears were in her eyes as she pleaded with him.

"What is it?" he asked. "What's wrong?"

"There are people. . . ." she said. "People waiting for you. They're going to . . . to *kill* you."

"What?" Laika said. "Who?"

"I don't know. But they're waiting for you . . . on that road. They *will* kill you."

"Not now," said Joseph, and Tony couldn't tell from his tone whether or not he was serious. "Now that we know they're waiting."

Miriam shook her head. "It doesn't matter. It doesn't matter that you know. There are too many of them. You can't go—please, please don't. You will die, please believe me."

"Okay," Joseph said. "I've had enough dreams and

visions. Dr. Kelly, Dr. Antonelli, I suggest we get in that car and drive. We can keep our eyes peeled, but I don't see the point in letting someone's so-called second sight dictate our procedure."

"What do you mean, 'so-called'?" Tony said. "We have seen proof over and over again of Miriam's . . . abilities."

"Wild talents, eh?" Joseph sneered.

"Call it what you like," Tony said, "but she saved our asses once from that rock slide when we picked her up that first night. She saw two of the drawings—got the designs dead on, *and* the two towers of Spider Rock. That's pattern *and* location. It wasn't on the news before she told us, so there's no way she could have known about it beforehand. And you saw how hard she was hit just now. I think it's just plain *stupid* to tempt fate by ignoring this." He turned to Laika. "Dr. Kelly, it's your call, but I feel very strongly about this."

Laika thought for a moment, then looked at Joseph. "What are our alternatives?"

"Oh, Christ," Joseph muttered. "We'd have to backtrack halfway to Gallup and cut across to 666, then go north through New Mexico—Jesus, that's another *state*."

"Thanks for the geography lesson," Laika said.

"Wait, there's another way," said Miriam, as though she had just remembered. "An oil road over the Chuska Mountains. It takes you out onto 666 near Shiprock, but just a few miles north you can get 64 West again."

"What do you mean, an oil road?" Laika asked.

"It's a road the oil company made over the mountain. A dirt road. The public doesn't know about it, though they've used it as a detour already. The Navajo use it all the time."

"And your crystal ball says it's safe?" Joseph asked.

"I don't know," Miriam said simply. "All I know is that the other way isn't. Please. . . ." She looked at Laika. "If you've ever believed that I have any ability to see these things, believe it now. I swear to you, your lives are at stake.''

Laika looked hard at Miriam for a good ten-count. "We'll change our route. . . .''

"Oh shit," Joseph said.

"We'll change our route on the condition that you come with us.''

"What?" Joseph said with mock delight. "Now we've got our own resident psychic? It's not bad enough we've got Tor Johnson in the trunk, now Shirley MacLaine's riding shotgun?''

"Dr. Tompkins," said Laika, "see if you can't suppress your ebullient sense of humor until later in the day.'' Then she turned back to Miriam. "I half believe that you do have some abilities, though I might not call them psychic. I believe in them enough to have us go out of our way and lose some time. But I want you to come with us to the other side of the mountain. If there are other consequences to our detour, I want you there to share in them. Do you understand me?''

Miriam understood all right. This Florence Kelly, she thought, is not someone who will die alone.

But when Miriam looked at Tony, she knew that she not only had to go with them, but wanted to. "If that's the only way I can convince you to change your route, then of course I'll go with you. I'm not afraid.''

It was a lie. She was afraid, just a little—not of death, but of damnation, if God thought what she had done was wrong.

"Let's go, then," Laika said, walking toward the car.

Joseph gestured to the rear. "What about Trunkboy?''

"I don't think we want to open that here," Laika said, then looked around to make sure no strangers were watching, and leaned down and spoke through the crack. "Are you all right?''

A deep grunt came from within.

"An eloquent affirmation," Joseph said.

They got into the car. Laika drove, with Joseph beside her. Their pistols, with extra clips, were under the seats. Tony sat in the back with Miriam, and had his weapon beneath the seat in front of him, next to Joseph's.

As they headed southeast on 12, Laika thought that she really might have gone crazy, believing in Miriam's powers enough to make her change their route like this. But if the girl was trying to steer them into some other danger, at least Laika had been smart enough to take her along with them. Whatever happened to them would happen to her, too.

And whatever happened, they were ready. They might not have been as alert without Miriam's warning, but now they were edgy. She saw Joseph's eyes dart constantly to the side of the road, ahead, then to the mirror of his lowered sun visor to check the road behind them. She found that she was doing the same thing, quick checks that she might have made automatically, only now she was more aware of them. And Tony, despite his proximity to Miriam, was still another pair of searching eyes. It would be a cagy opponent that could take them unexpectedly, at least on this road, with high, open desert all around them.

Just before they got to Lukachukai, Miriam told them to turn onto a wide dirt road that led toward the mountains. Once they were on it, they saw only one other vehicle, a pickup truck coming the other way. "Indians and locals," Miriam said. "They're the only ones who use this road, and even then not very often."

They found out why when they got to the mountains and entered the cover of the pines, where the road became steep and deeply rutted. It also narrowed severely so that passing another car would have meant holding your breath and hoping for the best. In places, the surface was like a washboard, the result of recent rainstorms. Tree roots jutted up through the dirt, helping to make the ride even more bone shaking.

At times Laika had to slow to a crawl to negotiate their

way around a combination of ruts, roots, and rocks, not to mention the frequent trenches on either side of the road. Still, they proceeded upward, reaching an altitude that closed Laika's ears, so that she had to yawn to open them.

"We're almost at the top," Miriam said. "Well over a mile up from the valley floor. It's a beautiful view when we cross over."

Laika assumed she meant crossing over the summit, but the phrase stayed uncomfortably in her mind as a harbinger of disaster. She sure as hell wasn't ready to cross over Jordan yet, beautiful view or not.

At last they reached the summit, and Laika saw that Miriam was right. The view was both breathtaking and terrifying, since there were no guard rails. If the tires slid too much on the loose earth, it seemed as though they would go over the edge and continue to fall until they hit the valley floor. She hugged the middle of the road as closely as possible.

She had her foot on the brake most of the time now, and the cold metallic taste in her mouth increased every time the Camry continued to slide of its own accord, though she was always able to control it in time. Her attention was focused on the road in front of her, and the next hazard she might encounter, so she wasn't immediately aware of the car that was suddenly behind them until she heard the first shots.

Chapter 33

*I*t was about time, Popeye Daly had thought, when the car had crossed his line of vision. He had started the engine as soon as he heard it approach, knowing full well that the operatives would never hear it over the sound of their own tires skidding and skittering on the loose dirt.

He had only had time for a brief glimpse of the car and passengers as they passed, but it was enough to positively ID the Camry, with Stein in the front seat and Luciano in the rear. "That's it," Daly barked, as he spun the Blazer out of cover and onto the road.

The Indians didn't have to be told twice. Their assault carbines were immediately punching shots at the Camry just ahead of them. They were aiming for the back window, but the condition of the road was throwing their shots high, wide, or low—anywhere, it seemed, but at their target. Bullets popped through the metal of the trunk, skimmed off the roof, and smacked into the bumper, but the glass remained intact.

The car speeded up, and Daly thought, Great, do my job for me and run off the goddamned road yourself. The brake lights lit up, and the Camry fishtailed around a turn, its rear wheels only inches from the edge of the precipice. "Just not built for this kind of driving," Daly whispered, as one of the Indians changed clips while the other continued to fire.

Daly's Blazer negotiated the turn tightly, and now the

car was only ten yards away, on a temporarily straight stretch. The Indians fired, and Daly was finally rewarded with the sight of the car's back window shattering to pieces. "*Yes*," he hissed. He could see only the head of the driver, probably Harris. Had they damaged the other two, or were they just staying low? Since they weren't returning fire, maybe they'd been hit.

He pressed them some more, racing forward until his reinforced steel bumper slammed against the rear of the sedan. It skidded toward the edge of the cliff, and Daly saw Harris jerk the wheel in that direction, then back, straightening out just in time.

But there was another turn ahead, and he knew that she was going too fast to make it. It swung to the right, with the mountain's face rising on their left. The Camry's wheels slipped on the dirt and stones, and its rear shot to the left, spinning the car so that its back left tire dropped solidly into a storm ditch, stopping the car as firmly as if a giant hand had grasped it.

Daly hit the brakes, stopping the Blazer just behind the car. "Box it in!" he shouted to the Indians, as he grabbed his weapon and pushed open the door.

They spread out as they ran toward the car, but Daly didn't expect much opposition, so he was surprised when three of the sedan's doors burst open at once and the operatives came out shooting.

The Indians were ready, but not for the kind of skill that Harris, Stein, and Luciano brought to the party. The bastards must have planned it all out. Daly was able to get off some rounds, but Luciano and Stein had targeted him, and fired directly at him a moment after he had pulled his trigger. He caught one round in the lung and another in the gut, and his shots went wild as he fell.

Harris had targeted the Indian on the right, who was hit with a string full in the chest and fell without firing a shot. Daly saw the second Indian manage to get a burst off before he was hit in the shoulder by Luciano, and his rifle went flying. Stein's fire took the Indian's legs out from under him, and he went down on his face in the dirt, where he tried in vain to push himself to his feet.

God damn it, Daly thought. A lifetime of wet work, a fortune in his grasp, and he had blown it by hiring bush leaguers. He was too used to working with pros, and he had depended on the undependable. It was one helluva time to make a fatal mistake.

But maybe, he thought in the few retrospective seconds he had left, maybe these three sonsabitches were just *better* than he was.

"He's dead," Laika called to Tony, who was advancing in a running crouch toward the man she had hit full in the chest. "Watch him," she added, gesturing with her gun barrel to the one who was trying to push himself to his feet. His chestnut skin and long black hair told her that he was an Indian. "Miriam okay?" she asked Tony.

"Yeah." He patted down the wounded Indian, found no other weapon, left the man in the dirt, and joined Laika and Joseph over the gutshot white man in the brown leather jacket.

The man was lying on his back, and Laika could see that he wouldn't live much longer. He had been hit in the chest and stomach, and blood was trickling from his mouth. His breath rasped in his throat.

"Hey," Joseph said, "I think I *know* this guy." Laika thought the man looked familiar herself, but couldn't place him. "Where have I seen you before?" Joseph asked. "Who are you, pal?"

The man shook his head slightly and coughed up some blood. "Nobody. Just . . . someone who wants . . . to disappear. . . ." A final breath wheezed out of him on a cough, and more blood poured from his mouth, as though something had been broken deep inside him. His eyes partly closed, and the pupils saw nothing.

"I've got it," Joseph said. "Langley."

"Company man?" asked Tony.

Laika nodded. "That's it. That's where I saw him. The

parking lot, the cafeteria, somewhere. I can picture him in a suit, Joseph."

Joseph was already going through the man's pockets. There was no wallet, just a thick money clip loaded with several thousand dollars' worth of twenties and fifties. "No ID at all." He ripped open the man's shirt. "He's got his share of scars, though. And Jesus, look at those arms. Strong bastard."

"Popeye," Tony said softly.

"What?" asked Joseph.

"It just clicked. I didn't recognize him at first, but I remember now. In the gym. The guy could out-benchpress anybody. Had arms like hams. They called him Popeye."

"What the hell was he trying to kill us for?" Joseph asked. "Skye?"

Laika looked back toward the car, her mind working out the betrayal. But then she saw the bullet holes in the trunk. "Oh, shit," she said. "Come on!" If Ezekiel Swain had been harmed by the bullets that had penetrated the metal, their search was going to be a lot tougher.

She sprinted to the car, yanked the keys out of the ignition, and jammed the trunk key in the keyhole. She had barely turned it before the lid flew up, startling her into a split second of immobility. It was all the time Ezekiel Swain needed.

The thing that leaped at her from the trunk was barely recognizable as Swain. It rather resembled the dried brown corpses Swain had left behind. But all Laika knew at the moment was that some nightmare was upon her. It bore her to the earth with the force of its attack, and she felt its brittle skin cling to her clothing like some ancient dry and crusted glue, reeking of things far worse than rendered horseflesh.

Swain's face was only inches away and coming closer to hers, its mouth open in a round "O" like the sucking beak of some deep-sea creature. Laika tried to push it away but discovered that she couldn't use her hands or arms, which seemed bonded to her attacker.

She closed her eyes to shut out the horror, but then the pain hit her. It was as if a thousand fiery hollow needles sank into her flesh, and she felt her life and humanity being drawn away, not from a single wound, but from an infinity of wounds, as though her entire body had been stripped of flesh and salt poured upon the exposed tissues.

But even worse was when the thing was pulled away.

Laika felt as though someone had reached into her mouth and down her throat all the way to her bowels, and then quickly yanked her inside out. It lasted for only a second, but a second was enough for the pounding agony to bludgeon her into the darkness.

Chapter 34

*L*aika awoke only seconds later, and all that remained was the memory of the pain. She could still feel it, but it was physically gone from her.

Tony and Joseph were holding the thing that had been Ezekiel Swain. Each had hold of a wrist and stretched it apart so that it could not reach him with its body. It looked as if they were holding a rabid tiger, so furiously did Swain twist his leathery torso and whip his legs back and forth. His head writhed and jerked, and from his mouth there came a high-pitched squeal again, like the scream of a cat. His frenzy to feed had taken him beyond speech.

"The sonofabitch," said Tony, struggling to get the words out and hold the fury, "is *hungry.* . . ."

That had to be it. Laika had nearly been *fed* upon, and unless Swain feasted immediately on the diet of blood and fluids he had grown to need, he would prove too strong for her colleagues. Laika quickly pointed to the dead Indian. Perhaps his gaping chest wound would make it easier for Swain to feast.

Tony and Joseph staggered over to the dead man, then fell to their knees, dragging Swain down with them, and positioning him atop the body. But the attempt was futile. Swain screamed louder and higher, and struggled so desperately to avoid contact with the corpse that he seemed almost to levitate in his efforts. Apparently, Laika thought, the meat had to be alive.

Then she looked at the wounded Indian, the one shot in the shoulder and the leg. He had given up trying to get to his feet and now was just lying on the road. The earth had turned dark from the blood running out from him, and she thought that, depending on whether or not the wound in his shoulder had punctured his lung, he might not live until medical help arrived, if it ever did. She and her fellow operatives were certainly not going to call for it. The Indian had tried to kill them.

On the other side was her knowledge of what had been done to her by Ezekiel Swain. It was not so much the death itself as the sheer horror of it, and she would have to stand there and watch this man experience it.

Ezekiel Swain shrieked again and thrashed about as Tony and Joseph managed to get to their feet. They looked at her as if begging to be told what to do, and that look reminded her that she was the leader, and there was a job to be done.

They were near the end of their long search. Resolve crept into her again. Almost without thinking, she shot a finger at the wounded Indian and gave the two men a look that would allow no challenge.

She thought that they feared for their own lives as much as they feared disobeying her order. They stumbled with their ferocious burden to where the Indian lay. The wounded man rolled over on his side to see what was approaching him, and when he did, he yelled and threw up his good arm, collapsing once again.

"Are you *sure?*" Joseph cried, a mixture of frustration and pity wrenching his face.

"*Do it!*" Laika shouted back. Tony moved first, thrusting Ezekiel Swain down toward the Indian, and Joseph, running the risk of being attacked himself if he did not let go, did the same.

Swain fell upon the unfortunate Indian with a sound like the cry of a panther. His body seemed to mold itself to the Indian's, trunk, legs, and arms slapping together as if drawn magnetically. Even his mouth came down upon the Indian's in a blasphemous kiss, the kiss that Laika would have suffered had her team not saved her.

The sight of it feeding, and the memory of what it had done to her, brought up the little that she had remaining in her stomach. It tasted sour and bitter, of bile and acid, and when she thought that those exact fluids were even now being taken from Swain's victim, she continued to heave until she could banish the thought from her mind.

"Are you okay?" asked Tony, as he put a hand on her shoulder.

She shook it off and straightened up. "Yes. I'm fine." She looked at Ezekiel Swain atop the Indian, telling herself that she would not be sick again, that she could look at this thing and take it.

The Indian looked dead. His body size was only half what it had been, and Swain's bulk was increasing in direct proportion to the dead man's shrinking. Swain seemed contented now, like a baby sucking from its mother's breast. In another minute he would be filled, his thirst slaked. Then other difficult decisions would have to be made.

Laika looked toward the car and saw the form of Miriam Dominick sitting in the backseat. Then Laika looked at Tony with hard eyes. "And how are *you*?"

He knew what she meant. He looked embarrassed, angry at himself, and as betrayed as all of them felt. Joseph's face was solemn as he listened, with no trace of smugness.

"No matter who that agent was working for," Laika said, "one thing's for sure. A trap was set for us that was going to work only if we took this road. And there was only one person responsible for us taking it. It was a set-up, and I was fooled as easily as you were, Tony."

"From the very start . . . the rock slide," said Joseph softly. "It was all set up to make us believe in her. And whoever did the drawings—she was in on it with them. She knew beforehand what and where."

Laika looked at Joseph apologetically. "And you were the only one who saw the truth."

"No," said Joseph, looking as contrite as she'd ever seen him. "You saw the truth whether you realized it or not, because you had her come with us. No matter what else I said, I *believed* in her. I believed in her even more than you did, but I wouldn't let myself say it." He shook his head. "What a sucker. It was all so obvious, and I didn't see it—because I didn't *want* to." He smiled. "If you want to believe, you won't let facts and logic stand in the way, and I didn't, God damn it. And I almost got us all killed. I'm the skeptic, and I didn't do my job."

Laika looked at the car. "I'm going to do mine," she said. "I'm going to find out who the hell is behind this, and if it's Skye, I'll go to Langley and I'll kill the bastard with my bare hands."

She stormed toward the car, and Tony and Joseph followed. Tony felt as though he were being ripped apart. He—all of them—had been betrayed, led to their intended deaths by the woman he thought he had loved, the woman whose lies would have sent him to his death, had Laika not, he now realized, called her bluff. He had loved her, and now he might have to be a party to her death.

"All right," he heard Laika bark, as she pulled open the door on Miriam's side, "who the hell are you with, and what—" Her words stopped in a sudden hitch of breath. In another second Tony was at her side, looking into the backseat.

Miriam was sitting up, but her face had gone white and was damp with sweat. The seat back all around her was red with blood.

"A round went through the car," Joseph said, moving past Laika and Tony and easing Miriam onto her side. A heavy blood trail followed as her body shifted. There was no exit wound. The bullet, spent by its passage through the trunk lid and the backseat, had lodged in her body.

Joseph moved her gently so that he could see the entrance wound in her back. He winced and shook his head. Tony knew the bullet would have been deformed by its passage through the metal. By the time it struck her, it had probably been as large as a silver dollar.

Miriam was breathing hard and seemed to be trying to talk. Tony knelt on the ground by the open door and put his face close to hers. "I'm . . . sorry," she said slowly. "I love you. I came . . . with you. Wanted to . . . die with you."

"You came," Laika said coldly, "because it would have given your game away if you hadn't."

"Shut *up!*" Tony said, opening his eyes wide in the hopes that no tears would come.

"No . . ." Miriam said. "She's right . . . I had to come."

"Who are you with?" Laika asked.

Miriam closed her eyes, then opened them again. "Good people," she said, looking past Tony at Laika.

"And what do these good people know?"

"Everything."

"They know where we're heading?"

Miriam nodded slightly. "The mission." Her face twisted with sudden pain, and she looked back at Tony. "Take my cross," she said to him, and her gaze moved downward to indicate the gold cross that hung on the chain from her neck.

He reached behind her head, at the soft curls on the back of her neck, and undid the clasp. Then he held the cross and the chain in his hand. "Keep it," she said. "Remember me . . . I didn't know—"

She paused, her eyes fixed on his face. It took a long moment for Tony to realize that she wasn't going to continue.

He didn't move when he felt Laika's hand on his shoulder. "We have to get on our way," she said, but he remained on his knees, looking into the open eyes of her dead face. "Come on, Tony. We don't have the time for this."

He whirled around and looked up at her. "Leave me alone," he said. "Will you just *leave me alone?*"

"For what, Tony? To grieve? If you're planning to

grieve for her, just remember one thing—until I said that she had to come with us, she was ready to say goodbye to you this morning. She was going to stand there and watch you drive away up the mountain. You just think about that in your grief.'' Laika turned away from him. ''Come on, Joseph, we've got some cleaning up to do.''

Tony stood up, wiped the tears from his eyes, and slipped the cross and its chain into his pocket. Laika was right: Miriam had betrayed him. He didn't want to believe it, but he had to, and now he had to help his team.

Chapter 35

*E*zekiel Swain was sitting on the road next to the wizened corpse of the Indian from whom he had fed. A satisfied smile bubbled from his round face.

Laika choked down her revulsion. "You're through with this?"

Swain made a deep rumble in his throat. "Hit the spot."

Laika took in the situation at a glance. They had four bodies and a vehicle to get rid of, and it looked as though Tony was ready to help again. The Blazer was a more sound choice for mountain and desert driving, which made the Camry expendable.

The three of them extricated the car from the ditch and removed their belongings, then put the corpses of their three attackers into the car with Miriam's body. Laika offered Tony the option of burying the woman, but he declined. "No time for that," he said shortly.

They pushed the car over the cliff at a place where the brush was heavy, and listened as it continued tumbling downward, until the sound of a massive crunch indicated that it had fetched up against several trees. There was no sign of it from where they stood. It might be months, even years, before it was found.

Then they covered up the blood on the road by kicking loose dirt over it. As they were finishing, Joseph said to Laika, "We just have one problem with the new wheels.

There's no trunk. So where does Mr. Gobble ride?''

"With us," Laika said, glancing with distaste at the oily, corpulent body and edematous limbs of Ezekiel Swain. "He is, like it or not, our guide on this great adventure."

"Might be a good idea to keep him tied up."

"I was planning on it."

"Think he'll mind?"

"He didn't mind riding in the trunk."

"Are you sure?" Joseph said. "He didn't seem too happy when he popped out this morning." Laika recalled the pain of the attack, and stopped moving for a moment. "Sorry. What was it like?"

"I've heard the worst possible pain for a man is a kidney stone," said Laika. "You ever have one?"

"Once."

"Multiply it by a hundred, and then add sheer terror."

"Ouch." Joseph nodded toward Tony, who was putting their things in the Blazer. "You think he's okay?"

"No, I don't. I think he can function as well as ever, but *okay?* Would *you* be?"

He answered with another question. "Who the hell are these 'good people' she was talking about? Was she working for Skye?"

"I don't trust Skye. I think he might have been behind the surveillance that was placed on us in New York, and I think he might have had something to do with that mass assassination. Kyle McAndrews, the sole survivor, certainly thought so.

"Still, I don't see how Skye could be behind *this.* Why would he want us dead? And those sand drawings, however they were done, had to be beyond what he could have ordered up. A hoax of that magnitude? You can run an operation like he's doing with the three of us fairly quietly, but somebody would start asking questions if Skye was requisitioning helicopters—*if* that's how it was done."

"What if somebody above Skye is behind it?" Joseph

suggested. "That at least would account for Popeye's involvement."

She shrugged. "Or it could just be that some outside party was paying Popeye more money. Agents have turned before." She looked around at the ground, and saw no trace remaining of the battle or the deaths, except for a sisal cowboy hat that had fallen from one of the Indians' heads. She picked it up and dusted it off. "Time to talk to Swain."

Ezekiel Swain, now replenished, was amenable to traveling in restraints, once he realized that it was the only way the operatives would take him to the Divine. "Symbiosis," he said, and the heavy word sounded like a bass section of a choir.

"Or cooperation," said Laika. "Call it whatever you like." She placed the hat on his head. It was much too small, but at least it covered part of his face. "You mind wearing this? In case anybody in a passing car looks over. You, uh, look a little. . . ."

"Dead?"

"Yeah."

Joseph sat in the back seat with Swain, who was bound with strong nylon cords. He sat on the passenger side, since Laika didn't want him behind the driver. They kept the windows open to reduce the stench that came from Swain's body, but even so, Joseph was pressed all the way over against the door.

As they slowly made their way down the mountain, Swain seemed to enjoy the predicament, and grinned at Joseph. "Sorry," he said. "Forgot use deodorant, this morning. . . ." Then he gave a low, gurgling laugh.

"Jesus," said Joseph. "This is like being in *Weekend at Bernie's* with Sam Kinison in the title role."

"*Liked* that movie," Swain said. "Sequel sucked."

At the bottom of the mountain, they came out into the open again, a land of sage and rocks. They went north on 666 toward Shiprock, passing the rock formation that had given the town its name, but turned left on Route 64, went back into Arizona, and headed northwest. They crossed the Utah border near Mexican Water, and traveled due north.

"We're going to start needing some guidance right about now," said Joseph, after they had passed the town of Monticello. "You have any feelings about which way we should go?" he asked Ezekiel Swain, as he closed up his laptop.

The big head nodded. "Keep going. I'll tell. When."

A half hour later, they turned at Swain's direction onto an unmarked dirt road that led straight into the desert. After less than a mile, it started to descend, winding its way down among constantly rising canyon walls, twisting and turning until the ops seemed to have no idea in what direction they were headed.

Several other roads crossed theirs, but seemed to go nowhere in particular, like the one they were on. "Are you sure this is right?" Laika asked, glancing at Swain in the mirror.

"Right," he grunted, and smiled. "Close."

As they turned a corner and momentarily emerged from a high-sided canyon, they were surprised to see, in the sudden distance across the rims of several canyons, a great manmade wall. "What the hell is that?" Laika asked.

Joseph opened his laptop and consulted some maps he had downloaded. "It must be the dam that created Dead Horse Reservoir," he said. "Yum. Wouldn't you love to drink out of *that*?"

"No," said Swain, then smiled. "But, Dead *Man* Reservoir...."

"Nice," Joseph said.

They descended once again into a canyon, and from then on drove in shadow, for the rock walls on either side were so steep that the sun's rays penetrated them only briefly, if at all. After what seemed like several more miles, they came to the narrowest canyon they had seen. A closed gate of rusted metal spanned its width.

Laika and Tony got out and examined it. There was no lock, and it swung open easily enough. "It's been opened recently," Tony said. "See here, where the rust flaked off?"

They got back in the vehicle and drove through the gate. The road wound through more canyons, and then went uphill slightly. "Almost," said Swain. "Almost here. . . ."

At last the mission lay before them. They had come around a sharp corner of sandstone wall and saw it fifty yards ahead, up a slight incline. "That's it," Joseph said, with such awed certainty that Laika was sure it was the mission he had seen in his dream.

The building was not large, only forty feet wide. It appeared to be constructed of adobe from which the whitewash had long ago peeled. Despite the mission's small size, its facade was imposing. It was two stories high, and surmounted by an open hump of a bell tower whose bell had fled it long before. Two smaller humps stood on either side of the roof line. A second-story balcony with a wooden railing covered a dirt-floored portico, and a single door stood in the center of the front.

There were several acres of open space around the building, and arid patches of ground with rotted fence posts dividing them. Someone had once tried to farm here, without much luck, Laika thought.

Though no occupants were visible, they could see a large panel truck and a weathered Jeep parked nearby. "Looks like we beat the competition. And I don't think they're going to slip him out as easily this time," said Laika, "unless there's another way out of here down that canyon." She pointed to a narrow opening in the walls of sandstone to the right of the mission.

Then she turned to Joseph. "Is this what you saw in your dream?"

He nodded, and a wheezing laugh came from Ezekiel Swain. "Be damned. You got, too. We . . . *brothers.*"

Laika could tell Joseph was disturbed when he didn't give Swain a flip reply.

She stopped the car. "Take your weapons," she said, "and let's hope we don't need them."

"Amen to that," said Tony. "I mean, there are probably priests in there."

Laika turned to Swain. "You stay here—you'll see the Divine soon."

Swain grinned, and fluid dripped onto his lap. "Goodie. Professional, armed force. You can, free him."

"We have to find him first," Laika said, opening her door.

The three operatives got out and listened, but heard nothing. Slowly they walked toward the building. They were only a few feet from the front door when it opened. They brought up their guns quickly, pointing them at the dark opening, but lowered the muzzles slightly as they saw two men dressed in black clerical garb come through the door, their empty hands clasped together in front of them in an attitude of prayer, beatific smiles on their faces.

"Greetings, sister, greetings, brothers," said one of the men. "Welcome to the Mission of San Pedro. Please, put down your weapons. You have no need of them here."

"I'm not so sure of that, Father," said Laika. "We're the good guys, but there are some bad ones coming. You may need some help to . . . protect your prisoner."

She was expecting a look of surprise, but didn't get it. The men just continued to smile. "That won't be necessary," one said.

"Look, Father, you don't understand—"

"No, my child—*you* don't understand. But perhaps if you look above, wisdom will come to you."

Laika looked up slowly. There on the balcony were half a dozen armed men wearing fatigues. They were holding cutting edge assault rifles whose muzzles were glaring down at Laika and her team.

She kept her eyes on the shooters, but raised her gun muzzle just enough to cover again the priests standing in the doorway. "I think the bad guys have arrived, after all," she said.

"That depends on your point of view." said the man. "We consider ourselves to be *very* good guys. The best, in fact. The ones truly sent by God."

"Be that as it may, I believe we're in a bit of a Mexican standoff here."

"How do you mean?"

"If the boys upstairs fire at us, we fire at you."

"That won't matter," said the man. "We'd like to take you alive, but if you won't put down your guns, we'll be happy to die for our cause, and our brothers upstairs know it. So either you drop them now, or you will be shot. Your killing us doesn't enter into it at all."

Laika had been in enough situations to recognize a bluff, but these men weren't bluffing. They could try to spray the armed men above, but their position was bad. She and Tony and Joseph would be cut down before they could even aim. They had nothing to lose by surrendering. If these people had wanted them dead, they'd have killed them already.

"All right," she said to the others, "set them down." She crouched and put her weapon on the ground. The others did the same.

"Ah, see," said the fake priest, taking off his robe to reveal fatigues beneath. He was the same man who had been in the front seat of the Buick at Spider Rock. David, Miriam's lover, was the man at his side. "You *have* learned wisdom. Of a sort. But the fear of the Lord is the beginning of *real* wisdom, to add a single word to the psalmist."

"Well," said Joseph, who had recovered his aplomb, "though you're not a man of the cloth, you sure talk the talk, Father Flotsky."

The man lost his smile. "My name is Commander John Bowman. And this is Captain David Richardson. And don't you dare criticize our faith or our God. Especially not you, Jew." Two more armed men came from inside the mission and handed rifles to the two impostors, then picked up the operatives' weapons. "Now, let's get your companion from inside the car," Bowman said, gesturing with the muzzle of his gun. "And tell him that we will cut him to pieces if he doesn't do as we say."

They walked to the car, and Laika opened the door for Ezekiel Swain. "We have to go with these men," she said.

"Is he a man or a demon?" asked Richardson, staring at Swain. Laika thought his question was serious.

"He's been sick recently," Joseph said.

"Why is he tied up?" asked Bowman.

"He has a tendency to get violent," said Laika.

Swain got out of the car, his constantly weeping eyes looking at Bowman and Richardson from deep within the fleshy pouches that surrounded them. "Hiya. Godboys," he said. Before a reddening Bowman could reply, he added, "Where's Divine?"

"Yes, you'd be looking for Him, wouldn't you? Just the type the enemy would use." Bowman swung his rifle in the direction of the mission. *"Get moving."*

Bowman and Richardson took Swain and the operatives through the unimpressive sanctuary of the mission, in which nearly two dozen cadre members were gathered, and back into a warren of smaller rooms. A guard was standing outside a heavy wooden door, which he opened to reveal a rickety wooden stairway leading down.

At the bottom was a windowless cellar, empty except for some mounds of something under a canvas tarpaulin at the far end, and several burlap mattresses thrown on the floor. The burlap seemed to be stuffed with dried grass, and a white-haired priest was sitting on one of them, his legs stretched out in front of him on the dirt floor. A dank smell pervaded the low-ceilinged chamber.

"I hope you'll be quite comfortable here. It hasn't killed the old papist yet, anyway," said Bowman. "Of course, *Father* Alexander has only been here a few hours." The man made a mockery of the title.

"Papists, Jews," said Joseph. "Anybody you do like?"

"Those who serve the Lord," said Bowman, "and walk in his ways."

"Lets *me* out," said Swain, with a gurgle that made Bowman shudder. "Where's Divine?"

"Don't worry, he's quite safe. For now. We have all of you to thank for locating the enemy for us. You've done us a great service. Just one question, however. Where is Miriam Dominick? Captain Richardson is particularly anxious to know."

Tony spoke before Laika could. "She's dead. Your men killed her."

Richardson turned pale, and looked at Tony with wide eyes. *"Our men?"* said Bowman.

"The ones who tried to shoot us, run us off the road," Laika explained. "The ones Miriam Dominick set us up for. Only she came along with us. I guess that wasn't in the plan."

"You killed her," Richardson said to Tony. "You filthy papist, you found out who she was and you killed her!" He would have attacked Tony if Bowman had not held him back.

"No," Tony said bitterly, shaking his head. "We just had sex."

"Captain!" Bowman barked, as Richardson, trembling in fury, raised his weapon and pointed it at Tony. "You will lower that weapon. The orders were that these people were to be kept alive if they got here, and they did." Then he turned to Laika. "And where are 'our people' who tried to . . . delay you?"

"I wouldn't expect them anytime soon," said Laika coldly.

Bowman took Richardson by the arm and guided him back up the stairs, keeping an eye and his gun muzzle trained on the ops as he went. The heavy door at the top closed behind them, and they were alone with the old priest.

Father Alexander had gotten to his feet. He looked at

Laika, Joseph, and Tony curiously, and at Ezekiel Swain with seeming dread. At last he spoke. "You're the ones, aren't you? The ones from the government?"

"Yes," Laika said. "The National Science Foundation. . . ."

She trailed off as the priest waved a hand and smiled knowingly. "No, no . . . not that branch of the government. I know, you see. I know that you've been looking for him, I know about New York, I know . . . more than I really care to." He shook his head. "We might have been able to reason with you, but with these people . . . I don't know. We've kept him safe all these centuries, but now fools have taken possession of him—yes, fools."

Laika wanted to keep him talking. "When did they arrive?"

He pressed his lips together as he struggled to control his emotions. "At dawn. They burst in here like commandos, like they were taking an armed fort. We weren't ready, we had no idea that anyone would determine his whereabouts so quickly. Three fine young men, good and brave priests, tried to stop them, but they shot them down." Father Alexander shuffled over to the covered shapes, crouched down, and drew back the tarpaulin.

Beneath it were three dead men lying on their backs. Their bodies, clad in black cassocks, were riddled with bullets. Even their faces had been shot away. "They had no weapons," the priest said. "But they shot them down anyway."

"They didn't try to kill you?" Laika said, wondering how Father Alexander had survived, and wondering if he had been planted by their enemies. They had proved quite adept at infiltration.

"No. I . . . ." He pulled the tarpaulin back up over the dead men, as though he could not admit it in their presence. "I hid when I heard the gunfire. When they found me, they knew that I was no threat to them. I think I amused them." His voice choked at the memory of his cowardice. "I should have died with them," he said.

"They'll kill me eventually. After they make me watch their triumph."

"Who are they anyway, Father?" Tony asked. "Cultists? Satanists?"

The priest looked at him oddly. "Satanists? *Unwittingly* guided by Satan, perhaps, but why would *you* think they were Satanists?"

"They referred to the prisoner as the enemy. How could you refer to such a person that way unless you were . . . on the other side?"

"My son," Father Alexander said gently, "who do you think this prisoner is?"

"Well—" Tony paused for a moment. "From all we've been able to gather . . . we thought he might be Christ, Father. Jesus himself."

The old priest's smile was filled with sympathy. It was the look of a father about to tell his growing son the truth about Santa Claus. "No, my son. It is not Christ who is the prisoner. It is quite the opposite."

Joseph's jaw dropped as he remembered what the dying Scot, the last of the Knights Templar, had tried to tell them.

"McAndrews," he said. "Remember McAndrews's last words?"

Laika nodded, her face lined with thought. "Yes—*andra*, or *anda* . . . you thought it referred to Johann Andrea, a Rosicrucian connection."

"I was wrong. Now I know what he was trying to say. He was telling us who the prisoner was. He was *warning* us. Against the greatest enemy of all to the Christian faith. He wasn't saying 'andra,' he was trying to say something else. Isn't that right, Father?"

The priest nodded. "The greatest enemy indeed, my son. The Antichrist himself."

" 'Antichrist,' " Joseph repeated. "That's what McAndrews would have said, if he'd had the strength."

"Is it true, Father?" asked Tony, sounding shocked and lost. "Is it the Antichrist?"

But before the priest could answer, Ezekiel Swain started laughing a laugh that sounded like lava bubbling. "Was *right*, was *right*. . . ." He gave a deep sigh that exuded not only air, but a spray of yellow liquid that the earthen floor soaked up. "My . . . *main* . . . man."

Father Alexander crossed himself. "God save us from all evil things," he said.

"Father, we've come a long way," Joseph said, "and we've got a lot of questions. I don't know how likely we are to get out of this alive, so I'd really appreciate it if you could tell us as much as you can."

The old priest nodded. "I think we may all die today. I've been sworn to silence, but I suspect even the Holy Father would not disapprove of my telling you the story to assuage your curiosity, and perhaps comfort your souls."

Chapter 36

*I*t began in the seventh century (Father Alexander said). The creature can be first traced to a small village at the foot of the Apennines. A troop of soldiers came through the village one day to find every resident dead. It appeared as though they had slaughtered each other. Even the children and the babies in their cradles had been killed. Indeed, some of the young children had died clutching bloody knives and axes, as though they had been among the attackers. As far as the soldiers could make out, half the population had risen up against the other half, and then they'd all turned on each other, fighting until they were all dead.

Only one man was left alive. He was sitting on a bench in the middle of town, smiling at the soldiers. When they asked him if he'd witnessed the slaughter, he said that he'd not only witnessed it, he'd been the cause of it. When they asked him how, he replied that he'd simply told the townspeople to begin killing each other, and half of them had responded in such a savage manner that the other half had had little opportunity to defend themselves.

The soldiers thought the man was mad. But then he began to tell them of the results of various crimes that they had come upon as they'd carried out their duties in the previous few years—unexplained deaths, and murders in which a man might have killed all the members of his family, and then turned his weapon on himself—and numerous rapes that had begotten multiple progeny—twins and triplets to double and triple the victims' shame.

The women and survivors had described the man who had been the rapist or the murderer, or in the vicinity when the uncanny events had occurred. He was a tall man, well formed and with light brown hair and beard. They all said that his face was handsome, even radiant, and his eyes were of a piercing blue. And that was the precise description of the man who had confessed his crimes to the soldiers.

Naturally they took him into custody, but when they bound his arms behind him, he somehow burst his bonds, and said that he would go with them not because he was forced to, but because it pleased him to do so. He had grown weary of killing in secret, he said. Perhaps confession would keep him amused.

They rode to a larger town and took the man before a magistrate. The man confessed to a multitude of crimes and then said that he did not repent of any of them, and intended to continue in such a manner as he had done. A boy was brought in who had survived the mass murder of his family. His father had killed himself after slaying his wife, his own mother, and four of his children. The boy identified the man as a traveler who had eaten supper with them that night. He said the man had told his father to take up a carving knife and kill everyone in the room, and then himself. The boy swore that the man was the devil incarnate, for his father had done precisely what he was told, with the exception of killing the boy, who had run outside and hidden.

That was enough for the magistrate. He ordered the man to be hanged for his crimes, such sentence to be carried out immediately. But the man ordered the magistrate to smash his own face on the table in front of him, and the magistrate did it, breaking his nose in the process. The man laughed and said that they had better hang him quick, or else he would order all the men in the room to sodomize the magistrate in the town square.

Then the soldiers tried to take the man to the gallows on the outskirts of town, but he commanded them to loose him, and they obeyed. He said that he would go to be hanged because it amused him, but he wished for everyone in the town to come along to watch him die.

Quite a procession followed him and the soldiers to the gallows. The man mounted the platform, walked up to the rope, put it around his own neck, and ordered one of the soldiers to open the trap. The soldier did, and the man dropped through. There he swung at the end of the rope, smiling, his hands spread as if he were proud of his achievement.

Several soldiers leapt at his body, as was the custom of the time, and dangled from his legs, adding extra weight to the man's to choke him. But he did not choke, and he did not die. With a laugh, he fell to the ground, while the rope, its noose still intact, dangled above him.

By this time, some of the onlookers were saying that the man was a demon, and the magistrate and soldiers were starting to agree with them. Nevertheless, if they could not execute him in one way, they would execute him in another. The captain in charge of the soldiers offered to sever the man's head from his body, for that was known to be an effective way to destroy those sent from Satan.

The man consented, and lay his head upon a wide stump, but when the captain swung his sword down across the man's neck, the blade went right through the man's flesh and thudded against the trunk. The man got up, totally unharmed.

At last people began to cry out, "Burn him!" and that seemed like a good idea, so they put together a great pile of wood, and spread pitch all over it, and the soldiers tied the man to a post in the center. As soon as they lit the fire, the man brought his arms forward. They were untied. And he merely stood there, unbound, as the flames rose about him and burned off his clothing. But neither his flesh nor his hair caught on fire. Everyone could hear his laughter over the crackle of the flames.

Then he pointed to the magistrate and said, *"Vieni,"* Come. The magistrate started walking toward the flames. Though the soldiers tried to stop him, he threw them off like a man possessed. He walked directly and firmly to the fire, and then into it, so that his clothing caught on fire. The crowd watched in horror as the magistrate's hair and flesh began to burn, and he started to scream, but the man beside him told him to be silent, and he was. He stood there until he could stand no more, and collapsed into the leaping flames.

Then the man stepped out. He was naked, for all his clothing had been burned away, and the records tell that he was . . . priapic to a great degree, causing women to scream at the sight of him, yet so beatific was his expression that they were drawn to him at the same time.

A priest who had been watching from the crowd declared him to be the Antichrist, and demanded in the name of Christ that he accompany him to Rome to see the Holy Father and stand before his judgment. The man agreed, saying that he would like to see this pope he had heard so much about. He was given some clothing, and put into a coach, and the priest and the soldiers accompanied him to Rome.

There is no record of his having caused any trouble on the way. On the contrary, he spoke often with the priest, asking him about the Holy Church and the Holy Father, and the priest told him what he could, at once fascinated and repelled by this creature.

At last they arrived in Rome and were taken to an audience with the Holy Father and all his cardinals, an audience kept secret from the populace. Having been informed of all that had happened, the Holy Father questioned the man, but the man made no answer other than to laugh at the Holy Father and tell him that Christ's kingdom would vanish from the world and be replaced by his own, that murder and terror and fear would reign on the earth, for he was impervious to harm.

The Holy Father then feared that the end times might be near, and, before those who were present, declared the creature to be the Antichrist. But he ordered that his existence should be kept secret until such time as he or his successors thought it best to reveal it. Then he ordered that the creature be submitted to all manner of torture and peril, to see if there might be any that would end its foul existence. The Antichrist cooperated wholeheartedly, telling the Holy Father that once he saw that he could not be harmed, the Holy Father could then step down or be carried dead from his throne, whichever he chose, leaving it to the Antichrist.

They tried in all ways possible to destroy the Antichrist, but only when they immersed him in a vat of molten lead was there any marked lessening of his strength. Priests entrusted with the Antichrist often felt ill in his presence, as though they might suddenly go mad, and it was only at the Antichrist's whim that they did not.

But when his body was lowered into the molten metal, they all felt as though a great weight had been lifted from their souls. The feeling lasted until the Antichrist was raised from the lead, and the metal dripped off him. He seemed changed, as well, as though he were actually frightened, and ordered them to remove his body from where it dangled in chains over the vat.

The attending priests found that odd, for before, when he had wanted to be free of his bonds, he'd simply passed through them. But now, if he passed through the chains, he would fall again into the lead, and they sensed with certainty that another immersion was the last thing he wanted.

Several of the priests hastened to follow his orders, but one of them, a strong-minded soul named Father Ignatius, pushed them away and turned the wheel that lowered the Antichrist back into the lead. He screamed at Father Ignatius, but the bold priest continued, even as several of the others actually attacked him to make him stop.

But those attacks ceased once the Antichrist sank beneath the surface of hot lead. It was as if the other priests had come to their senses, and they apologized to Ignatius for trying to stop him. Then they knew that lead could contain the Antichrist's power.

This they reported to the Holy Father, who ordered that a leaden cell be made, and a lead casket in which the Antichrist might be transported. Ever since, the Antichrist has been imprisoned in lead under the deepest security. But his strength has grown over the centuries, and there are times when his mind can burst through its leaden prison and touch those who, for unknown reasons, are particularly susceptible to his wiles.

The Antichrist calls upon them to find him and free him, or to commit terrible acts in his name. There are things done that no one can explain, deeds so horrible that humanity shudders at them. Sometimes those who commit them, if they are not caught or do not take their own lives afterward, search for the Antichrist and follow his voice in their heads, so the Antichrist must be moved from time to time, lest these dark disciples of his track him down.

The last remaining members of the Knights Templar were approached by the Holy Father a few centuries ago when this dreadful activity was beginning to peak. They dedicated themselves to investigating strange occurrences to try and determine if the Antichrist was involved. They were the eyes and ears and hands of the Vatican, where the Antichrist was concerned.

If there was too much activity, if the acts were the type for which the Antichrist was most often responsible, then the Knights would act, eliminating those murderers and madmen who sought to do the unholy creature's bidding. The Knights would also alert his captors to relocate him once again, to have the captive vanish, to leave another dead trail for the Antichrist's followers, so that they would have to pick up the scent anew.

But now the Knights Templar are all dead, felled at

last. There is no one left to stand between the Antichrist and the world he would destroy. And now fools who know nothing of his power are going to try to destroy him. If they fail, and they can do nothing but, then the world is his.

Chapter 37

*F*or a long time the three operatives just stood there, looking into the face of the old priest. Then Tony spoke. "Father, why didn't they just seal him away forever somewhere? Put him somewhere where his . . . disciples would never find him."

"If they'd done that, my son, it would have had to have been at the bottom of the sea, or down a bottomless hole in some deep cave. If that had been the case, there would be no possibility for redemption."

"Excuse me?" Joseph said.

Father Alexander nodded. "This has been a dream of the Holy Fathers through the centuries, for this Antichrist to redeem itself, repent of its sins, and use its powers for good in the world."

A noise came from Ezekiel Swain like vomit striking cement. "Fat. Chance."

"So basically," Joseph said, "the church is endangering the world by keeping this insane whatever-the-hell-he-is accessible, in the eventual hopes of good PR, or maybe to use his power in its own interests? Is that the skinny here?"

"The church's interests," said Father Alexander, "are *good*."

"So are everybody's, Father," said Joseph. "Everybody's always got our best interests at heart, including, probably, the soldier boys out there now. Who are they, anyway?''

The priest had opened his mouth to answer when they heard a dull throbbing, like a huge heart beating all around them. ''Helicopter,'' Tony muttered.

In another second, the door at the top of the cellar stairs opened, and Commander Bowman trotted down. ''We'd like to invite you outside,'' he said. ''There's something that you should see—the coming of the leader of a new Holy America.''

''Well,'' said Joseph, ''how could we possibly refuse an offer like that?''

''Not him, though,'' said Bowman, pointing at Swain. ''He smells.''

Swain, still bound, rolled his massive head on his shoulders and looked at Bowman. ''*You* try, being dead.''

The three operatives and Father Alexander followed Bowman to the top of the stairs, where they were joined by four armed men who kept their weapons trained on the little party. They were led through the mission and outside, where, on the patch of land that had once been farmed, the first of two helicopters was landing.

''Black,'' murmured Laika, shielding her eyes from the sun with her hands.

Joseph nodded. ''Nice touch.''

As the first helicopter touched down, they could see the second behind it. Beneath the second one, Laika saw a wide-wheeled motorcycle dangling from what looked like a thick cable. ''Now I get it,'' Joseph said. ''Remember our sunburnt hippie and his mother ship and baby ship? There they are. The bike's attached to the copter by a rod.''

''You mean the cable?'' asked Tony.

''Uh-uh, not a cable. That is a flexible rod, probably retractable, operated by hydraulics. Look—you can see the tanks next to it. They lowered the cycle by the rod, and the rod's rigidity stabilized it. No feet in the sand; it just dropped right down. Then the copter flew in tandem with the bike—skated across the sand, like that witness said—lifted it when it was done, and *presto,* no entrance or exit path. Sonofabitch rod is probably a hundred yards long or more, so that's why the sand wasn't disturbed. The copter didn't get close enough to the ground.

"Look," said Laika as the second copter came closer. "The tires have no tread."

"Wouldn't need to, with the copter providing the horsepower," Joseph said. "All the motorcycle was was a motorized pencil. My compliments to the chef. Very simple, very effective."

"And who the hell *is* the chef?" Tony asked, then glanced at Father Alexander. "Sorry, Father."

"No, my son, you're quite right. Who the hell, indeed? For whoever this man is, it is the devil's own doing that brings him here to free his son."

They didn't have to wait any longer to find out. The door of the first helicopter opened, and a man holding a video camera stepped down from it. He aimed the camera back at the copter door and began to shoot the next man who came out. There was no doubt that this second man was the leader, for his bearing stated that he was used to being deferred to, and that was only a step away from being worshipped.

He was a few inches over six feet, and his carefully coiffed dark hair was gray at the temples. A moustache flecked with gray adorned his upper lip, and he was wearing a perfectly tailored set of fatigues, along with a red beret that Joseph suspected he wore because he thought it made him look dashing and jaunty, when he really looked like a militaristic French waiter.

But even out of the suits and ties the man always wore in public, they could not fail to recognize him. His picture had been in a thousand newspapers and TV news reports, as well as on all the covers of his bestselling book.

"Mr. Christian," Joseph said so softly that only Laika could hear. "Michael LaPierre himself, come to save the world for Jesus."

Chapter 38

L aika tried to put it all together. "The book," she said. "LaPierre's book—it was there on purpose."

"Right," said Joseph, "to keep us on the trail."

"But that means LaPierre had to be behind the code as well," said Tony. "And that means his people were in New York. . . ."

"It means that Michael LaPierre has been in on this every step of the way. Somehow he's been steering the ship," Laika said.

"And I bet it's heading right," said Joseph. "*Far* right. Or should that be far starboard?"

Bowman was talking to LaPierre now. Though Laika couldn't hear the words over the sound of the copter blades, she knew he was telling LaPierre about them, for LaPierre was looking over at them and smiling like a cat with a mouthful of canaries. Two big men with big weapons had gotten out of the copter with LaPierre, and continually flanked him as he moved.

The quartet of LaPierre, Bowman, and the bodyguards now came over to where the operatives and Father Alexander were standing. "Thank you all," LaPierre said to them.

"I didn't notice us applauding," Laika said, "though the entrance was dramatic."

"Sons and daughters of Ham," LaPierre said, shaking his head in mock dismay. "Always so *sassy*." Laika hadn't been called sassy since she was a little girl, and she couldn't ever remember being called a daughter of Ham.

"Of course," LaPierre went on, "I suppose working for this godless government brings out the worst in people. Be that as it may, I wasn't thanking you for any recognition per se, but for helping us achieve our most cherished goal."

"And that is?" Laika asked.

"Why, finding the enemy, of course . . . the Antichrist. So now at last we might destroy him."

"You got here first," Laika said.

"Oh yes, but we never would have, had it not been for you. We've been following you for a long time."

"Why?" Laika asked. "What got you started?"

"I'd be happy to tell you all about it, so that when you stand before the Lord you can tell him of the part you played in destroying the greatest enemy of Christ. Then perhaps he will weigh that in the balance and have mercy on your souls." LaPierre turned to the priest. "But for you, papist, there can be no mercy. The Church of Rome is a blasphemy, and you are condemned to hell, as are all those who accept its teachings."

"Like me?" said Tony tensely.

"Like you, Mr. Luciano."

Laika's eyes widened. "You know our names?"

"More than that." LaPierre turned to the four armed men Bowman had assigned. "Two of you, take the old man back to his prison. As for the others, come with me. We'll sit together, have a glass of water, and I'll tell you of your part in all this."

Bowman led them to a shaded area behind the mission building where canvas folding chairs had been set up, along with a table, glasses, and pitchers of water and ice. As they walked, Laika saw men in fatigues taking supplies from trucks that had appeared since they'd been taken to the cellar. LaPierre's men had probably hidden them up the canyon in anticipation of the agents' arrival. Several of the men were setting up a large tent, the type a Victorian general might have used while invading some third-world backwater. LaPierre did have style.

"The Goldfinger syndrome," Joseph said to Laika. She almost smiled.

"Something to share with the rest of us?" said LaPierre, who had overheard.

"Yeah," said Joseph. "Goldfinger, or Hugo Drax, or Doctor No, or Blofeld, or. . . ." He made a slight bow. "Michael LaPierre. It's a cliché. Asshole in charge tells back story to temporarily beaten heroes. But they always do it. They can't just kill them right off, they have to bore them to death first."

LaPierre wasn't smiling. "Would you rather die not knowing? I'd think it would be a comfort to go before the Lord in full knowledge of what good your acts have done, even if, Mr. *Stein*, your people have not accepted Christ as their personal savior."

"That's why they call us Jews."

LaPierre looked puzzled. "I don't understand."

"It's a Jewish thing. You wouldn't."

LaPierre gave what he must have thought was an appreciative chuckle for the jibes of a lesser being, then told them to sit down. "Humility is something I've struggled to attain for many years, often unsuccessfully. So I don't mind admitting to you and to the Lord that part of my telling you my story is born out of pride. I try to subdue it, and I trust the Lord will forgive me for slipping up one more time. Now. I have been told that you are responsible for the death of your fellow CIA agent Paul Daly. True?"

"Like we told Bowman," Laika said, "don't expect him anytime soon."

"That's a pity." LaPierre shook his head and took a sip of water. "One reason is that I have no doubt the man is in hell as we speak. I never got the impression he believed in anything, let alone Jesus. He worked for us for money, nothing more."

"You turned Daly?" Laika asked.

"It didn't take much. Money. Your government is cheap with the people whose loyalty they need. God has been so generous to me that I needn't make the same mistake. I wanted someone within the CIA the way I have others within other agencies, including your Vatican, Agent Luciano. It was from him that I first heard the stories of how the Church of Rome was sheltering the Antichrist. It's no wonder. They'd have used him for their own ends as they've always used any kind of power. The Antichrist, through the papist church, rules this world. But once the Antichrist is slain, then the true kingdom of the Lord will be at hand."

"That's nice," said Laika dryly. "But how did you get tipped off to the three of us?"

"Daly had been entrusted by your superior, Mr. Skye, with the knowledge of your activities. He was supposed to keep a watch on you."

"So Skye's never trusted us," Tony said bitterly.

"I don't know that," LaPierre said. "One of my very few areas of ignorance. From what Agent Daly said, I assumed it was not so much a case of not trusting you as of trusting Daly *more*, which goes to show what dreadful judges of character federal bureaucrats can be. But then, character has never been a requirement for civil service. That will change, too."

"So Daly told you about the Holberg affair," Laika said.

"Yes. We had been informed that seemingly paranormal occurrences might be indications that the Antichrist was in the vicinity. As evil as he is, he is still a miracle worker. So when Daly told us about the sculptor's disappearance and the destruction of his final sculpture, we began spying on the spies."

Laika nodded. "You put the bug in the warehouse where Holberg made the sculpture, and we reassembled it."

"Correct. And we also saved your lives in the subway station when those Satan worshippers tried to kill you.

And it was us who you were shooting at in the vacant office building where the Antichrist was being held. We'd have had him then if it hadn't been for you.''

"I doubt it," Laika said. "We tripped the alarm system and warned the priests. You'd have done the same. If we couldn't catch them, your people wouldn't have."

"Yes, but you didn't have Jesus on your side."

"I didn't notice Jesus and his pals being able to out-shoot us." Then something occurred to Laika. "And is human sacrifice part of your religious services?"

"Ah, you mean that boy. Yes, that was a shame, but it was a contingency put into place in case the Antichrist escaped. You see, if that happened, we never intended to kill you. We needed you to find him for us again. We knew that he spoke to one of you, that one of you was a minion of his, whether he wished to be or not. Naturally, we suspected the Jew."

Joseph nodded in acknowledgment. "Naturally. The traditional minions of Satan."

"We have no such people in our organization, of course. If we did, then they would no longer *be* in our organization. We couldn't tolerate anyone akin to the Antichrist, whether by blood or by other . . . affiliations. So we had to keep you on the trail, and the best way of doing that was to plant our evidence that it was *Christ* that was being held by the papists. We knew that at least one of you," here he nodded at Tony, "would wish to free him. The young man who provided the book code was sacrificed for Jesus, and he lives now in eternal bliss in the presence of his Lord."

"We didn't even kill him, did we?" Laika said. "One of your people shot him down." LaPierre only pursed his lips. "And you rigged it with Miriam Dominick so that we'd stumble across your book."

"Eventually, we had to," LaPierre said. "No offense, but we thought you'd have cracked the book code much sooner than you did." He smiled. "I suppose I shouldn't expect *everyone* to be familiar with my work. Pride again, you see. I struggle against it.''

"Doesn't put up much of a fight, does it?'' said Joseph.

LaPierre shook his head. ''Sassiness. There should be a commandment against it.''

"Maybe you can write one,'' said Laika.

The man smiled automatically. ''But you are right, Agent Harris. We knew that you would be investigating Miss Dominick, so we placed the book in her backpack. We chose her well, don't you think? Right in line with Agent Luciano's weaknesses. Vibrant, attractive, and a good Catholic girl, to boot.''

"Why did you follow us when we came west?'' Laika asked. ''You couldn't have known there was a link between the mummified body and . . . the Antichrist.''

LaPierre shook his head. ''No. We didn't know anything about the body. You see, we learned from our informants within the papist church that the Antichrist would stay in the United States for the time being, but was being moved west. That was as much as we were able to get. His location has always had top-secret status. So when the three of you went west, we naturally assumed you were on his trail, and followed.''

"And Daly eventually told you about the body?''

"That's right. When we learned you weren't specifically after the Antichrist again, we decided to bait the trail, as it were, to keep you in the area, in case this mummified corpse turned out to have a natural explanation. We thought that eventually Agent Stein would be 'contacted' by the Antichrist again, if he remained in the west long enough. That was when we began to stage the sand drawings. At night, of course, and using infrared lights. This is a desolate land, you know. Even near the roads, the chances of actually being seen were slim. And even if we had been, what would they have reported? Large, dark shapes moving through the night sky—what UFO sightings are made of.''

"An expensive prank," Joseph said. "But I guess you don't have to worry about money."

"I don't worry at all. The Lord is my shield. And if you want further proof that He is on our side, just look at the splendid coincidence of your dried corpses appearing near the places where we did our drawings."

"Who decided where the drawings were going to be?" Laika asked, a half-formed idea eating at her mind.

"Miss Dominick made the suggestions."

"Any particular reason?"

LaPierre shrugged. "She was closest to you. She knew your thoughts and your plans. We followed her advice, and it seemed to work. Uncanny, isn't it? But in her choices, she seems to have followed the very trail of the Antichrist itself, as though she were guided by the Lord."

"Or," said Laika, "as though she were guided by someone else. Did you ever think that she might be a . . . minion, too?"

LaPierre looked uncomfortable, but just for a moment. "No. Never."

"That's debatable," Laika said. "But the sand drawings had another purpose, didn't they? They added to the illusion that Miriam Dominick was psychic, and that was your trump card."

"Yes. Her 'psychic abilities' would entice you, of course, draw her closer to you. But it also set you up for the final blow—or what was to have *been* the final blow."

"Our near-fatal mountain trip."

"Correct. Once we knew where the Antichrist was, you three had served your purpose, and it was time for you to meet the Lord. That time has been pushed back just a bit, so that you may behold the destruction of the Antichrist."

"One little problem with your timeline," Joseph said. "The first sand design was found before we were even assigned to come out west. You couldn't have done that one."

"No, we didn't. But it gave us the idea to do the others."

"Then who did the first one?"

"You don't know?" LaPierre laughed as if at an ignorant child. "The Lord God Himself, of course. It was a true sign from heaven, sent to give us the idea and show us the way."

"Silly me," Joseph said. "I thought it was some high school kids with a Harley."

LaPierre shrugged. "Maybe it was, but if so, the students were tools in God's hands. It doesn't really matter, though, does it? All that matters is my final goal, not how we get there."

"Shades of the Thousand-Year Reich," said Joseph.

"Don't try and bait *me*, Jew. This is no political crusade. Everything that I do I do to glorify the Lord God almighty and His son, Jesus Christ. We're going to make this country a land ruled by God, not man. We have millions of people ready to rise up and take this country back for God. All they need is a leader."

"And that's you," said Laika.

"That's me. I have been called, and I will serve." LaPierre stood up and walked a few steps toward the sandstone cliffs, looking high above their red rims. "This was not of my choosing. But God gave me the money and the talent and the energy and the power to pull believers together. The current rulers of this country are hand in hand with the Antichrist. And with him destroyed, we shall rise up and take America and lead it into a revival of faith such as the world has never seen."

"And what about the existing government? What about the Constitution?" asked Joseph.

LaPierre whirled and looked at him with intense, almost mad eyes. "The only law any country requires is the law of the Lord as proclaimed in the Bible."

"Reconstructionism," Joseph said. "Old Testament law. Where you execute gays and adulterers and disobedient children. And I believe the method of choice is public stoning?"

LaPierre's face took on a grim and puritanical cast. "It

will take severity to bring an entire nation back to God,"
he said.

"What about all those annoying dietary laws?" Joseph
said. "And what about not cutting your hair or your
beards? I couldn't help but notice that so many of you
have moustaches. Is that dictated in the book of Leviticus,
or do you all just think it looks macho?"

"The blood of Christ did away with the need for many
of those Jewish laws," LaPierre said.

"And who's going to decide which to obey and which
to ignore, Mr. LaPierre? You and your . . . minions?
You'll be the ones to do the interpreting."

"No. *God* will show us the way. *He* will tell us what
laws still remain."

"Ah," said Joseph, nodding. "With a little help from
his friends, no doubt. And how are you going to bring
about this overthrow—by appealing to reason nation-
wide?"

"You know that's not possible. Most in this country
are still allied with Satan. It isn't the liberal atheistic scum
who have the weapons, Agent Stein. They believe too
much in the danger of guns to own them. But you'd be
surprised how many good, right-thinking Christians have
access to firearms."

"No," said Joseph. "I don't believe I would."

Laika cocked her head at LaPierre. The man was crazier
than she thought. "Are you telling me that after—or *if*—
you kill this so-called Antichrist, you intend to take over
the U.S. government by force of arms?"

LaPierre nodded. "We have leaders in every area of
this country, 144 sections altogether—the number of cu-
bits in the wall of the New Jerusalem; 144,000 is the
number of the Lamb of God's faithful followers. But there
are far more than 144,000. These men have hundreds
more under their control, and each of those, more hundreds. When the call comes from the Lord, the people of
the Lord will respond, believe me. Millions of them, men,
women, and youth. They will overtake every government

office, every police station, and every military installation in this country.''

"And what are the police and soldiers going to say about that?'' Joseph asked.

"For all your seeming sophistication, Agent Stein, you are really very simple.'' LaPierre's voice softened so that they could barely hear him. "Do you have any idea of how many policemen and soldiers are already ours?''

The thought stifled any quick comeback. Laika felt sick to her stomach. It wasn't the thought of dying that frightened her, but the all too real possibility of the country— *her* country—under the control of this fanatic and his followers. She had always thought that the extreme religious right wing had been very vocal, but that the numbers just weren't there to affect much other than local school board elections.

But what if LaPierre was right? What if these reconstructionists who followed the Bible literally had the numbers and the weaponry to take over the country at the local level? It was a damned scary thought, but not an impossible one.

She knew that fundamentalists, be they Islamic or Christian, often had a passion and a fury that the more liberal and tolerant Christians and Muslims did not. For most of them, there was no middle ground, no compromise. That was what made them dangerous, whether they were bombing school buses in Israel or abortion clinics in New Jersey. And that was what made Michael LaPierre's scenario all too conceivable.

But what the hell could Laika or her team do about it?

Her reverie was startled by the sudden movement of the guards as they pointed their weapons at Tony, who had moved his hand to his right pocket. "Don't shoot,'' Tony said in a calm voice tinged with sarcasm. "I'm just getting out something you all know and love.'' From his pocket he withdrew Miriam's gold cross on its chain. He put it around his neck and let the cross slip down into his shirt.

"This belonged to a friend of mine," he said. His voice was soft now. "Somebody whose mind you took and screwed up. You've made this cross, and who it represents, very ugly to a lot of people. But you're not going to do it to me. I know what this cross really stands for. Its message is love, not hate. Tolerance instead of bigotry. Not judgment, but forgiveness. That's what *my* God offers. This is *his* symbol. And if you want to use it, Mr. LaPierre, I suggest you bend and twist it the way you bend and twist its message. Bend it into the *crooked* cross, the swastika. That's the cross that suits you."

LaPierre met Tony's gaze for a long moment, then slowly clapped his hands together three times. "A very nice sermon, Agent Luciano. But by making it you only prove yourself aligned with the Antichrist."

LaPierre stood and slowly paced back and forth. "The meanings in the scriptures are all too clear. But you haven't read them, have you? You haven't studied them the way you should. Because if you had, you would know who it is that contends with the devil himself, who it is that defeats the great dragon in the Book of Revelations. It is the archangel. . . ." He stopped pacing and turned toward them, spreading his arms wide as if inviting them to behold him. "The archangel *Michael.*"

"And what," said Joseph, "if your mother had named you *Herbie?*"

"Mock on, Agent Stein," said LaPierre. "We'll see if you mock tomorrow, once you witness the destruction of the Antichrist."

"From what we've heard from Father Alexander," Laika said, "others have tried and failed."

"Old legends perpetrated by a blasphemous church that kept the Antichrist alive when it could have destroyed him. The Book of Revelation tells how the devil may be destroyed. Do none of you know?"

"I hate pop quizzes," said Joseph.

Tony cleared his throat. "He's cast down into a lake of fire."

"A-plus, Agent Luciano," said LaPierre, beaming. "The 'eternal fire prepared for the devil and his angels.' Fire will destroy him, and it will be the fire of Michael that shall help to light tomorrow's dawn, a dawn that will signal a new beginning, a new age for America, and eventually for the world."

Chapter 39

"*T*he man is definitely on a power trip," said Joseph, after they were taken back to the basement of the mission.

"He's crazy," said Tony. "Absolutely insane. What do we do about it?"

"What happen?" Ezekiel Swain, still sitting against the wall, rumbled. "Where Divine?"

So Laika told him, as she might tell a child, what Michael LaPierre had done, and that on the following day, he intended to destroy Swain's "Divine."

But Swain only laughed, and said one word: "Won't."

It seemed to Laika that he had shrunk somewhat in stature, and they tightened his bonds reluctantly, dreading any contact between his flesh and theirs. "For our own safety, you understand," Laika said, by way of apology, though why she should apologize to this monster, she had no idea. Even as disgusting as he was, there was still something charismatic about him, something that commanded respect.

"Father," Laika said when they were finished, "is there any way out of this cellar? Any . . . secret passage to escape Indians, or anything?"

Father Alexander smiled sadly and shook his head. "When this mission was built, there was no longer any danger from the natives. No, the only way out is through that guarded doorway. Or breaking through the three-foot-thick adobe walls, or digging through solid earth.''

It seemed fairly hopeless, but Laika drew Joseph and Tony to the far end of the cellar where neither Father Alexander nor Swain could hear them. ''Our only chance for escape will be tomorrow,'' she said. ''We're stuck here tonight.''

''Don't know if tomorrow looks much better,'' Tony said. ''This bunch doesn't look like the type to let down their guard.''

''We'll just have to stay alert for an opportunity,'' said Laika. ''But the most important thing now is getting through the night alive.''

''You're talking about Fat Boy,'' Joseph said, glancing at Ezekiel Swain.

''Yes. He's a monster, a murderer. I'd have no compunction about killing him. If we could.''

''Iffy,'' said Joseph. ''He's already dead. Maybe La-Pierre can torch him tomorrow, along with his *Antichrist*.'' He said the last word with contempt.

''You don't believe the story?'' Tony asked.

''No. The more I think about it, the more I'm convinced that there isn't anything religious or supernatural about this at all.''

''How can you say that?'' Tony asked. ''After everything you've seen.''

''Just because we don't understand things doesn't mean we have to ascribe a supernatural origin to them. For example, there has to be an explanation as to how Swain has managed to stay alive and feed off the living. It's not like he just sucks in their 'life energy,' to use a New Age term. He requires physical contact. There's some organic process at work.''

''When he was on me,'' Laika said, ''it felt like burning needles.''

''Exactly. We could theorize that his individual cells merge somehow with his host's.''

''But he was *dead*,'' Tony said. ''What brought him back to life in the first place?''

"Some force that we don't understand. Maybe some force derived from this being who everybody's calling the Antichrist. But I'd bet my life that it's got to be explainable by natural laws. It's just that those laws aren't in our lawbook yet. I don't know, maybe Stephen Jay Gould or Edward Wilson could explain it. I can't. I'm not smart enough."

"Well, whatever makes him tick," Laika said, "Swain is dangerous to us."

"Those ropes are tight again," said Tony. "And strong. He's probably tried to get out of them already, and he hasn't succeeded. But we can keep a watch on him in shifts."

"I'd rather kill him." Laika glanced at Swain, then at the priest sitting across the room from him. "But even if I knew how, it's not something I'd want to try in front of a priest. Let's just keep watch."

Laika took the first watch while the others lay on the burlap mattresses, trying to get comfortable enough to catch some much needed sleep. Ezekiel Swain closed his eyes, too, and several hours passed uneventfully.

At eleven, Laika woke up Joseph. She drifted into sleep eagerly, surprised at how easily it came.

Hours later, she awoke to the sound of a long, drawn out, "Ahhhhhh. . . ."

When she looked up, she saw Ezekiel Swain on his hands and knees. He was as bloated and corpulent as ever, and beneath him was a brown-skinned mummy smothered in a greasy, gleaming black robe.

Tony rose from his sitting position, and as he ran to Swain, Laika figured out what had happened. Tony had fallen asleep just before Swain had lost enough mass to slip out of his bonds. Hungered, he had attacked the priest, and now Tony, enraged at his own failure as well as at Swain, was going after the monster.

"You *sonofabitch!*" Tony yelled as he tackled Swain. He landed on top of the man, and went sliding across the floor on the slick surfboard of Swain's moist and slimy body until they hit the wall. Tony struck at him, but his fists sounded as though they were pounding into plastic garbage bags filled with brie, a thick, pulpy sound. The only sound Swain made was a wet *whoosh* every time Tony hit him, as though the air was sputtering out of him.

Finally Tony grasped Swain's thick neck, trying to strangle him. But he could not encircle it with his fingers, and the glutinous flesh seemed to slide right off it. It looked, Laika thought, as though he were trying to throttle a lump of bread dough.

Together, she and Joseph were able to pull Tony off the man just as the door opened above. "What's going on down there?" a voice said, and then several men came down the stairs, their weapons in front of them. They stopped when they saw the bizarre tableau. "What's happened here?" one of the men said, trying to make sense of a scene from hell.

"Got. Hungry," said Ezekiel Swain, and the stench that the words rode as they came through his lips was abominable. They all winced, but the young man with the gun retched, and fragments of his morning's breakfast dribbled from between his lips and onto the floor.

"Mmm," said Swain, eyeing the puddle. "Dessert."

"We'll get Mr. LaPierre," said the man behind the one who'd been sick. Then all of them went up the stairs again, leaving the ops, Swain, and the mummified priest locked in the cellar again.

"You bastard," Laika said to Swain, who was still lying on his back like a tremendous roly-poly toy, chuckling and snuffling. He spread his sausage-fingered hands in a gesture of submission and smiled. The usual exudations appeared.

"You, criticize me, for my, *nature*."

"Your nature," Joseph said, "is killing people for their bodily fluids. You can see how one might be critical of that."

"Cheer up. Could have, been *you*."

The three agents sat together at the opposite end of the cellar from Swain, who now rolled himself up to a sitting position. "Damn it," Tony was saying to himself. "*God* damn it. He hadn't moved for hours, not for *hours*, and I was just too tired. I fell asleep, and because of it the priest died."

"You woke up fast," Joseph said.

"Go to hell."

"Maybe, before the day is out."

They heard the door above open again, and now Michael LaPierre came down the steps, bodyguards before and after him. He looked at the priest's corpse, then at Swain's corrupted and reeking flesh. "A demon," he said. "This man is a demon of Satan, feeding on his own kind."

"How do?" said Swain, waving a hand in a manner meant to be jaunty.

The gesture did not amuse LaPierre, who wrinkled his nose. "You'll die today, demon. Right after you witness the destruction of your master."

"Ooo. *Scared.*"

If LaPierre's eyes could have shot flames, Ezekiel Swain would have been a pile of bubbling ashes, Laika thought. "Bring them up," LaPierre ordered his guards. "It's nearly dawn."

Martin Reigle drove his car across the dam crest as he did every morning. But this morning he didn't look out across the reservoir, as he always did, to see the first rays of the rising sun over the water. No, this morning Martin's attention was on what he had to do, and how to do it. He was thinking about what was wrapped in the thick wax paper in the cardboard box in the backseat.

At the end of the roadway he turned left and drove down to the parking lot near the powerhouse where he worked. He parked his car in his usual space and walked to the powerhouse, carrying the cardboard box with the wrapped cylinders.

"Heya, Marty," said Joe, the guard, as he waved him in. "Subs? Shame on you—you didn't tell it was sub sale time again."

Martin smiled sheepishly. Once a month his two kids in junior high school sold subs for their church's bell choir, and Martin hit up everybody he knew at the dam. "Sorry, Joe," he said. "Forgot to get you this time. You want one if somebody's out sick today?"

"Yeah, sure." Joe sniffed the air. "Don't smell any onions."

"Nobody ordered any. Sorry." He walked past Joe and into the building. He went to his locker right away and put the wrapped cylinders inside, then threw away the box.

Then he sat down on the wooden bench in front of his locker and thought about just what the hell he was going to do. He knew he was going to die today, and when he thought about that, he didn't want to do it. He knew how badly Susan and the kids would miss him, and they wouldn't understand at all why he had done it. But he didn't really have a choice. Once the voice had spoken to him, he knew that he would do whatever it told him.

He thought that it was God. Anyway, he hoped so. Because if it was God, then He would take Martin to be with Him when Martin died doing what God wanted done. He couldn't conceive of it being anyone *but* God. Who else could speak to you in your head and tell you to do something that you never would have dreamed of doing yourself in a million years—and then you went out and did it?

He didn't understand why God wanted this *particular* thing done, but it wasn't his to question, it was his to obey. That was the weird thing. He couldn't consider, even for a minute, not obeying. There seemed to be no option. If God wanted the Dead Horse Reservoir dam blown up, then Martin Reigle would do it.

Chapter 40

*O*utside the Mission of San Pedro, the guards tied Laika's, Tony's, and Joseph's hands behind their backs. Laika glanced at the others to see if they were considering making a break, but it would have been suicide. Two of LaPierre's soldiers held the muzzles of their guns to the operatives' heads while a third did the tying.

The soldiers did an even better job with Ezekiel Swain, winding heavy nylon cord several times around his stinking body, between his legs, and around his wrists, so that he had to hobble out to the military truck into which the guards directed their four captives.

LaPierre reappeared and climbed into a humvee loaded with his troops. Three trucks besides the one the ops were in followed the humvee as it headed toward the narrow canyon Laika had noticed when they'd come in. She estimated that LaPierre might have five or six dozen men with him, not counting the few who remained to guard the mission and the helicopters.

"Not flying to our destination?" Laika asked a guard.

"Couldn't land a chopper in the terrain," the man said.

Laika tried to follow the maze of canyons they drove through, in case they had to find their way out again. She prayed to God they would, but was afraid the truck was taking them to their deaths.

At last the truck slowed and the procession came to a halt. Laika could see that they were in a round canyon

305

larger than most of those they had come through. She guessed the area was thirty to forty yards across, small enough that only the humvee and the truck they were in parked within it, along with a Jeep that was already parked against the curved wall. The men sitting in it had probably been there all night, guarding the place. The other trucks simply stopped in the narrow canyon that provided access to this one. When Laika looked up, she noted with unease that the upper walls of the canyon were actually curving in on them, as though they sat at the bottom of a round vase.

The unseen sun was far to the east and just above the horizon, so the deep canyon was still in heavy shadow. Yet as soon as they had climbed from the truck, there was enough light for Laika to see the circle of ancient stones. They were in the center of the canyon, thirty feet across, fitted together, a foot wide and perhaps nine inches high. At one side of the circle was a squared-off area that extended a few feet outward from the circle.

"My God. . . ." she heard Joseph whisper.

"It's your keyhole, isn't it?" she asked him. "The giant keyhole you saw in your dream."

"Yes," he said, nodding. "What is it?"

"It's a kiva," said Laika. "An underground ceremonial room. It must be where they have the . . . the prisoner."

Michael LaPierre, along with four cameramen, came strutting up to them. "Tie them to that," he said to the guards, gesturing to a large cross constructed out of thick wooden beams. It was planted in the sandy soil just outside the stone circle. "I want you all to have an excellent view," he told Laika. "And it may as well be from the symbol that you have spurned."

"Quite the Kodak moment," Joseph said, gesturing to the cameramen. Two held videocameras, and the others were still photographers.

"Of course," said LaPierre. "It's a great moment, to be preserved and shown to rally our cause. Think of what it would be like to actually witness St. Patrick driving the snakes from Ireland, or St. George slaying the dragon. Although those were lies of your papist church, Agent Luciano, the similarity between them and LaPierre destroying the Antichrist are clear. Only what I do today will be seen by millions.''

''Thanks to the miracle of videotape,'' said Tony.

LaPierre nodded to the guards, who prodded their captives over to the cross and tied them to it, one by one, with strong nylon cords. The beam of the upright was a foot thick, and Laika was bound to the front of it, on the side facing the kiva, her back against the wood. Tony and Joseph were lashed to the sides, so that they could see the kiva by turning their heads, and Ezekiel, already tightly bound, was tied to the back, his face against the rough wood. Laika heard him laughing softly, his head inches from her own, and shuddered at the droplets that struck the side of her face.

''What's the cross for?'' Joseph asked.

''Maybe a palliative the priests set up against the old magic,'' said Laika.

''Little did they know how useful it would be for Michael LaPierre,'' said Joseph.

Now LaPierre's troops were taking weapons out of the back of one of the trucks. Laika saw several flamethrowers and a number of machine guns. One of the men handed LaPierre a flamethrower, which he aimed toward the canyon wall and fired. A bolt of yellow flame shot through the air, scorching the dust of the stone wall. LaPierre turned back to his men. ''Open the entrance!'' he shouted.

Immediately two men went to a small crane and fired up a gas engine that ran it, while two more attached a cable to an iron ring in a slab that sat in the center of the stone circle.

''Yesss. . . .'' Laika heard Ezekiel Swain say. ''Free him. Morons.''

Slowly the slab rose until Laika could see the lead sheathing that covered the bottom of it. Several men shifted it to one side, and the crane lowered it to the ground, revealing a large rectangular passage to whatever lay below.

"Secure the prisoner!" LaPierre barked, and three men, one with a flamethrower and the others with machine guns, slid a wooden ladder down into the gaping hole. Then they lowered an electric lantern on a cord, and one by one climbed down into the pit. Laika thought they looked nervous as hell, and if what LaPierre claimed was down there really was, they had good reason to be nervous.

LaPierre walked to the hole and looked down inside it. "Is he there?" he called. Laika couldn't hear what the men below said, but it seemed to satisfy LaPierre, on whom the cameramen and photographers had fixed their lenses. "Open it, then," he said, "and tell the creature to come forth out of its hole!"

He stepped back and grinned in triumph at Laika, who had been working against her bonds, trying to loosen them, but to no avail. She heard from below a dull, heavy thud, as though something had struck the dirt floor of the kiva. Then, nearly a minute later, one of LaPierre's men appeared at the mouth of the opening. She could hear his words to LaPierre: "He's down there, but he won't come up. He says that the earth is his strength, and that the true servant of the Lord must meet him there, or be a coward all his days."

LaPierre straightened up, and Laika saw an angry, fiery look come into his eyes. "Very well, then! We will wage the battle on righteousness in the very den of evil itself! Descend!"

He gestured to his men, and half a dozen went down the ladder ahead of him, half with flamethrowers, and the other three with guns. A video cameraman and a still photographer followed. "Brave guy," said Tony. "I'm surprised he doesn't lob a couple grenades in there before he goes down."

"Now, Antichrist!" LaPierre bellowed. "Prepare to

meet your master, the devil, in the fires of hell!'' With one final look of triumph at the prisoners bound to the cross, Michael LaPierre, a flamethrower in his arms, descended the ladder and disappeared from view.

It wasn't hard for Martin Reigle to evade the scrutiny of his co-workers at the Dead Horse Reservoir dam. Martin was the assistant manager of dam maintenance, which meant that when something went wrong, he was the first to try and fix it. If he couldn't, he knew who to contact. He carried a beeper so people could get ahold of him, but he didn't have to tell anyone where he was going unless he wanted to.

So, at 7:14 in the morning, Martin was at the center of the eight taintor gates, in the shelter of one of the large concrete piers near the dam crest. He knew that there was no way, with the small amount of dynamite he had, that he could blow the whole dam and make the entire contents of Dead Horse Lake roll down into the canyons south of the dam. But what he *could* do was blast apart the center gates, which would easily reduce the depth of the lake by twenty feet.

He didn't know exactly how much water that would release, but since Dead Horse Lake was nearly a mile long and a half mile across, he suspected it'd be more than enough to do whatever he hoped was God intended it to do.

He finished setting the dynamite sticks where their detonation would do the most damage, then looked at the sky one last time. In the east the sun was rising. It looked beautiful, and he wished he could see it over the lake, the sparkles of light dancing on its surface. But he wouldn't have that luxury. He didn't have a timing device, and there was no need for one, really. He could just set it off by hand. That meant, of course, that the last sight he saw would be the sun across the high desert, not the faces of his wife or his kids.

But he knew without a doubt that the next face he would see would be God's.

Chapter *41*

*T*hey were such fools, such complete and perfect fools.
They had him, safe and sound and trapped under lead,
and now here they were, opening his casket, offering him
freedom. For the first time in centuries he had contact with
the world again. There was nothing now between him and
the outer air. The slab had been removed, and they had
unsealed and taken the lid off the leaden casket.

Sensations flooded into him. He felt minds and souls
and thoughts galore, as though they were pouring into his
brain. Yet he was able to isolate and sort every single
one, analyze it and learn how malleable it was. And there
were many among these who were touchable.

Before they'd come and opened the casket, he had been
starved for contact. There had been the single strong one
at first, but then, just as he was in the middle of *pushing*
at him, bringing the mortal's mind to bear on where he
was so that the man might come and free him, the contact
had been violently broken.

Frustrated, he had pushed out harder, weakening himself in the process. But there'd been nothing there. He felt
only the woman, whose power was far weaker than the
man's. He tried to reach her, but it was agony, like one
of these mortals trying to push over a tree with only his
hands. They might be able to make the leaves tremble,
but to crack the bark and splinter the trunk? Never.

So he searched, searched until he found the man again,

310

the one whose dreams he had managed to breach before. But he was difficult to reach. Disbelief was a strong boundary.

Then there was the girl, who seemed ignorant of his existence, never responding to his mental touches, but still moving toward him as he'd instructed her, like a sleep-walker, oblivious to all.

And then at last the man nearby, who had made this desert land his home. The ties must have been close with this one: he was so obedient, so simply accepting. When he told the man what he wanted him to do, there was not a mental pause or a question, only pure submission. The prisoner had thought that if the water did nothing else, it would at least draw attention to this barren area to which they'd brought him. It might also cause chaos and death, and that was not to be slighted. Maybe some of these very priests who had imprisoned and guarded him would be drowned, and that would be a delectable outcome.

But now, as it turned out, he didn't need that oh so pliable man. For here were fools opening the cage door so the bird could escape without any bursting dam or floods of water. He sat up in his casket, glad for the chance to stretch his false human form, and probed the nervous men around him, sensing which of them he could use, could bend to his will.

Then the legs of one more man appeared through the opening to the world, and the prisoner watched as his liberator descended the final steps of the ladder, stepping into a hell which he would never leave alive.

So this, at long last, was the Antichrist. Michael La-Pierre stood at the foot of the ladder, his throat feeling suddenly dry, his stomach churning with fear.

The creature was not what LaPierre had expected. He had thought he would look demonic and evil, while this man sitting up in the casket appeared to be almost angelic. He was clothed in a simple white shift, and his long hair and well-trimmed beard were a light brown. His eyes were blue, and his light-brown flesh was perfect, with not a blemish. As the man turned his head and LaPierre saw him in three-quarter profile, he realized that he was nearly identical to the standard pictures of Jesus that hung on every Sunday school wall in the country.

"Impostor!" LaPierre shouted, and the man's gaze slowly moved back to him. This Antichrist looked entirely unconcerned about anything that LaPierre might say or do, and that infuriated him all the more. "You *are* the Antichrist!" he said. "We see you for what you are, a vile servant of the devil! And now our sacred fire shall cleanse the earth of you, so that God's people may take possession of this land and God's law may rule it!"

The creature only smiled at him. No, it wasn't a smile, it was a smirk, and in it LaPierre saw all the evil that dwelt in the monster's soul.

"Die!" he shouted, turning the flame on full and directing it straight at the Antichrist, only a few feet away. A thrill went through LaPierre's heart as he saw the white clothing burst into yellow ribbons of fire, and with a laugh, he shut off the flame to see what damage he had done. He hoped the videocamera had caught his expression of righteous indignation.

The creature still sat there, smiling. Not a hair on his head had been singed, although what was left of his clothing hung on his flesh like black scabs. Slowly he raised his hands and brushed the charred and still burning cloth away. Then, for the first time, he spoke to LaPierre.

"Has that flamethrower, by any chance, been blessed by the Church of Rome?"

The mockery infuriated LaPierre, and he turned to the nine men huddled against the wall behind him so as to avoid the flame from his weapon. "Kill him!" he shouted to them, and they fanned out into a half circle around the Antichrist, shooting their weapons and turning on their own flames to bathe the monster in a storm of bullets and fire, while the cameramen recorded it all. The kiva burst into savage light amid a cacophony of gunfire.

*   *   *

You, the prisoner thought, giving commands faster than the velocity of the bullets that passed through his body like fish darting through water. *You, you, you, you, you, you.*

There were seven of them, seven of the ten soldiers down there he could reach, men with already violent natures whom his blood had touched, and though he did not touch their minds with words, not even *you*, his powers sought them and made them his own, and he used them like a man would his fingers, and turned them on the others.

So it was that Michael LaPierre was amazed to see John Bowman, one of his trusted inner circle, turn on him with his machine gun and fire at his legs, literally cutting them from beneath him so that LaPierre fell to the dirt floor of the chamber in agony, his blood soaking the earth. LaPierre, unable to rise or use his own weapon, looked in disbelief at the Antichrist, who smiled disingenuously and gave a theatrical shrug.

Boys will be boys.

Although LaPierre saw the Antichrist's lips move with the words, he heard them only inside his head, for the gunfire and the roar of the flamethrowers would have drowned them out had they been simply spoken. The flames shot through the small chamber. His men were shooting and turning their torches on each other. He had been wrong: this creature's power was greater than he had thought. Perhaps it wasn't the Antichrist at all.

And as the fire from David Richardson's flamethrower leaped out, blinding and searing him, Michael LaPierre had just enough time before he died in agony to realize that he had been fool enough to come into the lair of Satan himself, and that the flames of hell now burned him and would burn him forever, for his terrible sin of pride.

*   *   *

"Something," said Joseph Stein, hearing the streams of gunshots and seeing smoke and stray gouts of fire tear upward from the opening of the kiva, "is not going according to plan."

"I think you're right," said Laika. "That could be good."

Then LaPierre's men started to appear at the top of the kiva entrance. The first one up was Richardson, the man who had been with Bowman when they were first captured. When his feet were on the ground, he pointed his flamethrower at LaPierre's troops and unleashed its fire. The flames shot out, enveloping several men in orange fire and nearly touching the agents tied to the cross. Laika could smell the pungent odor and feel the heat.

"*Or*," Joseph said, "that could be *bad*."

By the time the rest of the soldiers came up from the kiva, both photographers on the surface and four of the troops had been torched by Richardson's weapon. One man was standing only a few feet from Laika, and she saw his uniform burst into bright flames. He screamed, but the scream was quickly cut off as the fire surged down his throat. He stood there for a moment after the flame had passed over him, his flesh blackened, his hat still burning, looking like a giant candle. Then he toppled over, smoldering and stinking of charred skin.

When the men above realized what Richardson was doing, they opened fire on him and shot him down. But now the ones who had been below savagely began to attack the others, some of whom had also begun to turn on their comrades. It was pure chaos. No one could be sure whether the man next to him was friend or foe, and Laika saw men turn on each other a second after they had been firing at some common enemy.

The bound operatives, however, seemed to offer no threat, and so far had been ignored by the combatants, when suddenly the earth seemed to lurch beneath them, and there followed swiftly the sound of a faraway explosion which they felt rather than heard. The cross to which they were tied loosened in the earth.

Rocks at the top of the canyon's walls crumbled from the shock, and huge stones fell, striking the warriors, wounding and crushing some of them still unharmed by the flames and bullets of the general melee. Those untouched strove to aim their weapons once again, and the sound of gunfire reclaimed the canyon for a moment.

But then a roar louder than that of the flamethrowers or even the explosion sounded in their ears, an ever-strengthening pulse that not only buffeted their ears, but shook the ground beneath them. The water was upon them all even as they saw it burst from the narrow canyon that opened to the north.

It was a solid wall that reached nearly to the top of the hundred-foot canyon. The bottom of the wide bowl of stone in which stood the warriors and their vehicles and the kiva and the operatives bound to their cross filled up in only seconds with violent rushing waters that plucked up men like dried leaves and swept them away, into the instant whirlpool that the round canyon had become, or out the narrow opening to the south.

Laika was aware only for an instant of the bodies of men, dead and alive, being lifted and tossed away. From the corner of her eye she saw one man slammed against the sandstone, bursting open, leaving a splatter of red that was instantly washed away.

When the water first hit her, she was afraid it would cover them and they would drown, lashed to the cross. But she had not reckoned on the power of the water. It wrenched the heavy wooden upright from the earth like a man plucking a flower, and spun them away into the maelstrom.

Though the cross twisted and turned in the moving waters, Ezekiel Swain's bulk provided its center of gravity. His weight, heavy with fluids, flipped the cross so that he was on the bottom and Laika was facing the sky, with Tony and Joseph flanking her. At first she had no problem breathing, even as the waters swept over her, and she could hear Tony and Joseph catching breaths as the cross bobbed up and down in the swells. She couldn't hear Swain breathing at all. Perhaps, she thought, he didn't have to.

They circled the canyon once, the upright ends and the crosspiece of their holy raft taking most of the impact as they struck the canyon wall. Then they were swept through the southern mouth, down into the narrow slot canyons through which they had previously driven.

What followed was a nightmare of water and rocks, of striking against stone while water rushed over and around her, pouring down her throat while she lay on her back, making her turn and cough it up, burning through her throat and nose, blinding her. And always the constant battering of their craft against harsh stone, the ceaseless pummeling, the scraping of wood and sometimes flesh against the unforgiving rock.

Then, over the sound of water slapping her ears, she heard either Joseph or Tony yell, "Christ! He's grow—" The words were smothered by another torrent, and Laika heard the speaker choke and cough.

She turned her head, flinching against the expected surge of water, and from the corner of her eye could see past the gasping Joseph, could blurrily see Ezekiel Swain's head and the top of his body. Whoever had shouted was right. *Swain was growing.*

His head was the size of a beachball. His eyes were nearly popping from their sockets; his tongue, a fat red sponge, protruded from his mouth; and the cheeks were Gillespied out to the size of babies' heads. His upper torso had become nearly twice as distended as it had been before.

He's soaking it up, she thought in horror, as another wave smacked the side of her face so that she looked front again. *He's soaking up the water.*

The passage ahead of them narrowed again, and they slowed momentarily as the water gathered force. Then it shot them through the opening so that for an instant they were airborne, above the water. The cross hung upright in the air, jagged rocks close on either side. Then it twisted so that Laika was turned to the left, while the back of the cross, with the filled-to-bursting Ezekiel Swain bound to it, smashed against the sandstone wall.

He exploded like a water balloon. There was a loud bursting noise and shards of Swain's flesh peppered the rolling tide like hail, while the water and fluids that had filled him shot past Laika's eyes like a pink cloud and were instantly swept away by the flood. Ezekiel Swain was gone, his corporeal body dissolved by the waters so thoroughly that he might just as well have been still buried beneath the desert sands.

Chapter 42

*T*he flood rushed on, but Laika noticed that her bonds had loosened, and suspected that contact with the rough stone had finally sawed through the tough cord. At the same time, she became aware that the waters were slowing, and soon they were moving through the canyons with no greater velocity than that of a steadily flowing river.

"Tony?" she called. "Joseph?"

"Here," she heard Tony gasp, and Joseph muttered, "Yeah. . . ." They were alive.

They drifted for a while longer, the current continually slowing, the flood continuing to divide itself among the labyrinth of canyons, until Laika finally felt the wooden cross begin to scrape against the canyon floor. At last it stopped upon sand sodden with the water's passage, while snakelike rivulets still ran past them, seeking the lowest ground, creeping until they could go no further, then sinking lifeless into the soil.

For a long time the three simply lay where they were, now tied but loosely to the wood, breathing hard, letting their tense muscles relax, getting used to being on land again.

Tony was the first to move, sliding his body down toward the bottom of the upright until the cords around him dropped off the end. Then he worked at the nearly torn through section of Laika's bonds and freed her, and together they helped Joseph get loose. Weak, shaken, but whole, they stood uncertainly on their feet and looked around.

"We came through here," said Laika. "I think the mission is through that passage, and a bit further on."

"If that's true," Joseph said, "I take back everything I ever said about there being no God."

Laika's memory had been correct. After a half-mile walk, they reached the mission. The helicopters and vehicles were still there, but the guards who had been left behind were nowhere to be seen. The old building, on its slight rise of land, seemed to have been spared the ravages of the floodwater.

"Where'd the guards go?" Tony asked. "You think up the canyon after the flood hit?"

"I don't know," said Laika. "But before we do anything else, I suggest we arm ourselves from the Blazer, if they didn't already confiscate the guns."

They made their way quickly to the vehicle, but the weapons in the back had all been removed. "Let me just see," said Tony, reaching up under the front passenger seat and removing a loaded Glock. "Thanks, Popeye," he said. "Never knew a Company wet work man yet who didn't stash one more piece." He pushed back the slide and snapped it forward, putting a shell under the hammer.

"Let's go," said Laika. "We'll check the mission and then get back to that kiva. The waters must have subsided by now, and I want to know what the hell happened to whoever or whatever was down there."

As they walked up the rise to the mission and the ground in front of the door came into view, they saw what had happened to the guards who'd been left behind. Three fatigue-clad bodies lay in puddles of blood. No weapons were near them. Then the heavy front door of the mission drifted open, and Joshua Yazzie walked out of the shadows, pistol in hand.

"Where's your Fury?" asked Laika.

"Oh, I parked around back after I got done talking with

these fellas. They didn't give me a very friendly reception.'' His tone was flat and dry. ''Another funny thing—I found three dead priests and another one of those dried-up bodies inside. Maybe you'd like to fill me in on what's happened.''

''This is beyond you now, Officer Yazzie,'' Laika said. ''And we're not on the reservation anymore. So I suggest you drive away and forget all about this and all about us. And I mean right now.''

Yazzie shook his head slowly. ''I don't take my orders from you, Agent Harris.''

Agent Harris? Laika drew in a sharp breath.

''That's right. And Agent Stein and Agent Luciano, too. I know who you are and who sent you. And I've got people who want to know what the hell this is all about. You've been within U.S. boundaries doing black ops, but the game's over. You lose.''

Laika took in the situation. Yazzie's pistol was trained directly on Tony, the only one of them holding a gun, and that gun was down at his side. She didn't know who the hell Yazzie was with, but she felt certain he could fire that pistol before Tony brought his up.

''All right,'' she said. ''The way I see it, it's a standoff. Now we're going to go and get in that Blazer and drive out of your life. You're welcome to whatever you find here.''

It was half true and half a bluff. As she turned her back on him, and Tony and Joseph followed suit, she was half hoping that he would call it.

He did. ''Stop,'' he said. They kept walking. ''If I have to shoot one of you to make the others stay, I will.'' She knew it would be the one with the gun, and so did the others. She kept walking.

''If you don't stop immediately, the next sound you hear will be a gunshot.'' He wasn't lying.

From the corner of her eye she saw Tony start to turn, but not in surrender. He was bringing up his Glock.

Yazzie fired and Laika saw the bullet strike Tony in

the chest. As he fell backward, the Glock continued to rise automatically, and Tony's finger pulled the trigger before Yazzie could get off a second shot.

Tony's bullet hit Yazzie in the center of the forehead.

Yazzie's head jerked as though someone had slapped him. Then he fell to his knees and over onto his side, dead.

Laika and Joseph rushed to Tony, who was lying on his back, breathing hard, his eyes staring at the sky. Laika knelt next to him and ripped open his shirt so that the buttons popped off. A large bruise, turning purple as she watched, suffused his chest, and blood oozed from his flesh where the sharp edges of Miriam Dominick's metal cross had cut into it. But that same metal had stopped the bullet.

"Jesus Christ," said Joseph, as Tony pushed himself up on his elbows. "You are one lucky bastard . . . La-Pierre could've put this one in his *book*."

"How do you feel, Tony?" Laika asked.

"Chest hurts like a sonofabitch, but it didn't penetrate." He took a deep breath and pushed himself to his feet, but stayed bent over. "Yazzie?" he asked.

"You didn't see?" Joseph said. "You're a goddamn amazing shot, Tony. Right above the eyes. Why didn't you go for center mass?"

"I didn't go for anything. He shot me first, and I just pulled the trigger as I went down." He smiled without humor. "Yeah, lucky shot. Another miracle. Or a third— that's twice a cross saved my life today." He straightened up and hissed with the pain, rubbing his chest.

After she was sure Tony was all right, Laika had gone to Yazzie's body and begun to search it. She was going through his wallet when the others came up. "Anything interesting?" Joseph asked. "Pretty weird that an Indian Affairs guy broke our covers."

"He's got Bureau of Indian Affairs creds, all right. But they're *his* cover." She held up a card they all recognized.

"Brian Foster. Federal Bureau of Investigation. We've killed a fed."

"Oh, my God," Tony muttered, looking genuinely stricken.

"Take it easy," Joseph said. "Don't forget he'd have killed you." He shook his head. "It does make things tricky, though."

"Maybe not," said Laika. "Who's necessarily going to know that we were responsible? True, somehow Yazzie—or Foster—followed us here, but it's possible he hadn't reported it yet. We get his body out of here, along with his car, and who's to know he was ever here in the first place? And if we take along Father Alexander's corpse, there's no link to us at all."

"Sure," said Joseph. "After all, what have they got? Dead priests, black helicopters, more dead men in fatigues, and Michael LaPierre's fingers all over everything. The doctors from the National Science Foundation's Division of Special Investigations were never even here."

"That means we've got to work fast. The explosion we heard must have been the dam breaking, and the flood was a result. Investigators will be all over this place in a few hours. But the first thing we *have* to do is get back to that kiva."

They took a truck and drove it back up through the canyons. The sand and the soil was wet, but no more than it might have been after a desert rainstorm. Puddles in rock indentations were the only indication of how great an amount of water had flowed through the canyons. It was amazing, Laika thought, how thirstily this land soaked up moisture. Like Ezekiel Swain himself, she thought, and grimaced at the memory.

Between the three of them, they retraced LaPierre's route easily enough. They frequently came across the corpses of LaPierre's men who had been drowned in the flood. They were badly battered by their contact with the rocks. Despite their mutilations, some of them still showed bullet wounds, now washed clean by the water, and others were burned red or charred black by the flame-throwers of their comrades who had turned on them. None was alive. The combination of the flood and the prisoner, whatever he was, had left no wounded.

In twenty minutes they arrived at the mouth of the round canyon. There were more corpses here. From their condition, it was obvious that most of the deaths had come from people being swept against the rocks rather than drowning, and Laika realized once again how lucky they had been to have been tied to the massive cross, which had taken most of the impact of their wild ride.

The trucks had been tipped over, but they found a still working flashlight in one of them, and shone it down the dark mouth of the kiva opening. The dim glow revealed a sodden mess of charred and shot corpses. The reek of burned flesh and mud was overwhelming, but Tony volunteered to climb down and see if there was any trace of the prisoner who had been there.

"Forget it," Joseph said. "Not with that hit you took. I'll go."

The ladder had been swept away; Joseph dropped down inside. It was only a few feet, but he landed sickeningly on a body half covered with mud. Laika tossed the flashlight down to him, and he began his search.

"There are five bodies," he called back up. "All are wearing fatigues. One of them's LaPierre. He's badly burned, but his ID was in his back pocket—it's still readable."

"Leave it there," said Laika. "Any sign of the prisoner?"

Joseph was silent for a moment. Then he called up, "An empty casket lined with lead. The mud's thick down here, but if he's got a human form, I'd see him. He's not here."

They extended their arms down into the kiva, and when Joseph jumped up and grabbed them, they pulled him out. The three looked around the canyon, and their gazes hung for a long time on the opening that led north through more canyons, and eventually out to the desert.

"We'd never find him now," said Laika, expressing what they were all thinking. "Those canyons are a maze for miles. He could be hiding in any of them, or he could keep moving, out onto the desert. We couldn't even start the search before this place will be crawling with officials coming in to see what damage the flood caused."

"But we can't just let him go," Tony said, holding his chest. "You heard what Father Alexander said—he's dangerous. There's no end to the trouble he could cause."

"We have no choice," Laika said. "We leave now." Her firm stride back toward the truck left no room for argument.

Back at the mission, they took Special Agent Foster's body and Father Alexander's dried corpse and placed them in the trunk of the Fury. Then Joseph got into the Fury and Laika and Tony climbed into the Blazer, and they drove away from the Mission of San Pedro, passing no one on the way.

When they came out onto the paved road several miles from the mission, they could see, far to the north, the black dots of small planes moving toward the area south of the Dead Horse Reservoir. They continued to drive south for another twenty miles before Laika pulled off onto a dirt road and drove blindly into the desert.

When the road ended, Laika and Tony got into the Fury, and Joseph drove it another few hundred yards over the dirt and scrub until they found a small gully. They took Foster's ID, and buried him and Father Alexander in a shallow grave, setting flat rocks over it in as natural a pattern as they could, to keep away predators. Then they turned off the Fury's engine and rolled it down into the gully. Someone would have to be right on top of it to notice it, and Laika thought the chances of it being found anytime soon were remote.

Then, in the Blazer, they headed back toward Gallup. It was a long drive, but they would arrive before dark.

They stopped just over the New Mexico border near Ship-rock, and Laika made a call, informing the person who answered with a simple "Yes?" that Kelly would need another vehicle in Gallup. "Acknowledged," the voice said, and Laika knew a car would be waiting for them when they arrived back at the motel.

The news on the radio finally reported the incident at the Dead Horse Reservoir. An explosion had blown away two of the dam's taintor gates and piers, allowing half the contents of the reservoir to rush unimpeded into the canyons south of the dam. There was as yet no explanation for the explosion, but investigators were on the scene, and foul play had not been ruled out. At least three people at the dam were known to have been killed as a result of the explosion, but it was not yet known whether the flooding had caused any loss of life.

"You know what I think?" said Joseph, when the story was over. "I think the prisoner somehow got through to somebody, the way he did to Swain, and talked them— or *thought* them—into becoming a saboteur."

"Why?" asked Laika. "Didn't he know that LaPierre and his troops were coming?"

"Doubtful. That might have been just a very pleasant surprise for him. And that the bomber struck when he did turned out to be a very pleasant surprise for *us*."

"But why would the prisoner have wanted the area drowned?" Laika asked.

"Shit happens," Joseph said. "At the very least, it might have destroyed his jailers, and by drawing attention to the area, he might have been found by someone other than the clergy. Red Cross or the park service finds a bunch of drowned priests and a closed casket, they open it to see what's inside. When they do . . ."

"When they do," Tony concluded, "the same thing happens that happened when LaPierre did it."

Joseph nodded. "The shit hits the fanatics. The big question now is what you report, Laika."

She had been thinking about that very thing for miles.

"At least we know," Laika said thoughtfully, "that Agent Daly didn't try to kill us at *Skye's* order. He was with LaPierre all the way. So I think we can at least report our involvement in the LaPierre business. And there's no reason we can't report that Daly turned and tried to kill us. Hell, we might as well give the location of the car with his body."

"Don't see why not," Joseph said. "But isn't it likely Daly had to be out here on Company business? And I suspect his official assignment was to keep an eye on us, though we don't have to mention that to Skye. But that brings up one niggling thing that really bothers me. I don't think any of us believe Skye's been open with us about the whole reason for our operations. I think he's looking for more than just supposed paranormal occurrences for us to debunk."

"But if he is," Tony said, "it would have to come down as a directive from above."

Joseph nodded. "Right. And if it *were* from above, why the hell would it be a CIA operation within the United States in the first place? Why not the feds? It's *their* jurisdiction, not ours. Foster bird-dogging us—as well as his willingness to kill one of us—shows that there's no interagency cooperation on this project. On the contrary, the feds *suspect* us of something. And if all that's the case. . . ." Joseph looked out the window at the desert dusk. ". . . Then maybe somebody turned Skye the way LaPierre turned Daly."

Laika saw the picture. "Skye's looking for the prisoner, too. And as far as he's concerned, we're just his stooges."

"He knows about the weird occurrences that happen when the prisoner's near," said Tony, picking up the thread. "And he's sent us out to debunk these things just to narrow his target area."

"And," said Laika, "in the hopes that maybe we'll latch on to a *real* paranormal incident, one we can't explain away. When that happens, he's got a good idea where the prisoner is.'' She sighed. ''It makes sense, but we don't have any proof.''

''It's solid enough a theory, though, that it might be wise to keep our knowledge of the prisoner from Skye,'' Joseph said. ''He doesn't know about it in New York, so why tell him about any of it?''

Chapter 43

*T*he report from Laika Harris was waiting for Richard
Skye the next morning. It had come in over an en-
crypted data line at midnight. Skye was not totally surprised by what it said. He had suspected that his three
operatives might have been somehow involved in the
LaPierre incident.

All he had known about it was that Michael LaPierre
had been found dead, along with approximately seventy
other men dressed in military fashion and bearing weapons, near the site of an old mission in southern Utah. The
deaths were due primarily to drowning after the flood-
waters of the bombed dam had rushed down upon them,
although some of the bodies had been shot and burned by
flamethrowers. But no one could explain precisely what
LaPierre and these men had been doing there. Laika Harris's report filled in the gaps.

It seemed that the operatives had infiltrated LaPierre's
operation, but had been captured, and LaPierre had revealed the entire plot to them before they were able to
escape by turning LaPierre's troops against each other.
The breaking of the dam did the rest. The report read in
part:

> The mummified corpses as well as the sand
> drawings were the first part of the plot by
> Michael LaPierre to overthrow the United

States government and establish a right-wing theocracy, with himself at the head. The disparate and bizarre elements of the plot were intended to fulfill LaPierre's distorted view of biblical prophecy, and act as a trigger for a radical right revolution using 144 cells in areas throughout the country. Some of the matches between prophecy and LaPierre's actions seem rather illogical, but after having been in contact with LaPierre, we are all of the opinion that he was quite mad.

The desert setting was to fulfill the prophecy that the Messiah (LaPierre himself, in his view) would come out of the wilderness: "Prepare ye the way of the Lord, make straight in the desert a highway for our God." (Isaiah 40:3)

The bombing of the dam was carried out by one of LaPierre's agents, but the timing was in error, and was to have come after LaPierre and his people had vacated the area. The biblical injunction was: ". . . in the wilderness shall waters break out, and streams in the desert. And the parched ground shall become a pool, and the thirsty land springs of water. . . ." (Isaiah 35:6–7)

The sand drawings were to be interpreted as the "signs and portents" that would herald the Second Coming, with LaPierre as the new Messiah: "And I will show wonders in heaven above, and signs in the earth beneath." (Acts 2:19) The drawings were executed with one of the helicopters and an attached motorcycle found at the site.

LaPierre admitted being responsible for the mummified corpses, though he did not say how the drying process had been accomplished, and we saw no mechanisms at the site that might give an answer. The corpses were intended to frighten those who would oppose LaPierre and were based on a verse from the Book of Revelation: "And if any man will hurt them [referring to the prophets, of whom LaPierre considered himself one], fire proceedeth out of their mouth, and devoureth their enemies." (Revelation 11:5)

LaPierre's men murdered the priests at the mission as a first shot in an intended holocaust that would include any practitioners of faiths not aligned with LaPierre's own narrow views. There is also the possibility that LaPierre may have been considering using nuclear weapons, as we witnessed a lead-lined underground facility at the site where the revolutionaries had gathered, but saw no actual nuclear devices.

There was more in the report, including the information that Agent Paul Daly had been turned by LaPierre's people, and had tried to kill the operatives. So that was why Skye hadn't heard from Popeye, the bastard. Skye had sent him west to keep an eye on the operatives, and unknowingly sent him right where he would do his real employer the most good.

Skye smiled thinly. He supposed he couldn't really blame Daly. *Let he who is without sin,* as long as he was in the biblical mood. After all, Skye had been bought and paid for by Mr. Stanley, who would be mightily disappointed that none of this seeming paranormal activity had borne fruit. Ah well, there would be other opportunities to find the mysterious prisoner he and his patron sought.

In the meantime, Skye would pass along Harris's warning that the proper agencies should infiltrate and ferret out the revolutionary cells LaPierre had established. And Skye knew, once he sent this classified information through the proper channels, that it would be done. The president would be delighted to have a right-wing religious fanatic military plot revealed, particularly since it had self-destructed so nicely. Unfortunately, Skye would be able to take no credit for it, since the operations of Harris, Luciano, and Stein were for his eyes only.

He sighed and wondered what his three operatives might be keeping from him. He wondered most about that "lead-lined facility" Harris had mentioned. Though he believed much of her report, the tidiness of it gave him the same sense of discomfort he'd felt when he'd read her report on the Holberg incident in New York. It all seemed a little too neat, too precise, with all the loose ends tied up in a pristine bow.

It seemed, he feared, like a clever fabric of lies.

"Agent Brian Foster is missing."

The words brought Quentin McIntyre's head up fast. Alan Phillips stood in the deputy director's doorway, looking like he had wanted to report anything but the words he had just spoken. "Missing?" McIntyre repeated, and Phillips nodded.

"We haven't heard from him for forty-eight hours, and there's no response from his cell phone."

"Jesus Christ," McIntyre muttered. "Did they make him? Break the Yazzie cover?"

"I don't know."

"Hell, even if they had, they wouldn't have *killed* him, would they?"

"I don't know, sir. I have other agents in a four-state area looking for him. The last we heard from him was that he was following the signal from the device he had placed on their car, but then he lost it. His last report from northeastern Arizona said he was going to try to reestablish contact."

"What about the Company operatives? Any sign of them?"

"Yes sir. We sent someone to the motel in Gallup late

this morning. They spent the night, and checked out before eight." He shook his head. "They're gone again."

McIntyre sat back in his chair, feeling unaccountably weary. "All right," he said to Phillips, waving a hand of dismissal. "Let me know as soon as you find anything." Phillips nodded and left the room.

Goddamned sonsabitches, McIntyre thought. The only thing that made any sense was that they'd either killed Special Agent Foster or left him somewhere out in the desert. Either way, the FBI had succeeded in losing Harris, Stein, and Luciano again.

But if they'd found them once, they could find them again, now that he knew what Skye's little squad was up to. Paranormal phenomena: that was what had drawn this bunch of rogue ops, and the next time something like that occurred, the FBI would be there.

In fact, maybe they could even create their own little unexplainable incident. And when Skye's team took the bait, they would find themselves in a trap. If they wanted to play rough, they would be the ones at the muzzle end this time. They had no legal standing at all, not in this country.

They were fair game, and McIntyre intended to set a deadly trap for his quarry.

When the man took off Taylor Griswold's blindfold, he found himself in a windowless room with only one lamp. It sat on a small bare table next to the wooden chair in which they'd placed him.

Griswold hated this cloak-and-dagger shit. Getting blindfolded and driven twenty or thirty miles to be told he was an incompetent asshole was not his idea of a good return to New York City. He was fairly sure that was what this Scotsman was going to say, and when the man came through the door and slammed it shut behind him, he was positive.

"You lost them," the man said. "You had them and you lost them, on straight, simple two-lane roads." His

voice was low but jagged with burrs. It was a voice that
pricked at you, making you deeply uncomfortable.

The man stepped closer, into the pool of light the lamp
cast, and Griswold saw his angry face. The wild red hair
that blazed atop his head like a flame only made his coun-
tenance look more fierce. He couldn't have been more
than thirty, Griswold thought, but the clefts of his rugged
face and the wisdom of his deep blue eyes aged him beyond his years. He glared down at Griswold from his six
and a half feet as though demanding some kind of atone-
ment.

"Christ, I'm not a cop, I don't know about tailing people like that. I got as far as the roadhouse, which was
pretty far without them spotting me, and then they tore
off after some guy speeding away, and some other guy
was yelling something about murder, and even *then* I kept
following them, but when they pulled off the road and
went gangbanging back into the desert, there was no way
I was getting involved in *that* action, so I just got the hell
out of there, I admit it."

"All right, Griswold," the Scotsman said. Griswold
had to admit to himself that he usually liked hearing him
say his name. The Scots pronunciation gave it a couple
extra syllables. But this time it sounded like a Scottish
curse. "I know you only help us for the money you get
paid, but that's coming to an end. You've been pretty
useless to us. I admit, you've put us on the trail of the
three, but you can never stay with them until we arrive.
We're going to have to use different measures now.
Here's the deal—you get anything that looks like the genuine article, you inform us and you'll be paid. But stay
away from the three from now on, ye ken?"

"Huh?"

"Do you *understand?*" the man said, as though Griswold were stupid.

"Yes. Yes, I understand."

"Because if you try and come in contact with them
again, or if you try and contact us beyond your usual

method, or if, by any chance, you should try to write this up into a story for your sad rag of a newspaper, believe me, we will kill you, Griswold.''

Griswold felt beads of sweat on his upper lip, but didn't dare move his arm to wipe them off. "I understand," he said again.

The Scotsman nodded. "Tread lightly, Griswold." He picked up the man's blindfold from the table and dropped it into his lap. "Now, be on your way."

Griswold tied the blindfold tightly around his eyes as he heard the Scotsman cross the room and open the door again. Someone else came in, and he felt a hand on his shoulder. He left the room without speaking or hearing more. But as he went, he listened nonetheless. He wanted to be able to judge where, approximately, he was. Maybe he could find these men again.

Yes, he was frightened of them, but he had been threatened before—hell, reporters were *always* threatened, but he was still alive. And if this Scotty thought that he was going to let go of the story of the decade when he had it by the balls, he was sorely mistaken.

Or maybe, he thought, that should be *sairly*.

Left alone, the tall, red-haired Scot sat in the wooden chair in the darkened room and rested his head on his right hand. The chair and the darkness had looked comforting at first, but as he closed his eyes, he knew that he could not find peace, no matter how dark or how quiet his surroundings. Battles were waged within his brain.

At least they were well rid of Griswold. The man was a greedy fool with no courage. Guts were not courage. And he had no sense of honor. His only country was his wallet. Best to pass on men like that. They had ruined causes before and would do so again.

The Scot had had his soldiers contact the man a year earlier. He had thought it valuable to have someone on the payroll who was close to the weird and bizarre, who could separate the wheat from the chaff. So they had hired

Griswold through several layers of secrecy, in hopes that the man might be able, by design or accident, to bring them news that would lead them to the one the Catholics called the Antichrist, the one whose dark activities the tall Scot's father had monitored as a Knight Templar.

Colin Mackay, son of the late Sir Andrew Mackay, sat in the near darkness and thought about his father, and the grail that had given him youth, and the people who had taken his immortality from him.

He thought about his task, about his poor, sad country, bound by impure, inbred fools whose only claim upon it was a stolen crown.

He thought about the news stories that mentioned the empty leaden casket in the desert earth, and about the creature, guarded so long, now set free on an unsuspecting world.

And he thought about what the power of that creature might do, set loose upon the might and kingdom and soldiers of those royal idiots.

He wished with all his heart that he could return to his home, to his Scotland. But that day was not yet to be. It would come only when he was ready to give his country the freedom it deserved. To make that day come, Colin Mackay was willing to shake hands with the devil himself.

And perhaps that circumstance was not as impossible as it seemed.

He stood alone in the desert, watching the sun, staring directly into the fiery ball, eyes open, never blinking. It had been centuries since he'd been able to move freely, to see the natural qualities of this world.

He remained there, watching as the earth rotated and the edge of the planet rose to block out its sun. He watched as the stars began to appear, and remembered, so long ago, the routes he had taken through them. He drank in the sight of the sky; he tasted his freedom fully.

He had wandered since that day of blood and water that had freed him, observing rocks and plants and the creatures that dwelt in this arid land. He touched the sand and the rock and the water of the infrequent streams, and saw only one human being in all that time, who he'd told to saw open his throat with the edge of a sharp rock, and the human had obeyed.

He had watched as the human's blood had sprayed out when the artery was severed, and when the human had fallen to the sand and died. It was interesting, but not, for any reason he could name, as interesting as the land. Here he and what constituted his mind were free to roam, unfettered by that foul dark substance through which neither he nor his will could pass, but by extreme effort.

So he roamed that land. There would be time to pay back those who had kept him bound for so long, and he would repay them. He would make the world run red with blood from a billion self-severed necks.

But for now he would simply wander, enjoying his freedom, even though bound on this world. He did not know how long he might wander. Perhaps for forty days and nights, like the dead Jesus his captors kept droning about.

Or perhaps it would be forty years before he would war on these puny creatures again, find his allies among them, those thirsty for lives. Yes, since time meant nothing to him, perhaps forty years.

Or, if he got bored, forty minutes.

"Here's to our continuing good health," said Laika, raising her glass of wine.

"Something," said Joseph, "that's getting more and more difficult to maintain."

Tony said nothing. He smiled slightly and drank his wine. It was two weeks since they had left the southwest for some well-deserved rest and recuperation in San Francisco. Now they sat on the deck of a waterfront bistro overlooking the bay, breathing in moist air instead of dry, and seeing the setting sun through clouds.

"The fuss is dying down at last," Joseph said.

"Over the 'Armageddon Plot'?" said Laika. "In the big media, maybe, but I suspect that the Internet and the alternative publications will feast on it for years. It's a conspiracy theorist's wet dream—a real, honest-to-God *conspiracy*."

"And they don't know the half of it."

"Neither do we," said Tony, looking out to the edge of the sea. "We still don't know who killed the Templars, or who made that first sand drawing. We don't know a damn thing about that Grail in the lock box back in New York, and we don't know who it was who escaped that lead casket.

"We don't know how he does what he does, how he puts dreams in Joseph's head and murder in other people's minds, how he raises a dead man so that he can suck the life out of people, or how he makes someone blow up a dam. We don't know where he is, or what he has in mind." He looked back at Joseph, then at Laika, and out to sea again. "When you get right down to it, we don't know much at all."

"But we will," said Joseph quietly. "We'll know it all."

"You really think that's possible?" Tony asked.

Joseph thought for a moment, then nodded. "Yes. Everything is there. If it's beyond our reach, that's only temporary."

"You're wrong." Tony shook his head heavily. "There are some things we won't know. Ever." His hand went unconsciously to his chest, where Miriam Dominick's cross had hung, and where his flesh now bore the shape of it, a white cross, a scar that would stay with him always.

"But that won't stop us from searching," Laika said. "Will it?" Her eyes looked into Tony's, and he thought that maybe she knew what he was feeling, the depth of his loss and his bitterness. She too had lost someone she'd loved, someone who'd betrayed her.

Her question hung in the air unanswered. He didn't

know. It was only one of so many things he didn't know.

But among the things he did know was that another face had joined the throng that haunted his nights, an oval face framed by chestnut brown hair, a face with sky blue eyes and a small nose and wide mouth that somehow went together perfectly. It was one more face among the many that would walk the night with him for the rest of his life.

The silence was broken by a muffled whirring sound. Laika tensed, then reached into the handbag at her feet and took out a cellular phone. She opened it, said, "Yes," and listened to the voice at the other end.

Then she silently mouthed the name of the caller, the identity of whom, in spite of their ignorance of so many other matters, they had all known as soon as the phone had rung.

The word, formed but unspoken, was *Skye*.

Their time of rest was over. The search would continue.

Readers wishing to further investigate the reality of the paranormal will find much of worth in the following books: *The Encyclopedia of the Paranormal* edited by Gordon Stein, Ph.D.; *The New Age: Notes of a Fringe Watcher* by Martin Gardner; *An Encyclopedia of Claims, Frauds, and Hoaxes of the Occult and Supernatural* by James Randi; *Why People Believe Weird Things: Pseudoscience, Superstition, and Other Confusions of Our Time* by Michael Shermer; *The Demon-Haunted World* by Carl Sagan; and the publications of the Committee for the Scientific Investigation of Claims of the Paranormal (CSICOP) at *http://www.csicop.org*.

If you have enjoyed the Searchers' adventures in *The Searchers Book One: City of Iron* and *The Searchers Book Two: Empire of Dust*, watch for the thrilling conclusion to the trilogy, coming soon from Avon Books.

In *The Searchers Book Three: Seige of Stone*, Tony, Laika, and Joseph face their greatest challenge yet—the Prisoner, free, and ready for revenge . . .

After centuries of captivity, the unholy Prisoner is finally free, and ready to recruit allies in his plan for mass destruction. Hiding from the FBI and their own superiors, the Searchers are sent to Scotland to investigate a series of "ghost" sightings that could be anything from fairies to aliens. Meanwhile, the Prisoner joins forces with a band of nationalist terrorists, and together they begin a series of horrific attacks across England. But the Prisoner has his own, larger plans—to destroy the world—and it's up to the Searchers to stop the demonic force before he starts Armageddon.

The Searchers Book Three: Siege of Stone will be published in March 1999.